W9-ARD-463

Forever After

**Center Point
Large Print**

Also by Deborah Raney
and available from Center Point Large Print:

Almost Forever
A Hanover Falls Novel

**This Large Print Book carries the
Seal of Approval of N.A.V.H.**

Forever After

a hanover falls novel

Deborah Raney

CENTER POINT PUBLISHING
THORNDIKE, MAINE

This Center Point Large Print edition
is published in the year 2011 by arrangement with
Howard Books, a division of Simon & Schuster, Inc.

The text of this Large Print edition is unabridged.
In other aspects, this book may vary
from the original edition.
Printed in the United States of America
on permanent paper.
Set in 16-point Times New Roman type.

ISBN: 978-1-61173-152-1

Library of Congress Cataloging-in-Publication Data

Raney, Deborah.
Forever after : a Hanover Falls novel / Deborah Raney.
p. cm.
ISBN 978-1-61173-152-1 (library binding : alk. paper)
1. Fire fighters—Fiction. 2. Large type books. I. Title.
PS3568.A562F67 2011b
813'.54—dc22

2011010814

For Max Daniel

Acknowledgments

My deepest gratitude to the following for help with research, ideas, proofreading, and "author support."

My critique partner and dear friend, Tamera Alexander, Kenny and Courtney Ast, Ryan and Tobi Layton, Terry Stucky, Max and Winifred Teeter, Courtney Walsh, the writers of ACFW, and especially the Kansas 8, who give wings to my ideas.

Steve Laube, best agent in the whole wide world.

Deep appreciation to my amazing editor Dave Lambert, and also to Holly Halverson at Howard Books/Simon & Schuster for great direction and encouragement.

My amazing husband, Ken, and our growing family—precious children, grandchildren, and the wonderful extended family God has given us: you all bring me so much joy!

Therefore I tell you, do not worry about your life,
what you will eat or drink;
or about your body, what you will wear.
Is not life more important than food,
and the body more important than clothes?
Look at the birds of the air;
they do not sow or reap or store away in barns,
and yet your heavenly Father feeds them.
Are you not much more valuable than they?

MATTHEW 6:25–26

1

Thursday, November 1

Lucas Vermontez clutched the mask to his face and forced out a measured breath, scrabbling to remember everything he'd learned in training. His air-pack fed a steady line of filtered, compressed air, but the thick bank of smoke in front of him carried him to the brink of claustrophobia.

The concrete beneath his feet shuddered. Next to him, he felt his partner, Zach Morgan, drop down on all fours. Lucas followed suit. Catching a glimpse of Zach, he wondered if his own eyes held the same wild fear.

He sucked in air and exhaled again, fighting panic. This was no training exercise. This was the real thing. Statue-still in the smoky darkness, he strained to discern the voices he was sure he'd heard seconds earlier. But his helmet and hood created their own white noise, and no sound pierced them save the roar of the fire overhead.

A split second later an explosion rocked the building, throwing him flat on his belly and knocking the breath from him. Debris rained down on them, and when he could breathe again, he scrambled for protection.

Zach motioned frantically behind them toward

the entrance they'd come in. In the aftershocks of the explosion, the copper pipes overhead trembled and the thick wooden beams bowed beneath the weight of the building.

Lucas forced out a breath and counted, trying to slow his respiration. If the structure collapsed, they didn't stand a chance. They were in the belly of the beast—the basement of the former hospital that now housed a homeless shelter—with three stories stacked on top of them.

"Go!" He motioned Zach out, his own voice ringing in his ears.

Zach scrambled ahead of him, hunkered low trying to stay in the two-foot clearing beneath the bank of smoke.

Lucas sent up a prayer that they'd gotten everybody out. His father, the station captain, had radioed moments ago that all but one of the shelter's residents were accounted for. He'd ordered the crews to evacuate and had sent Lucas and Zach in to search for the missing man.

It always filled him with pride to hear Pop's commanding voice. Manny Vermontez was the best fire captain Hanover Falls—or the state of Missouri, for that matter—had ever had. And that wasn't just the opinion of a proud son. Pop had worked hard to get where he was, and the whole family rightfully had him on a pedestal, even if it sometimes caused conflict at home. Ma swore her prematurely graying hair came from having a husband, and now a son, who put their lives on the line almost daily.

"Lucas!"

He spun at the sound of Pop's voice. Not on the two-way like he expected, but inside the building—down here.

"Pop?" He turned back, straining to see through the thick smoke. He saw no one. "Zach?"

His partner must have gone ahead to the entrance. Good. Zach would make it out okay. But what was Pop doing down here?

"Pop? Where are you?"

Nothing. The crew from Station 1 must have arrived. Either that or somebody was still trapped inside the building. Pop would never leave the control engine otherwise.

The smoke banked downward and he had no choice but to crawl on his belly, commando-style. He still had air, but everything in him told him to get out. Now.

But he couldn't leave. His dad was down here!

The building groaned and shuddered again.

"Lucas!"

There it was again. He rolled over on his back and propped himself on his elbows, trying desperately to figure out which direction the shout had come from. He listened for a full ten seconds but heard only the deep roar of the fire above him.

He started belly-crawling again, but in the orange-black he was confused about which way he'd been headed. He needed to follow the sound of Pop's voice. His dad would lead him out. But where had they come in? Everything around him looked the same. Panic clawed at his throat again.

Once more he heard the voice. Weaker this time, but he didn't think he was imagining it. The old-timers told stories about hearing voices, seeing things—hallucinations—in the frantic moments where a man hung between life and death. But he wasn't in full panic mode—not yet. And he *knew* his father's voice.

He crawled deeper into the blackness, forearm over forearm in the direction of the voice, grateful for the heavy sleeves of his bunker coat. But he heard nothing now. Nothing except the raging fire and the ominous creak of beams somewhere above his head.

He stopped again and listened. He smelled smoke and the unique odor of the air-pack, but there was something else, too. Something had changed.

A new sound filtered through his helmet. The clanging of engines? A crew from Station 1 had been requested. That must be them arriving. But the sound was coming from behind him. He'd been heading deeper into the building.

He reversed his direction. Thank God for those engines. Their clamor would guide him out. The taut thread of fear loosened a bit. Help was on the way.

"Pop?" he shouted. "You there?" He waited for a reply before moving forward. His air supply seemed thinner than before. Smoke choked him. He couldn't stay down here much longer. He would have sold his soul for a two-way radio right now. He prayed Zach had gotten out . . . that his buddy would let them know he was still down here.

At that moment, a faint glimmer caught his eye. The voices of his fellow firefighters drifted to him. He crawled faster, heading toward the light.

"Hey! It's Vermontez!" Molly Edmonds shouted. "Lucas is out! Tell the chief!"

Lucas collapsed on the damp concrete outside and felt strong arms pull him out, then help him to his feet.

He stripped off his mask and hood, gulping in the sooty air. "Where's Pop? Where's my dad?"

"He went in after you!" Molly yelled over the roar of the blaze. "Didn't you see him down there? What about Zach?" She jogged back toward the building.

"Anybody seen the captain?" someone yelled. "Where's Manny?"

"Morgan's still in there, too!"

Yanking his headgear back on, Lucas stumbled to his feet and jogged after Molly.

He heard the men shout for them to retreat, but he didn't care. His father was in that inferno looking for *him*.

Molly disappeared into the mouth of the

building. He followed. A split second later another explosion rocked the earth, knocking him to his knees. *Oh, dear God! No! God, help me!*

He scrambled for the entrance, but the opening had disappeared. Someone grabbed him in the darkness. He clawed at the rubble around him, but he couldn't move. Couldn't feel his legs. Something was pinning him in.

He heaved against the weight on his calves and searing pain sliced into his thigh. He tried to move again, but the pain robbed him of breath. He found a crumb of comfort in the fact that he still had feeling in his legs.

"My dad's down there!" His voice was raspy from the smoke. He couldn't seem to get enough air to propel his words. "Somebody get down there! Pop! God! Help!"

The wail of sirens drowned his cries, and everything faded into blackness.

One year later, Saturday, November 1

*L*ucas jerked awake, sitting straight up in bed. He put a palm to his racing heart, then wiped a fine film of perspiration from his forehead. Sirens wailed in the distance outside his bedroom window. Or was that only part of the dream?

He stilled to listen and heard only the quiet rustle of his bed sheets, and the frantic *rat-a-tat-tat* of a woodpecker in the backyard.

Through the haze of sleep, he eased leaden legs over the side of the bed and reached for his cane. It felt like an extra appendage after all these months.

He stretched his legs out, averting his eyes from the crazy-quilt of scars that stitched from knee to ankle on his left leg, and the mottled burn scars that went from the top of his foot up his calf on the right. More than thirty bones in his legs and feet had been shattered. He hadn't known the human body contained that many bones. His long, muscular runner's legs had been his best feature before the fire. They'd inspired Cate Selvy to affectionately nickname him "Legs."

Before pity could seize him, he forced himself to look in the corner of his room where the folded wheelchair was parked, and beside it an aluminum walker. He murmured a prayer of gratitude. It could be worse. *Had* been worse. He should probably store the wheelchair and walker away now, but they were good reminders of how far he'd come in one year.

Today was an anniversary he'd never wanted to celebrate.

His bedroom door nudged open a few inches, and Lucky slinked through the opening, purring loud enough to be heard across the room. Lucas clicked his tongue and the large tom tiptoed over last night's dirty laundry. Lucas ran his hand over the silver gray fur.

He'd adopted Lucky—then a nameless kitten—two years ago after rescuing him from the ruins of a burned-out warehouse on the outskirts of the Falls. Once the cat's scorched paws and singed whiskers had healed, he'd turned into a handsome animal.

Lucas hobbled into the bathroom with Lucky trailing him. His physical therapists—and his mother—had tried to talk him into getting rid of Lucky, worried the cat would trip him up. But Lucky was one of the bright spots in his life these days. One of the few.

Now *there* was a depressing thought. But he wasn't about to get rid of one of the few friends who'd stood by him through it all.

He opened the medicine cabinet and stared at the bottle of Vicodin, steeled himself to not need it today. He'd been off pain meds for almost three months now, but the memory of the torment he'd endured wouldn't let him throw the bottle away. Not yet.

In the kitchen down the hall, dishes rattled in the sink. Any minute Ma would be in to badger him to eat a breakfast he wasn't hungry for.

He bent over the sink and splashed cold water on his face, waiting for the nausea to hit him, as it had every morning since that awful night. The sick feeling came in waves as the icy water shocked him awake. *Pop is dead. And the other firefighters . . . Zach is dead. Molly. All of them.*

16

Why did that truth have the power to crush him again with each new day?

Because he should have gotten Zach out. Because Pop had died searching for Lucas, trying to save him. He heard Pop's voice inside his head now, clear and strong, telling his family, "Anyone who calls on the name of the Lord will be saved." Pop had quoted the words again and again.

Well, Lucas Vermontez had called out to God that awful day. And maybe God had heard him. He didn't know. God hadn't saved Pop. And since He *had* saved Lucas, Pop's oft-quoted verse begged the question: saved for *what?*

Because it was starting to look like Lucas Vermontez wasn't worth being saved.

2

Wednesday, November 5

Jenna Morgan stared at the numbers on the bank statement in front of her and punched the figures into the calculator one more time. It was her third try at reconciling her checking account, and for once she wished the stupid checkbook *hadn't* balanced. This couldn't be right! Her account was overdrawn by almost eight hundred dollars.

Trying to quell the panic rising in her throat, she got the bank's number off the statement and dialed it. She hadn't even paid the mortgage yet, and it was already two days late. That would set her back another two thousand dollars, plus the late fee, never mind that she'd paid last month's payment with a credit card.

The statements spread on the table beside her laptop warned that she was over the limit on two of her three credit cards already.

A recording, a woman's soothing voice, came on the line and offered Jenna half a dozen choices she knew would only get her to someone else's voice mail. She punched "0" and got another recording. She dropped the phone in its cradle. The beginnings of a headache niggled at the back of her eyes.

Something had to give. Even with her in-laws paying Zach's funeral expenses and buying his pickup from her, in the year since his death, she'd blown through what little insurance he had and spent his meager pension checks as fast as they came in, just trying to keep up with the bills.

She glanced up at the clock and gasped. She was late. Zach's mother had somehow wrangled her an appointment with a new girl at Cutlines. "And don't worry about the cost, darling," Clarissa had said. "It's already taken care of. Get the works."

She'd better get "the works" because once Clarissa discovered the state her finances were in, that would be the end of salon perks for the next decade.

• • •

*T*wo hours later Jenna stretched behind the wheel of her Volvo to check her hair in the rearview mirror. Her naturally blond hair sported highlights—or lowlights, the salon owner called the technique. She liked the look, but she wasn't sure it was worth the hundred dollars it had cost Clarissa—not to mention the basketful of products Jenna had been coerced to purchase to "maintain" the look.

Zach had never really cared about her hair one way or the other. Whenever she talked about changing her style, he'd assured her, "You're beautiful just the way you are."

Clarissa, on the other hand, always had opinions. She'd been expressing them since the day Zach first introduced his mother to her. Jenna had been a junior in high school then, in St. Louis, where she and Zach both grew up. Zach was away at college in Springfield, and she'd lied to her mom and sneaked out to visit him one weekend. Clarissa showed up on campus unannounced, but Zach had been unflustered and treated the two of them to lunch in Springfield. Standing on the sidewalk in front of Bruno's that day, Clarissa reached up and brushed Jenna's bangs off her forehead. "You really should let these grow out and show off your beautiful bone structure, darling."

Jenna had taken it as a compliment and started

growing out her bangs that day. Remembering the moment, she fingered the fish-shaped charm hanging from a silver chain around her neck. The necklace, fashioned of white and yellow gold—real gold—was an engagement gift from Clarissa. It was the first thing of any value Jenna had ever owned. Years after Clarissa had presented the necklace, Jenna read in a magazine that the goldfish was the Chinese symbol for prosperity and wealth. She wondered if Zach's mother knew that. Probably.

At any rate, even after Jenna had collected a whole jewelry box full of more expensive treasures, the goldfish necklace remained her favorite. A talisman of sorts. She took it off only to shower.

Clarissa had quickly become the mother Jenna's own mother could never be to her. She'd never treated Jenna like trailer trash, but taught her how to dress, how to do her makeup, and later—after she and Zach were married—taught her how to hold her head high and act as if she deserved to carry the Morgan name.

It had taken a dozen years of Clarissa's mentoring, but most days Jenna could almost believe she was worthy to associate with Bill and Clarissa's crowd. Could almost believe she deserved to live in a beautiful home in the Brookside development and that she wouldn't be turned away trying to gain entrance to her in-laws' home in Clairemont Hills, the new gated community on the outskirts of Hanover Falls.

She pushed away the sudden vision of her anemic checking account and turned off Main Street, heading to the east edge of town.

She entered the passcode and waited for the iron gates to slide open, then wound her way through the wooded enclave to the Morgans' rambling property.

She pulled onto the circle drive in front of the elegant Tudor-style home. Clarissa met her at the door, her little Shih Tzu, Quincy, yapping in her arms. Clarissa shushed the pup while she gave Jenna the usual once over.

Her eyes lit when she noticed Jenna's hair. "Look at you! Lovely!"—she twirled her free hand—"Let's see the back."

Jenna obliged.

"Simply stunning. Do *you* like it?"

Jenna tucked a wayward curl behind her ear. "I think so. It's a little shorter than I'm used to, but I—"

"Well, of course you like it! Who wouldn't? I told you that new girl was good. Dottie said it usually takes weeks to get in with her."

Jenna took the hint. "Thank you again for getting the appointment for me. And for taking care of the bill."

"Oh, heavens . . ." Clarissa waved her off, right on cue in this game they'd played for over a decade. "I was glad to do it. Come in, come in . . . Quincy doesn't like this cold."

Clarissa disappeared into the house and Jenna followed, closing the front door behind her. The scent of cinnamon and cloves wafted from a tray of candles on the carved mantel.

"Do you want coffee?"

"No, thanks." She wiped sweaty palms on the thighs of her jeans. "I . . . I need to talk to you about something."

Zach's mother must have heard the tremor in her voice because she looked up, deep furrows etching her forehead. "What's wrong, honey?"

"Maybe I will take that coffee."

The lines in Clarissa's forehead deepened, but she beckoned Jenna to the kitchen and pulled fancy mugs from a cupboard.

Jenna watched her, searching for a gentle way to break her news. After they'd lost Zach in the fire a year ago—a tragedy that killed four other firefighters from the Clemens County Fire District—Bill and Clarissa had taken Jenna under their wings, encouraging her to stay in the home she and Zach had built in the upscale development on the west side of Hanover Falls, and helping her out financially as they had all through her and Zach's marriage.

His parents continued to pay for little extras like Jenna's hair appointments and manicures, and season tickets for the Springfield Little Theater season. Just last week Clarissa had presented Jenna with a pair of tickets for the new season, saying, "I know it won't be the same without Zach, but you can bring a friend."

Jenna smiled wryly to herself at the thought. First of all, Clarissa meant a female friend. Perish the thought she should ever start dating again. Second, Clarissa's "it won't be the same without Zach" didn't wash since Zach had gone with them to a show exactly once. He'd never been a fan of theater and always managed to somehow pull an extra shift the night of a production.

Clarissa placed two steaming mugs on the table and motioned for Jenna to sit down. "What's on your mind?"

Jenna stirred creamer into her coffee and inhaled the fragrant steam. "I . . . I'm late on the house payment. I think I'm going to have to—"

"Why didn't you say something?" Clarissa jumped up and slipped her checkbook from her purse. "How much do you need?"

Jenna wadded a paper napkin and dabbed at an invisible spot on the tablecloth. "The house payment is two thousand, but . . . I put it on a credit card last month and I really need to pay that off, too." She didn't mention that she'd also put the groceries on a credit card.

The pen in Clarissa's hand stilled and she eyed Jenna. "You don't want to get behind on your credit cards, honey. The interest will eat you alive.

It might make sense to take some of Zach's pension and get your credit card paid off."

If Clarissa had any clue how far in debt she was, how many credit cards she'd maxed out . . .

But Clarissa resumed writing the check. "Will five thousand be enough?"

Jenna nodded. "Thank you. I'll pay it back as soon as I can, but . . ." She took a deep breath, hearing Zach's disapproval in her head. He would have been mortified at what she was about to tell his mother. "I think I'm going to have to sell the house, Clarissa."

"Oh, no!" Clarissa shook her head, alarm in her voice. "You don't want to do that. The house is an investment. You want to build as much equity in it as you can. Besides, where would you go? You'd pay at least half what you're paying on the mortgage to rent anyplace decent. Besides, there's not a rental in this town that isn't a dump."

"I don't know that I have a choice, Clarissa. I can't keep up with the payments. I'm so far behind right now . . ." She waited for the familiar words that always brought relief: *"Don't worry, honey . . . we'll take care of it."* She hated herself for hinting, for always depending on the Morgans to bail her out.

Clarissa frowned and pointed at the check lying on the table between them. "This will get you caught up, right?"

Jenna couldn't meet her eyes. "No, Clarissa. Not

quite . . . Not even close, actually," she whispered.

Clarissa straightened. "Exactly how far behind are you?"

"I think—" She swallowed hard. "I need to sell the house," she said again, trying to sound firm. "I'm getting further and further behind."

Her mother-in-law shook her head. "I don't understand. What's happened to all your money? You have Zach's pension and the insurance. That can't all be gone. . . ."

"It's gone to pay the bills. Every cent." She was glad she could say that honestly. But as quickly as the thought came, so did the image of the beautiful eighty-dollar sweater she'd ordered online last week.

Clarissa sat with her jaw hanging open. "How on earth could you let this happen?" Her voice climbed an octave. "Especially when we've been pitching in every month? Why didn't you say something sooner? I can't imagine where all this money has been going! You surely haven't blown through your savings, too?"

"We never *had* any savings, Clarissa. We were living . . . beyond our means. Way beyond our means." She willed her voice not to tremble. "From the very beginning."

"What are you talking about? Not before Zach—"

"Yes." Jenna shook her head. "Then, too. Neither of us wanted to admit it, but we could never quite make it on what Zach made."

"Even after we helped you with the house?"

"We couldn't *afford* a house like that, Clarissa."

"Then, why in heaven's name didn't *you* get a job?"

Jenna bristled. There were few jobs in the Falls that weren't beneath a Morgan. She'd broached the subject once, years ago, and Clarissa and Zach had both had a fit. "Zach was determined to prove he could be a good provider, but—"

"Prove? To whom?"

Jenna didn't miss the accusation in her voice. She bit her tongue and collected herself. "To *you. You* and Bill. And I would have gotten a job, but *you* didn't want me to."

"I don't know what you're talking about," Clarissa sputtered.

Zach had spent the ten years of their married life trying to prove to his parents—and to her—that he could provide a good living on a firefighter's wages. But the Morgans had a very different definition of "good living" from Zach's. They'd never tried to conceal their disappointment that their only son had chosen firefighting over a "professional" career.

Thankfully, once Zach and Jenna were married, his parents had quit hounding him about going back to college. Of course, given the fact that Jenna was three months pregnant on their wedding day, they'd had other things to worry about.

Though Clarissa had the decency not to say so, Jenna suspected she was relieved when the pregnancy ended in a miscarriage three months later, saving the Morgans the humiliation. Instead Clarissa had milked it for sympathy. Jenna had overheard her tell a friend at church, "Poor Jenna got pregnant practically on their honeymoon, but at least she was only a couple of months along when she miscarried."

Let Clarissa fudge on the numbers if she thought it saved face. Never mind that Jenna's "wedding dress" had been tent-shaped because she was already showing by then. She wondered what Zach's mother would say if she knew the whole truth.

To Zach's credit, he'd somehow put a stop to their blame game. She'd probably be out on the street right now if he hadn't smoothed things over between her and his parents.

"Zach didn't want me working either, especially not with the baby coming."

"The baby?" Clarissa's carefully penciled brows lifted. "What does that have to do with anything? That was years ago." Her eyes narrowed to silvery gray slits. "Just how deep in debt are you?"

It felt wrong to reveal their secrets when Zach wasn't there to defend himself. Zach may have fooled his parents, may have even fooled himself, since Jenna was always the one who paid the bills. But the truth was, they'd been up to their eyeballs in debt long before Zach died. And without insurance on their mortgage or any of their credit cards—a decision Jenna had pushed for—she'd inherited over a quarter of a million dollars in debt at Zach's death. And only a little more than half of that was the mortgage.

She might be sorry later for what she was about to say, but she wasn't just hinting this time. She was merely telling the truth about her options. "I—I'll probably have to declare bankruptcy to keep the house from foreclosure."

Clarissa gasped. "You'll do no such thing! I will not let our—*Zach's* good name be destroyed that way. Wait until Bill gets home and we'll work something out. You may have to sell the house," she conceded, "but you will *not* declare bankruptcy."

Jenna tensed and bit her lip to keep from saying something she'd regret later. It drove her crazy the way Clarissa had perched Zach atop a pedestal the day he died a hero's death. If only Zach could have had his parents' support while he was living. She reminded herself that it was Bill and Clarissa's generosity that allowed her to have the kind of life she'd never dreamed possible before meeting Zachary Morgan.

Relief flooded her. As difficult as it was to confess the truth, she should have known Zach's parents would take care of things. Clarissa might hold it over her head for a while, but at least they would help her get out of the mess she was in. She should have let them know how much she'd struggled financially long before now.

But it meant she had no choice but to lay open her bank statements and confess the truth to them. The truth about their finances anyway.

Other truths—one in particular that haunted her still—Jenna Morgan would take to her grave.

3

Friday, November 7

*L*ucas deposited his breakfast dishes in the sink and, using the counter to steady himself, worked his way to the dining room. He was growing steadier on his feet each day and rarely used his cane in the house anymore. But he wasn't fooling anyone, least of all himself. He was a long way from being ready to go back to work. Back on duty.

He'd wished a thousand times that he was one of the fallen. To have died a hero, to have left loved ones grieving his death—

An image of Jenna Morgan, weeping over Zach's casket at the graveside service, filled his mind, and he was tempted to entertain it. Ironically, the image wasn't even one he'd distilled from real life. He'd still been in the hospital—unconscious—when they buried his father and the others. The haunting image of Zach's wife came from a newspaper photograph—one that had run in the *Hanover Falls Courier* the day after the funerals and had been picked up by the AP and run across the nation.

He'd stared at the half-page photo from his hospital bed and wished it had been he who'd died instead of Pop. Instead of Zach. He would have traded places with any of them in a heartbeat.

Zach was an engineer. He should have been manning the truck. He *never* should have been in that building. Jenna should not be a widow.

The truth—wrong as it was, guilty as it made him feel—was that he'd envied Zach even when his buddy was alive. To have a woman like Jenna love you . . . he could only imagine.

He tried to banish the disturbing scenes from his mind, but Jenna's lovely image resisted, hovering at the fringe of his thoughts. Lucky appeared around the corner and came to rub against his leg, begging to be stroked. Lucas nudged the cat away, as if he could push away thoughts of Jenna as easily. No need to add lust and envy to his already lengthy list of sins.

But memories bombarded him. Among the things he'd lost in the fire was the barely blossoming love of the woman he'd started dating three months before the fire.

Cate Selvy didn't hold a candle to Jenna

Morgan, but he'd been in love with Cate. Or so he'd thought. She'd visited him in the hospital. Once. At least according to his mother. He had no recollection of seeing Cate there. And except for one awkward encounter at the Hanover Falls Pharmacy a few weeks after he'd been released from rehab, he hadn't seen her since.

So much for true love.

Recalling that day in the pharmacy still made the blood rush to his face. He would never forget the look on Cate's face as he maneuvered his wheelchair away from the counter after paying for his prescriptions. Trying to avoid hitting the person behind him, he'd backed into a display of vitamins. Bottles clattered to the ground. Mortified, he reached to pick them up. Cate knelt to help, only then recognizing that it was him in the chair.

She tried hard to cover her surprise with a pasted-on smile, but the revulsion in her eyes spoke the truth of her feelings.

After an interminable, awkward silence, she mumbled something, ducked her head, and veered down the cosmetics aisle.

She'd called him once after that. He hadn't answered. A few months later his sister Victoria told him Cate had moved to St. Louis.

Not that it mattered. Not that she had ever mattered. He was over her. And Cate was no Jenna Morgan.

He hadn't had a date since Cate—despite his sisters' concerted attempts to set him up. Even from their out-of-state colleges, Gina and Victoria had been relentless matchmakers. And although he assured them and his mother otherwise, he doubted he would ever date again. Certainly not marry. Even if he were interested, what kind of woman wanted half a man?

"Lucas?"

"In here, Ma." He limped toward the dining room, grateful for the distraction. His poor mother had put up with his whining for a year now. He inhaled deeply. Time to shove the gloomy thoughts back into the closet of his mind.

"Oh! There you are." Emily Vermontez appeared around the corner, her trademark smile in place even before she spotted him. "Did you have breakfast already?"

"I made toast. You want some?"

"No, I was going to offer to make pancakes."

"Thanks, but I'm good."

A strange look lit his mother's eyes. "Do you mind fending for yourself for dinner?"

"Again?"

"Mmm-huh." She turned away, grabbing a dishrag and scrubbing at the already pristine porcelain of the sink. "Geoff heard about a new place in Springfield he wants to try."

This was getting suspicious. His mom and Geoff Morrison had been hanging out together for several months, but this was at least the third time they'd gone out this week.

He opened his mouth to ask what the deal was, then thought better of it.

His mother turned toward him, weaving the dishrag between slender fingers. Her usually clear nails were polished a bright shade of orange. Her thick black hair was pulled off her face, and it struck Lucas that the deep crows' feet that usually marked the corners of her eyes had faded, making her look ten years younger than her fifty-four years.

"I've been wanting to talk to you about Geoff." A smile bloomed across Ma's face, and her brown eyes glinted with a spark they hadn't held since before tragedy took Pop from them.

He cocked his head, bracing for what he already feared was coming. "What's up with you two? I thought Geoff was just a friend."

She lifted one shoulder in a shrug. "He is a friend. A very dear friend. And—" She let loose a breathy sigh. "It's turning into something more, Luc. It's getting a little . . . well, serious."

"Serious? What's that supposed to mean?"

"Geoff wants to marry me." His mother actually blushed.

Lucas froze. "You're kidding."

"Would I kid about something like that?"

"You're not seriously considering it?"

A determined glint flashed in her eyes. "Yes, Luc. I am."

"It's only been a year, Ma." Even though he'd somehow known this news was inevitable, he'd hoped it would be a long time before his mother and Geoff moved beyond friendship.

She came and wrapped him in a hug. He steadied himself against the countertop, returning her embrace with one arm. She trembled against him, but when she looked up at him, she wore a peaceful smile, not the tears he expected.

"I loved your father with all my heart. No woman could have loved a man more. You know that."

He did know that. So why couldn't that be enough for her?

As if she'd read his thoughts, she sighed and stepped away from him, smoothing the wrinkles from the front of his shirt with slender, olive-skinned fingers. "Your dad isn't coming back, sweetheart. Geoff is a good man. If I live to be as old as my mother, I still have a lot of years yet to live. I don't want to be alone the rest of my days on this earth."

"Ma—"

She reached up and pinched his cheek playfully. "I don't want *you* to be alone either, Luc."

He placed a hand over hers. "Don't go trying to change the subject on me." The lighthearted tone he'd tried to find failed miserably. "Besides, I've got Lucky to keep me company."

She ignored his sorry attempt at levity. "Honey . . .

I understand how hard this news is for you. Your dad was the closest thing to a saint this side of heaven and—"

"News? Are you trying to tell me you've made a decision?"

She bit the corner of her bottom lip and nodded slowly. "I'm going to say yes to Geoff. I love him, and he treats me like a queen. He wants to get married right away and—"

Lucas held up a hand, wanting to make it easier for her, even while his heart ached. "And you need me out of here by the end of the month. . . . I can take a hint."

His mother laughed her musical laugh, and he felt his heart softening.

"Not so fast, buddy. No, actually, the bank has offered to move me to one of their Springfield branches. Geoff and I will live in his house in Springfield after we're married."

Geoff Morrison was a professor at one of the smaller universities in Springfield. Lucas couldn't even remember which one. He liked the guy fine, but that didn't make it any easier to think about him and Ma—together.

"I was hoping you'd stay on here," Ma continued. "I don't know if your sisters will come back to live over the summer, but if they want to, I'd like them to have a place. This will be hard enough for them. . . ." A shadow crossed her face, but then a teasing spark came to her eyes. "You could keep paying the same rent you've been paying."

Which was zero.

"But"—the spark in her eyes grew to a twinkle—"don't think for a minute that I'm going to come over and cook and clean and wash your underwear for you."

"Aw, come on, where's the fun in that?" He tried to rumple her hair—a ploy guaranteed to elicit a girlish squeal—but she ducked out of reach, almost sending him sprawling. He clutched the counter and steadied himself.

She shook a finger at him. "I am also not going to hound you about your rehab and exercises, but I'd better not find out you've skipped so much as one session." She said it jokingly, but he knew she was dead serious.

If not for his mother's nagging, he would have given up a hundred times over the past year of grueling rehab. If it weren't for her, his butt would probably still be glued to that wheelchair.

"I'm a big boy," he teased. "I think I can handle things. And I will start paying rent the minute I get back to work."

"I know you will, son."

"Only . . . what about Pop's flowers?" He hadn't meant to turn serious on her again, but Pop had turned their backyard into an oasis of flower gardens and flagstone paths. It would kill him, and his sisters, too, to see it all go to seed.

She sighed. "I don't know, honey. I can't really expect you to keep them up. It's practically a full-time job. Maybe I can hire someone to come in once or twice a week . . . at least keep things from becoming a jungle. We may have to just turn it all back to lawn."

"Don't do that," Lucas said too quickly. Since Pop's death the backyard was the one place Lucas still felt his father's presence. "Let's see if we can find someone to take care of it. I'll do what I can."

But he couldn't pretend to possess his father's green thumb, even if he had the physical strength to take on such a project. He hesitated, not really wanting the answer to the question he was about to pose. "So have you and the professor set a date?"

Ma shot him the same look she'd doled out routinely back when he was a mouthy teen. But her scowl softened. "Not yet, but . . . we're hoping soon after Christmas."

He stared at her. "Whoa. You're not messing around, are you?"

"I love him, Luc."

"I know, I know . . ."

He wasn't sure if the tears that welled in her eyes now were happiness because of Geoff or sadness because of his father.

He pulled her in for a brief hug. "I tell you, it's pretty sad when a guy's mother can get a date before he can."

Her laughter was just the response he was going for, but his joke hit a little too close to home. He and Ma had grown close over the past year. She had nursed Lucas through days he thought he couldn't go on. For much of that time, he'd been too gripped by his own agony to realize how deeply she was hurting. There was no way he would deny her a chance at happiness with Geoff.

But he was glad when Ma hurried out the door to go to work. She would have seen right through his plastic smile.

4

*Y*ou have a lovely home. I don't see why—even in the current market—we can't get your asking price, or very close to it anyway." Maggie Preston smoothed a nonexistent wrinkle from the jacket lapel that bore a shiny Realtor's pin.

Jenna had spent two full days cleaning, getting the house ready for the real estate agent's walk-through. Apparently her efforts had paid off.

She stifled a sigh of relief. As much as she dreaded the move, it would take a huge load off her mind to be out from under the mortgage payments. The grief books she'd read all said it was wise to wait at least a year after a loss before making any major life changes. She wondered if Bill and Clarissa had taken that first anniversary—less than a week ago—into consideration when they'd invited her to move in with them.

The invitation still surprised her. But she was grateful. She'd stayed with Bill and Clarissa for a few weeks following Zach's funeral—when she simply couldn't face going home to the empty house. They'd gotten along well, and she thought it had comforted the Morgans a little to have her there . . . the closest thing to having their son back.

She'd moved back home only when she could no longer deny—or conceal—a truth she didn't have the strength to face then. Memories bombarded her, but she fought them off. *Not now. This wasn't the time. . . .*

"I have a little house you might be interested in." The Realtor's voice pulled her back, and she brightened, grateful for the interruption.

"Thanks, but I'm going to stay with my in-laws for a while."

Maggie looked at her like she couldn't be serious.

"Don't worry," Jenna assured her. "They have a huge house—in Clairemont Hills. I'll have their lower level, a walk-out basement, to myself. It's practically a little apartment."

"Oh, well, that's different," Maggie said.

Would it be? Jenna couldn't deny how good the Morgans had been to her. The memory of their many kindnesses pricked her conscience. There'd been tears in Clarissa's eyes the other day when she'd invited Jenna to move in with them. "It's the least we can do for our son's wife."

Jenna wondered then, was she still Zach's wife? Would she forever wear the identity of "Zach Morgan's widow"?

Walking Maggie to the door a few minutes later, she glanced at the clock. Bryn Hennesey was due to pick her up for lunch in a few minutes. It had been several weeks since she'd last seen her friend, and she was looking forward to a chance to catch up on each other's news.

Maggie buttoned her jacket and reached for the doorknob. "I'll try to give you as much warning as possible before I show the house, but you might want to be ready on short notice. I expect this one to go pretty fast. It's a desirable neighborhood and you've done a beautiful job staging the house."

Jenna shrugged. "I didn't do anything special. Just cleaned."

"Well, your decorating style is just right for a home on the market." She turned back toward the living room and swept an arm over the view. "Tidy and a bit spare, nothing too personal on display, furniture arranged to make the rooms look as large as possible . . . Nice work."

Jenna followed Maggie outside and stood on the porch as the Realtor pulled a For Sale sign out of her trunk and planted it in the front yard.

Jenna smiled and waved as she drove away, but

she couldn't get the woman's parting comments out of her mind. She'd never thought of her home as "spare and impersonal" or even tidy, for that matter. She wondered what that said about her.

She brushed the questions away. They didn't matter now. She was selling the house and moving in with Zach's parents. She kneaded the spot between her eyebrows where a band of tension thrummed. She knew Bill and Clarissa would expect her to find a job. Clarissa had said as much the day she'd agreed to move in with them.

Not that she had any choice. Even if she got her full asking price for the house, she would net very little—nowhere near enough to pay off her debts. Never mind that most of the down payment on the mortgage had come from Bill and Clarissa. It had been a gift. She only hoped they wouldn't expect her to pay it back now.

Back inside, she walked through the rooms of her house, trying to see them through the eyes of a potential buyer. The house was only four years old and looked almost new. The granite counters in the kitchen were shiny and clear of clutter, and dark cherry cabinets stood sentinel over the adjacent dining room, Jenna's favorite spot in the house.

The doorbell rang and she ran to let Bryn in.

"What's up with the sign?" Bryn swept a strand of dark hair off her forehead and hooked a thumb over her shoulder toward the front lawn.

Jenna looked at the floor. "I'm selling. I just can't keep up with the payments."

"Oh, Jen . . . I'm sorry. Where will you go?"

She accepted Bryn's sympathy hug. "Would you think I was crazy if I told you I was moving in with Zach's parents?"

A shadow crossed Bryn's face. "Not necessarily crazy, but"—she dropped her head—"I guess that'll be the end of our lunch dates."

"I won't let that happen, B. Clarissa and Bill don't control my life." She didn't even want to think about the Morgans' reaction if they found out how close she and Bryn had become over the last few months.

Last January, Bryn had come forward and confessed to being responsible for the fire that had killed Zach and the others, including Bryn's own husband. It was all a tragic accident—a candle left burning—but Bryn had been convicted of involuntary manslaughter and had served hours of community service for her mistake.

Bill and Clarissa were outspoken in their anger over what they felt was far too lenient a sentence. They'd been furious when Jenna offered Bryn forgiveness, and for a while—to her shame— Jenna had avoided Bryn on the Morgans' account.

Her friend's silence now spoke volumes, and Jenna felt her defenses rising. "It's just for a while, until I can find a place of my own. But I promise, this won't change our friendship, Bryn."

Bryn gave her an enigmatic smile and looked at her watch. "Hey, I've got Sparky in the car. I need to drop him off at the vet. And if you don't mind, I'd like to stop by the shelter and pick up some stuff from Susan before we go eat."

Jenna tensed, mentally bracing herself for an encounter with Bryn's dog, but she kept her voice light. "No problem. I've got the whole afternoon."

"Must be nice."

"Oh? Do you have to work this afternoon?" Jenna felt bad for flaunting her freedom. Bryn not only worked part-time at the public library, but she still volunteered at the new homeless shelter—work that served as her community service.

"No, but I sure wouldn't mind having every afternoon off."

"Well, don't envy me too much. As soon as I get the house sold, I'll be joining the ranks of the gainfully employed, too. I can't expect Zach's parents to bail me out forever."

Bryn's eyebrow went up. "Yeah, I'm thinking that will end about the time you bring a boyfriend home."

"Oh? You have someone in mind for me?" Jenna teased.

Bryn laughed. "No. But I'll start looking if you want me to."

Jenna shook her head, sobered by the turn the conversation had taken.

Bryn's voice softened and she put a hand on

Jenna's arm. "Hey, girl, it's been a long, hard year. You deserve to find somebody wonderful. When you're ready, of course." Bryn looked down, fumbling with the keys in her hand.

Jenna knew she meant their shared tragedy, but of everyone who'd lost loved ones in the Grove Street fire, Bryn had surely suffered most. She had lost her husband, whom she'd loved deeply. But to also carry the burden of being responsible for the fire . . . Jenna shuddered to think what it must be like living with that guilt.

What happened to Bryn could have happened to anyone. And yet, in some ways Jenna envied Bryn. Bryn had grieved Adam deeply, but now she had a wonderful man in her life. She and Garrett Edmonds planned to marry as soon as Bryn completed her obligation to community service.

Jenna forced herself to brighten and turned the subject back to Bryn. "Speaking of somebody wonderful, how's that guy of yours?"

Bryn's smile set her face aglow. "He's great. Ready for Christmas break, I think, but he has a pretty good group of kids this year."

Garrett taught at Hanover Falls Middle School. His wife, Molly—a firefighter—had also died in the Grove Street fire. It seemed nothing short of a miracle that Garrett had been able to forgive Bryn. Jenna was glad she'd found happiness again with Garrett, though the sadness in Bryn's brown eyes would probably always dwell there.

Jenna tried not to feel envious of the relationship Bryn and Garrett had, but sometimes she wondered when it would be her turn. Or had Zach been her one chance at love?

If so, she'd blown it. Big time.

She held back a sigh, not wanting to reveal her thoughts. Bryn was the only one she didn't have to pretend with about what her and Zach's relationship had actually been, but she wasn't in the mood to talk about that today. She would be in "pretend mode" full-time when she moved in with Zach's parents, and today would be a good rehearsal.

Bryn unlocked the car and opened the back door a couple of inches. "Sparky, stay!" She reached in and held the collar of the excitable black Labrador while Jenna climbed into the passenger seat of the Honda Accord.

Wrinkling her nose at the smell of doggy breath, she spoke to the dog, trying not to let Bryn see how nervous he made her. "Hey there, Sparky."

She sat forward in the seat, keeping as much distance as possible between her and the dog and trying to keep her voice steady. "I thought he was staying out at your dad's."

Bryn frowned. "He is . . . most of the time, but I think I'm going to have to bring him back into my apartment. Dad's had some more spells with his heart."

"Oh, Bryn . . . I'm sorry."

"They don't think it's anything serious, but keeping up with Sparky is just too much for him." She laid her arm across the seat and turned to back down the driveway. "But Garrett says we can't have both Boss and Sparky, so I'm going to have to figure something out. You don't know anybody who'd like a nice Lab, do you? He really is a great dog."

"Can't think of anybody offhand, but I'll let you know if I do." Dogs made her nervous, to put it mildly. As a child she'd been petrified. The Morgans' little Quincy had helped her get her fears somewhat under control, but she avoided large dogs if at all possible.

When they pulled up in front of the new homeless shelter a few minutes later, Jenna forced herself to be brave and wait in the car with the dog while Bryn ran in to talk to Susan Marlowe, the shelter's director.

The dog paced the floor of the car's backseat from window to window, letting out a low growl. Grateful for the high seat backs that created a barrier between her and the animal, Jenna tensed and grabbed the door handle, poised for a fast escape. "What's wrong, buddy?" Zach had always told her dogs could sense her fear, but it was impossible to keep her voice from trembling.

She did not like the way this dog was acting. Quincy sometimes yapped, but Sparky was five times the size of the Morgans' dog and his growl held menace. The Lab stuck his nose out the crack in the window behind her and let out a sharp bark, then pawed at the glass.

"What's wrong, boy?" she said again. Cautiously she unlatched the door handle. Feeling a little foolish, she slipped out of the car, closing the door behind her. While the dog kept up the racket, she leaned against the fender, trying to think how she would explain her exit from the vehicle.

She was relieved when Bryn pushed through the shelter's front door carrying a stack of manila envelopes. She must have heard the barking because she took off at a jog toward the car. "Is everything okay?" She eyed Jenna. "What happened?"

Jenna shrugged. "He just . . . started barking."

Bryn pushed the dog's nose back inside the car window and spoke harshly. "Sparky! Hush!" She went around and climbed into the driver's seat, tossing the envelopes on the console. "Has he been barking the whole time?"

"For a while."

"He must have seen a squirrel or something."

"I didn't see anything."

Sparky kept it up even when Bryn put the car in gear. "Something's really bothering him." She shifted back into Park and got out of the car.

Jenna followed suit.

"I've never seen him like this. Except—" A strange look came over Bryn's face.

"What's wrong?"

"He got all wound up like this the night of the fire. It was before any of us even smelled smoke, but I've always wondered if Sparky tried to warn us."

Jenna sniffed the afternoon air and smelled only the pungent scent of earth moist from recent rains and leaves decaying on the grass. She looked across the street to where the original shelter had stood. "Do you think he remembers?"

Bryn followed Jenna's gaze but shook her head. "Surely not after a year. It's not like there's anything there now that he'd recognize. But you do hear stories about dogs finding their way home from hundreds of miles away, so maybe he remembers something familiar about this place."

The burned-out shelter was nothing more than a deep gouge in the lot now. According to Bryn, Susan Marlowe hoped to someday put a park on the property so the children of families staying at the shelter would have someplace to play. Susan was also a widow of the Grove Street fire.

Bryn checked her watch and opened the car door. "If you don't mind, I'm going to let him run a little bit. He's been cooped up in the car all morning and he'll have to be kenneled at the vet. Sorry, I know you're probably starving." She gave Jenna an apologetic look.

"No, it's fine." Jenna shrugged, not excited about the idea, but feeling at Bryn's mercy since it was her dog and her car. "Lunch will taste that much better when we finally get there."

Bryn clicked her tongue and Sparky shot across the shelter's patchy lawn, then quickly changed direction, darted around the side of the building, and disappeared.

"Sparky!" Bryn shouted and took off after him.

Jenna followed, not thrilled at the turn this day was taking. She picked her way through the tangle of weeds behind the building, trying to stay on the path Bryn had tromped down. Even as she followed, she plotted a route of escape in case Sparky headed her way. Not that she could outrun him.

The dog was digging in a pile of rubble behind the building. Bryn crouched near him and when she rose, she held up what looked like a soggy white handkerchief. "Come on, Sparky. Come!"

He ignored her and she finally dragged him by the collar with her free hand, still holding the rag in her other. When she got closer, Jenna saw that the rag protruded from a plastic water bottle with an inch or two of amber liquid in the bottom.

"What is that?"

Bryn sniffed the bottle gingerly, wrinkling her nose. "It smells like gasoline. Sparky went straight for it."

Jenna started back for the car, keeping plenty of distance between her and the dog.

Sparky fought against Bryn all the way back to the car. "I don't know what his problem is," she growled, manhandling him into the backseat again. But instead of going around to the driver's side, Bryn held up her find. "I think Susan needs to see this. I'll be right back. . . ."

"I'll come with you." No way was she going to be left alone with that dog again.

She followed Bryn to the front entrance. The door was locked, but Bryn pounded loudly, then peered through the glass door.

A few seconds later they heard keys rattling and Susan opened the door. She looked past Bryn. "Jenna! I haven't seen you in ages."

Not since Bryn's sentencing, probably. "Hi, Susan."

"Bryn said you two were having lunch." She turned to Bryn, then noticed the bottle she carried and furrowed her forehead. "What's that?"

Bryn explained how Sparky had dug it up from behind the building. "It smells like gas. I don't know if somebody was cleaning paintbrushes or what, but it seemed a little dangerous to have it lying around. I could just imagine one of the guys going out for a smoke and . . ."

Susan winced at the suggestion. "Nobody's been painting for a couple of weeks." She took the rag from Bryn and sniffed, then made a face.

"Sparky went straight for it."

"Show me where you found it."

Susan led them inside, where Bryn took the lead, walking through a large dayroom furnished with a mismatched collection of sofas and

50

recliners. She pushed open a back door by the kitchen and pointed out the spot where she'd discovered the odd find.

"Maybe the crew that mowed the lawn left it?"

Susan rolled her eyes. "As you can see they never got around to mowing the place last summer." She took the bottle from Bryn, who sniffed her fingers, then bent to wipe her hands off in the dry grass.

"I think maybe I should show this to Pete," Susan said. "After everything that's happened I don't want to take any chances—" She stopped short and her face turned crimson. "I'm sorry, Bryn. I didn't mean—"

"No, it's okay. I think you *should* report it. It seems pretty suspicious."

Susan seemed relieved that Bryn wasn't offended by her remark. She quickly changed the subject and led them back to the front door. "Thanks for letting me know about this. You guys have a great lunch."

"Thanks," they said in unison.

Back in the car Sparky had calmed down, but Jenna gave an inward sigh of relief when they dropped him off at the vet a few minutes later.

By one o'clock she and Bryn were enjoying fragrant cream of potato soup in bread bowls at the new deli downtown, but Jenna couldn't seem to put all her worrisome thoughts aside and simply enjoy the afternoon with her friend.

5

Monday, November 10

*J*enna, it's Maggie. Sorry to bother you on such short notice, but I have a couple here who'd like to look at the house."

"Hey, don't apologize for doing your job." Jenna tucked the phone between her ear and shoulder and started loading breakfast dishes into the dishwasher. "Give me fifteen minutes and I'll be out of here."

Thank goodness she'd cleaned up the kitchen after baking this morning, and the house was perfumed with the scent of homemade blueberry muffins.

"I don't want to get your hopes up, but I think your house might be just what they're looking for."

"Let's hope so." She put more conviction behind the words than she felt. Not that she had any other option but to sell her house, but she'd spent the weekend mourning the nicest home she'd ever lived in—and trying to imagine what it would be like living with Bill and Clarissa. The Morgans' house was twice the size and ten times as fancy as this one, but she was starting to have second thoughts about losing her freedom.

Maybe she should take Bryn's lukewarm reaction when she'd heard Jenna was moving in with Zach's parents to heart. Not that she'd come right out and said she thought it was a bad idea, but Jenna could read the skepticism in her friend's expression. What choice did she have, though? It would only be for a while. Until she could find a job and a place of her own.

She finished straightening the house—an easy task since she'd cleaned top to bottom before it went on the market last week—then grabbed her purse and car keys. Maggie Preston had shown the house only once before today, but she assured Jenna things would pick up once the listing appeared in the *Courier.*

Winding her way down her street, she met Maggie's car and they waved. Maggie had promised to call her cell with the all clear when she was done. Jenna decided to drive through for coffee and maybe pick up a sandwich to take home for later. Surely it couldn't take that long to show the house. She'd probably only have to kill an hour.

There were four cars in line at the drive-through at Java Joint. It would be quicker to go in. She could find a cozy chair and wait for Maggie's call. She parked the car and went inside.

There were half a dozen people seated inside, and two women in line ahead of her. A lone barista was trying to handle both the counter and the drive-through traffic, and from the look of things she wasn't having much success. Jenna inhaled the wonderful fresh-brewed coffee aroma and lopped her jacket over a comfy armchair in the corner to reserve a place.

She was paying for her latte a few minutes later when she heard a familiar voice.

She turned to see Lucas Vermontez coming through the door. Zach's buddy walked with a pronounced limp, and with aid of a cane, but Jenna was surprised he was on his feet at all. He'd been in a wheelchair the last time she'd seen him. And in the throes of depression. At least, that was what the Hanover Falls grapevine rumored.

Almost a year ago.

Lucas had been one of Zach's best friends at the firehouse. He was the only survivor of the crew who'd gone inside the homeless shelter the night of the fire. Lucas's father, the captain of Station 2, had died in the blaze that night, too. Jenna had met Manny, but hadn't known him well. He was one of Zach's bosses when he and Lucas were rookies in the same training class.

Lucas had hung out at their house sometimes for Monday night football and pizza—when the guys weren't pulling a shift. And he'd helped Zach hang Sheetrock the year they finished out the basement family room. Jenna felt as if she knew him better than she really did because Zach talked about him so much. Zach practically idolized

Lucas—the way he would have a big brother—even though she thought Lucas was a few years younger.

Lucas seemed thinner than she remembered. His Cuban heritage was evident in his jet-black hair and olive skin, and it was good to see him smiling. She noticed his entrance turned more than a few female heads in the coffee shop, and it wasn't because of his shuffling gait or the cane. Yet he seemed oblivious to the female eyes following him.

She was tempted to pretend she didn't recognize him. What if he didn't recognize her? There was talk that he might have suffered a degree of brain damage.

But he seemed like his old self, greeting strangers with a friendly nod and grinning at the toddler perched in a highchair at a table by the door. She didn't want to be rude, so she picked up her order from the counter, gathered her courage, and wove her way between tables.

She caught his eye. "Lucas?" She held out a hand. "I don't know if you remember me . . ."

His eyes lit. "Jenna!" He switched his cane to his other side and shook her hand firmly. "Of course I remember. Good to see you again."

He sported the same crooked smile she remembered—as if he were about to burst out laughing—but the smile didn't quite make it to his dark eyes.

Nodding at his cane, she brightened. "You're getting around a lot better than the last time I saw you."

He shrugged and dipped his head, and Jenna wondered if he remembered that the last time they'd come face-to-face was just a few weeks after the funerals—which Lucas had missed because he was still in the hospital.

"Well . . . I'm glad to see you back on your feet." She cast around, looking in vain for a graceful exit. The line at the counter had grown longer while they exchanged greetings, and she grabbed at the excuse. "Sorry . . . I've made you lose your place in line."

"Not a problem. I'm in no hurry. Just . . . killing time." He glanced around the sunny room where tables were quickly filling up. "Are you staying? Would you mind sharing a table?"

"Oh . . ." She glanced toward her chair in the sunny corner near a book-lined wall. "I'm over there. In that chair. It doesn't look like—"

"Help yourself." An elderly man in the chair adjacent to hers apparently overheard. He rose slowly, plopping a worn fedora on his head. "I was just leaving."

"Are you sure?" She wasn't in the mood for conversation, but she could hardly say that to Lucas.

"Absolutely." The man winked and tipped his hat. "You kids enjoy."

Settling in the chair, she moved her jacket to reserve the other spot for Lucas while he ordered. She scrambled to think of something they could talk about that didn't involve the fire.

He carried his coffee over and set it on the wide windowsill behind their chairs, then used his cane to lower himself into the low-slung chair.

Leaning the cane carefully against a nearby bookcase, he let out a sigh and gave her a sheepish grin. Pushing his forearms against the chair's armrests, he joked, "I may need a crane to get out of this chair when it's time to leave."

She glanced around, then felt silly, realizing she must look as if she were searching for a crane in some hidden corner of Java Joint. "Uh . . . we'll figure something out."

Lucas didn't seem to notice. He took a sip of his coffee, then searched her eyes. "So how are you doing?"

She was never sure what people expected when they asked that question. In the first weeks after Zach's death, there was no doubt they were referring to her loss. But now that the first anniversary of the tragedy had passed, she never knew whether to answer the question in relation to Zach and the fire, or in relation to her "new normal."

She took a risk with Lucas because at least he understood what the fire had cost the community, even if he didn't know her own pain. "I'm hanging in there. How about you? How is your mom?"

A shadow darkened his countenance. "She's doing well. Moving on."

"Moving on? As in . . . literally moving?"

"It looks that way. It's not public knowledge yet, so don't say anything, but she's . . . I think she's getting married."

"Oh, that's wonderful." Too late, she saw in his eyes that he didn't agree. "I'm sorry. I'm sure that isn't easy for you."

He shrugged. "She's happy. She wasn't for so long, I really can't begrudge her this."

"I hope she's not moving too far away."

"Just to Springfield. That's where Geoff lives. Geoff Morrison."

"Well, tell Emily I've been thinking about her." She looked at her lap. "You too. I'm glad to see you're doing so well."

He grunted. "If you can call it that."

"You were in a wheelchair last time I saw you— with casts up to here." She drew a line above her knees, then gestured to his cane. "I'd say this is a huge improvement."

He shrugged. "I'll consider myself improved when I can get back to work."

"Any idea when that might be?" She felt as if she was prying, and worried he heard the skepticism in her voice. He didn't look anywhere near ready to return to the rigors of firefighting.

But he didn't seem offended. "I really don't know. Ma just told me a few days ago—about Geoff. I'm still trying to wrap my brain around it."

"I'll bet."

He grinned, obviously trying to put her at ease. "Oh well, I'm a big boy. Twenty-seven next month. It's probably time I was out on my own."

"Where will you go? Have you looked at apartments yet? I'm going to be looking one of these days, too," she confessed.

"You're moving, too?"

She nodded. "Not leaving the Falls, but I can't afford to keep our house." It made it seem so real to speak the words aloud. "I've got it on the market. Actually, that's why I'm camped out here. The Realtor's showing the house right now. I'm a little afraid it'll sell right away."

"Maybe you can just move in here." He winked and pointed toward the counter. "All the coffee you can drink, bathrooms in the back . . ."

"I'm moving in with Zach's parents for a while. And *I* just turned twenty-nine." She smiled, realizing the irony.

He cocked his head. "*Really* twenty-nine, or the twenty-nine all women claim after a certain age?"

"No, *really* twenty-nine."

He looked skeptical. "And you'll be thirty on your next birthday? Or twenty-nine again? Just checking."

"No really. I swear. I may stop counting at

thirty-nine, but honest, I'm twenty-nine right now. For real." She held up three fingers in a Scout's honor gesture.

He laughed. "Okay, okay, I believe you. It's nice you have someplace to go. I do, too, just so you know. Ma's renting the house to me as long as I want to stay."

"Over on Bramblewood, right? I always liked that house. Not that I've ever been inside . . ."

"Yeah, it's home. But it's going to feel awfully strange rattling around in there by myself. Me and the cat."

"Yeah. I know what you mean. And I don't even have a cat."

His face fell, as if he'd just realized the implications of his words. "I'm sorry, Jenna. You already know what it feels like—to be alone."

"Hey, I don't have a corner on the market. You've been there, too." She was saying the things she knew he expected her to say. She'd watched Bryn and Susan Marlowe carefully, learned to imitate the grief that always colored their voices when they spoke of their beloved husbands.

Lucas didn't seem to notice. "It's not the same. Sure, it was awful losing Pop, but I watched Ma go through what you've been through. It's different losing your . . . other half."

"But you had this to deal with, too." She nodded toward his cane, wishing she could erase this whole thread of their conversation.

He took another swig of coffee, then set his cup on the windowsill. "I have an idea: let's not sit here and try to figure out who has it worse."

She smiled, relieved. "Very good idea. Change of subject."

He turned and looked out the window, playfully craning his neck to look beneath the wide awning that covered the window. "Lovely weather we've been having, isn't it?"

"Not really," she deadpanned.

"Okay. That was lame. How 'bout them Chiefs?" He lifted a fist in a rah-rah gesture.

"Nope. I don't speak 'sports.'"

"Politics?"

"Definitely not."

He raked a hand through a head of gorgeous black curls. "Religion?"

She winced. "I'd rather not."

"Wow . . . I give up then. Your turn."

"Coffee?"

"Ah. Coffee. Now there's a fascinating topic. So what do you think of the caramel latte? Be honest now." His eyes flashed with mischief.

"Haven't tried it yet."

He blew out a sigh, obviously enjoying their lighthearted exchange. "So what's your poison?"

"House blend, black."

"Boring, boring. But that's probably why I've got this spare tire around my waist and you've kept your girlish figure." He patted his belly, which was a far cry from being a "spare tire."

She smiled but studied the nearly empty coffee cup in her hand, not sure how to respond to his compliment.

Lucas must have sensed her discomfort because when their eyes met again, his expression had turned serious, even guilty. She could almost read his mind: he'd been flirting with his buddy's wife—a married woman, as far as he was concerned.

"Listen, Jenna. I've wanted—" He twisted the lid from his coffee cup with long, slender fingers. "This might sound strange, and I hope it doesn't bring back bad memories—stuff you've tried to put behind you, but I've wanted a chance to talk to you."

She frowned, curious. "About what?"

"Zach and I got pretty close working together. I just . . . I hope you know how much he cared for you. How much he loved you. The guy's whole face would light up when he talked about you. He—" He closed his eyes and shook his head slowly. "That's probably enough. I'm sure I don't have to tell you how your husband felt about you, but someone told me something similar—about my dad, how he was proud of me. And it—it helped." He stopped, looking embarrassed.

But when he met her eyes again, he looked so sincere, it made her want to cry.

"It helped a lot," he said. "And I just thought

you should hear the same from Zach. From someone who heard it from his own mouth."

Jenna felt frozen to her chair. She pasted on a smile and murmured a shallow "thank you," but she felt as if Lucas Vermontez—however innocently—had punched her in her already-bruised heart.

She'd never doubted Zach's love for her. Didn't doubt for a minute that he lit up when he talked about her to the guys at the firehouse.

But how long could she pretend that she'd loved him the same? And how long would she carry the ache inside her because she hadn't?

6

Tuesday, November 11

*L*ucas retrieved the morning paper off the drive-way and trudged back to the kitchen, greeted by the smells of burnt toast and fresh-brewed coffee.

His mother appeared in the doorway. "Good morning, sunshine."

He grunted, not ready to engage yet this morning. He was still lost in a dream about Jenna Morgan. A guilty dream, but one he wasn't ready to surrender yet. It had been good to see her last night, good to laugh with someone and talk about mundane things.

But why did he have to go and bring up the fire? It had obviously upset her—and why wouldn't it? She'd clammed up after that. They'd talked for a few more minutes . . . about her move, about his desire to get back on at the firehouse. But thanks to him, the meeting had ended on a tense note.

After he got home yesterday, he'd considered calling her, maybe try to apologize for the direction their conversation had taken, and casually invite her to meet him at the coffee shop again. Now, in the light of day, that seemed like a stupid idea. But he'd already decided he would find excuses to hang out at Java Joint, just in case she showed up there again.

Too bad she was having to put her house on the market. He tried to imagine how he'd feel if Ma were to sell this house—the only home he could remember, and a place where memories of Pop seemed to reside in the very walls. Difficult as it had been at first—to be reminded of Pop in every room—those memories offered comfort now.

His mother opened cupboards and rummaged noisily through a jumble of travel mugs, mumbling as she tried to find a matching lid, then scolding Lucky when he got underfoot. "This stupid cat is going to put one of us in the hospital!"

The commotion pulled Lucas from his dreamworld. Just as well. His fantasies were just that.

Ma poured coffee into a tall mug and screwed the lid in place. She wore a smile that said she was in her own la-la land. He knew exactly who she was with there, too.

He hobbled across the kitchen to refill his mug. She handed him the creamer, and that's when he saw it. A ring twinkled on her finger. Not the simple anniversary band Pop had given her, but a sparkly diamond with tiny blue stones set on either side.

For a minute he couldn't breathe. So she was really going to do this.

"Oh, by the way," she said, gathering her purse and the bag she toted library books in, "I won't be here for dinner, honey. Can you fend for yourself?"

"I don't suppose this has anything to do with that big honkin' ring on your finger?"

She gave a little gasp and clasped her hands, covering the ring. But she couldn't camouflage her smile.

He held out a hand. "Let me see."

She presented her hand, turning her wrist so the stones caught the light.

"How long have you been carrying this rock around?"

"Since about nine o'clock last night. Isn't it beautiful?"

He shielded his eyes, pretending to be blinded by the glare.

She rewarded him with a schoolgirl giggle.

"I'm happy for you, Ma. I really am." The sudden lump in his throat took him by surprise. He swallowed over it and cleared his throat. "So, have you set a date?"

"Not yet, but we don't want to wait too long. It will be a quiet, private ceremony. We've talked about one of those wedding cruise packages." She looked up at him with a little shrug, as if trying to gauge his opinion of the idea.

"Well, let me know when you decide. I'm trying to set up some people to come in and tear out a couple of walls, maybe paint a room or two black."

She stared at him. "You're going to paint—?"

"Kidding, Ma. You can breathe now."

"Oh, you!" She landed a playful punch to his shoulder.

"Ow!" He rubbed the spot in feigned agony.

But she turned serious, cupping his unshaved cheek in her palm. "It's good to have my Luc back. Even if I do want to clobber him sometimes."

He wrinkled his nose and grinned at her.

She looked at the clock. "You'd better get moving. Don't you have PT this morning?"

He nodded. "I don't know why I'm bothering, though. I don't think it's helping."

"Yes, it is." She shook a finger in his face. "You're just too close to see it. You're so much better, Lucas. Don't you dare give up now."

He rolled his eyes. "Okay, I'm goin', I'm goin'. . . ."

"That's more like it." She slung her purse over one shoulder. "Speaking of which, I'd better get a move on, too. I might be late tonight—don't wait up."

He shook his head. "Man, is *that* a strange switch of roles."

"Hey, at least I never miss curfew, which is more than a certain young man I remember can say." Laughing, she went out through the garage.

He went to the sink and watched her car back out of the driveway. As hard as it was to think about Ma married to anyone but Pop, he had to admit it was good to see her smiling again. And Geoff was a good guy. A little stuffy, maybe—especially compared to Pop. But he was good to Ma, and he obviously made her happy. He wouldn't begrudge her that.

He thought about what his mother had said. He *was* better, at least emotionally. There had been some dark days after the fire. He didn't remember a lot of them, didn't want to remember. Even after he'd graduated from the wheelchair to the walker last spring, he'd plunged into a depression so deep he hadn't been sure he would ever find his way out.

He'd never told his mom—maybe she'd guessed—but there had been days he'd prayed to die. He never could have done anything . . .

desperate. That would have killed Ma after losing Pop. But he could beg God to take him. And he had.

But it wasn't his mental health Ma had been talking about this morning. She meant his physical condition. *Was* the physical therapy making a difference? Was he still improving, getting more mobility back? His legs were a mess. Flesh and muscle had been torn and scarred, and he was full of enough plates and pins to send airport metal detectors into conniptions.

It would have been bad enough if he'd only injured one leg, but to have both of them messed up was too much to deal with. His left leg was the worst. Since the surgeries, he'd had almost a year to heal. His doctors said he'd likely seen most of the improvement he was going to see. If that was true, those hunks of concrete had crushed more than his legs.

But maybe the doctors were wrong. He dumped his coffee in the sink and put his mug in the dishwasher. He needed for them to be wrong.

He couldn't let himself think too hard about what life would be like if he had to live with this limp, with the cane, if he couldn't get in good enough physical shape to get back on with the fire department. It was the only thing he'd ever wanted—from the time he was a kid. To be a firefighter like Pop. And with Pop gone, he wanted it even worse.

Otherwise, nothing made sense anymore. Nothing.

7

*J*enna stared at the boxes stacked five-deep in the living room and wiped her forehead with the sleeve of her T-shirt.

As relieved as she was to have sold her house in less than two weeks—and for the asking price—it was sobering to realize that as of next week's closing she would officially be homeless. Not homeless as in needing the homeless shelter, of course, but homeless in the sense that she was twenty-nine years old and couldn't even provide for herself. Thank goodness she still had Bill and Clarissa.

For some odd reason, as she'd packed up her belongings and looked around this place that had been her home for a decade, she'd had flashbacks of her childhood home.

Sometimes when she closed her eyes she could smell the stale cigarette smoke and the mold growing in the corners of the bathtub in the two-bedroom mobile home in a run-down trailer park in St. Louis. She could hear the mice skittering behind the walls, and the Jacksons next door launching words at each other that even her mother didn't use.

Shaking off a reality she didn't want to claim any longer, she reached for the goldfish charm at her throat and rubbed it till it grew warm beneath her fingers. She ran her palm over the smooth finish of the dining room table and its matching chairs and hutch. Dug her toes into the plush carpeting as if she could tether herself to the luxury it represented.

This house wasn't rich by many standards, certainly not in Bill and Clarissa's eyes. But compared to where she'd grown up, it was a mansion. It had taken years of pinching herself to believe she could possibly deserve to live someplace like this. That she could be trusted to care for a real home with nice furniture and original paintings on the wall, and carpet that wasn't embedded with oil and spaghetti sauce and blood.

She wouldn't be here to watch the trees grow tall, or to see the flowers and perennials she'd planted come to life next spring.

It was beginning to hit her: she'd be at the mercy of Bill and Clarissa—for everything—while she was in their home.

She still hadn't mentioned Bryn Hennesey to Zach's parents. Every time she and Bryn got together, she was afraid Clarissa would ask where she'd been, and afraid Bryn would ask if she'd told the Morgans they'd been spending time together. She feared running into Clarissa when she and Bryn were together, though that was unlikely, since they didn't frequent any of the Morgans' high-class haunts.

She wasn't about to give up her friendship with Bryn, but something told her she'd better wait until she was firmly ensconced in the Morgans' house before she let that cat out of the bag.

She hauled three boxes out to the garage and came back inside to start working on the kitchen. Sitting cross-legged on the floor, she separated stacks of newspaper and began wrapping breakables. Thanksgiving was next week, but she wouldn't need her dishes since the Morgans had invited her to spend the holiday with them. Last year, Thanksgiving—and Christmas, too—had gone uncelebrated with Zach so recently buried.

Oddly, packing up this house that she and Zach had shared, wrapping dishes that had been wedding gifts, and storing away decorative items she would have no use for at the Morgans' had made her think more about Zach than she had in months.

She took a small measure of comfort in the fact that in the act of leaving this home they'd shared, she felt twinges of the emotions she'd feigned so well in the past year. Perhaps she'd loved Zachary Morgan more than she gave herself credit for.

But shouldn't a woman *know* whether or not she loved the man who'd been her husband for more than ten years? She'd thought she was over the

71

agony of wondering why Bryn and Susan Marlowe, Emily Vermontez, and even Garrett Edmonds could all mourn the loss of their spouses passionately and publicly, while she had to pretend.

Why couldn't she have loved her husband wholeheartedly? Even with the tension that was sometimes between them, Zach treated her with kindness. He had been a good man in life—and a hero in death.

Lucas's words about how much Zach had loved her were disturbing. In a deep way. She hated that she'd grown so adept at pretending. She'd become an actress . . . to the point that sometimes she even convinced herself.

The phone rang, echoing in the empty space. Crumpling the last sheet of newsprint, she jumped up and grabbed the phone on the third ring. "Hello?"

"Jenna? Hey, it's Bryn. How's the packing going?"

"It's going."

"Do you need a break?"

"I need one . . . not sure I have time to take one."

"What if I bring pizza over? I can help you pack until five or so."

"Hey, I can't turn down an offer like that!" She smiled into the phone. "Make it half pepperoni and you've got a deal."

Thirty minutes later, the two of them sat on

barstools at the kitchen counter washing down pizza with Diet Coke.

"I keep forgetting to tell you." Bryn wiped pizza sauce from the corner of her mouth. "Remember that day we stopped by the shelter and Sparky found that gasoline?"

Jenna nodded, remembering how anxious the dog's barking and growling had made her.

"He did it again the other day. At the shelter. Sparky almost never acts like that, so I let him take the lead. It was the craziest thing. . . . It was like he was a bloodhound or something. He led me to a pile of debris beside the Dumpster east of the building—sniffed out a can of paint solvent that was buried in all the remodeling trash."

"Somebody needs to haul that stuff off before there's another fire."

"No kidding. But you should have seen Sparky. He just stood there beside the Dumpster, waiting for me to praise him."

"Why would a dog sniff out something like that? I could see if it was a rabbit or a cat or something, but paint solvent?"

"I know. It's almost like he's been trained to detect it."

"Maybe he was. Does anybody know where that homeless guy got him?"

"No, I'm pretty sure Sparky was just a pup when Charlie got him." She frowned. "But now that you mention it, I'm not sure where Charlie adopted him from. I always assumed it was the Humane Society, but I'll ask him."

"You still see him?" Charlie was a homeless guy Bryn had taken a liking to when she volunteered at the shelter. He'd been moved to another shelter in Springfield after the fire.

"Once in a while," Bryn said. "We're trying to move him back to the Falls once the shelter is up and running. Susan Marlowe wants him to come on staff."

"On staff? She has a budget for that?"

"Well . . . not exactly paid. We're still dependent on volunteers. But she could give Charlie room and board. That's the arrangement he has now in Springfield, and Susan said she'd offer him the same."

"Maybe Charlie could take Sparky back. Aren't you still trying to find a new home for him?"

"I thought of that, but Susan wasn't crazy about the idea. She's not sure they're even going to let clients keep animals this time around. Since we're coming up against a lot of opposition to reopening the shelter, she's trying to avoid anything the least bit controversial."

"What will you do about the dog then?"

Bryn's shoulders slumped. "I don't know. I feel bad Susan is having to fight every step of the way. If it wasn't for the fire—"

"Hey, it's not your fault. From what I hear, it's really not the fire that has everybody so skittish."

74

"Well, it sure hasn't helped."

Rightfully or not—Bryn shouldered some of the blame for the community's resistance to the shelter. Letters to the editor in the *Courier* had been running two-to-one against the shelter, and some of them bordered on malicious.

Jenna tried to reassure her. "From what I've heard, it has a lot more to do with the assault." A few months before the fatal fire last winter, a man staying in the shelter had tried to rape a teenage resident. After that, Bryn's husband had forbade her to volunteer at the shelter. She'd secretly continued against Adam's will, which only added to her guilt. "People are just worried about the kind of people a homeless shelter brings in to town."

Word got around that James Friar had been convicted of the assault at the shelter, and when people learned that Friar was not only mentally ill but an addict as well, opinions of the shelter and its mission soured quickly. It didn't help that Friar's family had been vocal about the shelter's supposed negligence in protecting the teen. The Friars were long-time residents of the Falls, but they lived—in Clarissa's words—on the wrong side of the tracks. A ranting letter to the editor from Friar's mother had been published with embarrassing misspellings and grammatical errors intact. Jenna had to wonder if the paper edited letters from people on the "right side of the tracks."

"I don't have a clue what I'm going to do about the dogs." Bryn seemed eager to change the subject.

"You really can't keep him?"

Her friend shook her head. "There is no way Garrett and I can have both of the dogs at his place. And believe me, it will be easier to find a home for Sparky than for Boss."

Jenna grinned. "I see your point." Boss was Garrett's bulldog mutt.

"Besides, Garrett's a lot more attached than I am. I'm more worried about how my dad will feel to see Sparky go to someone else."

Jenna frowned and an idea started brewing. "You don't think the fire department would take him, do you? I remember Zach talking about Springfield using arson detection dogs. He was always wanting to get something like that started here. Maybe somebody at the station could train Sparky to be an arson dog?"

Bryn lit up. "That's not a half bad idea. He's definitely got a nose for it."

"Maybe I could talk to someone for you. Actually, I ran into Lucas Vermontez the other night at Java Joint. He might know who to talk to at the station."

Bryn's eyebrows lifted. "I didn't realize he was back to work."

"He's not. But he's hoping to be soon."

"Really? Susan said they weren't sure he'd even walk again."

"He was walking with a cane the other night. He has a pretty bad limp. . . . He's obviously not ready to be climbing ladders yet, but he looked great." She felt herself blush and wondered if she'd sounded a bit too enthusiastic.

But Bryn didn't seem to notice. She sighed and closed her eyes. "I'm so glad. That's good to hear."

Jenna recognized the faraway look in her friend's eyes, and she put a hand on Bryn's arm. "Stop it right now, B. I see where your mind is taking you. You don't have to carry this weight anymore. You've done everything you could possibly do to make things right."

Tears seeped from beneath Bryn's dark lashes, but she nodded and produced a crooked smile. "Thanks, Jen." She pushed a plate of pizza crusts away from her and slid off the stool, brushing her palms together like she meant business. "All right, then. If we're going to get you out of here before the new people move in, we've got work to do."

Jenna was grateful for the change of subject, but while they worked, she rehearsed her phone call to Lucas.

Tuesday, November 25

Jenna dialed the number from the Hanover Falls phonebook, surprised it was still listed as "Manuel Vermontez" more than a year after the fire.

The phone burred once. She blew out a breath and quickly placed the receiver on the hook. Her home phone was scheduled to be disconnected in a couple of days. Maybe it would be better to use her cell phone so Lucas would have her number in case he needed to call her back.

She flipped open her cell phone and punched in the number again, hoping it wouldn't be his mother who answered.

"Vermontez residence. This is Emily."

So much for hoping. "Um . . . hi, Mrs. Vermontez. This is Jenna Morgan. I'm—" She started to say she was Zach's wife, then thought better of identifying herself that way. Surely Emily would remember her, even though they hadn't seen each other since the funeral. "I don't know if Lucas told you, but I ran into him the other night."

"How nice to hear from you. I wasn't sure if you were still in the Falls or not."

Jenna loosened her grip on the phone and cleared off a place on the sofa. "Yes, I'm still here.

For now anyway. Lucas may have told you that I sold my house."

"Oh? I didn't know. You say you saw him the other night? He didn't mention it."

Jenna plunged ahead. "We just ran into each other at the coffee shop. It was good to see him looking so well."

"He's doing wonderfully. Better than we ever expected after the first surgeries. God has been good." Her voice wavered with emotion.

How could Lucas's mother say God was *good* after all they'd been through? Jenna cleared her throat. "Does Lucas happen to be home? Could I speak to him?"

"Sure, hang on a minute. He's here somewhere. It's nice to talk to you. We've missed seeing you at Susan's."

Bryn had told her about the other wives—and Garrett—gathering at Susan Marlowe's house in the months after the tragedy. The group had raised money to get the new shelter opened as a memorial to the fallen firefighters. Jenna had never taken part, despite repeated invitations from Susan. Back then she'd only wanted to put the tragedy behind her. More than that, she hadn't wanted to risk being exposed as the fraud of a widow she was to Zach.

"Oh, here's Lucas now. Luc, it's for you." Emily's stage whisper carried over the line. "It's Zach Morgan's wife."

Jenna cringed, but a moment later Lucas was on the line, his voice deep and matter-of-fact. "This is Luc."

"Lucas? Hi . . . It's Jenna Morgan."

"Hey, Jenna."

"I'm calling because I thought you might be able to help me with something."

"Well, if I knew what the something was, I just might." His voice held the teasing smile she remembered from the other night.

She relaxed a little. "This might sound strange, but I'm calling about a dog. A Labrador Retriever." She explained how Sparky had ferreted out the gasoline at the shelter. "According to Bryn, he went straight for it like he'd been trained as an arson dog. It's happened at least twice now."

"Do you think he *is* trained?"

"No . . . Bryn said he was just a puppy when Charlie got him, and she—or her dad—has cared for Sparky since the fire. But she needs to find a home for him. She's getting married in a few months, which is why I'm calling. Garrett already has a dog. . . ." She paused for a minute, and the silence on the line made her wonder if they'd been cut off.

But then he sighed. "I'm not sure . . . how you think I can help."

She could almost see his thick black eyebrows knit in question.

"Zach mentioned once that the fire department had entertained the idea of working with accelerant detection dogs. I have no clue how that even works, but Bryn and I got to talking and we wondered if maybe someone there would be willing to take Sparky . . . maybe with the idea of training him. To be an arson dog . . ." she finished lamely.

An uncomfortable silence filled the line. Finally Lucas cleared his throat. "I'm not back to work yet. You knew that, right?"

"Yes. But that—that's sort of why we thought of you. But maybe you don't have time for something like this. I just thought since—"

He gave a low grunt. "Pop had dogs when we were kids, but they were hunting dogs. I wouldn't know how to teach a dog to sit and stay, let alone train one for accelerant detection. I'm sure there's a science to it."

She cleared her throat. "Actually, Bryn says he's already got the sit-and-stay stuff down. Her dad has been working with him a little." She could almost hear him scrambling for a way to extricate himself from her proposal.

"I suppose I could talk to someone at the station. I'm not sure who would handle that, but I guess we'll find out."

"Oh, that would be great. Thanks, Lucas." She tried not to sound as surprised as she felt, and before she lost her nerve added, "Would it be all right if I bring Sparky by sometime? So you can meet him?"

"I guess that'd be okay. When were you thinking?"

"What works best for you? I'm sure you have plans for Thanksgiving, and I'm moving this weekend anyway, but I could do it about anytime the following week. Oh, Bryn will be so relieved!"

"Hang on a minute—I haven't agreed to anything yet."

She inhaled sharply, then giggled. "I know. Sorry. Didn't mean to make you nervous."

He echoed her laughter. "You did have me a little worried there. Tell you what, let me talk to somebody at the station. I'll see what I can do. And um . . . just so you know, I'm more of a cat person."

"Really? I wouldn't have guessed that."

" 'Fraid so. Cats rule, dogs drool."

That made her laugh, even though she was disappointed that he didn't seem too enthused about her and Bryn's idea. She must be crazy to have agreed to transport that stupid dog to Luc's, but she was excited at the prospect of seeing him again.

She'd forgotten what it felt like to just have fun with a guy. Or maybe she'd never known. In sixth grade she'd had a crush on a boy, but Zach was the only guy she'd ever dated. They'd been together all through her high school years, even after he graduated and left for Springfield to study fire science, and later when he moved back to the Falls to work.

"So, what do you think?" Lucas's voice broke through her rambling thoughts.

"I'm sorry—what was that?"

"I wondered if you want to go for coffee again. After you get moved in, I mean. I could pick you up . . . Tuesday? Think you'll be settled by then?"

If she didn't know better, she'd think he was asking her for a date. But she smiled into the phone, happy he wanted to see her again. "I'd like that."

"Good. I'll give you a call. Hope your move goes okay."

"Thanks." She hung up, feeling a little bewildered. What had she gotten herself into?

9

Sunday, November 30

There! That's done!" Bill Morgan secured the plastic tarp over the furniture Jenna was storing in the Morgans' garage and brushed the dust off his hands. "You're sure everything else goes inside?"

Jenna nodded and wiped her face on the sleeve of her T-shirt.

"Okay, then." He pulled down the garage door behind them, and Jenna followed him around to the front of the Morgans' house on the circle drive.

Clarissa waited on the front porch, holding the door open. The three of them had spent all day moving Jenna's things out of her Brookside house and into Bill's fourth garage bay.

It had taken longer than she'd anticipated, and despite the brisk November wind, she was sweaty, tired, and hungry.

And homesick.

She supposed one could say she'd moved up in the world. She had the most desirable address in the Falls now—Clairemont Hills. But already she missed the Brookside house—and everything it had represented about how far she'd come.

Today, locking up the house for the last time—the house she and Zach had shared—had hit her harder than she'd expected. It didn't help that Clarissa had kept up a teary running commentary about her "sweet Zachary" the entire time they were loading boxes.

Bill looked up at the gray skies and mumbled under his breath. All day he'd lamented having to move his precious restored Karmann Ghia to make room for Jenna's things. The vintage car had gone in the bay where Bill's woodworking shop was. She felt bad about that and had offered to rent a storage unit for her furniture. But she couldn't afford the monthly fee and they knew it. Bill would have ended up having to pay that bill, too.

So many things to worry about. At least tonight she would keep busy setting up her new digs in the Morgan's walk-out basement. She grabbed a suitcase from the back of Clarissa's vehicle and headed toward the front door.

Bill shouldered a stack of boxes and started down the hallway that led to the bedrooms. Quincy followed, yapping and wagging his tail furiously.

"Wait, Bill. . . . Those go downstairs. To my room."

He turned and looked past Jenna to his wife, confusion drawing his brows together.

Clarissa waved him on down the hall. "No, go on. You're right." She glanced at Jenna, looking sheepish. "I thought I mentioned . . . We're going to put you in the guest room up here instead. We just got to thinking that if you took over the basement, it would leave us without any place to entertain, so . . ."

"Up here?" She sounded like a squawky parrot. But surely she'd misunderstood.

"This guest room is twice as big as either of the downstairs bedrooms. You'll have a bath all to yourself. I've got everything cleaned out of there. And of course, you're more than welcome to spend time downstairs when we don't have guests.

But we just didn't want to give up the media room and space to entertain down there."

Jenna worked to unclench her jaw. She could not believe they would pull a bait-and-switch like this on her.

Numb, she followed Clarissa into the guest room.

Zach's mother smoothed the bedspread, looking smug. "I think this will work just fine." She went to open the drapes. "See what a lovely view you have?"

It was indeed a gorgeous view to a golden meadow behind the house, and beyond that the Morgans' wooded acreage. But Jenna saw it through a haze of unshed tears. Zach's parents didn't owe her anything, and she was grateful for their financial help and for their offer of a place to live. But this was not an option. The guest room was directly across the hall from the master suite. She would have no privacy whatsoever. And neither would they. To get downstairs, she'd have to tromp through the main rooms of the house. And now, instead of having her own little suite, she would be sharing the family room with Bill and Clarissa.

This was not what she'd agreed to! The thought made her feel like a spoiled brat, and maybe she was, but she felt betrayed, too.

Bill brought another load of boxes in, and Jenna waited for him to leave before she turned to

Clarissa. "I wish you'd mentioned this before." She would be a guest in their home—company. And how many times had she heard Clarissa say that fish—and company—start to stink after three days?

"We didn't really think about it until a couple days ago," Clarissa said, looking apologetic. "But I thought I'd mentioned it."

"No, Clarissa, you didn't mention it." She closed her eyes and forced down the roiling anger. Jenna had always known Clarissa wasn't above a little white lie, but—as far as she knew—this was the first time she'd been on the receiving end of one. "The only thing we ever talked about was me moving in downstairs."

"Well, I'm sorry. But we realized that just wasn't going to work for us. The guest room should suit just fine."

Jenna forced a smile and took a step forward, hoping Clarissa would take the hint that she was ready to be alone.

Bill came to her rescue, bringing in the last of her clothes on hangers. He deposited them in the guest room closet and wiped his hands on his jeans. "That's everything." He put his hands on his wife's shoulders and turned her toward the door. "Now let's leave this girl alone so she can get settled in."

"Come on, Quincy." Clarissa scooped the dog into her arms and took him out.

Jenna shut the door behind them and plopped onto the queen-size bed. She loved Zach's parents, but this was *not* going to work. She had to find a place of her own, had to get a job and get out of here.

She began to unpack boxes, but her heart wasn't in it. Besides, there wasn't room for half of this stuff in the guest room, even though it was large as bedrooms went.

She riffled through the junk piled on the floor in search of her cell phone. When she finally located it, she dialed Bryn's number. It went straight to voice mail, and Jenna hung up without leaving a message.

She'd made a colossal mistake. She had to go someplace—away from here—where she could think things through.

She changed into clean clothes, finger-combed her hair, and grabbed her purse and car keys.

Halfway down the hall to the front door Clarissa intercepted her. "Oh . . . do you still have boxes to carry in? I thought we got everything."

"No. We did. I'm just . . . going out for a while."

"Out? Don't you want to get moved in first? I'll be glad to help if you like. I just thought you might want to be alone while you got settled into your room."

Into my prison, you mean. "I'm fine, Clarissa. I won't be long."

"Well, I'm making chicken and dumplings for dinner. It'll probably be ready around six."

"Oh . . . Thanks, but don't count on me for dinner."

"Oh? I didn't realize you had plans for this evening. Where are you going?"

Smile. Count to ten . . . "I'm really not sure."

Clarissa gave a nervous laugh. "Not sure? Or not telling?"

Jenna pretended to rummage through her purse for some imaginary missing item.

"You know, darling, it's not like we're going to monitor your activities every minute, but if you're going to live here, we'd appreciate it if you'd let us know where you'll be. I'd feel awful if we assumed you were one place, and instead you're lying in a ditch somewhere."

Was the woman *serious?* It took physical effort to keep her jaw from dropping. "I'm going over to Bryn's."

"Bryn? Bryn *Hennesey?*" Clarissa's hand went to her throat as though Jenna had slapped her. "I . . . I don't understand."

"She's my friend, Clarissa. You may as well know."

"Friend? You don't mean that. You wouldn't do that to us." Her voice wavered.

"Clarissa, what happened—the fire—was an accident. It could have happened to me, or even you." She regretted the tone of those last words, but she'd jumped in with both feet, so she may as well start swimming. "Bryn has asked for forgiveness, she's still serving community service. She's done everything except bring back the dead, and she'd do that if she could. But she can't, Clarissa. Nobody can."

Clarissa gave a little gasp, and Jenna put up a hand in apology but went on. "I've chosen to forgive her. If you don't like that, I'm sorry."

The color drained from Clarissa's face. "I cannot believe what I'm hearing."

"I'm sorry." Jenna took a step backward toward the door. "I'll be back by nine. Or I'll give you a call if it's going to be later." She brushed past Clarissa, feeling like a wayward teenager. But she kept going out the front door. If she stayed one more minute, she'd say something she could never take back.

She threw her purse across to the passenger seat, got behind the wheel, and slammed the door. Easing down the long drive, she managed to keep the car below twenty until she rounded the curve that trailed behind a curtain of evergreens, then she punched the accelerator to the floor.

Did they think she was back in high school? Would they give her a curfew, too? Good grief! This was not at all how she'd pictured life with Zach's parents. And she was barely moved in.

She navigated the winding avenues of Clairemont Hills and forced herself to calm down before turning onto Main Street in the Falls. She drove by her house—her *former* house—and burst into tears of self-pity. The new owners' moving truck wouldn't arrive in the Falls until Monday, but she'd already turned the house keys over to Maggie.

She swung by Bryn's apartment, but there were no lights in the windows. No doubt she was out with Garrett. After all, it was Saturday night. Date night for most of the civilized world. The tears came faster.

Jenna drove up and down the streets of Hanover Falls, trying to sort things out, trying to think where she could go to get away from the suffocation of her new living arrangements. One thing was sure: she couldn't go back there. Not until she could lock herself in her room and play possum. She hadn't thought to check, but it wouldn't surprise her if there wasn't even a lock on the guest room door.

The way things were going, Bill and Clarissa would probably give her a lights-out curfew, since from the master bedroom they could no doubt see the light shining under her door.

She laughed at the absurdity of it and gunned the engine. She thought about finding a corner of the public library to hang out in, but the library was closed until Monday.

It was too cold to go to the park and she wasn't in the mood to see anybody, which ruled out Java Joint or a restaurant.

She reached to turn the heater up a notch and

noticed the gas gauge. She was almost on empty. There was a Rhodes station on Fifth Street. She could fill up there.

She pulled under the canopy and started the gas pumping, then got back in the car to stay warm while the tank filled. A knock on the hood made her jump.

She looked up to see Lucas Vermontez laughing at her through the windshield.

10

Lucas hobbled around to the passenger side door and leaned in to speak to Jenna through her partially open window. "Sorry about that. Didn't mean to scare you to death."

She gave a nervous laugh and rolled the window the rest of the way down. "I didn't see you coming."

He'd been surprised to spot her pumping gas next to where he was filling his truck. "So did you get all moved in?"

"Just finished." She turned to look past him at the gas pump racking up the gallons. Neon lights from the gas station canopy illumined traces of tears that had worn a trail down her cheeks. All was not well with Jenna Morgan's world. He felt like a jerk scaring her the way he had.

"Everything okay?"

She looked at him as if to gauge whether he really meant it. Apparently he looked sincere because she sighed and put a hand to her forehead. "Actually, I could use a friend right now."

"You want to move that coffee date up a couple days to . . . say, right now?"

She rewarded him with a smile. "I'd love that."

The gas pump clicked off and Jenna started to climb out of the car. He put a hand on her door. "I got it. I'll just follow you to Java Joint, okay?"

He hung up the hose, gave the gas cap a final twist, and popped the lid shut. The acrid odor of gasoline stung his nostrils. On the other side of the island, a car pulled in behind Lucas's truck and the driver tooted his horn. Lucas held up a hand, motioning for the guy to be patient. Navigating the maze of concrete back to his pickup, he did his best to hide his limp, praying with every step that he didn't trip and fall on his face in front of her.

He followed her to the coffee shop, but as they turned into the parking lot, he saw the sign on the door. Closed. Pulling into the parking space beside her, he motioned her over.

She climbed out of her Volvo and he leaned across the bench seat. He unlocked his passenger door and popped the handle.

"Climb in." He patted the seat. "Want to drive through the Dairy Bar for something?"

"Sure." She climbed up into the truck and slammed the door behind her.

He backed out and headed west on Main Street, energized at the way things had turned out. Behind the wheel of his pickup he felt blessedly normal. Here he didn't limp, didn't hobble, didn't get the sympathy nods he'd grown accustomed to. And here the hated cane could stay hidden away on the floor beneath his seat.

They ordered hot chocolates, and Lucas drove slowly down the main drag of Hanover Falls, trying not to feel like a high schooler on his first date. "So talk to me. Was it harder than you thought to leave your house?"

She shrugged. "It's not that so much as—" In the seat beside her, Jenna's purse started ringing.

She cringed. "Sorry. Hang on a second." Balancing her drink, she retrieved her phone and slid it open. "Hey, B. What's up?"

She listened for a minute, frowning. "Oh, I'm so sorry. When did it happen?"

After another minute of listening, she threw Lucas an apology with her eyes. "Um . . . sure. I don't mind. I can look in on him. Does it need to be tonight?"

He couldn't make out the other end of the brief conversation, but judging by her expression, it was bad news.

She closed the phone and slipped it back in her purse.

"Is everything okay?"

"Bryn's dad is in the ER. They're having trouble

getting his blood pressure regulated and they want to admit him. She's going to stay with him overnight. She wants me to check on her dog—oh, hey!" Her eyes lit. "It's Sparky. Remember? The one with the nose? You wouldn't want to go with me, would you? It'd be a chance to meet him and see if you think they might be able to use him at the station."

"Sure." He wasn't crazy about going to see a dog, but he grabbed at a chance to have some unexpected time with her. And maybe the kick in the pants he needed to go talk to Chief Brennan.

"We don't have to. I can go later tonight." She must have misread his hesitance.

"No, I don't mind. Like you said, it's a chance to check out the dog."

"Oh, good." She sighed over a sheepish grin. "I—I'm not exactly a dog person either. They make me a little nervous, to tell you the truth."

"Really? You're scared of dogs? This one, or all dogs?"

"*Most* dogs. Big dogs for sure. Sparky's not mean or anything. I don't know why . . . he just makes me nervous."

"Don't worry, I'll be your bodyguard."

She giggled. "Thanks."

"Is he at Bryn's place?"

She nodded and gave him directions. He navigated the streets of the Falls to the apartment, praying Bryn lived on the ground floor. Steps were still a challenge, and the last thing he wanted tonight was Jenna's sympathy.

His prayers were answered, and a few minutes later she retrieved the key from Bryn's hiding place under the eaves and unlocked the door to a barrage of barking.

When Jenna flipped on the lights, a large black Labrador came bounding down the hallway, tail wagging like crazy. Lucas braced for the dog's enthusiastic greeting, but Jenna screamed and scrambled behind him. He shielded her from the dog, but she clutched the back of his jacket as if it were a life preserver.

He grabbed for the wall to regain his balance. She kept her death grip on his jacket and he started laughing. "It's okay . . . I've got him."

He felt his jacket go slack and turned to face Jenna, still laughing. But the genuine fear in her eyes wiped the smile off his face. "Hey. It's okay. He's not going to hurt you. He's just glad to see us. Hey, boy, it's okay." He reached to place a hand on the dog's head. "He is a boy, right?"

Jenna let go of his arm and took a measured breath, keeping one eye on the dog. "Yes. He's a he."

"Here, let him smell your hand." He demonstrated, offering the back of his hand for the dog to sniff. "If you hold your hand like this, it lets the dog know you're not threatening it."

He leaned his cane against the wall and

crouched in front of the dog, placing his palm on the floor for support. Pain shot up his leg, but he shook it off and concentrated on keeping his balance. Slowly he stroked the sleek black fur, then gently took Jenna's hand and flattened her palm between his and replaced his hand with hers on Sparky's head. She kept her palm flat and stroked from forehead to neck. She seemed to breathe easier now.

"Talk to him in a soothing voice. That lets him know you're a friend. Right, boy?" He patted the dog's flanks.

"Hey, Sparky," she crooned, her voice warbly. "You hungry, boy? You wouldn't eat *me,* would you, buddy?"

Lucas let himself laugh at that. At the sound, Sparky looked up at Jenna and cocked his head, a quizzical expression in his round, golden eyes. Lucas scratched him behind one silky ear and turned to Jenna, smiling. "See? He likes you."

She looked sheepish. "Sorry about that. I honestly don't know what I'd have done if you weren't here. That dog might just be going hungry."

"In that case, he just *might* eat somebody. And by the way, I was only kidding when I said I'd be your bodyguard. I didn't think you'd take take it literally."

She laughed and ducked her head, blushing. "I'm really sorry."

"Just teasing. You would have been fine. He wasn't going to hurt you. What's the deal? You get bit once or something?"

"No." She shrugged and turned back to Sparky, petting him tentatively. He sensed she wanted to change the subject.

His leg was tightening up on him. If he didn't get his weight off of it soon, she might be the one rescuing him. He reached for his cane and hoisted himself to his feet, disguising a grimace as a smile. "So you just need to feed him?"

"And let him out, but Jenna said he's quick. It won't take but a minute." She unlocked the back door and the dog made a beeline for it.

"I'll go get him some fresh water." She hurried to the kitchen and he followed.

Jenna gestured toward the closet at one end of the small kitchen. "Bryn said his food is in the broom closet. Do you mind looking?"

"Sure." He found the large bag of kibble and filled the measuring cup inside the bag.

A minute later they heard a bark at the door. Jenna opened it, putting the door between her and the dog.

Sparky went straight for the bowl of dog food. He ate a few bites, then looked up at Lucas and nuzzled his knee.

Jenna grinned. "I think he wants to go home with you."

Lucas felt an instant affection for the dog—the

girl, too, but he dismissed that thought as quickly as it came. Sparky was a beautiful animal and he'd seemed to take a liking to Lucas, too. The thought of having a companion in the empty house after Ma and Geoff moved to Springfield was comforting—Lucky wasn't much company. "So, Bryn's definitely looking for someone to take him?"

"I'm sure she is now, with her dad in the hospital. Are you considering it?"

The eagerness in her eyes made him laugh again. "Wasn't that the whole point of dragging me over here?"

"Guilty as charged." She cringed, but her tone turned playful. "Just so you know, I didn't put Bryn up to that phone call. That really wasn't part of the plan to manip—"

"The plan?" He grinned. "So you're admitting there *was* a plan."

"No! I just meant—" She looked up, and seeing him laughing silently, she slugged him in the bicep. Hard.

"Ow!"

Her hands went to her mouth and her eyes grew wide. "I'm sorry."

He rubbed the tender spot, impressed with her punch. "You must have grown up with brothers."

She giggled. "No. A sister. But she was a tomboy."

"Well, now that you've managed to change the

subject and deflect the blame, I guess I have no choice but to consider ol' Sparky here." He bent to scratch the dog behind the ears again. "When does Bryn need to know?"

Jenna shook her head, blond curls bouncing against her cheeks. "Probably the sooner the better. I know it would help her out so much if you'd take him. Thanks."

He held out a hand in protest.

"I know, I know, you're just considering. That's all I'm thanking you for."

"Okay. Glad we got that straight." He grinned.

She answered with a smug roll of her eyes. "You ready to go?"

He was in no hurry to end their time together, but she started turning off lights, so he followed her outside and waited for her to lock up Bryn's apartment.

Walking to his truck, he fumbled for an excuse to prolong their conversation. *Duh, Vermontez.* The whole reason he'd invited her to go for a drive in the first place was the tears streaking those pretty peaches-and-cream cheeks.

"Do you want to talk about . . . why you were crying?" he risked once they were settled in the cab of his pickup again.

She fiddled with the charm on her necklace, and stared at her lap.

"Sorry." He shook his head, feeling chastened by her silence. "None of my business."

For a moment that seemed to go on forever, she didn't say anything.

But then she looked up at him with a sigh, and the dam seemed to break. "I guess I didn't think very far ahead. I—didn't realize how much freedom I'd be losing by moving in with my in-laws—*former* in-laws," she corrected.

That seemed like a no-brainer to him, but he refrained from saying so. He glanced at his watch and shot her a grin. "So, do you have a curfew?"

She gave an unladylike snort. "How'd you know? Clarissa said they—meaning *she*—didn't want to have to worry about me lying in a ditch somewhere."

Lucas laughed. "Oh, boy, I've heard that one before. My mom," he explained, turning onto Main Street.

She cast a sideways glance. "Don't tell me *you* have a curfew?"

"No, but not for lack of trying on Ma's part."

She looked sympathetic. "Don't get me wrong—Bill and Clarissa have been wonderful to me. I don't know how I would have survived without them this past year. But I'm kind of at their mercy, and I'm not sure how long I can—"

Jenna stopped short as the wail of sirens broke the silence of the nighttime streets. On instinct Lucas hit the brakes and checked his mirrors. He knew those sirens as well as he knew his own voice. Clemens County Fire District. Adrenaline shot through his veins. The sirens were coming from Station 2.

As if on autopilot, he headed toward the station. Cresting the hill, he switched on the police scanner radio under the dash and fiddled with the dial, trying to catch the frequency. He hadn't turned the thing on in weeks. No reason to.

The strobe of red-white-and-blue lights on the street ahead made him punch the brakes. The ladder truck and a pumper were pulling out of their bays, lights flashing, sirens blaring.

The radio squawked to life and the dispatcher's voice cut in and out. "Fire reported in progress . . . Engines en route . . . Grove Street homeless shelter . . ." The cryptic phrases Lucas could catch sent a surge of adrenaline through him. It was a good feeling.

He hit the gas, swerved to the outside lane, and headed toward the back of the station.

11

Lucas screeched into the parking lot behind the station, and Jenna reached for the grab handle above the passenger door and braced her feet against the floorboard as if she had a brake pedal on her side of the vehicle. What was he doing?

The truck fishtailed and he slammed on the brakes and shoved open his door. Using the door as a crutch, he slid to the ground in one smooth motion.

She gripped the handle tighter. "Lucas? What's going on?" Surely he wasn't going to try to go help.

Not answering, he took off across the pavement toward the firehouse, his gait labored but steady. Jenna held her breath, watching through the windshield as he negotiated a patch of grass that ran between the curb and the sidewalk. She breathed easier. He really was doing so much better now—

He staggered and stumbled forward, apparently tripped up by something in the grass. He landed facedown on the sidewalk.

She gasped and fumbled for the door handle. "Are you okay?" She scrambled down from the pickup and ran to his side.

He groaned and rolled over, easing up to a sitting position. He grabbed his left leg, his face contorted.

"Are you all right?" she said again, offering him a hand.

But he ignored her and slammed his fists onto the concrete like a football player who'd just missed the winning touchdown pass. Jenna backed away, scrabbling out of his range.

She stood helplessly and watched as he rolled onto all fours and tried in vain to stand. Cursing, he fell prostrate, forehead to the ground.

She couldn't tell if he was writhing in pain or humiliation, but given his harsh rejection of the help she'd offered, she hesitated to approach him again.

The fire engines were out of sight now, the sirens fading into the distance. After a few seconds of indecision, Jenna went to the pickup and retrieved his cane from beneath the seat where she'd seen him put it earlier.

She slammed the door of the truck and took a step toward him. "Lucas?" She risked another step. "Do I need to get help?"

He looked up at her, agony written on his face. "I'm fine." His voice was stone cold. "There's nobody here anyway. They dumped the station on this run."

She held out the cane to him and he took it without a word.

"Do you want a hand up? How can I help?"

"I've got it. Thanks," he grunted.

She bit her lip. She was only trying to help. What did he think he could accomplish by going to the firehouse in the first place? If she'd understood the dispatcher, the alarm was at the homeless shelter. It might be nothing . . . a false alarm. She hadn't heard any other sirens. But why would they have sent all the engines? The thought stirred too many memories.

Before she could react, Lucas staked his cane in the ridge between the sidewalk and the grass and hauled himself to his feet. But he took one staggering step toward the truck and groaned.

She hurried to where he stood on one wobbly leg. "Let me help you—please." Not waiting for permission, she slipped her arm around his waist, bracing her legs to bear his weight. "You're hurt."

He didn't argue this time and used her shoulder and his cane like crutches, one tentative step at a time until they stood in front of the truck.

"Do you want me to drive?"

"No, I can drive. I'm fine."

"You don't look fine. You fell pretty hard back there." She pointed back at the sidewalk.

"I'm fine. Just give me a minute to catch my breath."

Stubborn man. She shrugged and skirted around the bumper. Climbing into the truck, she resisted the temptation to slam the door.

A minute later he was back behind the wheel, massaging his leg. He put the keys in the ignition, turned the engine, and threw it in gear. He started to back out of the parking lot, but instead slipped the gear back in Park.

He sighed and turned to face her. "I'm sorry I snapped at you. You didn't deserve that. I was . . ." He rubbed his face, hiding behind his hands. He stayed that way for an uncomfortably long time.

Several lights blazed inside the station, but she knew the building was empty. She wondered again how he'd intended to help if anyone had been left at the station.

Finally he put his hands down, his profile outlined by the lights. He turned to her but refused to meet her gaze, sitting instead with one elbow on the steering wheel, staring out the windshield. "That was humiliating," he finally whispered.

"I'm just glad you're okay."

"Don't be so sure. My pride may be fatally injured."

She laughed, relieved to see a glimpse of the Lucas she knew. "It was a very graceful fall actually." True, but that hadn't made it any less frightening to watch.

"Ha!" He peeked briefly in her direction. "I know better than that. But you're sweet to say so."

She folded her hands in her lap. "Not that it's any of my business, but where were you going?"

"I—" He rubbed the space between his dark eyebrows and shrugged. "Something just kicked in when I heard the sirens. I felt like . . . like I needed to be here. Like I had to help."

"Wow."

"I know . . . weird. You'd think after a year I'd be over it."

"No, no, I didn't mean it like that. I just meant 'wow' that you have that kind of dedication."

"Yeah, right." He rolled his eyes. "For all the good it does me."

"It's still a noble thing, Lucas. To have that desire." Her words felt stilted and awkward, but they were what came to her. Along with a memory. She hesitated, then decided to share it with him. "I remember once when we were on vacation in Colorado, we'd stopped for gas in some little town off the Interstate. We drove by their fire station just as the trucks were leaving. Zach followed them five or six miles out into the country. There was wheat stubble burning out of control, and Zach rolled up his sleeves and helped them fight that fire until it was out."

Lucas smiled, a faraway look in his eyes. "That sounds like Zach all right."

She hesitated, then risked putting a hand on his arm. "It sounds like you, too."

"Uh-huh. And here I sit helpless as a baby while my buddies are out there risking their lives."

She stared at him. Did he really not see? "Lucas. You're sitting in this truck, with that cane, because you *already* risked your life. Who knows how many more people would have died that night if it wasn't for you?"

"No." He shook his head. "I appreciate the thought, Jenna, but the shelter had been evacuated by the time we got there. We were looking for a man who wasn't there. Maybe never was there."

"It doesn't matter, Luc." She flushed. She'd shortened his name without thinking about the intimacy it implied. "What you did was an act of heroism. And you'll be paying—suffering—for it to some extent for the rest of your life." She pointed to where his cane leaned against the console.

"It doesn't feel like heroism. It feels like stupidity."

"Lucas, stop it. You act like it's your fault that you almost lost your legs in the fire. Your life! You were the lucky one. You made it out alive. You have so much to be thankful for. So much to live for." She knew even as the words left her mouth that they would sound empty and patronizing to him. She knew because they would have been the same to Zach. "I'm sorry. I know that sounds trite."

He offered a smile and met her eyes for the first time since he'd climbed back into the pickup. "I appreciate your intentions."

"Ah, good intentions . . . You know what they say about those—pavement for the road to hell."

"No, I mean it. I really do appreciate what you're trying to do."

She shrugged, just wanting to change the subject.

Lucas changed it for her. "You know what? I'm hungry. Let's go get a hamburger."

"Now you're talking some sense." She laughed, feeling as if this evening might turn out okay after all.

Her cell phone gave a muffled ring. "Sorry. Hang on." She dug the phone out of the belly of her purse and looked at the caller ID. Clarissa.

"Hello?"

"Jenna, is everything okay? Bill said he heard

sirens a little while ago. We're worried about you."

"I'm fine, Clarissa. I'll be home in a little while."

"Well, I've got dinner on. I'll keep it warm for you."

She willed her voice to remain steady. "No, that's okay. We're going to grab a burger. Please don't hold dinner for me."

"We? Are you with Bryn?"

"I'll see you this evening. I'll be home around nine or so." She hung up before Clarissa could grill her further. A low growl escaped her throat despite her efforts to hold it in.

"That was my—" Her phone trilled again and she checked the ID. "I don't believe this. Do I look like I'm twelve years old? Wait—don't answer that." She tossed her phone back into her purse and stuffed it under the car seat.

He cleared his throat. "I don't suppose it would be appropriate here to ask what on earth were you thinking, moving in with your in-laws?"

"I love my in-laws. I really do. Clarissa and I are friends. At least I thought we were. But lately it's like they think they own me."

"So, do I need to take Cinderella home, or are we still going for burgers?" His smile was closer to a smirk.

She sighed. "Burgers. Definitely."

"Burgers it is." He shifted the truck into reverse,

but keeping his foot on the brake, he turned to her, looking sheepish. "Do you mind if we make a quick sweep through town first . . . see if we can find out where the fire was?"

"Sure . . . of course."

"Just to make sure everything's okay."

"Sure." She tried to put him at ease with her smile, but right now he reminded her too much of Zach.

12

*L*ucas lopped an arm over the steering wheel, stuffed another French fry in his mouth, and tried to ignore the throbbing in his knee. That pain was nothing compared to the emotional trauma he felt reliving the fiasco from an hour ago. Heat rose to his cheeks and he was grateful for the cover of darkness the pickup's cab afforded.

Jenna's words soothed his embarrassment somewhat, but he felt ridiculous for thinking he had anything at all to offer the firefighters of Station 2. On their way back downtown, they'd met the line of emergency vehicles returning to the station, and all had appeared quiet when they drove by the homeless shelter.

He sighed. No matter how desperately his heart longed to be back on duty again, he'd proven tonight that physically he was not ready to sit behind a desk for more than a few hours, let alone fight a fire. He was worthless. And he had no business thinking of himself as a firefighter anymore. Those days were over. It was time he faced that fact.

Beside him, Jenna sat in silence. He'd felt helpless and small in front of her tonight. Why would a woman ever want to be with a man who couldn't even take care of himself, much less protect her?

He quickly wiped the thought away. How dare he even think of Jenna in that way. This was his best friend's wife he was thinking about. A woman in mourning who was living with Zach's parents, no less. He was crazy to be having these fantasies. Especially after tonight.

"You're sure you're all right?"

The genuine concern on her face only made him feel worse. "I'm fine." He choked down another bite of his hamburger. It stuck in his throat, despite how hungry he was.

He swallowed hard, took a deep breath. "Listen, Jenna. I—I'm sorry for how this night turned out. I really didn't mean for it to be all about me."

"Would you quit? I'm just glad you're okay. And hey"—she winked—"just look how you took my mind off my issues."

"You feel like talking? About your issues? Now that I've got your mind off of them." He gave a dry laugh.

She joined him, then shook her head, turning serious. "I don't know what I've gotten myself into. The whole town is probably wondering if I'm out of my mind. I'm not sure I really had a choice. The sad thing is, considering my options, moving in with Zach's parents is probably what I would have chosen regardless."

His face must have given away his confusion because she went on to explain. "My other options were getting a full-time job, finding a one-bedroom apartment somewhere. I—" She dropped her head and blew out a heavy breath. "I just couldn't face going back. I've come too far."

"Going back? I don't understand."

"Of course you don't. You don't know where I come from. *What* I come from."

He waited for her to explain, wondering at the faraway look that came to her hazel eyes.

"White trash."

"Huh?"

"You know how they always talk about the wrong side of the tracks? Well, that's where I grew up. I suppose my mom did the best she could, but my sister and I grew up with nothing. I never knew my dad. He bailed before I was born. If it hadn't been for food stamps and Goodwill . . ." She grimaced and closed her eyes as if speaking of her past was physically painful.

He tried not to let her see his shock at the revelation. For some reason he'd assumed she was a blueblood, like Zach. She'd certainly worn the role well as a Morgan. "Zach never mentioned any of this. But that has nothing to do with who you are, Jenna."

She rolled her eyes. "Yeah . . . Tell that to his mom. I met Zach, and when we got married, I swore I would never go back to that life again." Something like anguish flashed across her face, and he regretted steering the conversation this direction.

"Wow. I'm sorry." It seemed there was nothing they could talk about that didn't bring pain.

She met his eyes and changed the subject. "Sorry, ancient history. And I really do feel bad ragging on Clarissa like this. They've been good to me—her and Bill both. I guess I should be trying to put myself in their shoes. If the tables were turned, I would be none too thrilled about having my in-laws move in with me in *my* house." She made a comical face that said, "Heaven forbid!"

"So what are you going to do? Suck it up and live by their curfew, or start looking for a job and a place to live?"

"Ouch. You make it sound so cut-and-dried."

"Sorry. I didn't know there were other options."

She narrowed her eyes at him. "I'm going to assume that was tongue-in-cheek."

He smiled in reply.

"Even if I found a job tomorrow—a good job—

it'll be months before I save up enough to pay the bills." She looked at her watch. "You know what, it's getting late. I'd probably better get home—" She stopped abruptly.

He saw the stark realization cloud her face: she didn't have a home anymore. And he hadn't helped matters any. She'd needed a shoulder to cry on, and he'd only stirred up more pain.

He turned the key in the ignition and gunned the engine a little. "I'll take you back to your car."

She nodded.

They rode in silence to the coffee shop where her car was parked. He thought about the guys back at the station and actually felt homesick, remembering what it was like to come back from a run, comparing stories, debriefing, joking around if everything had turned out okay—and sometimes even if it hadn't, coping the only way they knew how.

It killed him not to know what was going on with the people he still considered family, with the place he still considered home. He should have been out there with them, working beside his buddies.

Instead he was here, making Zach Morgan's beautiful wife miserable.

13

$\mathcal{I}$t was ten after nine when Jenna pulled into the Morgans' driveway. Her breath caught. The porch lights and all the yard lights were on. And inside the house almost every window was aglow. What was going on?

Surely they hadn't called the police because she was eight minutes late? But there were no vehicles on the wide drive. She parked the car and ran up the brick walk to the front door.

Clarissa met her in the foyer.

"What's happened? Is Bill okay?"

"Bill's fine. He's in the kitchen. Where on earth have you been? What were all the sirens for? We were worried sick."

"I told you I was going out."

Clarissa pressed her lips into a hard line. "We need to talk." She turned on her heel and strode to the kitchen, the sirens apparently forgotten.

Mindlessly Jenna followed.

Bill was sitting at the head of the table, a cup of coffee in front of him, his head down.

"Sit." Clarissa indicated a chair on the side of the table that backed up to the wall.

Jenna pulled out the chair and sat, her back straight, hands in her lap, feeling like a schoolgirl who'd been called into the principal's office.

Clarissa didn't sit but placed her hands on the high back of the chair across from Jenna and closed her eyes. "If you are going to be living here in our home, as our guest, we need to get some things straight."

Ah, so that's what this was about. She stared past her mother-in-law but didn't say anything. This ought to be good.

"Bill and I have come up with a few rules. We're not trying to run your life, Jenna, but if you're going to live with us, we can't have you just going your merry way doing whatever you please whenever you please."

Jenna glanced at Bill, who was working hard to avoid her eyes. She knew that when Clarissa said "Bill and I" she meant "I and I alone."

"First of all, we need to know where you'll be. We're not going to give you a curfew, obviously." She gave a humorless laugh. "But it's not fair for us not to know your whereabouts. It would worry us sick to have to wonder every night when you're coming in—or *if* you're coming in. And certainly we need to know whether to expect you for dinner. As you know, I have club and guild luncheons several days a month, so we'll all do lunch on our own."

She seemed to forget that Jenna belonged to several of the same social organizations, though she hadn't attended any of the meetings since Zach's death.

Clarissa waited until Jenna proved she was paying attention by looking directly at her. "It would be nice to have dinner together several nights a week. Goodness, that was always important to us when Zachary was a child. It's what families *do*."

Bill had not yet uttered a word, and Jenna silently begged him to stand up for her. But Clarissa droned on with patronizing talk about how important it was for Jenna to clean up after herself in the kitchen and keep her room tidy. When she reminded Jenna to wipe her feet before walking on the expensive living room carpeting, that was the last straw.

"Clarissa, I am not a child!" She held up a hand, as much to calm herself as to apologize for her outburst. "I have no plans to trash your house or track mud on your precious carpets."

"Of course you don't." Clarissa's expression turned contrite. "I just thought we should go over the guidelines so we're all clear on what's expected." She looked at Bill as if to get his approval. He had scarcely moved since Jenna sat down and didn't budge now except to nod briefly at his wife.

Jenna tested Clarissa, scooting her chair back an inch. The older woman's hand shot up. "Just a minute. There's something else we need to discuss."

In a flash of insight Jenna understood what this

was really about. *Bryn.* Of course. All these rules and regulations were merely an introduction to what Clarissa really wanted to say. Moving her chair back up to the table, she braced herself, physically and mentally.

"I'm afraid Bill and I are going to have to insist that as long as you're living under our roof, you avoid Bryn Hennesey."

Jenna started shaking her head.

"No, Jenna. Hear me out. You can surely understand how difficult it is for us to have her living in the same town, let alone camped out on our doorstep."

"What are you talking about?"

"Well, that's exactly what it will be if we give our approval for you to run around with that girl."

"I've been running around with 'that girl' for months now. I don't see what difference it makes that I'm living here."

Clarissa's jaw tensed and the irises of her eyes turned to steel. "Then let me put it more succinctly. If you choose to remain here, you *will* have nothing to do with Bryn Hennesey."

"I can't believe what I'm hearing." She almost laughed at the absurdity of it—like an echo of an argument she'd had with her own mother when she was thirteen. "First you want to know my whereabouts twenty-four/seven, and now you're going to dictate who my friends are?"

"Call it 'dictate' if you like. We're simply saying

that if you choose to remain friends with that woman, you are, in essence, choosing to live elsewhere. I should think the reasons are obvious, but in case they're not, in case you can't defend the memory of your *husband,* then let me remind you that your so-called friend was responsible for the death of our only *son!*" Clarissa's voice cracked on the word. She pinched the bridge of her nose.

"Then I guess you've made my choice for me. I love you and Bill, but you are not going to decide who my friends are."

Clarissa pressed her lips into a firm line, and Jenna watched the color drain from them.

A flash of memory came, and for an instant she saw Clarissa as she'd been the day of Zach's funeral. A mother who'd lost her son. Her only child.

Something close to compassion tugged at Jenna's heart, but she forced herself to look away. She couldn't let anything distract her from what she needed to do right now. She cleared her throat. "I'm sorry."

Clarissa's shoulders slumped and she gripped the back of the chair, seeming to need it for support. "Fine. Then I'll need to ask you to pack your things and get out. Right now."

"Tonight? You're not serious?" Jenna stole a glance at the oversized clock on the mantel. "It's almost nine thirty! Where would I go?"

"That's something you'll have to figure out, I guess." She folded her arms and planted her feet. "Either that, or simply agree to distance yourself from that girl."

Jenna looked at Bill, but he refused to engage and sat silent, coming to neither of their defenses. For a fleeting moment she wanted to say whatever Clarissa wanted to hear. Just say the right words so she could go to her room and go to sleep.

But all at once things came into focus, and for perhaps the first time, she saw clearly that from the day she'd met Clarissa, she'd been acting out a script Zach's mother had written for her—a script she'd been handed the instant Clarissa realized she couldn't talk Zach out of marrying the girl from the wrong side of the tracks.

It had only gotten worse after Zach's death. But Jenna had been too busy pretending to be a grieving widow, and worrying about how to fund the comfortable life Zach—and Clarissa—had carved out for her.

She wasn't blameless by any means. Zach had offered her an escape from a life of near poverty and she'd grabbed for it. Being Bill and Clarissa Morgan's daughter-in-law had given her a position in society that she'd never dreamed she could have. For the first time in her life, she didn't feel invisible. Her Brookside home was admired—even envied—by her friends. She enjoyed being fussed over at the beauty salon and the civic club meetings. Never mind that all of it was a lie.

She'd grown accustomed to the perks of her social position in the Falls—even addicted to them maybe. Yet, after twelve years living as a "somebody," her nightmares were always about the same thing: being back in that shabby trailer in the Shady Groves Trailer Court with her mom and sister, and Mom's current boyfriend, some faceless man in a long string of losers. In her dreams a snarling rottweiler chased her down the alley while a man laughed at her terrified screams. Sometimes her mom's laughter mingled with the man's.

Her thoughts flashed back to the last time she'd seen her mother. More than a year ago, at Bryn's sentencing. Jenna's sister, Becky, had driven Mom to Springfield, all the way from St. Louis, and they'd sat in the gallery with her while the judge sentenced Bryn to community service.

Jenna hadn't known then that her mother was dying of cancer. Before that day she hadn't been in contact with Mom or Becky in six years. She hadn't seen Becky since, and she'd only seen her mother one other time before she died last March.

Jenna wasn't sure she'd have had the courage to walk into that courtroom by herself, given Clarissa's stance on the matter. She'd always been grateful Mom and Becky had showed up to be with her that day—in spite of the fact they'd both hit her up for money before heading back to St. Louis.

"Well? I'm waiting?" Clarissa's shrill voice broke through her tortured thoughts.

She would not betray Bryn. She scraped her chair back from the table. "I can't fit everything in my car in one load, but I'll come back for the rest later."

Trembling, she forced her feet to carry her down the hall to the guest room. She opened dresser drawers and emptied their contents into the cartons that were still scattered about the room.

She hauled the boxes out to her car, then came back for more. Bill and Clarissa had disappeared, but she heard the TV blaring from the media room.

She packed the Volvo as full as she could and still see out the back windshield. She did not want to have to come back here any sooner than necessary. She tossed her laptop on the passenger seat and threw a tote bag containing her hairdryer and makeup in the backseat on top of the pile of clothes.

Backing around on the wide driveway, she shifted gears, turned 180 degrees and followed the lane to the entrance, then to the street beyond. She had no idea where she would go, how she would pay for a place to stay. Rooms were at least $150 a night at the two hotels in the Falls. She had enough gas in her car to drive to Springfield, but even fifty dollars for a fleabag room there would put her credit card over the limit.

She picked up her phone to call Bryn but quickly disconnected when she imagined the conversation—in which it was Bryn's fault that Jenna had been banished from the Morgans' home. She couldn't do that to her friend. She would have to know eventually, but Jenna didn't want Bryn offering her a bed for the night out of guilt. And besides, she'd have to sleep with one eye open with Sparky there. She shivered at the thought of that dog jumping up on her in the middle of the night.

But going down the list of people she knew well enough to call, she was shocked to realize that, except for Bryn—and now Lucas—all her friends were the Morgans' friends. And she couldn't very well call Lucas about a place to spend the night.

The streets of Hanover Falls were dead at ten thirty at night. She drove slowly through Ferris Park, trying to figure out what to do. A teenage couple sat on top of a picnic table, huddled together, their breaths mingling into a single cloud of steam on the night air.

She turned onto Main Street and drove past the city limits where the pavement turned into a dirt lane. Susan Marlowe lived out here somewhere. She remembered driving out here one day, scouting out the location from the directions on one of the many invitations Susan had sent.

Clarissa had discouraged her from attending those meetings. "You don't want to become a band of merry widows." And on that, at least, Clarissa was right. It took too much energy to feign grief, especially around those who might detect her deceit.

She slowed, watching for the driveway, unsure what she intended to do when she found it. There it was, on the left, the yard light hitting a grove of trees, and a small spot aimed at a rustic sign carved with "Marlowe" and the house number. She turned onto the wooded lane, her tires crunching the gravel drive. It was too late to turn back now.

But when the house came in view, it was dark. If Susan was home, she was already in bed. What had prompted her to come out here anyway? She didn't even know Susan that well. Dimming her lights, Jenna turned the Volvo away from the house, hoping she hadn't wakened anyone. She retraced her route down the lane and headed back to town.

She meandered through the streets of Hanover Falls for the next hour, until she noticed the fuel gauge slipping below the Full mark. This tank of gas might have to last her a while. She couldn't waste it driving aimlessly.

She turned onto Grove and made herself look the other way as she passed the homeless shelter. But not before she noticed the lights in the building painting each window a warm shade of yellow. Smoke billowed from the furnace stack in welcoming puffs.

No way. Not even a possibility. She may not have a place to stay tonight, but she was *not* homeless. She'd find a place tomorrow—an apartment. Find a job and figure out a way to put down a deposit on a place of her own. She glanced at the shelter again. She was not about to lower herself to that.

She took a left turn at the next street and punched the accelerator.

Another half hour of aimless wandering and she drove back through the iron gates of Clairemont Hills. Jenna still had her pass card and she swiped it, waiting for the gates to part. For one awful moment she was tempted to go back to the Morgans' and grovel. Betray Bryn.

Rounding the first curve, she spotted a grove of trees and pulled off the narrow road beneath the overhanging branches, crossing her fingers that the ground under her tires wasn't so soft she'd get stuck. She parked the car but left it running while she rummaged through the boxes in the backseat for sweaters and extra socks. She pulled on layers of clothes until she could scarcely move.

Catching a glimpse of herself reflected in the dark windshield, she almost laughed. But the gravity of her situation stopped her short. How was this any better than the homeless shelter? But somehow it was. Thank heaven she owned her car free and clear.

She locked the doors of the Volvo and tried not to think about what animals might be hiding in the woods. At least she'd be safe in the car. The windows started to fog up, and she turned off the ignition and crawled over into the backseat, arranging the boxes into a cardboard cocoon. She fashioned a pillow from several pairs of sweatpants and spread her winter coat over herself for a blanket.

Within ten minutes the cold had breached her fortress and she lay shivering in the cramped seat. Her goldfish necklace hung at her throat like a hunk of ice. She tucked her collar underneath it.

The smell of woodsmoke filtered into the car's interior, and she imagined the blazing fire in the Morgans' hearth room. But the thought offered no warmth.

Around eleven o'clock she heard a car coming up the lane. She held her breath until the sound of the motor faded away.

She'd just drifted off when a sharp rap on the window near her head made her sit up with a start. Heart pounding, she swung her legs off the seat and tried to peer through the window.

"Open up! Hanover Falls Police."

She rolled the window down half an inch. "Hello?"

The uniformed officer bent to look in at her, his eyes the only thing showing above the frosted window glass. "Are you all right?"

"Yes. I'm fine."

He shone the light around the car. "Are you alone in there, ma'am?"

"Yes." For crying out loud, did he think she was some teenager out parking?

"I'm sorry, but I'm going to have to ask you to leave the property. This is a private residential area. How did you get past the gate?"

"I . . . have a pass."

"Excuse me?"

"I'm—I *was* staying with the Morgans on Brighton Way. We . . . had a disagreement."

The police officer pulled a notepad from his back pocket and aimed the light at it, reading. "That's not who reported you. Do you have ID on you? Could I see it, please?"

She started to reach over the seat and then hesitated. "It's in the front seat . . . in my purse. May I?"

He flashed the light into the front. "Go ahead and get it."

She leaned over the seat and rummaged in her purse until she found her wallet. She rolled the window down farther and handed her driver's license to the officer. Chill air poured in through the gap, but now it felt good on her flushed face and neck.

"You're a Morgan? I thought you said you were staying with the Morgans."

"They're my . . . they were my in-laws. My husband passed away."

"I see. I'm sorry, ma'am." He took a step away from the Volvo. "Do you need me to call your in-laws?"

"No. I'll leave."

"You have someplace to go for the night?"

"Yes," she lied.

He looked skeptical. "I can call the hotels, see if there's a vacancy. And you know there's always the homeless shelter over on Grove Street. You can follow me there if you like. They've got an eleven p.m. check-in, but I think we can still get you a bed for the night."

"No. It's okay. I can go to a friend's."

"If you're sure." He pointed to her car. "I'll wait to make sure your car starts okay. It's pretty cold out here tonight."

"You don't have to wait. I'm going."

But he shook his head. "I'll wait."

She shrugged and crawled out through the back door and got back in the driver's seat. She started the car and waved to the officer as she backed carefully across the shoulder and onto the roadway.

She watched in her rearview mirror as the policeman stood, legs spread wide, arms folded, watching her drive away.

When she and Zach were first married, and the

Morgans moved to the Falls—to Clairemont Hills—every time she drove up to the security gates, she'd been terrified she wouldn't be allowed admittance, that they'd see the girl from the trailer court trying to get in where she didn't belong, and they'd kick her out.

Looked like her fears had been justified all along. It just took them a few years to catch on to her.

"Oh, God . . . what do I do now?" Her own whispered words startled her. She'd never been much for praying, but tonight seemed to be challenging that. "If You're there, God, please show me what to do." Her words were not idle. She needed help and God seemed to be her only hope right now.

Where she would go now, she had no idea, but it would not be anywhere near Grove Street. That much she was sure of.

14

Monday, December 1

*L*ucas took a sip from the steaming cup of coffee and drove through the early morning streets toward home. He'd barely slept last night, reliving his embarrassment at the firehouse, and then Jenna's comforting words.

He pulled into the garage, for once wishing that his mom's car wasn't still parked inside. She'd been asleep when he went in search of the morning paper and a cup of coffee.

He was hoping she'd have left for work by the time he got back. The last thing he was in the mood for was a heart-to-heart with Ma. Especially with the cheerful attitude she sported lately. She was off-the-charts in love.

And he was happy for her and Geoff. He really was. As hard as it was seeing her with someone who wasn't Pop, he was glad she'd found the joy of loving again, of having someone to spend the rest of her life with.

But it was hard being around her with all her chirpy talk about the wonderful Geoffrey Morrison. As much as he would miss Ma, he'd be sort of glad when the wedding was over and she and Geoff had moved to Springfield.

He just wanted to move on to the next chapter of his life. Get healthy again and get back to work. He'd lost a whole year, a year when the force could have used him—except he was useless. It was time to do whatever it took to go forward.

He rubbed his knee where he'd landed on it outside the station last night. It hurt, but at least he'd gotten through the night without taking any pain meds. He had to quit foolishly pushing himself— taking risks like that—physically if it meant three steps backward for every one he moved ahead.

That applied to his friendship with Jenna, too. What he wouldn't give for an eraser that could make last night go away, give him a clean slate with her.

He limped to the door, steeling himself to hide his pain from his mother.

He should have known better. Ma met him at the door. "What's going on?"

Lucas forced a smile. "What kind of greeting is that?"

She looked pointedly at the take-out cup he held. "Since when are you in the habit of going for coffee at this hour?"

"I . . . just felt like getting out." He pushed past her into the kitchen, but his knee gave way and he caught himself on the bar stool at the high counter.

"Lucas? What happened?"

"Nothing happened, Ma." He forced himself to look her in the eye.

"Don't you stand there and tell me nothing happened." Nothing got by Emily Vermontez—at least not when it came to him. "I can see it in your eyes. Something's going on."

"I banged up my knee a little last night."

"What? Did you fall?"

"I'm fine, Ma. Don't worry about it."

"Don't worry about it?" She glared at him. "Let me see. What'd you do?"

He brushed her off and took his coffee to the counter by the sink, doctoring it with sugar and creamer, his back to her. He grasped for something to change the subject. "So, you and Geoff going out this weekend?"

"No." She sighed. "He's going to a conference in New York."

He smiled and turned to pat her on the back. "Poor Ma."

She laughed and playfully pushed him away. "Don't act like you really care."

"I do. I just think you can probably live a few days without seeing the man."

"Oh, I can live. I just won't be happy about it."

"Have you set a date yet? For the wedding?"

"Valentine's Day." She beamed and shook a finger at him. "Save the date. Gina and Victoria are both coming home."

"Don't worry. It's not like I have a busy social calendar." His tactic worked and she was off, chattering about wedding plans and shopping for new furniture for Geoff's house in Springfield.

Lucas smiled and nodded in all the right places, but his mind went back to Jenna. He hoped the Morgans hadn't made things too difficult for her when she got home. Wasn't there a proverb or a rule or something that pointed out what a bad idea it was to move in with her in-laws?

He'd give her a call after he got home from his PT session this morning. Maybe she'd be up for talking over coffee.

An uninvited image popped into his head and

left him sick to his stomach. What must he have looked like chasing after that fire engine last night? He shook off the thought. But too late. Suddenly, asking Jenna Morgan to coffee didn't seem like such a great idea.

*J*enna squinted as sun poured in through the windshield. She tried to stretch her legs and winced. The combination of icy air and her cramped "bed" had left her joints stiff and achy. Her breath hung in a cloud in front of her.

A familiar roar outside the car window reminded her of the dream she'd been having. But she recognized the sound now. Not fire engines, but the trash truck. Monday morning.

Looking up through the windshield, she stared at the house. Her house. How could she have lost it? She'd driven here last night after getting kicked out of Clairemont Hills, not knowing where else she could park to spend the night. When she remembered that the new owners hadn't moved in yet, she risked parking here on the driveway close to the house. She'd hoped the L formed by the house and garage might protect her from the wind. But she'd barely slept all night, waking every half hour, freezing, to turn on the heater long enough to quit shivering. She'd been terrified someone would hear the car's engine and call the police.

She took in a sharp breath, clambered over the

car seat, and fumbled for the keys she'd left in the ignition. The car stuttered several times before purring to life. The clock on the dashboard flickered and displayed the time. Seven forty-five. The first day of December.

She could hardly move in the layers of clothes she'd slept in. Yet despite the layers, she shivered as cold air from the heater hit her face. She turned on the defroster and waited while the warming air cleared a porthole in front of the steering wheel.

The radio weatherman announced that it was "a balmy thirty-nine degrees" and headed for a high of fifty-six today. He declared the temps unseasonably warm. If *this* was balmy, she hated to think about spending a truly cold night in the car.

She didn't know what time the new owners were due to arrive today, but she didn't want to have to explain why she was camped out in their driveway. As the car warmed, she peeled off enough layers of clothing so she could move her limbs. Finally she put the car in gear and backed out of the driveway.

She couldn't remember when she'd ever been so miserable. Cold and damp to the bone, feeling claustrophobic in the cramped interior of the Volvo. She could not do this again tonight. She had to find a place to stay, had to find a paying job. But catching sight of herself in the rearview mirror, she knew she first had to find a place to shower and dress before she darkened the door of any business.

It was almost eight o'clock. Bryn would be up and getting ready for work by now. She punched in the number and scrambled to think what excuse she could give. She couldn't confess that she'd spent the night in her car, but neither could—

"Hello?"

"Bryn. Hey, it's Jenna. Can I ask a huge favor?"

"Sure . . . shoot."

"Would you mind if I use your shower and—hang out there for a while today?"

"Sure . . ." Her reply sounded like a question. "What's going on?"

She sighed. "Clarissa and I had a fight. I just . . . need to get away from there—from *here* for a while," she corrected. It wasn't a lie exactly. She needed to get away from this house, too.

"Already? Oh, Jen, what have you gotten yourself into?"

"I know, I know. And you tried to warn me. I should have listened."

"I'm heading to work in a little bit, but you've still got a key, right? And hey, thanks for taking care of Sparky last night."

"No problem."

"Listen, just make yourself at home. Ignore the mess. Garrett and I spent most of the weekend doing wedding stuff and the place is a wreck."

"Believe me, I'm not picky." She forced a laugh.

It came out more like a sob, but she covered it with a cough and Bryn didn't seem to notice. Or pretended not to.

"Oh, I usually shut Sparky up in the laundry room when I'm at work, but if you're here, you can let him out. Just be sure and close him back in there before you leave."

"Yeah, sure." She did not look forward to being in the same room—the same house—with that dog.

"Stay as long as you want. *Mi casa es su casa.* I'm going to run by and see Dad on my way home from work, so I probably won't be home till after dark."

Jenna had forgotten all about Bryn's dad still being in the hospital. Some friend she was. "How's your dad doing?"

Bryn sighed. "Not great. They still can't get his blood pressure straightened out. Hey, you didn't happen to talk to Lucas about Sparky, did you?"

"Actually, I did. He was going to check with somebody at the station, but he hasn't gotten back to me yet." She didn't tell Bryn that she'd seen Lucas again since that night at Java Joint. She wasn't sure how she felt about it herself yet. And now that she'd been kicked out of the Morgans' house, she wasn't eager to talk to anyone, including Lucas.

"Thanks, Jen. I appreciate it. Well, I'd better run. I hope you get things worked out with

Clarissa, but stay as long as you like. Between Dad and Garrett I'm hardly ever home anyway."

That relieved a little of her guilt. If Bryn wasn't there much, it wouldn't feel like such an imposition to be crashing at her place.

She cruised the back streets of the Falls, relishing the feel of the heater blowing warm air on her, and grateful that—at least for today—she had someplace warm to go.

She killed time until she felt sure Bryn would have left for work, then drove to the apartment, praying Sparky would be content to stay locked in the laundry room. The bathroom was at the opposite end of the apartment from the laundry. Maybe if she didn't make any noise letting herself in, the dog wouldn't even know she was there.

It wasn't as if she could afford to be picky. Right now it was a choice between facing Sparky or facing Clarissa, and for today at least, her fear of dogs paled in comparison.

15

*W*hy so glum this morning?"

Lucas felt his mother's eyes on him again and looked up from the newspaper to see her frowning.

"And why are *you* still hanging around? Don't you have to go to work or something?" He feigned a teasing tone he didn't feel, shook out the morning paper, and leaned back in the kitchen chair, pretending to read.

"Cut it out, Luc. You don't have to pretend with me. You surely know that by now. Now what's going on? Did you hurt yourself?"

"Nothing, Ma. I'm fine. I . . . tripped and bit the dust last night. . . . Made a fool of myself in front of a beautiful woman. It ticked me off, that's all."

Her eyebrows shot up. "You were out with a woman last night?" She slid into the chair across from him. "Who?"

"Well, hey, don't worry about me too much, Ma. I'm sure my leg will heal up in no time."

She laughed and reached across the table to pick up his hand and plant a kiss on his knuckles. "Poor baby. I'm so sorry. Are you okay?"

He rewarded her with a genuine smile. "I'll live. Nothing bruised but my ego."

"Okay, now let's hear about this woman."

He rolled his eyes. "Real subtle, Ma." But he told her about the fire run and even dared to mention that it was Jenna Morgan he'd been with.

"What were you and Jenna doing at the station anyway?"

"I ran into her at Rhodes. We were going for coffee and passed the station just as the trucks were leaving. You didn't hear anything on the news, did you? The scanner was sketchy, but they said something about the homeless shelter."

"Really? Fire?"

He nodded.

"No," she said, "I didn't hear anything. But I didn't have the radio on last night. I never heard sirens, though. What time was it?"

"Around nine, I think. But you probably wouldn't have heard them. They took the back way around. At least that's what it looked like from my angle—with my face planted in the sidewalk."

She smiled and scooted her chair closer. "Now tell me more. Jenna Morgan, huh? She called here the other night. Is this getting serious?"

"She has the hots for me, Ma. Like all the ladies. What can I say?"

"Can you be serious for two seconds? Sarcasm does not become you, son."

He gave her a cheesy grin he knew would get a laugh, but decided to risk being serious. "Like I said, I ran into her at Rhodes last night. We ended up spending the night together."

His mother's eyebrows shot up.

"Not that kind of spending the night." He laughed. Served her right for being so snoopy. "We just drove around for a while . . . talking."

She feigned a skeptical look, then beamed at him. "Are you going to ask her out again?"

"Ma. We're just friends. This is Zach's wife we're talking about."

"Luc. Come on—you don't think Zach would

want Jenna to curl up in a corner somewhere, do you? If you like her you should ask her out. She probably—"

He held up a hand. "No. It wouldn't be right, Ma. I couldn't do that to Zach." He shook his head slowly, but her words brought a strange hope, something he hadn't felt in a while. A long while.

"I worry about you, Lucas." His mother pushed back her chair and came to stand in front of him, framing his face with her hands, the way she used to when he was a little boy.

Her touch warmed him and embarrassed him at the same time. He gently pushed her hands away. "You don't need to worry about me. I'm fine. I'll be fine."

Concern crept into her eyes. "You aren't still struggling with . . . ?"

Her question—and the love in her expression—stabbed him in the heart. "Ma, you don't ever have to worry about that. I would never do anything—to hurt myself." What he must have put her through all those months when he was in the throes of depression, grieving Pop, grieving the loss of his career, and of his healthy body. He'd thought about ending his life many times in those first agonizing months after the fire. But now he would give anything to take back all the worry he caused Ma when she had so many other things weighing on her. "I would never do that to you. Or to Dad's memory."

"Oh, Luc . . . I just want you to be happy again."

"Yeah, me too."

"I know God will show you what He has for you next. You just have to ask."

"There's only one thing I want, only one thing I've ever wanted my whole life."

"I know." She sighed. "But for whatever reason that's not possible now. But God is perfectly capable of giving you something new, something you'll love just as much as firefighting. You just have to find out what that is."

"No." He shook his head again. "If I can't be a firefighter, then what was this all for? It's not worth it. Not worth losing Dad, losing Zach . . . all of them." He stopped, not trusting his voice. How had the conversation moved to this?

She knelt beside him, tears brimming in her dark eyes. "That's not true, Lucas. You know that's not true. You have so much potential! There are a thousand other things you could do, and do well. You just have to discover what God has in mind for this next chapter in your life."

"Well, He'd better start talking then because I'm not getting the message He's trying to—"

The phone rang and Ma patted his cheek and went to answer. Her smile grew. "Yes . . . Just a moment . . . he's right here."

Grinning, she handed him the cordless handset. "Speak of the devil," she whispered. "And don't you blow it."

Her smile lifted his spirits. Or maybe it had more to do with Jenna being on the other end of the line.

"This is Lucas."

"Hi." Her sigh held apology. "I'm so sorry to bother you, but I've got . . . a dog problem."

"Sparky again? What's up? He trying to eat you or something?"

Silence on the other end.

"Jenna? You there?"

"He, um . . . has me trapped."

He laughed. "Seriously? You're trapped?"

"Not exactly, but he's holding me hostage. I'm over at Bryn's—she's at work—and I can't get him back in the laundry room."

"Back in?"

"I accidentally let him out, but Bryn said to put him back before I leave and . . . he won't go. I tried calling Bryn, but she's not answering her phone."

"Did you try going into the laundry and calling him? He'll probably follow you."

More silence.

"Jenna?"

"I'm—I'm scared I'll get closed in there with him."

"He won't hurt you, Jenna. Where is he right now?"

"He's . . . watching me."

He scratched his head. "Um . . . Maybe the question is, where are *you?*"

"In the kitchen."

"He won't let you catch him?"

She sighed heavily into the phone. "Promise you won't make fun of me?"

He frowned, confused. "Promise."

"I'm up on the counter. He won't let me down."

He tried to picture her predicament and failed. "You're sitting on the countertop?"

"Um . . . crouching is more like it. He just keeps staring at me."

He couldn't help it—he burst out laughing at the image. "He probably wonders what in the world you're doing up there."

"Hey . . . you promised!"

"I'm sorry."

At the edge of his vision he saw Ma motioning to him. He turned his back on her, but she came around beside him, gesturing frantically and mouthing, "Go help her. You go *help* her."

"Hang on a second." Swallowing a new wave of laughter, he turned his back on his mother again and limped to the other side of the kitchen. "Jenna, if that dog wanted to hurt you, he'd rip you down from that counter so fast you wouldn't know what hit you."

"But when I start to get down, he won't let me."

"Listen, your only danger from that dog is being licked to death. But stay right there. I'll come and rescue you." He threw his mother a look meant to say, *There. Are you happy?*

Her smile said she was.

"Don't worry," Jenna said. "I'm not going anywhere."

"How am I going to get in?"

"I didn't lock the door."

"Okay. Sit tight—or maybe I should say, crouch tight." He hung up, chuckling.

"What's going on?" His mother wore an inquisitive grin.

Ignoring his aching muscles, he hauled himself to the closet for his jacket and his cane. "I have to go rescue a damsel in distress." He tried to sound annoyed, but from the grin on Ma's face, he didn't think she was fooled for one second.

16

*J*enna?" Lucas's tentative voice floated from the entryway.

"I'm in the kitchen," she squeaked from her graceless and uncomfortable perch on Bryn's kitchen counter. "Can you call him?"

"Sparky? Come here, boy." Lucas clicked his tongue, and without giving Jenna a second glance, the dog trotted around the corner to greet him. She heard Lucas baby-talking the dog, and then the sounds of patting and tail-wagging. *Stupid dog.*

She swung her legs over the counter, trying to affect some semblance of dignity. But she remained on edge, poised and ready to scale the counter again if necessary.

A minute later man and dog appeared around the corner. Lucas's smirk said he was working hard not to laugh. She no doubt looked laughable perched on the counter with her hair uncombed and her clothes a wrinkled mess from spending the night wadded in her car.

When she was sure he had a good hold on Sparky's collar, she slid off the counter and stood in the corner near the sink.

"Thank you." She knew her face must be ten shades of pink, but he didn't comment.

"You want him back here?" He pointed toward the laundry room, keeping one hand on his cane, the other firmly wrapped around Sparky's collar.

"Please."

He pushed the dog into the tiny laundry room and pulled the door shut. "Now stay, boy," he said, obviously for her benefit. He took a staggered step, grabbing the door handle for balance. Sparky answered with a muffled bark.

Lucas leaned his cane against a chair in the breakfast nook and steadied himself, then came around the bar to where she stood, her back still to the sink.

"Stupid dog." She rolled her eyes toward the laundry room, but she felt like the stupid one. "I barely opened the door and he got out and practically ate me alive."

"Yeah, I noticed that big chunk out of your arm." He grinned and leaned against the counter, bracing his hands behind him.

She lasered a ha-ha-very-funny look in his direction.

He ignored it. "You taking care of him for Bryn again?"

"Not exactly. I didn't want to let him out at all, but he was scratching at the door."

Lucas looked confused.

"Oh . . . Bryn said I could hang out at her place today."

"Things that bad at the Morgans'?"

"That bad and worse. They sort of, um, kicked me out."

"What? Seriously? You just got there."

"They forbade me to associate with Bryn as long as I was under their roof." She looked around the room as though Bryn might overhear.

"Ouch."

"Yeah, tell me about it. So I decided I can't live there."

"Good for you. But where *will* you live then?"

She looked at the floor, not wanting to confess to him that she'd spent last night in her car. "I don't exactly know yet. I'm going to look at some apartments today. You don't know of anything do you? In the Falls?"

He shook his head. "Sorry. I can ask around, though."

"That's okay. I thought I'd talk to the Realtor who handled my house sale."

"So you're staying here in the meantime?"

"I don't know. I don't really want to tell Bryn why I got kicked out."

"I see your point. But you can't exactly *not* tell her."

"No, I guess not. But it breaks my heart to think about hurting Bryn like that. She's already taken so much junk over this whole—" She stopped short. She didn't really know where Lucas stood on Bryn. After all, he'd lost his father in the fire. He had this limp and the cane because of the fire. And worse, he'd lost the job he loved. "I'm sorry," she said. "I know some people still . . . blame Bryn. For the fire. I guess I can understand how you might, too."

He shook his head slowly. "I did for a while. But I forgave her. A long time ago . . . thanks to my mom."

"I like your mom."

That brought a crooked smile. "Yeah, I do, too. She's one of the good ones."

His expression at the mention of Emily made Jenna a little jealous—and made her wonder if Lucas knew about her own mother. Had Zach talked with him about what she'd come from—her past—when they'd worked shifts together at the station?

Before she could decide whether to risk asking

him, he changed the subject. "Hey, you want to go for coffee?" He looked like a nervous kid inviting a girl on his first date.

And she did want to go with him. Very much. But she was in desperate need of a shower and a shampoo. And she had less than eight hours to find a place to stay tonight. "I'd love to, but I need to go apartment hunting—and job hunting before that."

"Wow. Big day."

"Yeah, I can hardly wait. Can I take a rain check on that coffee, though?"

"You bet." He went around the bar and retrieved his cane from the breakfast nook. "You'll be okay—with Cujo there." He grinned and pointed to the laundry room door where Jenna could hear the dog snuffling beneath the door.

"You wouldn't want to take him now, would you?"

He laughed. "You're relentless! And giving Bryn's dog away? Some friend."

She gave him a look. "I told you, I have permission. Seriously, though, she really needs to find another home for him."

He nodded and appeared to be considering the possibility. "I haven't had a chance to check yet whether the station would consider taking him in."

"But just think how nice it would be to have a furry companion in your house," she said, trying to close the sale.

He narrowed his eyes and shook a playful finger in her face. "Don't think I don't see through your clever ploy. This is all part of that 'plan' you and Bryn cooked up, right?" He looked from her to the laundry room door and back again. "And that 'furry companion' pitch sure sounds funny coming from a girl who just spent ten minutes trapped on a kitchen counter by one."

She didn't tell him she'd been crouched on the counter for more like thirty minutes. "Just trying to help. Final offer. Take it or leave it." She grabbed a damp dishrag hanging over the faucet and pretended to concentrate on scrubbing the counters.

"I'll take him."

She whirled around and did a double take. "Seriously? You'll take Sparky?"

"I will." He eyed the closed laundry room door. "I've been thinking about getting a dog. And I like this one."

She studied him, trying to figure out whether this was just one of his pranks. If it was, he had a great poker face.

"Assuming Bryn hasn't changed her mind," he said.

"I'm sure she hasn't. But let me call her and make sure she doesn't mind you taking him now." She dug in her purse for her phone and dialed Bryn's number. She would love nothing more than finding a new home for Sparky, especially if she was going to be spending any time at all in this apartment.

• • •

$\mathcal{L}$ucas pulled into the driveway, parking his truck as close to the back gate as he could. Cutting the engine, he watched Sparky in his rearview mirror. The dog trotted from the front of the pickup bed to the back, obviously eager to explore his new home. *What have I gotten myself into?*

But one glance at the passenger seat beside him made him think it may have been worthwhile. Jenna flashed him a smile and reached for the door handle. After he'd agreed to take the dog, it had been easy to talk Jenna into coming with him to get Sparky settled. She didn't get out but watched in the side mirror, nibbling at her lower lip.

"Don't worry, I'll put him on a leash."

She laughed nervously. "Is it that obvious?"

"Pretty obvious. Why *do* you hate dogs so much?"

"I don't hate them, I just . . . don't like them."

He waited, knowing that wasn't the whole story.

She glared at him but finally offered, "Vicious rottweiler next door to our—to where I grew up, okay? I really don't want to talk about it."

Ah, so the truth comes out. He held out a hand. "Come with me. I'm going to make you and that dog friends yet. Sparky's a teddy bear. You'll see."

She gave an adamant shake of her head, but she opened her door and climbed down.

He grabbed his cane from the floor of the cab and located the leash in the box of dog

150

paraphernalia Bryn had insisted he take. He went to the back of the truck and clipped the leash to Sparky's collar. He opened the tailgate and Sparky sprang down from the truck. But as soon as he realized he was on a leash, he stood at Lucas's side, panting.

Lucas clicked his tongue. "Heel, boy." He was impressed when Sparky obeyed. Jenna had mentioned that Bryn's dad had worked with the dog, but he wasn't sure what to expect— especially on foreign territory.

Walking Sparky around the truck, Lucas worked to keep his own gait even, aware of Jenna's eyes on him. He was constantly aware of his limp when he was with her, but he was beginning to think being with her might be better than PT. He didn't think it was his imagination that he'd learned to control his limp better. His disability grew more pronounced at the end of the day when he was tired, and he still didn't trust his balance without the cane, but he'd seen a little improvement, and that roused a faint hope in him.

Jenna eyed Sparky, keeping her distance while Lucas opened the gate for them. Once in the backyard he latched the gate behind them and bent to unclip the leash. Even Jenna laughed when Sparky charged around the corner of the house the minute he was free.

"He must think there's a rabbit back there. Or a cat."

She gave a little gasp, and her hazel eyes—gorgeous eyes—grew round. "Your cat's not out here, is she?"

"Lucky's a tom—a he. But if he's back there, he's climbed to higher ground by now." He pointed to a tall cottonwood that stood with its branches outstretched over one corner of the yard. "I doubt Sparky could get him way up there."

She followed his line of vision, then shot him a impish grin. "Lucky for Lucky, living with a fireman. In case he ever gets stuck up there," she explained.

He laughed. "You know, don't you, that we don't *really* rescue cats from trees."

She looked shocked. "And you call yourself a fireman? Seriously, what if I called you tomorrow and told you my poor little kitty was stuck in a tree?"

He laughed—and took note of the fact that she still referred to him as a fireman. "Well, I might come and hold your hand. Maybe bring a carton of milk for the kitty. But I'd just point out that we've never seen a dead cat in a tree and that he'll come down when he gets hungry."

"You're heartless. And actually, Zach did have to go on a cat-up-a-tree run. His first week on the job. A kitten."

He curbed a grin at her serious expression. "Really?"

"It was a telephone pole, not a tree, but same principle."

"Really? I don't think I ever heard that story. Must not have been on my shift." He didn't want to talk about Zach. Didn't want to be reminded that Jenna was his friend's wife. It didn't matter that Zach was gone. Regardless of what Ma thought.

Sparky came to his rescue, barreling toward them from the far end of the yard. Jenna squealed and scrambled behind Lucas, gripping his elbow as if her life depended on it.

He started laughing, but when he turned to tease her for being such a chicken, the near terror in her eyes stopped him.

He turned and spoke sharply to the dog. "Sparky! Sit! Stay!"

The dog stopped in his tracks and cocked its head as if trying to figure out what he'd done wrong. But before Lucas could grab hold of his collar, Sparky wove between his legs, almost tripping him. Jumping up on his hind legs, the dog pawed at Jenna's shoulders.

Lucas pushed him down and made him sit, holding his cane out like a shepherd's staff. Jenna clutched so tightly to his free arm he was afraid she'd take them both down.

He got Sparky calmed down a little, then took Jenna's hand. "It's okay. He just wanted to dance with you." When she didn't laugh, he tried again. "He's just being friendly."

She gave a curt nod, but her eyes said she didn't believe him.

"I'm not going to let him hurt you. He's just excited about being in a new place, that's all."

"Okay." Her voice was strained and breathless.

An idea formed and he twined his fingers with hers. "Come here." He whistled softly. "Heel, boy."

Sparky trotted beside them, looking up every few seconds, as if to be sure his new master noticed how well he'd minded.

Jenna came along willingly, but her grip on his hand was viselike.

Lucas led her around the corner of the house. She stopped short and unlaced her hand from his. "Oh, wow! What a gorgeous place."

"It's my dad's garden." Even in these waning days of autumn the place held a rare beauty. Being back here never failed to make him miss Pop. "You should see it in the spring," he said quietly.

With Sparky all but forgotten, Jenna turned a full circle, oohing and aahing. Lucas tried to see the garden through her eyes. Dry leaves skittered beneath the benches lining the flagstone pathways, and spent roses still clung to the arbors. The stone fountain, despite being littered with leaves, trilled a pleasant melody, but the garden begged for attention. "Pop would have a fit over the weeds and—"

"Oh, Lucas, it's stunning!" She turned to him, eyes wide.

He shrugged. "Ma and I tried to keep it up this summer, but neither of us has Pop's green thumb. I hate to think what will happen to it after Ma moves to Springfield."

"Can't you hire someone? It would be a shame to let it go."

"We haven't decided." He lifted his cane. "All I know is I sure can't do it."

Her gaze panned the garden again, and he took pleasure in her obvious enjoyment of Pop's creation. She was right. They couldn't let it go to pot. It would have broken Pop's heart to think of his garden being abandoned.

They laughed as Sparky lapped water from each of the fountain's four spigots. But before they could wipe the smiles off their faces, he galloped across the lawn and stood in front of them tossing his head. A fine spray of water—and slobber— flew off his whiskers.

"Ewww!" Jenna swiped at her forehead with the sleeve of her jacket and quickly moved behind Lucas, using him as a shield.

He didn't mind when she grabbed his elbow this time. This dog just might come in handy when it came to women. At least when it came to this woman.

"What's so funny?" She looked up at him with a question in her eyes.

"Nothing." He hadn't realized he was smiling and quickly wiped the grin off his face. Remembering why he'd brought her back to the yard in the first place, he started down the flagstone path. "Follow me."

Sparky ran ahead and she followed Lucas to a bench on the edge of the patio near the fountain.

He leaned his cane on the bench and sat, patting the spot beside him. She sat.

He held out a hand and whistled. "Here boy."

Sparky ignored him.

"Sparky!" He made his voice gruff. "Sparky, come!"

After several detours to sniff out the garden, the dog trotted over and worked his way between Lucas's knees, nuzzling his palms, begging to be petted.

Jenna recoiled, but he took her hand, guiding it to Sparky's head. "Remember how I showed you last time? Hold your hand out like this." He demonstrated, flattening his palm.

She resisted at first, but Lucas placed his hand over hers on top of Sparky's large head, stroking gently. The dog leaned into the massage and relaxed. Jenna seemed to do the same.

He spoke to Sparky in a soothing voice, then turned to Jenna. "See? I told you he likes you. He still just has some puppy in him. That's what makes him so frisky."

She frowned. "He's awfully big for a puppy."

"Well, a full-grown pup. Kind of like a teenager."

"Ugh." She wrinkled her nose. "That explains a lot."

He laughed. "Maybe that wasn't the best analogy. A big fifth-grader then."

"Even worse."

Sparky wriggled out from under their hands, and before Lucas thought to stop him, the dog moved to sit in front of Jenna. He placed his jowls on her knee and looked up at her, panting.

"Look, he's smiling!"

Feeling triumphant, but not letting it show, Lucas bent his head to check it out. Sparky sported what could only be described as a smile. He tried to sound incredulous. "I think he has a crush on you."

That earned him a giggle, which eased the "buyer's remorse" he'd been feeling for having adopted this crazy dog. He could just imagine Ma's reaction.

Sparky gave a sharp bark and rose to all fours.

A meow came from near the back door.

Jenna turned to look. "Oh, there's your kitty."

Sparky backed away from the bench, then spun around, ears on alert. Jenna grabbed Lucas's arm again.

But Sparky took a step forward and stood watching the cat, his tail thumping a steady beat on the bench behind him.

Lucky slinked through the flower bed in front of

the deck, keeping his eyes on the interloper. His thick gray coat was good camouflage on the weathered mulch, but Sparky wasn't fooled.

"Yep, that's Lucky. I bet he's been hiding out in the garage. Probably smelled dog."

"They're sure giving each other the eye."

"Yeah." He tensed, sensing Sparky's intentions. With Jenna clutching his left arm and his cane out of reach, he braced himself.

"What happened to Wonder Dog here?" He patted Sparky's neck. "With his reputation for sniffing things out, I'm surprised he didn't smell ol' Lucky right away."

"Maybe he did and he just wasn't interested."

He shot her a look. "A dog not interested in a cat? I don't think so."

She laughed and loosened her grip on his arm a bit. For a fleeting moment he considered siccing the dog on Lucky just to keep Jenna close.

Sparky must have read his mind because the pooch chose that moment to lunge at Lucky. The cat darted across the yard and scrambled up the fence, prancing along the narrow ledge like a tightrope walker.

Sparky took chase, and Lucas shouted to no avail. The dog charged the fence and stood on point there with his front paws high on the plank boards, baying as if he'd treed a coon. Lucky balanced atop the fence just out of reach, tail held high, daring the dog to come closer.

"Stay here," Lucas told Jenna. He grabbed his cane and hobbled across the uneven garden terrain, praying he wouldn't embarrass himself in front of her again.

17

Jenna held her breath while Lucas approached Sparky with an outstretched hand. The dog temporarily lost interest in Lucky, and Lucas snatched his collar and hauled him back across the lawn to where she waited.

Unable to overcome her fear, she jumped up from the bench and hurried around behind it, putting a wall between her and Sparky.

"You're not changing your mind, are you? About keeping him?" She tried to keep her expression from revealing that she feared just that.

"He just needs a firm hand. No self-respecting dog could resist a good cat chase."

Jenna smiled apologetically. "I just hope he doesn't scare Lucky off. He's a pretty cat."

"Don't worry. Lucky knows where his bread is buttered. They'll work things out."

"So you'll keep him?"

"We made a deal. I won't back out on it."

"I wouldn't blame you if you did." She hadn't really meant to say that out loud.

"Give me a week. I bet I can whip him into shape."

"You don't mean that literally, right?"

"No, of course not. Figure of speech." He gave her a smile that seemed to seal his promise.

A man of his word. She liked that.

The sun climbed high in a clear gray-blue sky, but a gust of wind sent a chill up her spine.

"You cold? Let's take this dog into the garage and get him settled, then I'll make you a cup of coffee."

"That would be nice." She *should* be downtown looking for a job and a place to live. Trying to get her life figured out. Spending time with Lucas this morning had taken her mind off her problems. Unfortunately, it hadn't *solved* a single one of them.

"If you'll give me your keys, I'll bring Sparky's stuff in."

"Great." He fished a key ring from his pocket and showed her which one opened the truck. It took two trips to haul all the stuff Bryn had donated along with the dog.

A lump rose in Jenna's throat, thinking about Bryn's teary response to Lucas's offer to take Sparky. She was grateful, but sad to let him go, too. Between having her father in the hospital and her upcoming wedding, poor Bryn's life was in upheaval. Still, Jenna felt a stab of jealousy. What would it be like to have a parent you loved enough to grieve over? And a husband-to-be who made you glow the way Bryn did since she and Garrett had fallen in love?

She slammed the pickup door and pushed the thoughts away.

Lucas met her in the backyard and let her in the house through the patio doors. The house smelled of day-old coffee, cinnamon, and woodsmoke.

"I'd start a fire, but I've got PT later on and Ma won't be home until late."

She liked the way he called his mother "Ma." And the affection with which he said it. "It's okay." She waved him off, then hugged herself, feeling warmer already. "It's nice in here." Looking around the large, cozy kitchen, she felt embraced by its charm. Clarissa would have considered the decor kitschy, and the painted cupboards and rag rugs outdated. And frankly, there was a time Jenna would have agreed. But somehow it all seemed just right for this house. Maybe it was the good-looking guy standing at the sink who made the difference.

Lucas rinsed out the coffeemaker and started a new pot. He seemed comfortable in the kitchen and moved around with ease, his cane apparently forgotten, though she noticed he kept close to the counters, using them to steady himself.

She settled into one of the high stools at the breakfast bar, watching him work. The heady scent of coffee soon perfumed the air and he joined her at the bar while they waited for it to brew.

Recounting Sparky's antics a few minutes ago, they laughed together, and for once, Jenna didn't feel her nerves standing on end at the very thought of the dog.

While they savored fresh coffee, they talked about everything and about nothing at all.

Spending time with him like this, Jenna realized that she and Lucas had already built a history together over the few occasions they'd been together. There was an easy comfort between them that she relished, even as she realized how different this was from what she'd had with Zach.

She didn't want to make comparisons. Zach came up short, and that didn't seem fair— especially when she didn't know Lucas that well. And yet she was beginning to feel as if she'd known him forever.

She couldn't have said how long they'd been talking, but she became aware of the sun on their backs, its bright warmth creeping in through the top of the tall west-facing patio doors.

"What time is it, anyway?" She looked around the room for a clock.

Lucas glanced at his wristwatch and gasped. "Oh, man . . . I'm late for PT."

"Oh, no. I'm sorry." She felt awful.

"It's not your fault. But I'd better get going." He slid off the stool and took his mug to the sink.

She followed with her mug and spoon and rinsed them out.

"Don't worry about the dishes."

"Listen, I can just walk back to Bryn's. I'm so sorry I made you late."

"Don't be silly. It's only two minutes out of my way to drop you off."

"You're sure?"

"You bet. Let me check on Sparky and lock up. I'll meet you at the truck."

They rode in silence back to Bryn's. Jenna regretted the abrupt end to their time together, yet the silence between them wasn't an awkward one.

When Bryn's apartment came into view, she gave an inward sigh. "Just let me off at the curb."

Lucas parked the truck, and stretching his right arm across the back of the seat, he turned to her, a boyish grin on his face. "Hey, you wouldn't want to go out tomorrow night, would you? See a movie or something?"

She shouldn't have been surprised at the invitation, but she was. He seemed a little startled by it himself, as if he hadn't intended to ask her out, but the invitation had popped out of its own accord.

She wanted to say yes more than she'd wanted anything in a long time. But she didn't even know where she'd be sleeping tonight. How would she get ready for a date from her rumpled "closet" in the backseat of her car? She couldn't very well tell him to pick her up for their date at "the gray Volvo in the parking lot."

"Lucas, I—"

He held up a hand. "I'm sorry. I assumed too much. I shouldn't have—"

"No . . ." Suddenly she was terrified he'd change his mind. "No, I'd like that. I'd like it a lot."

His smile melted her. "I'll pick you up around six then?"

She grimaced. "Where?"

"Oh. Where should I come?"

She'd just have to figure out a way to explain things to Bryn. "Pick me up here," she said, hating the deception, but unwilling to let the chance to see him again slip away. She'd park in the back lot of the complex here if she had to.

"It's a date then."

She climbed down from the truck and stood watching until he disappeared from sight. Should she be feeling guilty that she was so eager to see him again? Maybe she did—a little. *But not enough to say no, right, Morgan?*

What had she gotten herself into?

18

Tuesday, December 2

Lucas woke to a slice of sunlight on the wall of his bedroom. His first thought was of Jenna Morgan. His second was of Sparky, though he didn't think he'd mention that to Jenna. He wondered how the dog had fared through the night. He hadn't heard him bark once, and now he worried something might be wrong.

Easing his legs over the side of the bed, he automatically performed the series of stretches and isometric exercises he'd learned over the past year of physical therapy. He wasn't sure if they really helped or not, but he wasn't willing to face the ire of his therapists—or his mom—by missing even one day. His legs always functioned better early in the day.

He looked out the window and saw Ma dragging the trash cart out to the drive. He'd gone to bed before she got home last night, so he hadn't had a chance to tell her about Sparky. He threw on yesterday's jeans, grabbed his cane, and hurried out to help her, knowing the kind of greeting she was likely to get from the dog.

By the time he retrieved Sparky's leash from the garage and shambled down the driveway, Sparky was running circles around Ma. She seemed delighted, twirling one hand above the dog in graceful arcs, as if they were dance partners. He smiled at the contrast between his mother and Jenna. Jenna must have had a bad run-in with that rottweiler as a kid to have the extreme fear she did. She'd warmed up to Sparky a little before she left yesterday, but she had a long way to go.

He wasn't sure why it was so important to him to help her overcome this fear. He was taking a lot for granted to assume she'd have any reason to be around Sparky in the future.

Of course, he did have a date with her tonight. He smiled at the thought. But the smile faded at the sudden image of Zach. His best friend, beaming, his wife on his arm. It was a scene that came to him with disturbing frequency in recent days. His face heated at the remembrance of the way he'd flirted with Jenna at the company picnic a couple of years ago. Jenna had been merely polite, while he'd made a fool of himself. Zach hadn't seemed bothered, but then Zach couldn't have known that there was a lot more going on in Luc's mind than innocent conversation with his buddy's wife.

He threw up what was surely the thousandth apology to heaven, and to Zach, then shook off the memories and the shame. It was over. He could put it all behind him. *Easier said than done.*

"Hey, Ma."

At the end of the drive, his mother whirled to face him. "Well! You're up early."

He met her in the middle of the driveway and patted Sparky's head. "You want me to take him?"

"So I take it we have a dog now?"

"Sorry. I meant to say something."

"I like him. We were just playing. He did scare the stuffing out of me when I went out to the garage this morning. What's his name?"

"Sparky." Lucas cocked his head. "You're not mad at me for adopting a puppy?"

She gave him a you-can't-fool-me look. "This is no puppy."

He held out the coiled leash. "I'm going to take him around back and work with him a little." He clicked his tongue. "Here, Sparky. Here, boy."

He grinned to himself. He might have to come up with another name—something a little more manly—for the dog. Then again, if he was going to be a firehouse dog, Sparky had kind of a nice ring to it.

His mother started toward the house. "Just please be careful, Luc. Don't let him trip you up. He's pretty rambunctious."

"Ma! I'll be fine." He hadn't meant for that to come out so sharp, but as if someone had flipped a switch, her words grated on him. No matter how many times he reassured her, she still worried. He understood why, but all her babying was starting to get on his nerves. Sometimes he wished somebody would remind her that he was a grown man.

He put Sparky on the leash and walked him around to the back gate. A quick call to Bryn last night confirmed the training her father had done with Sparky. Later Lucas had spent two hours on the Internet reading up on the basics of training a grown dog.

For the next hour and a half, he tested some of the commands Bryn claimed the dog knew. Sparky seemed a little rusty at first. He kept one eye on Lucas's cane, as if he were afraid his new master might beat him with it. Lucas finally leaned the cane on the bench and took Sparky out to the giant oak in the middle of the yard.

By the end of the hour Sparky was responding amazingly well to simple commands of *sit, stay,* and *heel.* Lucas rewarded him with doggy treats from the box of stuff Bryn had sent.

After Sparky followed him around the fence line, heeling and sitting on command, Lucas took the dog to the stone bench where he and Jenna had sat yesterday.

He unclipped the leash and gave Sparky a good rubdown. "Good job! You did good, boy. Just wait till Jenna sees you. She'll be amazed. Yes, she will." The dog ate up the sweet talk and seemed content when Lucas went in to shower.

Twenty minutes later, his head swimming with inspiration that had come while he stood under the hot spray, he took a steaming mug of coffee to the computer. He entered *accelerant detection dogs* into the search engine and started reading.

Sparky would be a good fit for the fire station. And from what he read, there just might be a possibility of training him as an accelerant detection dog. Jenna got credit for that idea, of course. He'd thought it was a little far-fetched when she'd mentioned it, but the more he read, the more excited he became.

His elation was short-lived, though, when he came to the part about acceptance into the training programs. Most of the training sites required the handler to be in top physical shape. One application said dog handlers must be able to walk three to four miles a day.

Could he do that? Maybe, but not with any speed. And he'd pay for it dearly the next day.

He was up to two miles a day on the treadmill in PT. It wasn't pretty to look at. He was slow and clumsy, and continuous walking still caused him a good deal of pain, but still, two miles was two miles.

Inspired by the thought, he grabbed his jacket and headed for his truck. He carried his cane but didn't use it, instead using every ounce of his will to walk without the usual hitch in his step. He drove to the station and parked in the front lot, leaving his cane in the car. It felt weird to be going in through the front entrance, as if he were a guest.

"Hey! Look who's here! Vermontez!" Several of

the crew on duty were hanging out in the front office shooting the breeze. He saw several new faces, but even the neophytes gathered round to clap him on the shoulder or shake his hand.

"How you doin', buddy?"

"Lookin' good, man!"

They closed in, threatening to throw him off balance. Through sheer willpower, he managed to stay upright.

"Is Brennan here?" he asked.

"In the south bay, last I saw him." One of the new hires—Jerry Samuelson, according to his badge shirt—pointed past the living area. "Go on back. He'll be glad to see you."

He made his way down the wide hallway to the bay where the engines were garaged, inhaling the unique smells of the place—last night's spaghetti and cheap coffee, and as he got closer to the bay, diesel fuel, boot polish, and sweat. The old excitement swelled inside him, buoying him.

Peter Brennan looked up and surprise registered on his sun-weathered face. The chief greeted Lucas with the same enthusiasm the other guys had, pumping his hand and looking him up and down. "You're looking great, man. What can I do for you?"

"I want to come back. I know I can't do everything I did before, but I can work up to it. I'll do whatever it takes." He hadn't meant to blurt it out, but there it was anyway.

Brennan studied him hard, then hooked a thumb over his shoulder. "Come on back to my office. Let's talk." Lucas took a step forward and his knee hitched, shooting pain down his calf. He barely suppressed a groan, but quickly caught himself and kept walking, sensing Brennan's frank perusal behind him.

"So, what does your doctor say?" Brennan asked once they were settled in his office with Cokes from the vending machine in the mess hall.

He could see the chief's skepticism but forced confidence into his voice. "I'm getting better every day. Still in PT, and improving all the time."

"I'll need a doctor's clearance. Before I can even consider it."

"I know that." Lucas's hopes dimmed, but he held up a hand. "I want to run something by you." He took a deep breath and told the chief his idea about training Sparky. "I'd be his trainer and handler. I've researched it, and there are programs not too far from here that we could get hooked up with."

Brennan looked pointedly at Lucas's legs, doubt clear in the set of his jaw. "You'd have to pass the same physical as the other guys. Even with a dog, you'd still have to be on-site."

"I understand." It was the kiss of death. They both knew he couldn't pass that physical now—maybe not ever.

Brennan stood, smiling but dismissing him.

"You come back the minute you're ready and we'll administer the tests. I'd love to have you back, Vermontez, you know that."

He thought he'd steeled himself for it, but Brennan's rejection hurt far worse than he'd expected it to.

"How's your mother doing?"

Lucas gave him an answer, but his voice was dead with defeat.

He extricated himself from the premises as quickly as he could, not bothering to hide his limp. They'd never let him come back. Never take a chance on him.

And how could he blame them? Even if he was only working with an accelerant detection dog, if he wasn't 100 percent, he could endanger lives. He didn't need any more blood on his hands.

Behind the wheel of his pickup, he slammed the gearshift into reverse and gunned the engine, shooting a spray of gravel into the winter air.

19

*D*on't be silly, Jen. I don't mind one bit." Bryn patted Jenna's hand, then went to the closet and pulled out her winter coat.

"Thanks, B. I owe you." She watched Bryn, envious of the confidence—and a strange sense of peace—she seemed to have, even with everything that had happened. The tragedy—not just losing her husband, but the awful guilt she bore—had changed Bryn. And for the better. It was a mystery Jenna hadn't had the courage to ask her about, but she was intrigued.

Bryn had not only helped her set up a job interview for that afternoon, she'd generously offered to let Jenna stay with her until the lease on her apartment was up at the end of January. It bought her a few weeks.

Jenna was relieved Bryn hadn't asked about the source of her blowup with Clarissa. She was even more relieved she wouldn't have to sleep in her car again tonight. That she'd done so last night was a secret she would carry to her grave. *Along with a skeleton far more profound.* She pushed away the thought.

Bryn buttoned her coat and reached for the door. "I'll stay with Dad until late—and maybe go for coffee with Garrett afterward—so if you beat me home, just make yourself comfy." She shot Jenna a knowing grin. "And have a great time on your date."

"I will. But I've got laundry to do, so I won't be too late."

Bryn put a hand on her hip. "Listen, girlfriend, don't you dare come home early from a date with that gorgeous man to do *laundry!* Do you hear me?"

Jenna grinned. "Yes, *mother.*" But the teasing

tasted sour on her tongue. The term felt like an insult, though she knew Bryn wouldn't see it that way.

"Have fun. I mean it. Just enjoy yourself."

"And you just get on to work and don't worry about me." She waved Bryn off with a smile. "Oh, hey, where's your ironing board?"

"Laundry *and* ironing? What's gotten into you?"

"I don't have anything ready to wear to my interview this afternoon."

"Oh. In that case, the iron's in the broom closet and the ironing board is folded up beside the dryer." She opened the closet and showed her where things were, then headed out the door.

Jenna waited until she was sure Bryn was gone before going to get a few clothes and her laptop from her car. If she brought everything in at once, Bryn would know she'd essentially moved out of the Morgans' for good.

She did a load of laundry and ironed several outfits and hung them in the closet in the guest room where she was staying. What did you wear to a job interview to be a grocery checker? Surely they didn't expect anything too fancy. Any other time she would have asked Clarissa's advice.

A wave of sadness came over her. Those days were over. And sometimes—like today—she really missed Zach's mom.

She finally settled on a pair of black pants and a silk shirt. She could dress it up with a jacket for the interview and change into a more casual jacket before Lucas picked her up tonight.

She wasn't sure which event she was more nervous about.

*L*ucas glared at the computer screen, forcing himself to cool off, to start thinking rationally. Sparky sat beside him, looking at him with soft eyes.

He patted the dog's head and sighed. On his way home from the firehouse, a Hanover Falls cop had pulled him over. He had it coming. He'd been driving like a maniac, as if he could somehow exact revenge on Peter Brennan from behind the wheel of his truck.

He'd been lucky to get off with a warning—for speeding. It could have been a big fat ticket for reckless driving. He was sobered by the grace the officer had granted him and felt guilty because he knew the leniency had everything to do with Lucas Vermontez having been a "victim" of the Grove Street fire.

It wasn't fair to blame Chief Brennan for his decision. The man was only looking out for his able-bodied men. Lucas *knew* that. He'd expected exactly the response he got—his rational self had anyway. Pop would have made the same decision. But that didn't make the rejection any easier.

Rubbing Sparky's silky ears, he ran through the browser's history on his computer, checking out the websites of training facilities for accelerant detection dogs again. Lucky watched warily from the bed.

Maybe he could find someone else to take Sparky and do the training with him. Maybe one of the new guys at the station would be willing to take him on. But they were shorthanded as it was. Could they afford to give someone six to twelve weeks off—the length of most of the programs he'd researched?

He pressed his lips into a tight line. Already the thought of letting Sparky go was like a knife to his gut. He'd grown attached to the crazy pooch. And not just the dog, but the idea of training him to be a working dog. Something about that notion had taken hold of him and it wouldn't let go. Jenna had said Zach talked about training a dog for the station. Maybe this was one small way he could honor his friend.

He found a training school in Oklahoma. He'd have to make a trip there to have Sparky—and himself—evaluated as candidates. But that was only six hours away, and this facility seemed to have somewhat less rigorous requirements for trainers, with the idea that the eventual handler— at the station—would receive training once the dog was ready.

Tossing up a prayer, he filled out their application online, trying to be honest about his limitations while still answering in a way that wouldn't disqualify him before he ever got a hearing.

He needed two character references, so he put down Captain Peter Brennan's name, and on a whim, listed Andrea Morley, the fire investigator who'd handled the Grove Street fire. Andi had questioned him several times in the weeks after the fire. She'd been thoughtful and sensitive at a time when he was grieving Pop's death, and not sure he wanted to go on living.

Several times since, he'd thought about calling the investigator to thank her. He'd never gotten around to it. Now he had a good excuse to go see her, and thank her.

He shook his head, pushing away thoughts of Zach and the fact that he had a date with Zach's wife tonight.

If he hurried, he'd have time to get to Springfield and back before it was time to pick Jenna up. He'd talk to Andi Morley and maybe have time to stop by the bookstore and look for some books on dog training.

He checked his watch. On second thought, maybe Jenna would like to ride along. He fished his cell phone out of his pocket and rang her.

"Oh, I wish I could," she said, after he explained his plans. "But guess what?"

"You found an apartment?"

"Close . . . first things first. I found a job! Well, maybe . . . at least I have an interview in an hour and they sounded hopeful on the phone."

"Hey, that's great. Where?"

"Hanson's. The grocery store."

"Sure, I know it. Good for you."

"Bryn worked there for a while before she got back on at the library, so she got me an interview. I'd just be a checker. I don't really have the experience to do . . . well, much of anything."

"I doubt that. You could probably do anything you put your mind to."

"Not without a degree. There's not much out there unless—"

"Well, I'm happy for you, Jen." He cut her off before she could put herself down again. "When would you start? I mean, if you get this job? Have you told the Morgans yet?"

"I'm not sure. And no . . . I haven't talked to Clarissa since I left there the other night."

"You don't think they're worried about you? Zach's parents?"

"Oh, I guarantee Clarissa has done some calling around and at least knows I'm still alive. She has my number."

Lucas could almost hear her indifferent shrug over the phone lines.

"Besides," she said, "if I call her, I'm afraid I'll say something I'd regret later."

He hated the fact that she was at odds with Zach's parents. Sure, they were upper-crust and a little hard-line about the whole thing with Bryn, but they'd lost their only son in that fire. Few would blame them for wanting to keep their distance from Bryn.

But Jenna was all the family they had left. For their sake, he hoped she wasn't distancing herself from them for good.

He rubbed his free hand through his tangled mop of curls. "So what hours would you be working at Hanson's?" he said, choosing to change the subject before he talked himself out of their date.

"I don't know yet. Probably evenings for a while. But they don't stay open very late, so it shouldn't be too bad. I'm nervous, though. Would you believe the last time I went to a job interview was in high school?"

"You're kidding!"

"Zach—well, *Clarissa,* mostly—never wanted me to work. Didn't think it was befitting someone of my social stature. Ha!"

"She said that?"

"Not in so many words. It's what she meant, though. I guess I'll show her." She gave a dry laugh.

Lucas had always seen Jenna as sweet and optimistic. He wasn't crazy about the side of her he was seeing now. The bitterness in her voice wasn't becoming.

"Well," he said, trying to cover his pause, "I guess . . . I'd better get going—and let you get to your interview."

"Oh. It's not until two, but—" There was silence on her end for a few long seconds. "Thanks for calling," she said finally. "I'm sorry it didn't work out for me to go with you to Springfield."

"Sure. Good luck with the interview. I'll still see you around seven, right?" He almost wished she would back out on their date. Especially if she was going to be so moody.

"Seven is good. I'll see you then. Unless they hire me on the spot and want me to start tonight." Her laughter fell flat.

Jenna buttoned her jacket against the cold and followed Lucas to his pickup, glad she'd decided to change into jeans after her interview, since he wore Levi's and a plaid button-down shirt. He looked great.

He opened the door for her and waited for her to buckle in before coming around to crawl behind the wheel.

"So how did the interview go?" he asked, once they were on the road.

"Okay, I think. I didn't say anything stupid at least." She didn't tell him that she'd almost started crying when the manager who interviewed her asked where she lived. The emotions had taken her completely by surprise. Until that moment she hadn't allowed herself to think about losing her house, or about Bill and Clarissa's rejection. Much as she hated to admit it, she missed them. But it was horrible timing for an emotional breakdown.

"Well, that's always good." Lucas seemed strangely cool toward her tonight.

She shrugged. "I'm supposed to hear something by Monday."

"Did they say how many other applicants they were interviewing?"

She shook her head. "No, but there was a woman waiting for an interview when I came out of his office."

"I'll pray you get the job."

"Thanks." She didn't put a lot of stock in prayer, but it touched her to think of him praying for her.

"So you're staying at Bryn's tonight?"

"For a few weeks, actually."

"Really? You're not going back to the Morgans'?"

She shook her head but didn't dare look at him. "Not in the foreseeable future."

He turned off of Main Street, heading west, keeping his eyes on the road ahead. "It's too bad you had a falling-out with Zach's folks."

She stared at him, wondering where that had come from. "It *is* too bad. There was a time I thought Clarissa was my best friend, which is a little sad when you think about it."

"What do you mean?"

"How many women do you know who are best friends with their mother-in-law?"

"A few. I hope my wife—my future wife—will be friends with my mother."

181

"Friends is one thing. Best friends is another. Besides, it's more than that. Clarissa has . . . *had* this strange power over me, or maybe I should say I let her—" She stopped. Why was she dumping this on him? Still, she couldn't resist adding, "I just hope you understand that I didn't have a choice about moving out. Staying at the Morgans' would have meant ending my friendship with Bryn. I'm sorry, but that would have felt like I was betraying her."

He paused, as if digesting that information. "I understand," he said finally. "I didn't mean to sound critical. You did the right thing. I'm just trying to put myself in their place. I know they've got to be missing you. And—I think I understand why it was hard for them to see you hanging out with Bryn."

She frowned. "But you said you don't hold anything against Bryn."

"No," he said quickly. "I don't. That's not what I meant. But Bryn will always be a reminder to them of what happened."

She studied him. "Maybe we're all reminders to each other. All of us who lost someone in the fire. Doesn't seeing Bryn make you think about that night? Seeing *me* even?" Was that why he'd been so cool toward her? Since she and Bryn had grown so close, she rarely thought of Bryn's connection to the fire, to Zach's death.

"I thought about it that first night we talked at the coffee shop. But not since then. But maybe

Bryn reminds me a little," he admitted. "I don't blame her exactly. . . . But back to Zach's parents. What I meant is, you're all they have left of Zach. It's got to hurt to have lost you, too."

She pushed away the thought that came: he didn't know the half of it. And this conversation was getting too personal. "I don't *want* things to be like this between us. They'll come around . . . I think." She tilted her head. "You don't like conflict very much, do you?"

He shrugged. "I come from a family that never fights."

She rolled her eyes. "You must not ever *talk* then."

"No. We talk." He looked annoyed. "We've just always gotten along. And if not, we do whatever it takes to work things out."

"Yeah, well, if I'd done whatever it took, I'd be banished from associating with Bryn. Just so you don't think I'm the wicked witch in this scenario . . ." She worked to keep her tone even.

He held up both hands, palms out. "Sorry. I didn't mean to start World War III, not to mention it's none of my business." He offered a smile that was hard to resist. "Pretend I never said anything."

"No problem." She felt bad about getting testy with him, but he was right on one count. This wasn't his business. And besides, he didn't have all the details he needed to judge her fairly.

20

Did you save room for dessert? Maybe El Coco's famous merenguitos?" The perky server set a tray of dessert samples on the edge of the table and launched into a well-rehearsed advertisement for each offering.

Lucas leaned forward in the booth until he caught Jenna's eye across the table. She put a hand on her stomach and mouthed a decisive no.

He cleared his throat and the server stopped in the middle of a clever description of the coconut flan.

"Thanks," he said, "but I think we'll pass this time. We're ready for the check."

"Right away." The girl lifted the tray and headed for the next table.

"You must be as full as I am."

Jenna pulled a face that made him laugh because he knew exactly how she was feeling—stuffed to the gills. Happily so.

"But dinner was delicious," she added quickly. "Does your mom cook like this . . . all these Cuban dishes?"

"At Christmas. Easter if we're lucky." He laughed. "Why do you think I was so excited about eating at El Coco? I'm a third-generation American. Ma and Pop never set foot in Cuba. We like our hamburgers and corn dogs as much as the next American."

That made her smile, something she hadn't done enough of tonight. He took advantage of the moment and glanced pointedly at his watch. "Well, do you want to try and catch a late movie?" They'd had to wait for almost forty-five minutes to be seated, and the earlier shows would have already started.

"I think I should probably get back. I'm not sure what time Bryn will be in, and . . ." Her voice trailed off and she fiddled with the edge of her linen napkin.

"We can go," he said. "That's fine." He hoped she wasn't just making excuses because she wasn't enjoying the evening. Thanks to him and his big mouth, their discussion had almost turned into a full-blown fight on the drive to Springfield. But dinner had gone well and he thought things were smoothed over between them.

"You're sure you didn't have your heart set on seeing a movie?"

"Not at all. It's past my bedtime anyway."

"Eight thirty?" She looked at him like she thought he might be serious.

"Just kidding. But by the time we get home, it'll be close. I'm an early riser." That much was true. He didn't tell her that it was usually pain that woke him in the wee hours of the morning.

The server brought the check and Lucas paid

with cash. He retrieved his cane propped between his knees under the table. "Ready?"

She nodded and slid out of the booth. He followed her to the door, glad that good manners dictated she walk in front of him. Before they'd run into each other that night at Java Joint, he'd almost quit being self-conscious about the cane. He wasn't stupid enough to try to get along without it, but he tried more than ever to hide his limp and often paid the price the next day with his healthy joints and muscles stiff and achy. At least he hadn't resorted to pain meds. He was almost ready to throw away what he had left so the temptation wouldn't be there.

They talked all the way back to the Falls, and Jenna seemed to be in a better mood. Their conversation was casual and easy, the way he'd always talked with Zach.

The thought stopped him cold.

He was out on a date with his buddy's wife—the thought hit him again. His rational mind knew Zach was gone and not coming back. But he'd spent so much energy in the past working to *not* pay too much attention to Zach's gorgeous wife that it felt awkward.

"Everything okay?" Jenna's soft voice broke through the sudden silence.

He shook his head, more to clear it than in answer to her question. "Sorry . . . I was just thinking."

"Oh. Excuse me for interrupting." Even in the dark of the truck's cab, he could hear the wry smile in her voice.

He laughed, trying to remember what they'd just been talking about. "I didn't mean to space out on you there. And don't worry, you weren't interrupting anything important."

"Whew. That's good to know."

He liked this Jenna much better than the one he'd picked up four hours ago. When he pulled up in front of Bryn Hennesey's apartment half an hour later, it seemed like the most natural thing in the world to ask her out again.

She answered as if she'd expected the invitation all along. "I'd love to."

"What does Friday night look like?"

"Well . . . it depends on if I have a job by then. But if not, Friday sounds great. Can I let you know?"

"Sure."

She scooped up her purse from the floor of the cab and opened the passenger-side door. "Thanks for a fun evening."

He opened his own door and started to climb out of the truck.

"You don't need to walk me to the door. I've got a key." She reached in to her purse and produced a keychain. "Ta-dah! I'll be fine."

He couldn't tell if she was pandering to his handicap, or if she was afraid he was trying to invite himself in. He hated this part of dating. Of relationships, period. Why couldn't people just say what they were thinking?

"Seriously, I'm fine," she said again.

He wasn't going to argue with her. "Okay. I'll wait till I see the light go on." He glanced out the windshield to the darkened windows of Bryn's apartment.

"Thanks." She climbed down from the seat. "Well, . . . See you later." She gave a little wave and flashed a smile that made him forget every one of his reservations about dating her.

That is, until she'd disappeared into the apartment and he was driving home on the darkened streets of the Falls.

Was he crazy? He had nothing to offer a woman. Dating led—eventually, hopefully—to marriage. He didn't know what Jenna's dreams for her life were, but they surely included marriage and a family. It wasn't fair for him to waste her time with someone who *had* no future.

He corrected his thoughts. Of course he had a future. He wouldn't allow himself to get sucked into negative thoughts—thoughts that had led him down a very dark path in those early days after the fire. But he had to be honest with himself and with Jenna. He couldn't support a wife—let alone children—on his disability check and what little savings he'd managed to accumulate while living at home.

He scoffed at the thought. What woman wanted a man who lived with his mother? Of course that would change in a couple of months when Ma married Geoff, but still . . .

And if all of that wasn't enough, Jenna was Zach's wife. There would always be that.

What had she been thinking?

Jenna let herself into Bryn's apartment and went to the window to watch Lucas drive away. Obviously she *hadn't* been thinking when she agreed to go out with him again. It was all wrong. She was practically homeless, sponging off a friend, at odds with her in-laws. The fact she *had* in-laws should have been enough of a red flag.

Lucas made it no secret that he disapproved of the rift between her and Zach's parents. Given her reasons, she had no regrets about her decision. It bothered her that Lucas didn't seem to get why she'd put her foot down with the Morgans.

But she couldn't help taking his opinion to heart, even if he was wrong. She determined to be more positive when she was around him, because she liked him. A lot.

If she was honest with herself, what she was beginning to feel for Lucas was stronger than anything she'd ever felt for Zach—at least after they were married. If she thought hard enough, she could remember the misguided teenage passion that made her think she was in love with

Zachary Morgan—the same delusion that led to her getting pregnant. And married.

Cut it out, Morgan! Hadn't she just told herself this couldn't go on? She didn't even know if she'd be living in the Falls a few months from now. If she was lucky, she'd get the job at Hanson's, then be scheduled to work Friday night. At least then she'd have a decent excuse to tell Lucas no.

But she didn't *want* to tell him no. Like Bryn, Lucas seemed to like her for who she was. He didn't withhold affection until she fit an image he'd created for her.

She stopped herself. That wasn't fair to Zach. Zach *had* loved her. Even Lucas said so. But Zach had loved the *Pygmalion* version of her—the one his mother had fashioned. Clarissa had played Henry Higgins to her Eliza Doolittle. She'd been startlingly good at it, too.

But it was the blue-blood *Morgan* version of Jenna that Zach had loved. She'd been pretending for as long as she could remember. She'd never let Zach see the real her—the Jenna Whitmore from Shady Acres trailer park.

But she wasn't that person anymore either. So . . . who was she?

She closed the curtains and went to get ready for bed. Washing her face at the sink in the hall bath, she stared at her reflection. Who was she anyway? Too often when she looked in the mirror, she saw Clarissa Morgan—or a younger clone of

Clarissa—staring back. It was frightening not to know who you really were. What mattered to you.

She scrubbed hard at her forehead, suds fogging her view. She'd always hated that term *finding yourself*. It seemed like a devious way to focus on yourself at the expense of people you loved. But how could she expect anyone else to know her if she didn't even know who she was?

She hadn't been any more honest with Lucas than she had with Zach all those years ago. So how could she possibly think Lucas liked her for who she was?

She dried her face and went through the apartment turning out lights and checking the locks.

She went back to the guest room and lay on the bed, staring at the ceiling. She remembered she'd turned off her cell phone in the restaurant and went to get her purse to check her messages.

What would she do if she couldn't pay her cell phone bill next month? She couldn't find a job, let alone keep one, if an employer had no way to reach her. She pushed the nagging thoughts away. She'd go nuts if she thought too far into the future.

She started to flip her phone open, then heard Bryn come in and went out to greet her. One look at her friend told her something was very wrong. "Is it your dad?" she asked, afraid to hear the answer.

Bryn nodded and tears sprang to her eyes. "Oh,

Jen, he's not doing well at all. They're going to run some more tests tomorrow, but they still can't get his blood pressure down."

"I'm so sorry, Bryn."

"I may stay at the hospital tomorrow night." She tossed her keys on the kitchen counter. "I'm beat. I'm going to do a load of laundry and go to bed."

"You just go to bed. I'll take care of the laundry. I've got a couple more things I want to throw in the washer anyway."

"Oh, that would be wonderful. I'm so glad you're here, Jen."

Poor Bryn. She'd had some tough breaks. It puzzled Jenna how her friend had come through it all with her faith intact. You'd think God could give her a break after all she'd been through.

Jenna started the laundry and went back to her room and flopped on the bed again. She checked her phone and discovered a voice mail waiting. "Hanson's Grocers" appeared on the screen, and her heart kicked up a notch. She clicked Play. "This is Hal Iverson at Hanson's calling for Jenna Morgan. We'd like you to come in tomorrow morning at eight for training. If that time doesn't suit, please give us a call. Otherwise we'll expect you."

She sat up on the bed, feeling a little stunned. She *had a job*. Wow. She wasn't sure how to even feel about it. It wasn't as if there had been forty applicants for this position, but still she must have done okay with the interview.

What would she wear? She seemed to recall that the checkers at Hanson's wore smocks, but she hadn't noticed what they wore underneath. Street clothes?

She went to the closet where her clothes were crammed together at one end of the narrow space. She chose a pair of khaki pants and a sweater. Remembering how much the sweater had cost, she replaced it and chose a less expensive polo. If she could get back every dollar she'd spent on the clothes in this closet—never mind what was still in storage at the Morgans'—she'd have enough to pay a month's rent.

An idea started to germinate in the back of her mind, but she didn't have time to entertain it fully. She had a job. As of tomorrow morning she would be gainfully employed. A working woman. The thought brought a smile. And with it, a tiny glimmer of hope.

She heard the phone ringing out in the kitchen and ran to answer it before it woke Bryn. But she heard Bryn's low murmurs in the other room and assumed she was talking to Garrett.

She went back to the guest room, but a minute later there was a light rap on the door.

"Jenna, are you awake?"

"I'm up. Come on in."

The door opened and Bryn appeared, eyes

wide, the cordless phone dangling in one hand.

Jen sat up on the bed, her pulse quickening as she thought of Bryn's father. "What's wrong? What is it?"

Bryn gulped and shook her head. "It's Susan. There was a fire at the shelter tonight. They think it was arson."

21

*F*ire? What do you mean?" Jenna jumped off the bed.

Bryn stared at the phone in her hand. "Everybody got out, but they're trying to get the residents into churches for the night."

"The shelter burned *down?*" Surely this nightmare couldn't be happening all over again.

"No . . . No, Susan said they were able to put the fire out before it got out of control. But there's a lot of smoke damage. She said the fire trucks just left."

"What happened?"

Bryn shook her head. "She said somebody set the fire."

"How do they know that?"

"I don't know." She slumped into the chair at the desk. "Do you think she called me because . . . to see if I was home?"

Jenna stared at her, not sure what she meant, why she was so upset.

"Oh, Jen . . . do they think *I* did it?"

"Bryn, no! Of course not! Why would you even think that? Susan didn't *say* that, did she?"

Bryn drew her legs up onto the chair, curling into herself. She hid her face in her hands.

This had to be bringing back horrid memories. Jenna hurried to envelope her in a hug. "Bryn, stop it. No one would even dream you had anything to do with this." She looked around the room. "Where's the phone? I'll call Susan. We'll find out what happened."

Bryn didn't respond and Jenna spotted the cordless on the end of the bed. She hit the Callback button and waited, patting the curve of Bryn's back with one hand.

"Susan Marlowe." Her voice sounded clipped.

"Susan, this is Jenna Morgan. Bryn said there's been a fire at the shelter?"

"Can I call you back, Jenna? Things are crazy here right now. We're trying to find places for the residents to stay tonight, and if I—"

"Bryn isn't a suspect, is she? In the fire?"

"Why on earth would you think that?"

"I don't . . ." Jenna slipped into the hallway, pulling the door shut behind her. She dropped her voice to a whisper. "For some reason she thought you'd called to see if she had an alibi."

"Oh, dear Lord. I don't know what I could have said to make her think that. That's not it at all. We

195

don't know how it started. I just didn't want her to hear about it on the news."

The tension drained from Jenna's shoulders. "Everyone's okay then?"

"Yes. Our count was way down . . . and no children here tonight, thank goodness. But the smoke damage is extensive. We can't let anyone stay here until we get the mess cleaned up."

"And you don't know what happened?"

"No. The fire investigators are searching the place now. They seem pretty certain it was set—like the other—but they haven't really told me anything else. We've got all we can do to get everybody relocated. So far only one church is willing to house these people on a Friday night. I really need to go, Jenna."

"Of course. Is there anything Bryn and I can do to help?"

"Some extra bodies here would be wonderful. Believe me, I can find something for you to do."

"We'll be right there."

*T*he shelter was in chaos when they arrived. Jenna and a much-relieved Bryn pitched in to help the residents pack their things and vacate the building. An acrid odor hung in the air and made her cough and cover her nose.

The Presbyterian pastor and his wife had already picked up the four female shelter residents and taken them to the church for the night, but Susan hadn't yet found anyone to take in the men. "Tony X and Bobby took off—probably for the bar, which is bad news waiting to happen. Especially since the police want to talk to them about the fire."

"They're two of the younger guys," Bryn explained to Jenna.

"Are they suspects?" Jenna asked.

"Just about all the residents are suspects right now." Susan sighed. "But I can't worry about that right now. Even with those two gone, that still leaves nine men we need to put up."

"I don't know who you've already talked to, but I could make some calls for you." Jenna felt helpless.

"I've called all the churches and half a dozen members that pastors thought might be willing to put people up in their homes, but so far, except for Pastor Bryant, either they're not home or they said no. None of the Springfield shelters have vacancies." She grabbed a dog-eared phone book off the desk behind her. "Would you want to contact the hotels? There's no guarantee we can pay them a dime, but maybe we can get them to donate the rooms. Or get the churches to pay for them"—she rolled her eyes—"and give them a chance to assuage their guilt."

Jenna didn't blame her for being frustrated. What were churches for, anyway, if they couldn't pitch in during an emergency like this? But since the shelter had burned—the first time—the town had soured on the idea of having a homeless shelter in Hanover Falls. Most of the shelter's individual volunteers still came from the community's churches, but the churches themselves were hesitant to attach their names to the shelter.

Jenna took the phone book to a table in the corner and used her own cell phone to make the calls. She got turned down at the first hotel she called, but the small motel on the outskirts of town was willing to put up a few people.

She wondered if Lucas had heard about the fire. She looked at her watch. It was just after ten. He was probably still up.

He answered on the second ring, and she explained what was going on.

"I'm on my way," he said.

Not ten minutes later he appeared in the doorway, Sparky in tow. "How's it going?" he said softly, coming around to where she was sitting with the phone.

Her heart stuttered the way it always did in Lucas's presence. It was good to have him here. "We're still trying to find places for all the residents."

He looked around the room that housed the shelter's office and volunteer lounge, as if trying to determine the damage. Everything looked normal, but a heavy odor of smoke hung in the air. "Has the inspector been here?" he asked.

"I'm not sure, but I think she's still out there." She motioned to Lucas. "Follow me. I'll show you where the fire started."

*L*ucas held Sparky's leash loosely and went around to the back of the building. A couple dozen people huddled at the fringes of the site—harried city officials, curious neighbors wearing heavy coats over their pajamas, and a few others who, Lucas assumed from their stunned faces, were displaced shelter residents.

He spotted Andrea Morley, the fire inspector, talking with a Hanover Falls police officer. He waited until they were finished and went over to talk to her.

"Hey, Vermontez. Are you stalking me?"

He grinned. "No, it just looks that way."

She looked pointedly at his cane. "What are you doing out here? I thought you weren't back to work yet."

"I'm not." He motioned toward the back of the building. "Have you found anything yet?" Sparky tugged at the leash, barking.

She shook her head, then bent to scratch the dog's head. "Who's this?"

Lucas introduced her to Sparky and explained about the training program in Tulsa.

Andi smiled. "I'd say it sounded great if I wasn't afraid this pooch would put me out of a job."

He laughed. "I think you're safe." He wanted to

ask her if she'd ever worked with arson dogs, but this wasn't the time.

"This is the dog you're training?"

He nodded and didn't correct her present tense reference. It was probably premature to be talking about this, yet it felt good to have a plan. Something with purpose, something connected to firefighting. He just hoped he didn't have to admit later that he didn't make the cut for the training.

Sparky barked and tugged at the leash, straining toward the place where the fire had started. The milling crowd turned toward the commotion. A woman in a hooded sweatshirt wore an expression of fear that reminded Lucas of Jenna. He spoke to Sparky firmly and made a show of holding the leash tighter. He gave the woman a look he hoped was reassuring, but she turned away quickly, retreating with the other onlookers as police officers cordoned the area with yellow barrier tape.

Lucas was curious how Sparky would perform in the field, but letting him loose now would contaminate the scene. Sparky had yet to learn the discipline of waiting for Lucas's commands. Still, he couldn't help daydreaming about someday being able to bring Sparky to the scene of a fire and turn him lose.

And tonight was good training for the dog to experience the sights and sounds of a fire scene. Things were pretty calm here now. . . . It would be a whole different test with fire engines on the premises and sirens blaring. But Sparky wasn't too skittish, and he was obviously dying to get his nose into the action.

"You don't know what started the fire?"

"Oh, it was set," Andi said. "No doubt about that. Gasoline. Too soon to say much more, but we can hope it was just some kids messing around." She shook her head. "But this is the second time . . ."

"Third," Lucas said, immediately wishing he hadn't given the thought voice.

"Second *unexplained*." The inspector looked at him, then at the ground, sadness deepening the lines around her eyes. "I'm sorry."

Her words touched him and reminded him that the lives of his father and his buddy would not soon be forgotten. They'd all lost friends in the Grove Street blaze.

She turned all business again. "I'm starting to suspect Chief Brennan is right."

"What do you mean?"

"He seems to think somebody's trying to get a message across. Apparently there's a lot of opposition to the shelter reopening, and he thinks this is somebody's idea of a protest."

Lucas shook his head. "After everything this town's been through, a person would have to be pretty sick to use *fire* that way."

"Yeah, well, this is a sick world." She clapped his shoulder. "I'd better run. You take care."

"You too, Andi."

His leg started to ache and he went back inside to find Jenna.

She was gathering her things in the shelter's dayroom, looking weary but triumphant. "We found places for everyone. At least for tonight."

"Hey, that's great," he said. "Are we still on for Friday?"

"Oh! I didn't tell you." She beamed. "I got the job. At Hanson's."

"You did? That's great!"

She hesitated. "I don't have my schedule yet, so I might have to take a rain check."

"That's okay. How about I call you?"

"Sure. Thanks, Luc." She sounded as relieved as he felt that they'd struck a friendlier chord. But he couldn't let her think she was completely off the hook. He still had a few points to make. "It'll give us a chance to continue our discussion.

She groaned. "Aww, do we *have* to?"

He laughed. "This way you'll have time to gather some ammunition."

"Gee, thanks." She rolled her eyes, but he noticed they held a very promising spark.

22

*H*ere, boy! Come here!" Lucas leaned down to grab a rawhide bone Sparky had left on the back deck. "Sparky?" He shut the door behind him and navigated the uneven steps to the lawn.

An overnight dusting of snow had melted in the morning sun, but the grass still glistened with moisture. He'd let the dog out to romp in the snow an hour ago, but had gotten caught up researching canine training programs online and nearly forgot to let Sparky back into the warm garage.

He was pumped about the calm way Sparky had handled himself at the fire scene at the shelter the other night—he didn't run off, didn't fight the leash, despite his excitement. This dog had great potential. He just had a feeling about him. He hadn't heard anything more about the fire since that night except that they'd been able to let the residents back in. It was hard being out of the loop. Maybe he'd call Andi Morley later and see what she knew.

"Sparky! Here, boy!" He whistled again and walked around the side of the house, grasping at whatever handhold the railings and shrubs offered. More and more he'd been trying to go without the hated cane, but it would have been helpful on the wet grass this morning.

"Sparky?"

The dog bounded around the corner of the house straight for Lucas, wearing what Jenna would have called a smile. But before Lucas could brace himself, Sparky charged and jumped up on him.

Lucas's feet went out from under him on the slippery lawn. He heard a sickening *pop* a split second before he felt his leg give. He cried out, but knew no one would hear him. Like his mother, everyone in their close-knit neighborhood worked during the day.

When the first waves of pain passed, he caught his breath and pulled himself to a sitting position. He ran a hand down his leg, fully expecting to encounter blood and a protruding bone. "Oh, dear God. Help me." As if his life were flashing before him, all the agonizing surgeries and excruciating physical therapy of the past year paraded through his mind.

"Please, God, no. . . ." He didn't have the strength to start over.

Sparky stood beside him, panting, whimpering a little. He must have sensed something was wrong. "It's okay, boy." Lucas rolled onto his elbows and knees, but when he tried to put weight on his left knee, the pain that shot up his leg knocked him flat.

The ground was icy and hard beneath him, and

a wave of nausea made him shiver. Sparky whined and nudged at his shoulder.

He had to get into the house, take a look at his leg . . . see what he was dealing with. If he stayed out here much longer, he'd freeze.

He pushed himself up, this time putting all his weight on his good leg—or more accurately, his *better* leg. Sparky took the "heel" position at his side, then shadowed Lucas as he half crawled, half dragged himself up the stairs to the deck and inside the house.

Sparky followed him in, and Lucas didn't try to stop him, even though part of him wanted to throttle the dog for what he'd done. But it wasn't Sparky's fault.

Sitting on the floor by the back door, he untied his left shoe and gingerly worked it off his foot, shouting in pain as the shoe came loose. Something was messed up *bad*. It felt as if the pain was centered in his ankle, but it seared all the way up his calf. Already his ankle was starting to swell.

Lucas looked up and eyed the phone on the kitchen wall. He'd left his cell phone in his room by the computer. It would be easier to get to the kitchen phone. He prayed Ma was at her desk at the bank.

He closed his eyes and blew out a breath. He wasn't sure if the sick feeling in his gut was a physical reaction to the damage he'd done to his leg, or if it was because of the sure knowledge that he'd just been dealt a months-long setback.

The thought of having to regain hard-earned ground made him want to weep.

*O*h, Luc, I'm so sorry." Ma actually wrung her hands while sitting on the side of his hospital bed.

He stared at Dr. Broderick and swallowed hard, trying to find his voice. "I have to be off of it for a month?"

Broderick nodded, empathy in his grim expression. "I want to see you again in two weeks for evaluation, and we'll decide for sure then. But yes, likely a month to six weeks. You tore it up pretty good. Besides the obvious contusions and stretched ligament, there's this." He showed them the X-rays, pointing out a hairline fracture on one of the small bones in his foot. With all the bones he'd broken when the shelter collapsed on him, Lucas wondered how the doctor could tell this was a new injury.

"And what about the dog?" his mother asked.

Lucas shot her a "don't you dare" look, but she plunged ahead anyway.

"Dr. Broderick"—she avoided Lucas's eyes— "if you don't write it down on a prescription pad as doctor's orders, I know my son. He'll be out there tomorrow trying to pick up where he left off training that dog. I just want to hear it from your mouth if that's something you'd recommend." She shot Lucas a defiant glare.

The doctor looked between the two of them and gave a little chuckle. "Emily, I'm not going to get involved in that argument for anything. What happened was unfortunate, but it was a fluke, too. It could have just as easily happened tripping on the sidewalk. And you can't keep the man off the sidewalks."

The doctor turned aside and spoke to her in a stage whisper, aiming, apparently, for humor. "For what it's worth, that cast will slow him down a little."

She rolled her eyes. "I'll believe that when I see it."

Lucas remained silent, not amused that they were talking about him as if he were invisible. He swung his feet off the bed and slid to the edge of the mattress. He grabbed the crutches leaning against the wall and situated them under his armpits. "So I can go home?"

Broderick gave him a stern look. "If everything goes okay tonight, I'll discharge you in the morning if you agree to go straight to bed for a couple of days. And stay *off* the leg until I see you again. If you're careful, you could be back to where you were in a few weeks. I don't have to tell you this could have been a lot worse, Lucas."

Lucas merely nodded, feeling the familiar old anger seething just beneath the surface.

· · ·

Friday, December 5

*H*e awoke, groggy, from a midmorning nap. He was back home in the confines of his bedroom. His comfy bed may as well have been a prison cot.

At his insistence Ma had gone back to work this morning, and the house was quiet. He felt as if he were back at square one. Back to those days following the fire when he'd thought he might go stark-raving mad here—trapped, with no way to leave.

He reached for the crutches and eased his legs over the side of the bed. He'd barely used the crutches and already his armpits felt raw. It brought back too many memories of the days following the fire. Of course then he'd been too grateful to be out of the wheelchair to mind the crutches.

He made his way to the kitchen, careful not to bear any weight on his leg. He felt light-headed, even though he hadn't taken any medication since last night in the hospital. Why did this have to happen? The last thing he needed was a setback like this. "Can You cut me a break, God? Come on!" His own voice startled him.

He didn't usually pray out loud. Or did he dare call that a prayer? The words had come out more like a curse.

"I'm sorry," he whispered. It wasn't right to take

it out on God. He knew better than that. His faith had been tested almost beyond what he could bear in this past year. And still, God had proven faithful every step of the way. Lucas knew beyond doubt that he would never have made it through without God's presence with him every second. He'd pushed away the memory of the darkest moments of those awful days—times he'd actually prayed to die. God had been there, even then. He was thankful now that God had refused to answer those prayers. Eventually hope had quickened his passion for life again.

But now he felt the darkness frighteningly near. He closed his eyes. "God, are You trying to tell me something? What am I missing? What is it You want me to do? Because I'll do it if I just know what it is."

He looked at his computer on the desk. Application forms scattered the desk's surface. Tears of frustration welled behind his eyelids. "Lord, why did You put this desire in me if You don't intend me to do something with it? I don't get it." Exhausted, he plopped down in the chair and let the crutches clatter to the floor. He put his head in his hands, feeling numb.

"God . . . give me a right attitude. Show me what I'm supposed to do." With effort he bowed his will, and slowly a sense of peace washed over him. A peace unlike anything he'd experienced before.

After Pop's death, Ma had talked about God giving her "a peace that passeth understanding." The description had sounded like a trite sermon to him then. But now he'd experienced it for himself.

He blew out a slow breath and let the calm flow over him like a summer breeze.

23

Friday, December 19

*W*hat do you mean it's expired?" The woman hitched the slobbering baby up on her hip and glared at Jenna. "You're new here, aren't you? They've never checked coupons here before. They just run them through."

Jenna frowned. "I'm sorry, ma'am, but I was told not to accept expired coupons."

"That's ridiculous. I'll just take my business over to the IGA if that's the way you're going to treat your customers."

"I'm sorry ma'am. I'm just following—"

"I want to speak to the manager."

A cheery Christmas carol played over the store's intercom system, contradicting the mood of the moment. Jenna sighed and offered an apologetic smile to the two people in line behind the coupon queen. She glanced down the row of checkout stands, hoping Mr. Iverson wasn't on the floor.

This was the second customer complaint she'd gotten today, and the manager had been none too happy to have to handle the first one—a man on his lunch hour who griped because she was too slow.

"Just one moment," she told the woman, biting her tongue to keep her voice even. She picked up the intercom and depressed the Call key. "Assistance on register five, please, assistance on—"

"What do you need, Jenna?" Sydney Baer, a part-time worker with the high school's work-study program, came to her rescue, and within a few minutes the coupon lady was happily on her way.

"I thought we weren't supposed to allow expired coupons?"

Sydney shrugged. "Technically we're not, but I usually go ahead and take them. It saves a lot of grief."

"You don't get in trouble?"

"Not unless they're like five years old or something. The customer's always right, you know."

"Okay." She shifted to her other foot. Under the guise of retying her apron smock, she tried to rub the kinks out of her spine. Her back was killing her, but turning to the next customer in line, she pasted on a smile. "Welcome to Hanson's. Did you find everything you need?"

211

Two weeks—and as of yesterday, three Thursdays—had gone by, and Jenna hadn't heard a word from Lucas.

She was disappointed, but she might have been more so if she hadn't been so crazy busy trying to learn this job. The first two days of training had been a killer, leaving her frustrated and exhausted, and thinking she was the stupidest woman on the planet. But on the third day some cog or sprocket or *something* had clicked into place, and after that, running the cash register had become second nature. She hoped interacting with Hanson's customers would soon come as easily.

Even with the occasional cranky customer, she was actually rather enjoying the job. It felt nice to be earning her own way, to be independent for the first time in her life. Okay, so she hadn't seen her first paycheck yet, but checks were due out today.

She helped out three more customers before the store cleared out a little. A few minutes later Mr. Iverson came down from the office with a stack of envelopes. As if they'd been summoned, the bag boys appeared from the back of the store, and the other checkers lined up, waiting for Iverson to call their names.

As soon as she had a minute to herself, Jenna ripped open the flap and peered inside, holding the envelope to the light so she could make out the amount of the check.

She looked again. Surely there was some

mistake. Glancing around to make sure no one was watching, she slipped the check out of its envelope, unfolded it, and studied the numbers on the pay stub. After the various taxes, Social Security, and some deductions she'd never heard of were subtracted, her check was barely half what she'd expected.

It didn't take a math whiz to figure out that it would be months before she'd saved enough for an apartment, never mind the credit cards and the other bills she'd be responsible for. Thank goodness her car was paid for. When she got home tonight, she needed to take a good look at her finances and figure out where she could cut back. Again.

Sydney and Elma Johnson, who served as a greeter at the front of the store, whispered about something at Sydney's checkstand. Mr. Iverson walked by, clearing his throat loudly, and Elma scurried back to her station. Sydney grabbed a spray bottle and started wiping down her conveyer, and Jenna took her cue to get busy.

A minute later a grocery cart appeared in her lane, and Jenna started her spiel. "Welcome to Hanson's. Did you find—"

"Jenna?"

Her breath caught as she met Clarissa's eyes. "Clarissa . . . Hi." She forced a steadiness into her voice. "How are you?"

"You work here?"

No, I'm just standing behind the cash register wearing this smock as a fashion statement. She bit her tongue. "Yes. For a couple of weeks now."

"Oh, honey." Clarissa delivered the words as if Jenna had just told her her dog died.

Jenna chose to ignore them and shifted back into business mode. "Did you find everything you need?"

"Jenna. Please. Don't do this."

Jenna pressed her lips together. Was this woman for real? Feeling a slow burn, she picked up a cellophane bag of yellow peppers from the cart and placed them on the scale. She scanned the other items from the cart—expensive food from the store's deli and gourmet departments. Of course those departments were why most people shopped at Hanson's instead of the IGA.

"Jenna, listen to me." Clarissa leaned close and lowered her voice. "You're better than this. If you must work, surely you can find something more suitable than—" She stopped.

Jenna wondered how she'd intended to finish the sentence.

"Look at you," Clarissa said, sounding just short of horrified. "Your hair . . . your clothes . . . a *smock?* Oh, Jenna."

She thought Clarissa might burst into tears of sympathy any moment. Taking a step back from the register, Jenna dropped the polite checker persona. "You didn't leave me much choice. And for your information, I happen to like this job."

"Come back." Clarissa spoke the words as if the idea had just come to her. "I mean it. Come home with me now. We can work things out."

Jenna shook her head. She knew Zach's mother too well. Knew how she could manipulate things and people. Jenna had always watched others cave to Clarissa Morgan's wiles. Why had it taken her so long to see that she was just as susceptible?

Well, not anymore. She knew what "work things out" meant. It meant that Jenna would toe the line and Clarissa would continue to control her.

She couldn't resist goading the woman. "Then you're okay with Bryn and me being friends?"

Clarissa opened her mouth to speak, then closed her eyes and took a deep breath, as if composing herself. "I said . . . we'd work something out. And we can. I'm sure of it. You don't want to do this, Jenna. I know—"

"Don't tell me what I want to do."

Clarissa recoiled as if she'd been slapped. Tears welled in her eyes, and Jenna almost felt sorry for her. This woman wasn't accustomed to being told no.

She forced a softer tone, speaking slowly, measuring her words. "I'm making my own way, Clarissa. I should have done that long ago. I—I appreciate everything you and Bill have done for me. I really do. But it's time I figured out what I want to do with the rest of my life."

"I understand that, Jenna. Truly I do. But we can still help you. There's no reason for you to end up on the streets."

"What? What are you talking about? I'm not living on the streets." What brand of gossip had she been listening to? "I'm staying with Bryn right now, but I'm looking for an apartment."

"But you *have* a place to live." Clarissa's voice rose an octave. "You can stay with us. It's silly for you to pay good money for some dump when we are rattling around in that house."

Jenna thought about the gorgeous house in Clairemont Hills, about how it made her feel to drive her Volvo through those imposing gates, knowing that she had a passkey, a right to be there. She thought about the paltry paycheck in the pocket of her smock, and about how she was imposing on Bryn.

It would be so easy to untie her smock, walk out that door, load up her car, and go back to a life of luxury. She could probably even talk Bill and Clarissa into letting her have the basement—as they'd originally agreed. For a split second she almost caved.

Then she thought about that day she'd looked in the mirror and seen Clarissa staring back at her.

She couldn't go back. Somehow she knew that if she did, she'd never be free, never find her own way. If she gave in now, she would live in Clarissa's shadow for the rest of her life.

"I'll come and get my things as soon as I can. It may be a few weeks before I can . . . get everything worked out. . . ." She'd almost said "before I can afford the apartment," but she didn't want Clarissa to even consider that she might be hinting for help. She'd done that too often, and it shamed her now.

"Suit yourself," Clarissa said, her tone instantly frosty. "At least I tried." She was no doubt rehearsing what she'd tell her high-society friends.

Jenna scanned the rest of the groceries in silence, feeling every bit as inferior and unworthy as she knew Clarissa intended her to.

Not meeting Jenna's gaze, Clarissa paid for her groceries and slung her purse strap across her shoulder. She started to follow the bag boy out the door, but as if she'd sensed Jenna's temptation, Clarissa returned to the checkout counter and held out her hand, palm up. "I'd appreciate it if you'd return the pass card we gave you. To the gate."

Jenna stared. "I . . . I don't have it with me. I'll bring it when I come to get my stuff."

"You can mail it. You have our address." She whirled and strode after the bag boy.

Jenna sighed and realized her hands were trembling. She would be okay. She had a paycheck in her pocket—money that belonged to her alone. It was her first step toward freedom and

independence, toward discovering who she was—
or who she could become.

She hoped that person would be worth the things
she was sacrificing.

24

Wednesday, December 24

*A*re you sure you won't come, Jen? We'd love to
have you."

From her perch, cross-legged on the sofa, Jenna
closed the lid on her laptop and gave Bryn the
sincerest smile she could muster. "Thanks, B. It
means the world to me that you've gone out of
your way to make me feel welcome. And I do. But
I'm exhausted. I really think I need to spend these
few days off resting up." She was only half
kidding. Being on her feet all day at Hanson's had
taken its toll.

Bryn grimaced. "Yeah, I remember my
Hanson's days. It's a killer on the feet, that's for
sure. Hey, I have one of those pedicure soaking
tubs under the bathroom sink. Feel free to use it."

"I just might do that. Merry Christmas . . . and
tell your dad hi for me."

"I will." She beamed and Jenna heard the relief
in her voice.

Bryn's father was finally home from the

hospital, and Bryn and Garrett were spending Christmas with him before traveling to visit relatives of Garrett's somewhere in Kansas. "If you change your mind about tomorrow, call me and I'll give you directions out to my dad's."

"I will," she assured Bryn. But she wouldn't change her mind. It might be a lonely Christmas, but it would be worse spending the day with two lovebirds and watching Bryn with her dad. She brushed the thought off and found her smile again for Bryn's sake.

"Well, okay. I'm outta here. Love you."

"Love you, too. See you Saturday." The door slammed and quiet descended over the apartment. Jenna swallowed the sudden rush of emotion that came as she thought about her friendship with Bryn.

They'd grown so much closer over the last few weeks she'd been staying here. Like sisters. It made Jenna think of her own sister and wonder where Becky was spending this Christmas Eve. What was wrong with her—with their family— that they didn't even get together for the holidays? Guilt sliced through her. With their mom gone, she should have tried to get in touch with Becky. But it wasn't as if Jenna had a place to host a big turkey dinner. She didn't even know where Becky was living now. Wasn't sure she wanted to know.

Bryn Hennesey was more of a sister to her than Becky had ever been. Bryn had been more generous and patient than Jenna deserved, refusing to take one penny for rent and chiding her if she so much as brought home a few groceries to help fill the cupboards. Jenna just hoped she could keep her promise to be out of here by next month. Not that she had any choice in the matter. Bryn's lease would be up at the end of January, and she'd be giving the apartment up. Jenna looked out at the frosty night, remembering the night she'd slept in her car.

She'd been checking the *Courier*'s classifieds each week and had Maggie keeping an eye out for low-rent apartments, too. She could probably afford the monthly rent for a couple of the cheaper complexes, but one of them had no vacancies, and the other had a strict two-months-deposit-in-advance policy. And it was nowhere near as nice as Bryn's place. Housing was at a premium in the Falls, so almost everything was way over her budget.

She opened her laptop again and checked her e-mail. The no-mail gong reminded her that the whole world was out celebrating tonight. Christmas Eve. Who sat home alone on this night?

She wondered what Lucas was doing. No doubt the whole Vermontez family had gathered at Emily's. She could almost imagine the laughter around their table, even in the midst of bittersweet memories of Luc's father. This would be their second Christmas without him. Odd how the thought came before it dawned on her that this would be her second Christmas without Zach.

She had trouble remembering what he looked like. Right after the fire she'd sometimes thought she heard Zachary calling to her. And his voice was as sharp and clear as if he were in the next room. But now, when she tried to imagine what he'd sounded like, it was Lucas's voice she heard.

But Lucas had never called her back after they'd talked the night of the fire. She missed him. Missed the friendship she thought had been growing between them.

But maybe he'd had the same second thoughts she'd been having. Maybe it was better for them both that he'd backed off. After all, she'd been telling herself all along that she had nothing to offer him. That she needed to figure out who she was before she had anything to offer Lucas—or anyone else.

Things were different now, though. Slowly she was getting back on her feet. Learning that she was stronger than she'd ever imagined. Even though she would never get rich working at Hanson's, at least she had a job. And she'd eventually have her own place.

She glanced up, and the lights of the scraggly little Christmas tree in the corner caught her eye. Bryn and Garrett had put it up one night while she was working at Hanson's. She and Bryn had ordered pizza and exchanged gifts beside the tree

221

two nights ago. They'd both gotten a little teary-eyed remembering last Christmas and how fresh their grief was then.

She'd confessed to Bryn that night about how things had been between her and Zach. That she didn't think she'd ever really loved him—didn't know what love *was*. It was a relief not to have to keep up the charade of grieving widow with her friend. But she held her other secret close. She was starting to realize that her inability to love Zach had far more to do with her than with him. Zach had loved her as well as he knew how. Even Lucas had testified to that.

What purpose would it serve to come out now and declare that she'd never loved her husband? It seemed dishonoring to Zach—and certainly to the Morgans. The Morgans. There were two gifts left beneath the Christmas tree—fruit baskets Jenna had picked up at Hanson's yesterday after her shift ended. Mr. Iverson had marked them down to half-price, and before closing he gave the staff their choice at another 20 percent off. In a spurt of generosity Jenna had chosen one for Bill and Clarissa and one for Bryn, even though it was still beyond her budget.

She'd headed out to Clairemont Hills after work to take the basket to them but changed her mind before she even left the city limits. What would she say? Her last encounter with Clarissa had ended badly, and she hadn't heard from her since.

Looking at the elegantly wrapped basket, a twinge of shame played at her conscience. Whether Zach's parents had done so from a pure motive or not, they had been generous with her. Not just since Zach's death, but for as long as she'd known them. The Morgans had made it possible for her to crawl out of the mire of poverty she'd grown up with.

As a Morgan, for the first time, Jenna'd seen the acceptance money could buy. The acceptance and friendships that dressing a certain way and living in a certain kind of house brought.

Hmmm . . . Where were all those friends now? She pushed away the question. It was her own fault that she'd let Clarissa choose her friends. *Dictate* her friends.

She closed her laptop and went to the hall closet to gather her coat and purse. For all she knew, Clarissa wouldn't even allow her through the gate, but she would do the right thing and at least try to take the gift to them. A small token of her appreciation.

And a step in the direction of reconciliation.

*B*ill stood at the door staring at her as though he didn't know who she was. Had Clarissa not told him that she'd buzzed Jenna through?

Quincy yapped and pranced at Bill's feet. Behind him, Clarissa appeared from the family room. "Hello, Jenna."

"Hi. Merry Christmas." She glanced down at the fruit basket. The gift's elegance faded in contrast to this luxurious mansion, and she shrank, feeling as if she was just about to tip a waiter a nickel.

"I brought this," she said lamely. "It's not much, but I wanted to say . . . how much I appreciate everything you've done for me this past year."

Bill nodded wordlessly, looking at the basket, then back at her. She'd never recognized it before, but she saw now that he was waiting for a cue from Clarissa as to how he was to respond to Jenna.

"Come on in." Clarissa stepped back from the door to let her pass.

"Come in out of the cold," Bill said, coming to life now that Clarissa had given the okay.

It was sad, really. Bill was a nice guy, but he needed to get a spine.

The house smelled of cinnamon and pine, and Clarissa's fancy flavored coffee. The tree in the cavernous foyer was decorated the way Jenna remembered from Christmases past—except for last year. There had been no celebration, no decorations then, so soon after the fire.

As Clarissa led the way to the great room off the kitchen, Jenna took in the rest of the decor—a garlanded tree in almost every room, mantels overflowing with greenery and glitter, candles aglow and their Christmasy scents mingling, filling the house.

The television was on in the great room, a commercial blaring a holiday jingle, but the heavy loneliness of the house weighed on Jenna. She felt sorry for Zach's parents. This beautiful, massive home, and two grieving people alone in it. She wondered—no, she *knew* what her life would have looked like if Zach were alive. They'd be here making toasts and opening thousand-dollar gifts from each other. She and Zach would go home and fight about how much they'd put on the credit cards and how they were going to pay the bills.

For an instant she let herself imagine what it would have been like if she and Zach had children—if she could have ever carried a child to term. Their kids would have been pampered and coddled by Grandma and Grandpa Morgan. Clarissa would have tried to orchestrate their lives, and she and Zach would have let them because they wouldn't have been able to afford to do otherwise. They would have—

"Jenna?"

She shook herself from the daydream, embarrassed to realize that Clarissa was speaking to her.

"I'm sorry. What was that?"

Clarissa gave her a frosty look. "Would you like something to drink? We've already put the champagne away, but there's decaf still on if you'd like."

"Oh . . . no, thanks. I'm fine. The house looks beautiful."

Bill picked up the remote and turned the TV down a few decibels, but some program came on and he kept one eye on the screen while Clarissa launched into a high-strung recitation of all she'd done to get ready for Hanover Falls' annual holiday home tour. Jenna remembered that—except for last year—the Morgans had been part of the tour ever since they'd moved out to Clairemont Hills.

"I tell you," Clarissa said, getting wound up, "it gets harder every year to come up with something new. I must have shopped at five different stores in St. Louis before I found anything that wasn't boring and cliché . . . the same as everybody else." She gave a nervous laugh.

"Well, it looks beautiful," Jenna said. She shifted the basket awkwardly in her arms.

Bill kept inching closer to the television and notching up the volume until he'd effectively removed himself from their conversation.

How long did she need to stay to be polite? She'd learned a lot about social graces and etiquette over the years, thanks to Clarissa, but this was a circumstance Miss Manners hadn't exactly covered.

She cleared her throat, buying time, foraging for something to talk about that wouldn't start a fight.

Clarissa saved her the trouble. "So, you're still living with Bryn Hennesey?"

Jenna drew back, willing herself not to get defensive. "I'm only staying with her for a few weeks until I can save up enough for an apartment."

"Well, you've managed to make Bill and me look like the devil incarnate. I hope you're happy." Clarissa took the fruit basket from Jenna's hands and plopped it on the counter as if it were a sack of potatoes. She poured herself a cup of coffee and gestured for Jenna to take a seat at the table.

"Clarissa, I haven't said one word to anyone that would give them that impression." Not exactly true. She'd unloaded to Bryn, and to Lucas, but she trusted both of them implicitly. "If people in this town don't have anything better to do than gossip about our situation, then that's their problem."

"It's not gossip if it's true."

Oh? You mean you and Bill are the devil incarnate? She bit her tongue to keep from voicing her mental retort. But her conscience got the best of her, and she clarified her earlier statement. "The people I work with—at Hanson's—know I'm staying at Bryn's for a while. But I haven't said one word about why. The only people who know anything about what happened are Bryn and Lucas Vermontez, and I assure you neither of them would share what I told them in confidence. And Bryn doesn't know the whole truth about *why* I moved out. I didn't want to hurt her," she couldn't resist adding.

Clarissa frowned. "Why would Lucas Vermontez know anything about it?"

Jenna had no desire to reveal her relationship— or lack thereof—with Lucas. "He was Zach's closest friend. . . . We've talked—"

"You don't think I know he was Zach's friend? But why on earth would you be discussing our private business with him?"

"I discuss *my* private business with whoever I choose, Clarissa. Lucas and I are friends."

Clarissa sniffed. "Well, he's a nice young man. As much as we were opposed to Zachary's involvement with the fire department, we always liked Lucas." Her voice softened. "I was sorry to hear about his accident."

What was she talking about? It sounded as if she was referring to a recent accident. She wouldn't talk that way if she was referring to the fatal fire at the shelter.

"Do you happen to know if he's home from the hospital yet?"

"Lucas was . . . in the hospital? Recently? What happened?"

"Oh?" Clarissa raised an eyebrow. "I thought sure you would know about it, since you're *such good friends*. He reinjured his leg. Something

228

about an accident with a dog. Mary Harrison said it was that dog from the homeless shelter . . . the one Bryn Hennesey took in." She made a face and clicked her tongue. "I don't know what Lucas was doing with the animal, but I'll tell you, that establishment has caused nothing but trouble."

Jenna's blood turned to ice. Lucas must have been hurt badly if he'd been hospitalized. And if Sparky had something to do with it, she'd never forgive herself.

She didn't want to ask Clarissa for more details lest she prove how distant her friendship with Lucas had become. She blew out a breath. At least maybe this explained why he hadn't called her. He probably wondered why she hadn't called *him*.

Making an instant decision, she scooted her chair away from the table. "I need to go!" Without apology, she practically ran to the front door.

25

*Y*ou cheater! There's no way you could have drawn all those aces!" Gina grabbed for the cards fanned out in Lucas's hand, but he laughed and held them high in the air just out of her grasp.

"Gina," Ma warned, "don't you hurt him."

"Yeah, little sister, don't you hurt me," he mocked, still holding his hand aloft.

But Ma wore only mild concern beneath a smile

that testified to her joy at all her chicks being home together under one roof on this Christmas Eve.

Gina glared at him, but her smile gave her away. "Fine. But so help me, if I find out you cheated, I *will* hurt you!"

The doorbell interrupted their merriment.

Ma looked up at the clock. "Eight-fifteen? Geoff must have gotten away early!" Her face lit up and she slipped from her chair and started for the door. "I'll get it."

"You might wanna take your cards with you!" Gina smirked and hollered after her, "That is, if you don't want certain people peeking at them."

"What?" Lucas feigned outrage. "You don't trust me? Since when have I ever been a cheater?"

"Since tonight, for one."

His sister's impish grin prompted him to pop her in the bicep, then duck out of reach before she could return the favor.

It had been a good night. They all felt Pop's absence keenly, but unlike last year when their grief was so fresh, they'd been able to talk about Pop and even laugh together, summoning funny stories from Christmases past. Surprisingly, it had been a Christmas full of laughter and full of love. Lucas could almost feel Pop's presence in the remembering.

He'd been reminded especially of a Christmas Eve twenty years earlier when Pop had told the Christmas story the way he always did. Only on this night a seven-year-old Lucas had taken the story to heart. Pop had segued from Christmas story to Easter story, and Lucas had opened his heart to the truth of Christ's life and death.

He'd faltered from that faith over the years, but his father's example lived on, and recently Lucas had felt God's presence strong with him, the way he had as a little boy on that Christmas night.

He was three weeks into his recovery from the most recent surgery, and time was going far more quickly than he'd anticipated. It helped having his sisters home from college, especially since Gina had taken over Sparky's basic training for the time she was home.

He'd managed to keep plenty busy researching and filling out applications to the various K-9 and accelerant detection training schools around the country, and at the same time, he was working on developing a specialized program for training Sparky himself—just in case he didn't get accepted into any of the established programs.

One way or another—he was going to do this.

The day he'd come home from the hospital, he'd not only felt God's peace come over him—in a way so convincing he had yet to try to explain it to anyone—but he'd become convicted of God's calling. This passion he felt, the urgency to take Sparky and complete the training with him, was more than a whim. God was behind it somehow and had put Sparky in his life for a reason. He felt certain of that now. And he was going to do whatever it took to follow through. Unless he heard God say "no more."

Feminine voices—familiar voices—in the entryway drew him from his reverie.

Ma was talking in animated tones. "No, really," she chirped. "Please come in. I know he'd love to see you."

Next thing he knew, there stood Jenna beside his mom under the archway between the living room and the great room where they'd set up their rowdy card game.

Jenna looked decidedly uncomfortable and decidedly beautiful, her cheeks flushed from the cold and her hair in wispy waves about her face.

She put up a hand in an anemic wave. "Hi, Lucas. I heard . . . you got hurt. I thought maybe you were still in the hospital."

"I'm home. Have been for a couple of weeks." Scraping back his chair, he held her gaze, trying unsuccessfully to read what was in her face. He wondered if she was angry he hadn't called. He'd wanted to. Started to a couple of times. But then the words would come back to haunt him. Words he'd felt so strongly after the last time they were together: *She was Zach's wife.*

And then he'd gotten hurt and went into the hospital. . . . He shook his head to clear his thoughts and hopped over to where Ma had put his crutches.

"Oh, please don't get up." Jenna backpedaled toward the entryway. "I'm not staying." She turned to his mother, then back to him. "I'm really sorry to interrupt your family's Christmas. I just wanted to make sure you were . . . okay."

Victoria put her cards down and hurried around the table. "Nonsense. Pull up a chair. We were just about to beat Luc's socks off."

He shot Jenna a sheepish grin. "They were after more than my socks, let me tell you."

"Luc!" Gina and Victoria chided in unison as if he'd said something risqué.

He laughed and hobbled back to his chair, motioning Jenna after him. He was surprised— shocked really—that she'd dropped by like this. But he had to admit she was a sight for sore eyes.

Gina dragged another chair up to the table, and Victoria scooted over to make room beside Lucas. He patted the chair. "Come on, Jenna. Have a seat."

"I really didn't mean to intrude," she said again. But she sat beside him.

Ma made casual introductions, and Lucas was grateful she did it without mentioning Jenna's relationship to Zach. Victoria and Gina went out of their way to make Jenna feel welcome, offering her a glass of soda and dealing a new hand of cards to include her in their game.

It didn't take a genius to figure out that his sisters were in cahoots playing matchmaker. He wondered what they'd think if they knew this was his buddy's wife sitting beside him. As high schoolers, Victoria and Gina had met Zach at the station and shared a crush on him before they found out he was married.

But his mother knew who Jenna was, and she didn't seem to think it mattered. In fact, if he was reading things right, she was in on the matchmaking shenanigans.

He slid to the far side of his chair, not about to give them any satisfaction for their efforts.

While they were explaining to Jenna how to play the card game—Hand and Foot—the doorbell rang again.

"*There* he is." Ma's coloring heightened again, and she scooted her chair out. "Deal Geoff in, will you?"

Lucas reached for the pile of cards four decks high in the center of the table and counted out another set.

Geoff joined them and Lucas watched Ma with him—the way they touched every chance they got, the way she looked at him the same way she used to look at Pop. Gina and Victoria had struggled a little with the idea of their mother remarrying, but they hadn't seen how happy she was with Geoff—or perhaps more important, being off at school, they hadn't seen how heartbroken Ma was in those first months after Pop died.

He let himself imagine Jenna looking at him with that same longing. Her presence beside him was unnerving. The scent she was wearing made him want to move closer. But he kept his distance.

At first she seemed almost embarrassed to be there, but as the evening wore on, her laughter lost its nervous edge, and she even joined forces with Victoria and Gina in giving him a hard time. When she won the second round, she almost came off her seat with triumph. They all laughed good-naturedly and she blushed. But it made him happy to see her enjoying herself.

Had she been alone on Christmas Eve? This was her second Christmas without Zach.

After another round of Hand and Foot, which he won soundly—without cheating—his sisters wandered down the hall to the bedroom they shared. His mom and Geoff went down to the family room to watch *It's a Wonderful Life*, a tradition Pop had insisted they keep annually.

"Do you want to watch the movie?" Lucas asked Jenna.

"Oh, no. Thanks, but I need to get going. I really didn't intend to stay. I'm sorry for barging in on your Christmas."

"Cut it out. Around here the policy has always been 'the more the merrier.'"

"Well, I appreciate it. I . . . had fun."

"My rowdy family didn't scare you off?"

"Are you kidding? I love them!" She looked embarrassed to have blurted it out like that.

"Yeah, me too." He grinned, touched by her enthusiasm. He sought to set her at ease. "I was about to have some of Mom's pecan pie. How about a slice with some coffee? We've got decaf."

Jenna hesitated.

He winked and looked pointedly at the clock, which was about to strike ten. "You have a hot date or something?"

"No, but—"

"Stay." It came out more like a command than he intended, but she didn't seem to notice. He hopped up on one leg and grabbed his crutches. "Please . . . I want you to."

"Tell me where things are and I'll get them."

He cringed. "Have you *seen* the kitchen?"

She looked into the next room to where dishes and pots and pans were piled high in the sink and everywhere on the countertops. "Okay, on second thought, you come with me and talk me through it."

She led the way and he pulled out a high stool at the bar counter and straddled it. He watched her, thoroughly enjoying the view, while he directed her to what she needed for making coffee and dishing up pie.

"So you thought I was in the hospital, huh?"

She didn't look up from slicing the pie. "Clarissa told me about it."

"Did you try to see me . . . at the hospital?" he risked.

She glanced up briefly from her task. "No." She didn't elaborate.

When he hadn't called her as promised after their date, he assumed that would be the end of it. And he'd begun to believe that was for the best. Their relationship was too fraught with complications.

But having her here, watching her interact with his family, he was having second thoughts. Somehow, she seemed as if she belonged here, as if she'd always been a part of them.

While the coffee brewed, Jenna started washing dishes.

"Hey, leave those. Ma will have a cow if she hears I let a guest in this house do dishes while I sat here and watched."

"I don't mind. I'll just do up a few while we wait on the coffee."

Lucas didn't argue and went on watching her.

When the coffee sputtered its last, she brought the dessert plates and mugs to the counter and slid onto the stool beside him.

Looking pointedly at his cast, she frowned. "Clarissa said Sparky caused your accident." It wasn't a question and he heard the guilt in her voice.

"No," he said. "*Lucas* was the cause of my accident."

Her eyebrows arched in a question.

"The grass was slick with frost that morning. Sparky came running like he always does, and I just slipped. It was my own fault."

"I'm so sorry, Luc."

Her use of his nickname was endearing.

"Why would you apologize?" But he knew why.

"Because I'm the one who pushed Sparky off on you."

"Stop it. You didn't twist my arm to take him."

"No, I guilted you into it."

"Yeah, you big bully."

She made a face. "I really am sorry. I feel terrible." She eyed his cast. "How long do you have to wear that thing?"

"Is that why you came tonight? To apologize? Because I'm the one—"

"No, I came because Clarissa said you'd been in the hospital." She bent her head and stared at the coffee in her mug. "It—scared me. I didn't expect you to be here. I was just going to find out from your mom how you were doing. I sure didn't expect you to be up and hopping around."

He shrugged but couldn't help smiling. "Sorry to disappoint you."

She didn't return his smile, and the furrow in her brow deepened. "I'm relieved."

"Did you have Christmas with the Morgans?" He was ready to change the subject.

"I—just came from there."

"I'm glad. I was hoping you'd mend things with them."

She rolled her eyes. "I wasn't exactly there by invitation."

"Oh. Sorry." Wrong subject.

"No. I took them a gift. It—didn't go very well. I really don't want to talk about it." She fingered the necklace at her throat. The same goldfish she always wore.

"I'm sorry. I didn't mean to pry."

She waved him off. "No . . . *I'm* sorry. I didn't mean that to come out so rude." She rose and cleared their plates to the sink. "I'd better go. Thanks again for everything. I really enjoyed the evening."

"Hey, I didn't mean to run you off. Don't go." He slid from the bar stool and made his way to her, favoring his casted leg and using the countertops as vaulting blocks.

Supporting his weight against the counter, he circled her wrist with his fingers. "Please don't go, Jenna. I'd like you to stay. I—I owe you an apology."

26

*A*n apology? What for?" Jenna was keenly aware of his hand on her wrist. His warmth offered something she desperately needed tonight, and she stood stone still, not wanting to break the spell. Not wanting him to realize he was still touching her, and let go.

He studied the kitchen tile before looking up and holding her gaze. "I promised I'd call you and I never did. That night of the fire."

"Yeah . . . I noticed." She let a grin come, then waited, wondering what reason he would offer.

"I'm sorry, Jen. I should've—I *started* to call. More than once." He ducked his head as if to hide the boyish grin he wore. But when he met her eyes again, his expression had turned serious. "I wish I could say it was just because of the accident. Being in the hospital. But . . . It just all seems so complicated—you and me."

"It doesn't have to be," she risked. "We can—just be friends. If that's easier . . ."

He shook his head. "That's not where this is headed and you know it."

She acknowledged the truth of that with a nod. "Okay. Then we can take it slow . . . to wherever this is headed."

"Let's go sit in the living room." He rubbed at his knee. "My leg is killing me."

She cringed. "I am so sorry."

Swinging like a gymnast between his crutches, he gave her a stern look. "No more of that. I mean it. Come here."

She followed him into the living room, where the scent of pine enveloped them. Old-fashioned colored lights twinkled on a crooked pine—one that looked as if they'd cut it from the woods behind the house. The room was strewn with gift wrap and ribbon, evidence of the family Christmas that had happened here tonight. An acute pang of envy sliced through her.

With one broad sweep of a crutch, Lucas cleared off a space on the sofa.

She laughed. "That's one way to do it. Glad there wasn't anything breakable on there."

"Sit," he said, looking stern.

"You're awfully bossy tonight." But she obeyed.

He sat down on the opposite end of the sofa and tucked his crutches on the floor beneath his feet. The murmured conversation of Lucas's sisters drifted down the hall to them, bursts of girlish giggling interspersed. Below them, Emily and her fiancé watched the movie, their laughter mingling with the movie's soundtrack. What must it have been like to grow up in a house like this, surrounded by love and laughter?

They'd lost husband and father—had almost lost Lucas—in the Grove Street fire, and yet the pall of tragedy didn't lie over this house the way it did the Morgans'. They'd honored Manny's memory, speaking of him freely and fondly, even in Geoff's presence.

She tried to put it into words. "You guys seem so . . . at peace. About your dad, about everything you've been through."

He shrugged. "Christmas was a little easier this

year. As hard as it is to see Ma with someone else, it helps to see her happy again." A shadow passed over his face. "Forgive me. I'm sure it hasn't been easier for you—this year, I mean. Especially with things the way they are between you and Zach's parents."

"Lucas . . . I wasn't in love with Zachary." Why had she just blurted it out like that?

He drew back, looking stunned. "I don't understand. Is that why the Morgans are angry with you?"

"No." She shook her head. "No one knows—except Bryn. It's the whole thing with Bryn that set Clarissa off," she reminded him. "They don't know . . . the other. Please don't say anything."

"Of course not. But . . . how could you not—" He shook his head. "Zach was crazy about you, Jen."

"I didn't know. Until you told me that night at the coffee shop."

"How could you not know? The man was absolutely nuts about you. It's why—one reason—I've been so hesitant to—"

"Zach never knew. I . . . was a great pretender. I never should have said anything. Let's change the subject." She pressed her lips together. Why had she started down this road? It was Christmas Eve. She was a guest here. This was not the time. If there ever *could* be a time for such an ugly admission.

He turned toward her on the sofa and reached for her hand. "Why do you do that?"

She shook her head, not understanding.

"Every time we edge close to sharing something personal, you back away like a scared kitten."

She forced herself to look into his eyes. "I'm sorry. You're right. I don't know why." She was evading again, and it wasn't exactly true. She was starting to understand why. But she couldn't explain it to him.

"Well, stop it." His tone was gruff, but his eyes held that twinkle that warmed her from the inside out.

"There you go being bossy again."

He gave her a smug look.

But she couldn't tease him back. She wanted to change. Especially since Lucas seemed determined to get to know her—the real her. But surely that would scare him off. Then she wouldn't have to worry about him—or about learning to be more "real." She forced a smile. "Okay. I'll try."

His gaze traveled to her throat, and she realized she had a death grip on her necklace.

"You always wear that." It was a statement, but his eyes held the unspoken question.

She nodded, then laughed as she realized the irony. "Clarissa gave it to me—the first Christmas Zach and I were married."

"It's a fish. Is that supposed to be like an ichthys?"

"Ick-what?"

He laughed. "The Christian fish symbol—" He drew a fish shape in the air. "You know? It was like a secret code so the persecuted Christians would recognize each other?"

She shook her head. She'd never heard such a thing. She held her fish out and examined it, wondering if she'd been wearing a Christian symbol all these years without knowing it.

Lucas looked closer. "Oh . . . yours is more like a goldfish."

She nodded. "That's what it is. It's a Chinese symbol for prosper—" She stopped short. More irony. "It symbolizes prosperity and wealth." She laughed. "I wouldn't run out and buy one if I were you. I don't think it works."

He gave a wry grin. "I'll make a note. And hey, just to set the record straight, the ichthys isn't a charm. It's just a symbol."

"I wish I could believe like you do."

"What *do* you believe?"

She shrugged. "I used to think I believed in God. Now"—she shrugged—"I don't know."

"Because of Zach?"

She shook her head. "No. Zach . . . he was a good man. Our problems were mostly my fault." *Or Clarissa's.*

"Then why?"

"I didn't grow up like you did, Luc." She panned the cozy scene in front of her, and a wave of longing roiled inside her. "I didn't have a loving dad to teach me about those things. I didn't have a dad, period. And my mom—I don't think she believed in anything. She was trying too hard just to survive."

"I bet that was tough. For you, I mean."

She shrugged. "I didn't know there was anything else—" She caught herself and put her head down. "No—you're right. It was very hard. When Zach asked me out on our first date, and I saw how the rest of the world lived—or at least it seemed that way—it did something to me. I would have done anything to hang on to him at that point." She bowed her head, feeling the shame all over again. "Actually, I did do 'anything' . . . and I ended up pregnant."

His eyes went wide. "You—had a baby?"

She shook her head. As long as she was being real . . . "I miscarried a few weeks after our wedding. It took Clarissa years to forgive me."

"*Forgive* you? For what?"

"If you know Clarissa, then you know I wasn't exactly her first choice for her darling son. I think she thought I trapped him into marrying me. And . . . maybe I did." Her own words shocked her—because she recognized them as truth.

"Well, you were Zach's first choice. I know that for a fact. But he never said anything about you having to get married."

She nailed him with a look. "I really hate that expression, you know? We didn't *have* to get married."

He held up a palm. "Sorry. I didn't mean it that way." He repositioned himself on the sofa, stuffing one of the cushions under his leg and scooting closer to her in the process.

"I know. I'm sorry . . . I didn't mean to snap at you." She wished she could take back the whole conversation. Seeking to lighten the moment, she affected an exaggerated cringe. "Actually, remembering how Clarissa reacted back then, we probably *did* have to get married. She would have killed us if we'd disgraced her."

He winced. "That bad, huh?"

He leaned closer. Close enough she could smell the citrus tang of his aftershave.

"It was not a pretty scene."

"I'm sorry. But to hear Zach tell it, you hung the sun and the moon and most of the Milky Way, for that matter."

Why did he have to bring Zach up again? And the baby. *Babies* . . . But that wasn't a place she was willing to go. Not tonight. Maybe not ever.

Some secrets were meant to stay locked up. But a niggling fear wouldn't let her forget. Lucas would make a great husband . . . a great father. She could see that just watching him with his family tonight.

What if . . . ? She stared at the lights twinkling

246

on the Christmas tree and let herself inhale its piney scent. She pushed away the thoughts. She didn't want to ruin what was turning into the kind of Christmas Eve she'd always dreamed about.

27

*L*ucas heard Ma's footsteps on the stairway and sent up a quiet prayer of thanks. He took his arm off the back of the sofa and leaned away from Jenna.

He'd been *that* close to doing something he would have regretted. But oh, those pouty lips of hers begged to be kissed. He ran a hand over his face, trying to wipe the idea out of his mind. But how could he when she was sitting right here beside him looking like an angel in the soft light from the Christmas tree and Ma's candles?

If he hadn't had this bulky cast to deal with, he would have removed himself from the sofa—or maybe the room—by now. She was too close.

Geoff and Ma appeared at the top of the stairs. "We're making some hot cocoa," she said. "You guys want some?"

"Sounds good. How about you?" He looked at Jenna and thought her expression said she wanted an excuse to stay, but he didn't want to take that for granted.

She smiled. "That would be nice. Thank you."

After the couple disappeared into the kitchen, she repositioned herself on the sofa.

He didn't think it was his imagination that she'd done it purposely, to move closer to him. *Lay off, Vermontez. You're asking for trouble.*

He lifted his casted leg off the coffee table and hollered into the kitchen. "You need help, Ma?"

"We got it," Geoff called back. "You two stay put." Great. They were no help at all.

"Geoff seems really nice," Jenna whispered.

He nodded. "He's a good guy."

"He's a good guy, but . . . ?"

"What?"

"You said that with a shrug . . . like maybe you had some reservations."

"I didn't realize I shrugged. I thought I nodded."

"You nodded"—she narrowed her eyes—"but you also shrugged."

"Sorry. I didn't realize—"

"I wouldn't blame you if you did have reservations. But it's obvious your mom is really happy. And he does seem like a really nice man."

"Point taken."

"Not that it's any of my business. I just thought in case you hadn't noticed, I'd point out that he's really nice."

"Right." He raised his voice pointedly as Geoff appeared behind Jenna with a tray in hand. "And speaking of hot chocolate . . . Thanks, Geoff."

Lucas curbed a grin as Jenna's cheeks flushed three shades of pink.

Geoff helped her clear a space on the coffee table in front of them. "You guys want whipped cream?"

"No, thanks," Jenna said, finally risking a glance at Geoff. "This looks great. Thank you."

"Yeah, thanks, Geoff. That was really *nice* of you."

Geoff gave him a look that said he knew something was up, but then Ma appeared with a can of Reddi-wip. "Anybody want whipped cream?"

"Geoff already asked," Lucas said. "But thanks, we're good."

"Okay. You two enjoy." Ma beamed.

When she and Geoff disappeared back down the stairs with their own tray of hot chocolates, Jenna turned to him, cringing. "Did he hear me?"

Lucas burst out laughing. "No, but I wish you could have seen your face."

She hid her face in her hands, then looked up, feigning anger. "Thanks for the warning . . . and thanks a lot for your 'nice' comment."

"Sorry. Couldn't resist. He was just being so nice."

"Haha. Very funny. Well, he *is* nice. That's all I'm saying."

He laughed harder and she joined in.

They sipped hot cocoa in comfortable silence, letting the Christmas lights mesmerize them.

Lucas drained his mug and set it on the coffee table. "So, are you going home for Christmas tomorrow?"

"Home? No. There's . . . not exactly a home to go to."

"Your family's not in St. Louis anymore?"

"My mom died last March."

He tried to hide his surprise. "I'm sorry, Jen. I didn't know."

"How could you? I know I probably seem calloused about it, but we were never close. And where I grew up wasn't exactly . . . the kind of place you go home to for Christmas."

"I'm sorry," he said again, still stunned at her matter-of-fact revelation.

She squirmed a little and set her empty mug beside his. "I didn't grow up the way you did, Luc," she said again. "What you have is special."

She looked so wounded behind those soft hazel eyes. He remembered their earlier conversation and felt bad that they kept coming around to this. It was Christmas Eve after all. "We do have something special," he acknowledged. "I'm glad you could be here tonight. To share it with us."

"Me too." She looked as if she might cry.

"And just for the record . . ." He swallowed hard, praying for words that would heal and soothe—and feeling wholly inadequate to find them. "What Christmas is all about—it's . . . God making things right between us and Him." It felt odd, sharing his faith this way when he'd had so many doubts this past year . . . times when he wondered if he could keep on believing. But saying the words to Jenna now, he was convinced all over again.

She put her head down as if his words made her uncomfortable, but when she looked up again, there was a faraway glimmer in her eyes. "I remember going to this church one summer." Her voice was almost a whisper. "It was a Vacation Bible School or something—and they invited all the kids in the neighborhood. Mom made Becky and me go, and they talked about that—about Christmas. I thought it was so weird . . . talking about Christmas in July. But there was something I always liked about that."

"I'm going to go out on a limb," he risked, "and say maybe God planted a seed in your heart way back then."

She looked skeptical. "A seed that's supposed to grow into what?"

He grasped for an answer that wouldn't scare her off. "Into knowing Him. I think God knew we'd have this conversation one day. And I think He wanted you to know that you can know Him . . . just like you know me."

She gave a humorless laugh. "Wow. You and God are pretty tight, huh?"

"Oh, yeah"—he held up a hand and crossed his fingers—"we're like this." He wiped the smile from his face. "I'm only partly kidding, Jenna. I do feel that close to God. I'm dead serious about that part."

She nodded, leaning forward, so much hope in her eyes. "But how do you know, Luc?"

"You just know"—he placed a hand over his heart—"in here." *Oh, God, give me the words. I want her to know You.* A few minutes ago his reasons might have been less than altruistic. But now—even if nothing else ever came of their friendship—he only wanted for Jenna to know the love of a heavenly Father.

For the next hour he tried to make a case for the God who'd carried him through the past year. She asked earnest questions that made him examine the evolution of his own faith.

A few minutes after the schoolhouse clock in the kitchen struck midnight, Jenna yawned and rubbed her temples. "My brain is on overload."

He laughed. "Mine too."

She unfolded herself from the sofa. "It's late. I should go. I've got a lot to think about."

He reached for his crutches and struggled to his feet. "I'll walk you to the door."

"You don't need to, Luc. I'm fine."

"No, I want to." Leading the way with long strides of his crutches, he stood in the entryway in front of the door. He leaned one crutch against the door and put a hand on her arm. "Would you come for dinner tomorrow? Lunch, I mean. We'll probably eat around one. My grandparents will be here. I'd love for you to meet them."

"It's Christmas Day."

"Um . . . that's sort of the point."

"Lucas, it's your family's—"

"Jenna, in case you didn't notice, my family adores you. They'll love having you. *I'd* love for you to come."

She looked up at him and narrowed her eyes. "You just want a rematch on that Finger and Toe game."

"Hand and Foot," he said, cracking up, thoroughly charmed.

She grinned. "Whatever. And you're sure?"

In reply he leaned in and brushed a strand of hair from her cheek. Before he could think about what he was doing, he kissed her forehead. Overcome with emotions he couldn't quite identify, he threaded his fingers through her pale, thick curls and cradled her head in the palm of his hand. He had never wanted to kiss a woman so much in his life. And by the way she leaned into his caress, he thought she was feeling the same.

"Are you convinced yet?" he whispered.

"Lucas . . ." Her eyes held a look of desperation that only made him want her more. "I don't—"

"Shhh." He put a finger to her lips. They were like velvet beneath his touch and he traced their lines. Something snapped inside him and he drew her close, kissing her full on the lips.

She made a sound that was somewhere between a moan and a sigh. "I have to go," she said, eyes wild.

He hadn't intended to do that, but he couldn't apologize because he wasn't sorry. "Jenna, wait. I—"

"No. I . . . I asked for it."

"You did? Well, in that case—" He kissed her again, a teasing peck on the cheek this time, but it was only his dependence on the crutch that kept him from taking her into his arms and giving her what she claimed to be asking for. He intended to quiz her on that further, but right now if he didn't walk her out that door, he would regret it.

He opened the door and put a hand lightly at the small of her back. "Come back tomorrow. We'll both sleep on . . . what just happened. We'll talk about it then."

She nodded, looking dazed.

"Merry Christmas," he said.

"Merry Christmas, Luc."

He stood in the doorway watching her pick her way down the sidewalk and get into her car. After she drove away, he went back inside, praying his sisters had already gone to bed. Because he couldn't seem to wipe the silly grin off his face.

28

*J*uggling a fruit basket under one arm, Jenna wiped damp palms on the back of her pants before ringing the doorbell. Hearing footsteps inside, she stole a quick look at her reflection in the side panel window, hoping she didn't look as nervous as she felt.

"Jenna! Come in. Merry Christmas!" Emily Vermontez flung the door wide.

"Here . . . I brought this for you." She thrust her offering into Emily's arms, feeling a prick of guilt since this was actually the gift basket she'd intended for Bryn. But she thought her friend would understand.

"Oh! How nice. You didn't have to do that." She turned and called down the stairwell. "Lucas? Jenna's here."

Feeling a little more confident at the warm greeting she'd received—and the reassurance that Lucas was expecting her—she took a deep breath and stepped inside. The savory aromas of turkey and gravy and something cinnamony filled her nostrils and made her remember her manners. "Merry Christmas. Thank you so much for inviting me."

"We're delighted you could come."

Jenna took in the house in the daylight, warmed again by memories of last night.

"You look lovely," Emily said.

"Oh . . . thank you. I love your sweater," she said, pointing at the soft lavender cardigan Emily wore over black dress pants. She'd worried about what to wear today, but her crisp white cotton shirt and casual black pants felt just right.

"Thank you," Emily said, fingering one of the rhinestone buttons and looking pleased at the compliment. "I've had this for years . . . a Walmart special. I think I paid eight dollars for it. I wish I'd gotten one in every color."

Jenna was a little shocked—both at Emily's admission and by the fact that such a pretty sweater had come from a discount store. Clarissa would have died before she'd shop for clothing at Walmart. When she bragged on a bargain, it was a designer name she'd picked up for under a hundred dollars in St. Louis. Jenna was embarrassed to realize that she'd been guilty of the same thing under the guise of impressing her friends with her thriftiness, but in truth, designed to reveal how much she usually spent on her clothes.

Jenna had always thought Lucas's mother was a beautiful woman, but for the first time she became aware that Emily's beauty didn't come from designer clothes or expensive cosmetics—or even a great haircut. Her beauty was natural and understated, and due in large part to her warm, friendly manner. Luc had inherited that from her—along with his dark good looks.

Luc. She'd started to think of him by that nickname. Maybe it was from being around his family, who all called him Luc—unless they were lecturing him, and then he became "Lucas Alexander." Jenna had noticed that during the card game last night.

She'd awakened in Bryn's apartment this morning not sure if she had the courage to come back and face Lucas after their stolen kisses last night. But she'd loved being part of this happy, generous family too much to stay away.

Lucas's voice floated up from the bottom of the basement stairway. "Hey, you came! Merry Christmas."

She peered over the railing at him.

"Come on down . . . we're watching the game." He leaned on his crutches, seeming as unsure as she felt. Or maybe he was just uncomfortable with his mom watching them.

She turned to Emily. "Do you need help in the kitchen?"

"No, no . . . you go on down." She glanced at the clock. "We're still waiting on Luc's grandparents. I may enlist you and the girls when it's time to dish things up, but dinner won't be ready for a few minutes yet."

"Come on down," Lucas said again. "Hope you don't mind if I don't come up. It's a bear getting upstairs on these stupid things." He shifted his weight to one crutch and pointed at her with the other.

She hurried down the stairs. Smiling, Luc took her hand as if it were the most natural thing in the world. "How are you?"

So many other questions contained within his three little words. "I'm good. How are you?"

He squeezed her hand. "Better now."

"Hi, Jenna!" Luc's sisters called in unison from the family room.

From the look in his eyes, he was not happy with the interruption.

She laughed at him and poked her head around the corner to where Emily's fiancé, Victoria, and Gina were ensconced in mismatched sofas and overstuffed chairs. The cozy room was lit only by the big-screen TV.

Lucas poked Gina with the rubber-tipped end of one crutch. "Scoot over."

"Ouch! You could just *ask*."

"I did."

Jenna laughed, charmed at the little boy Lucas became in the presence of his sisters. Even though he was the big brother.

Lucas plopped beside his sister and pulled Jenna down beside him.

She settled in, letting Lucas take her hand again

in the dark. She pretended to watch the game, but as he twined his fingers with hers, her mind wandered far away, fantasizing what it would be like to be part of this happy family. What it would be like to have Lucas beside her every day, holding her hand, kissing her the way he'd kissed her last night. She almost couldn't breathe thinking about it. Wishing it would happen again, fearing it would. And wondering if things could ever work out between them.

Emily appeared on the stairway. "I don't suppose anyone could tear themselves away from the game long enough to help me in the kitchen."

"Luc would be happy to." Victoria grinned at her brother from her nest in a comfy chair.

He picked up a crutch and pointed it at her. "Have a little compassion for the handicapped, will you?"

"I'll help." Jenna untangled her fingers from Lucas's grip and pushed off the sofa.

Victoria and Gina shot from their seats, which made Lucas roar. "Oh, man! You guilted them straight out of their seats."

Jenna laughed, but she felt awkward as she followed the Vermontez sisters up to the kitchen. Emily put her immediately at ease, assigning her simple tasks and keeping up friendly chatter while they worked.

The doorbell rang while Jenna was slicing homemade bread.

"Abi and Baba are here!" Victoria shouted.

"Manny's parents," Emily explained, wiping her hands on a Christmas-y dishtowel.

Jenna thought she saw a glint of sadness in Emily's eyes when she spoke of her late husband's parents.

Victoria and Gina ushered an elderly couple into the kitchen. "Jenna," Victoria said, hugging the petite white-haired woman, "this is Abuela and Abuelo Vermontez."

"Nice to meet you," she said, coming around the counter to shake their hands.

"She's a pretty girl," the gentleman said to his granddaughters, as if Jenna couldn't hear him.

She smiled, mildly embarrassed, but Luc's sisters seemed not to notice.

"Baba, Abi, this is Lucas's friend, Jenna Morgan."

"Morgan, you say? Wasn't that the name of that rookie friend of Lucas's? The fellow who died with our Manuel?"

Emily came to her rescue. "Yes, Pop, Zachary was Jenna's husband."

"I thought you said she was Lucas's friend."

"She is, Pop." Emily smiled a friendly apology Jenna's way. "Any friend of Zachary's is a friend of our family."

Luc's grandfather removed the gray fedora from his head, placed it over his heart, and bent at the waist. "I'm very sorry for your loss, dear."

"Thank you." She swallowed back sudden tears. "And I'm sorry for yours."

"We've all had some hard times, haven't we?"

"Yes, we have." She managed to acknowledge his sweet expression of sympathy before her throat closed completely.

"Girls, take Abi and Baba's coats. Dinner's almost ready."

A few minutes later the adorable couple was settled at the table, and the food was arranged on the bar counter doubling as a buffet.

"Gina, go tell Luc and Geoff that dinner's on . . . and don't let them talk you into bringing plates down to them either. It's Christmas and we *will* eat a proper meal together." She winked at Jenna.

"Good luck with that," Victoria mumbled.

But within seconds Gina was back with Geoff in tow, and Jenna heard the muffled *thump thump* of Lucas's crutches on the carpeted stairs.

He reached the top and clumped over to greet his grandparents. After kissing both of them—kisses on both cheeks—he came to where she was standing near the table. "You hungry?"

Jenna nodded, butterflies fluttering in her belly. "Everything looks delicious."

Emily smiled her thanks and turned to Lucas. "Luc, will you say the blessing?"

He looked a little taken aback by her request, but he nodded and everyone bowed their heads. Jenna followed suit.

"Father God, we thank You for this day when we celebrate the birth of Your Son. Thank You, God, for the hope that gives us. It's been a year of—"

Lucas paused and Jenna realized he was choking up, struggling to regain his composure. Unexpected tears threatened behind her own eyelids.

"It's been a hard year," Luc murmured. His voice grew strong again. "But it's been a year of healing, too, and we're grateful for all Your blessings. Thank You that Abi and Baba could be here with us, and for each person You've brought around this table today."

He reached over and squeezed her shoulder.

"Bless this food and bless our time together," he finished. "In Jesus' name, amen."

A chorus of amens fluttered through the room, and Jenna bit her lip to keep it from trembling. This was a side of Lucas she'd only seen hints of. But his prayer unlocked something within her that she couldn't yet define. It moved her deeply to be standing here with this family. She could imagine what their lives must have been like two years ago, while Manny was still alive, gathered around this same table, unaware that tragedy would soon shatter their world.

And yet, here they were, three generations, laughing and smiling together, teasing each other in a way that exuded love. Seemingly whole again, and thanking a God they seemed to consider part of the family. How could they claim they'd been blessed after everything that had happened over the past year? And yet, looking around the room at faces that glowed with genuine joy, she knew it was true. How could eyes haunted by sadness also spark with such unspeakable joy? It was a mystery she felt compelled to solve.

Beside her, Lucas abandoned his crutches and tried to juggle a plate in one hand while he gripped the counter for balance with the other. She took his plate from him. "Here. Tell me what you want and I'll dish up."

"Thanks." He put a hand at the small of her back while she filled his plate. She thrilled at his touch but felt the watchful eyes of his family on them.

"Keep it coming, keep it coming," he teased as she scooped dressing and gravy onto the only empty spot left on his plate.

They ate amidst lively conversation, affectionate teasing, and love that was palpable. Jenna couldn't help but compare this gathering to last night at the Morgans', where the house—despite its grand decorations—had the feel of a mausoleum. What was it that made the difference in this family? The Vermontezes had arguably lost even more than the Morgans. Manny was a husband, son, *and* father with two daughters in college. And besides, they'd had to deal with the trauma and expense of Lucas's injuries, too.

Injuries that had been life-changing for Luc—for all of them.

Luc's Abi and Baba charmed her through dinner, though she really hoped his grandpa wouldn't mention Zach again.

When Luc was finished with his plate, he handed it to Gina. "Hey, little sister, save Sparky some of the scraps. And a nice turkey leg maybe?"

"No, sir!" Emily protested. "Not until I pick that bird clean. I've got a pot of turkey noodle soup started. Besides, I thought Sparky was supposed to be on a strict training diet."

Lucas pushed his chair away from the table. "He is. I'll make him work for it, but it's Christmas Day. Can't you give a poor doggy a bone?"

Emily rolled her eyes. "He can have a bone, but not till I get the meat off of it."

Gina gathered up everyone's offering of scraps. Lucas had told her that Gina was helping with Sparky's training while she was home, since he'd been sidelined by this latest injury.

"How's the training going?" She was sorry she asked when Luc grabbed his crutches and took the plate of leftovers from his sister, handing it to Jenna. "Come on . . . I'll show you."

She was still no fan of the dog, but she *was* a fan of Luc. Thanking Emily for the meal, she excused herself from the table and followed Lucas out the back door with the plate.

29

$\mathcal{T}$he cold air blasted him and every joint in his legs ached, but Lucas was eager to put Sparky through his paces and show Jenna how far they'd come.

She hovered close beside him in the garage, as she always did when Sparky was anywhere near. Not that he minded having her close.

"At least he's not jumping up on me," she said, rubbing her arms briskly. "I figured I was dead meat bringing a plate of food out here."

"Nope, he won't bother you until I give the command."

She looked up at him with a wry smile. "You sound like you've got plans to sic him on me."

He grinned. "Let me reword that. He won't bother that plate of food till I give the command." He rubbed the dog's head. "He doesn't eat until he works. That's part of the training, so I've got to put him through the paces before he gets his reward."

"Poor baby."

"Hey, when he's working, I'm working, so you should feel sorry for me, too."

Her brow puckered and she reached up and patted his cheek. "Poor baby."

"That's better. Okay . . . watch this." He

positioned himself in front of the dog. "Sparky, sit."

The dog obeyed promptly, panting and wagging his tail, obviously eager to show off for their guest.

Lucas put out a hand. "Stay." Sparky stayed put. "Follow me."

Jenna kept her eyes trained on the dog.

"Um . . . that 'follow me' was for you, not him."

She gave an embarrassed laugh. "How come he knew that and I didn't?"

"I guess you just have to be smarter than the dog."

"Hey!" But she laughed and obeyed his command, following him to the door that led to the backyard. He grabbed a canvas bag off a hook and handed it to her.

She opened it and peered inside. "Tennis balls?"

"Yep. See that?" He pointed to a row of plastic buckets lined up in front of the fence at the far end of the yard. "Go put one ball in each of those buckets. . . ." He pulled out the Ziploc bag containing the accelerant-doused ball. He unzipped the bag and held it up to her nose. "Can you smell that?"

She took a whiff. "Not really . . . smells like a tennis ball."

"This is the test ball. It has one tiny drop of 50 percent evaporated gasoline on it. And it's been in this bag for a week."

"He can smell that? One drop?"

"A tiny drop. Almost microscopic. And not full-strength gasoline either—evaporated."

"Seriously?"

"Here." He handed her the plastic bag. "Put a ball in each bucket and remember where you put this one. Oh, and try to dump it out of the bag without touching it, just so you don't risk getting the scent on you." He grinned. "We don't want it to be you he alerts on."

Her look of horror made him crack up. "Don't worry," he said, "I'm training him to be a passive responder."

"As opposed to an aggressive responder."

"Exactly."

"I was kidding. Do I even want to know what an aggressive responder does?"

"You'd probably still come out alive. Just barely." He winked.

"Gee, that's comforting."

"An aggressive response is barking and digging. A passive response—well, you'll see. Go place the balls and prepare to be amazed."

"Am I supposed to tell you which bucket this one is in?" She held up the plastic bag.

"You won't have to. Sparky will tell me."

She looked skeptical but jogged to the fence and deposited the tennis balls, then came back to stand beside him.

It was nice having an assistant, and it would be a good test for Sparky to have to work with a distraction. Who was he kidding? He was the one distracted. Quite pleasantly so.

He pushed off with his crutches and reached the garage door in two strides. He opened the door and gave a short whistle. "Sparky, come."

Sparky trotted after him, and Lucas waited until the dog came around and sat at his right side. "Okay, boy, it's time to work." He used his commanding "business" voice. "Show me, Sparky. Show me, boy."

Like a shot, Sparky headed for the fence. Within twenty seconds he'd alerted on the third bucket from the left, putting his nose on the ground in front of the bucket and waiting there for Lucas.

"Was that the right one?" He had no doubt it was. Sparky had been almost 100 percent with his alerts from the day Lucas had started the training.

"That was it," Jenna confirmed. "That wasn't a lucky guess?"

"Nope."

"So he could do it again?"

"He'll do it all day if I ask him to," he bragged. "Of course, we've only worked with two accelerants so far—gasoline and kerosene. But I think he's got the nose for it. I'm pretty confident he'll learn to alert on anything I teach him to."

"That's amazing. So that day at the homeless shelter, he was strutting his stuff, huh?"

He laughed. "I guess he was. Either that or just trying to impress you ladies."

She rolled her eyes. "Well, he didn't impress me! He scared the daylights out of me."

He noticed she was still keeping her distance from Sparky, but she hadn't climbed on any countertops recently that he knew of, and she wasn't clinging to him the way she had before in Sparky's presence. That was a definite downside of having a well-trained dog. He just might need to have a talk with Sparky about misbehaving a little when Jenna came around.

"What's so funny?"

Lucas wiped the smile off his face. "Nothing. Just thinking."

She didn't push him to explain. "Can we try it again?"

"You don't think he can do it?"

"I'm just not going to be impressed with one time. How do I know you didn't bury a hunk of steak under that bucket?"

"How would I know which bucket you would pick? But fine," he challenged. "Go put the ball in different one this time. And—"

"I know, I know . . . don't touch the test ball with my hands. Believe me, I'm not going to take a chance he'll alert on my hand."

He chuckled. "Getting the lingo down already. I'm impressed."

Jenna gave him a smug grin.

"How many substances do you have to train him for?"

"According to the training center in Tulsa, there are at least a dozen different accelerants they train their dogs to detect."

"Wow."

Lucas gimped across the yard, and bracing himself with his crutches, he patted his good knee, giving Sparky the signal to collect his reward—an abundance of ear scratching and praise that he hoped Jenna couldn't hear.

But her giggles told him she'd heard every word.

"I'll have you know this is an important part of the training," he hollered over his shoulder.

Her footsteps crunched on the grass behind him. She stood beside him—but still a safe distance from Sparky. Keeping his eyes on the dog, he kept up the baby talk. "Good doggy. That's a good boy. I think Miss Jenna is just jealous that she didn't get the cootchie-cootchie-coo treatment." He snuck a peek at her.

She gave an exaggerated frown and mimicked him. "That's right. Miss Jenna did such a good job hiding all those tennis balls so the big doggy could find the right one, and then the big doggy gets all the praise."

Grinning, Lucas pivoted to face her. "Poor baby . . ." He took her head in his hands and rubbed playfully behind her ears, talking baby talk exactly the way he had to Sparky.

Her hair was silk beneath his hands, and he wove his fingers deeper.

She stepped closer, and when she looked up, the expression on her face invited him to do what he'd wanted to do since the minute she'd walked through the door today.

He obliged, pulling her close, whispering against her lips. "Is that better?"

In reply she cradled his face between her palms and kissed him soundly. But when she shifted against him, he lost his balance. He caught himself and shuffled to regain a position that took his weight off his leg.

Jenna pulled away. "Are you okay? "

Trying not to wince, he nodded. "I'm fine. I just . . . landed on my bad leg." Ha. Like he had a good leg. He grasped for words that would get them back to where they'd left off but came up blank.

She backed away, brushing dried grass off her pants, obviously embarrassed. "I'm sorry."

Using his crutches for leverage, he hoisted himself up and reached for her again. "I'm fine, Jenna."

She closed her eyes and sighed. "I'm not sure *I* am." She wriggled out of his grasp and walked back to the garage.

Sparky took off after her, ready to play, but Lucas knew Jenna wouldn't see it that way. "Sparky! No! Come!" He whistled.

Jenna turned at the commotion and plastered herself against the house, fear in her eyes.

"It's okay, Jen. I've got him." Sparky ran back to him and she visibly relaxed.

He made the dog sit and vaulted across the lawn on his crutches. "Let me feed him real quick, okay?"

"Sure."

He put Sparky in the garage with the turkey scraps and went back to find Jenna staring out over the garden.

"Why don't we go for a drive? I'd take you for coffee, but I don't think anything's open."

"Luc . . . It's Christmas. You should be spending time with your family."

"I will. They'll all still be here tomorrow."

"But aren't you going to open presents?"

"We did that this morning. We need to talk, you and me. Let me just let Ma know where I'm going so she doesn't worry. I'll meet you at my truck—"

"No. I'll come with you. I want to at least thank your mom for dinner."

*J*enna watched Lucas from the corner of her eye as they drove through downtown Hanover Falls. The town was dead on this Christmas afternoon, and her heart felt a little the same.

In many ways this had been the sweetest Christmas she could ever remember. The way Luc's family had drawn her in and made her feel that she belonged. Sharing kisses with this man beside her—kisses that melted her, just thinking about them now.

Just outside of town he turned onto a dirt road and drove a quarter of a mile before pulling off onto a wooded lane. He eased the pickup under a copse of leafless trees and cut the engine.

She looked through the windshield at their secluded surroundings and gave him a wry grin. "If I didn't know better, I'd think you brought me out here for more of what created the need for this talk in the first place."

"Don't tempt me, woman." He unbuckled his seatbelt and scooted to lean his back against the door, stretching his bum leg out over the console.

She unfastened her own seatbelt and angled herself to face him.

"So . . . what are we going to do?" He looked at her as if she were a child who'd misbehaved and he was burdened with deciding her punishment.

But she knew what he meant. "About us, you mean."

Lucas nodded.

"Well, we can't keep going on like this."

"The kissing, you mean?" Was that a smile behind his eyes?

She glared at him. "I can't ever tell if you're being serious or if you're just joking around."

"About the kissing? Oh, I'm dead serious about the kissing, Jenna Morgan."

Oh dear. What had she gotten herself into? "No, Luc. Not about the kissing, about—"

"Wait, Jenna." He shifted in his seat, bumped his knee on the steering wheel, and winced. "Something's got to give. Every time we get together, we wind up the same way, which suits me just fine, by the way. But then you back off like a scared rabbit, and I am clueless about where I stand with you."

"Luc—I'm sorry. It's my fault. I didn't think—" She wasn't making a bit of sense and she knew it. "It's just that—"

"Whoa, whoa. Hang on . . . *what's* your fault?"

"The kissing," she squeaked.

"No." He wagged his head. "No, the kissing is definitely my fault. What I want to know is whose fault is the running away? And why does this have to be anybody's *fault?* Can't we just enjoy it and see where it leads?"

So there it was. "Luc, look at me. I'm sponging off my best friend, I'm up to my eyeballs in debt, I barely have enough money to pay my bills, let alone rent an apartment. I don't have the first clue what I'm going to do with my life . . . who I even am. I'm not ready for . . . kissing."

"And look at me," he countered. "At least you *have* a job. I seem to be doomed to live life on crutches . . . or in PT. For all I know, I'll never get my job back." He closed his eyes and a deep shadow passed over his face. "I'm sorry, Jen. I'm the one who should be apologizing. I can never offer you what Zachary could. I didn't mean to try to lure you in. . . ."

She smiled at him, loving him like crazy in that moment. Yet knowing what they'd both said was true. They had nothing to offer each other right now. Except maybe empathy. "Maybe what we both need right now is just a friend. Can we just be that for each other? For now?"

He shook his head. "I want more, Jenna. I want a house in the country, and I want to fill it with babies and a dog and a cat or two. And I think"—he looked at her as if he were about to dive into an icy lake—"I think I want all that with *you*. Is that so terrible to admit?"

"A . . . dog?" She could barely breathe.

He laughed. "The dog is negotiable."

But it wasn't the part about a dog that made her breath catch. Lucas wanted babies. After all he'd sacrificed, was it fair to ask him to give up a dog and babies, too?

She'd never told him about the second miscarriage. She'd never told *anyone*. It had happened on the first day of December. One month to the day after Zachary died. Spontaneous abortion, her doctor termed it, which made it sound more ominous than ever. And yet with Zach gone and her future so uncertain, she'd felt mostly relief.

Mostly. Except for the guilt that she'd never told

her husband she was pregnant again. Maybe she should have felt guilty that she hadn't told his parents either. But what purpose would that have served? They'd already lost their son, their only child. Her revelation would only have made their grief deeper. Wouldn't it?

And there'd been no reason for her doctors to explore the reasons she'd lost the baby. "These things happen. It's not something to worry about now," Dr. Harrison had said. But what if she could *never* carry a baby to term?

"Did you hear me?" Luc's voice cut through her thoughts. "I said dogs were negotiable."

"Can we just be friends for a while, Lucas?"

His expression changed. "Uh-oh . . . I know a brush-off when I hear one."

She hated that she'd taken the light from his eyes. "No. I really want to be friends. When we— when we both get our lives figured out, then we'll talk about . . . dogs."

"And kissing?"

She held up a hand. "One step at a time."

"Okay, okay." The spark came back to his eyes a little, flecking his irises with gold.

She was pretty sure her own eyes reflected that same spark.

30

Friday, January 16

*J*enna pulled up to the drive-through window and hurriedly endorsed the back of the paycheck she'd just picked up at Hanson's. She handed it to the cashier along with a deposit slip, trying to contain the smug smile that wanted to come.

This was her third payday since she'd started working, and thanks to Bryn's generosity at putting her up rent-free, Jenna had money in the bank, even after paying twice her minimum payment on each of her credit cards this month. It wasn't a fortune and it wouldn't go far—and she couldn't even let herself think about the money she owed Zach's parents—but it was a start. And there was more where that came from. Mr. Iverson had told her he'd give her some overtime hours if she wanted them. That paid time-and-a-half. She was working late tonight in fact, even though right now she felt her time might be best spent looking for a job that paid more. Of course, she hadn't said that to Mr. Iverson.

With the money safely deposited and a little cash in her wallet, she headed to the newspaper office to pick up a copy of the *Hanover Falls Courier*. The weekly paper's classifieds had yielded little in the way of rentals or jobs, and she was already a day late getting this week's edition. No doubt if there'd been anything good in there, it would have been snapped up by now, but she had to at least check.

She was starting to fear she might have to move to Springfield to find a job that paid a decent wage. She'd have more to choose from for housing in the city, too. But she didn't want to leave the Falls. And Lucas Vermontez was the reason why.

More than three weeks had gone by since she'd told him she just wanted to be friends. When they were together he was a perfect gentleman. But that was just the problem. She didn't *want* him to be. She was falling for him, hard. And more and more the things that had made it seem impossible for them to be together were fading away.

Her cell phone chirped from her purse, and she fished blindly until she found it. Bryn. "Hello?"

"Hey, Jen." Bryn sounded breathless.

"Is everything okay?"

"Fine. Listen, I can't talk long, but I wanted to let you know about this before somebody else grabbed it. Garrett just told me one of the teachers he works with has a place to rent out in the country. I'm not trying to make you feel pressured to get out or anything, but I know you've been looking and Garrett said they're only asking $350 a month for this place. Oh, and they'd probably only require one month's deposit since Garrett knows you."

"Wow. Are you serious?" She hesitated. "Is it cheap because it's a dump?" Not that she could be picky . . .

"I honestly don't know. I'm just relaying what Garrett said. But if you want to go look at it, I just happen to have the keys."

"Really?" This was getting interesting. "Are you at work?"

"I'm headed there now. I wish I could go with you to look at it, but if you can meet me in front of the library in a few minutes, you can have the keys. And I'll give you directions."

"Sure! I'm three minutes away right now. How far out of town is it?"

"A mile and a half. Out on the old refinery road. You know where that is, right?"

"I think so. I'll be right there." She flipped her phone shut, excitement fluttering in her chest. She'd just deposited the equivalent of two months' rent in the bank. She could afford this place! And not just an apartment, but a house in the country.

She glanced in the rearview mirror and laughed at the goofy grin on her face. "Somebody pinch me," she said to her reflection.

On a whim she grabbed her phone again and dialed Lucas. Since Christmas they'd met for coffee at Java Joint a couple of times, but those evenings had been too much of a temptation for both of them—by Luc's own admission—to repeat what had happened at Christmas. So mostly they talked on the phone or volleyed lighthearted e-mails back and forth. She wondered if he looked forward to those exchanges as much as she did. Lucas was becoming one of the best friends she'd ever had. But it was too hard to be "just friends" with a man when all you wanted to do was find a way to be in his arms, to have him kiss you . . .

She made herself put the brakes on that train of thought. She just wanted his advice, and someone along for moral support. His phone rang four times before voice mail kicked in. She glanced at the clock on the dashboard. Almost four. He was probably still at PT, but she could swing by before she headed out to the rental and see if he was home yet. It made her a little nervous to think about going alone into an empty house in the country. What if someone thought she was breaking in?

After picking up the keys from Bryn, she drove by the Vermontez home. Luc's pickup was in the driveway and the gate to the backyard was open. She heard his voice—and Sparky's barking—as soon as she got out of the car.

She went through the gate and spotted Lucas leaning against the huge oak tree that shaded the lawn. Hands tucked into faded Levi's, he was putting Sparky through his paces. His cane was propped against the trunk of the tree, and for a moment Jenna almost forgot his need for it. The man was definitely easy on the eyes.

He tossed a baton twenty feet in front of him, and Sparky dashed to retrieve it, then trotted back to accept Luc's words of praise. Lucas sat on his haunches and took Sparky's huge head between his hands. "Good boy! That's my good doggy, yes, it is," he cooed, scratching behind Sparky's floppy ears and hugging the dog as if it were a beloved child.

Hints of this softer side of Lucas always came out when he was with Sparky, but he usually seemed a little guarded in Jenna's presence. Now he spoke in a tone of total love and acceptance, the way he might have spoken to a child he cherished. *Or a woman.*

Tempted to slink away before he saw her, she cleared her throat loudly.

He looked up, surprise in his expression. "Jenna! Hi. What's up?"

She held up the keys. "You don't want to go for a little drive, do you?"

"Where to?" He gave Sparky a pat on the head and held out a palm. "Stay, boy." The dog immediately went down on his hindquarters, tail twitching, watching his master.

Lucas struggled to his feet and took a step toward her, blanching as his left leg hitched.

Looking self-conscious, he reached behind him for the cane.

Wanting to save him the distance, she closed the gap between them, picking her way over the uneven lawn, praying Sparky would stay where he was. She still wasn't 100 percent in love with the dog.

She told Lucas about the rental. "I wondered if you'd go out there with me. Just to look at the place."

"Sure. Let me shut the gate. You want me to drive? That way Sparky could come." He winked at her, but she could tell he was serious.

"Fine, but I call shotgun."

He laughed. "You got it. Let me shut the gate, and I'll meet you at the truck."

From her safe perch in the passenger seat, she watched him latch the gate, then put the tailgate down on the truck for Sparky. The dog jumped in and trotted up to peer in the back windshield at her.

Lucas climbed in the cab and started the engine. "So you found a place, huh?"

"Maybe." She couldn't control the smile that forced its way to her face, so she quit trying. She relayed the directions Bryn had given her and they headed out of town.

"You sure you want to live in the country?"

"Why not?"

"Boogeymen. Rattlesnakes. Wolves," he said with a straight face.

"There are no wolves in Missouri."

He gave her a look that said maybe there were.

She narrowed her eyes. "You're just trying to scare me."

"Okay, no boogeymen. But there are coyotes."

"Would you stop?" She looked up to see a mailbox in front of a long angled driveway. "Hey, I think this might be it."

He slowed the truck and waited while she checked the name on the box.

"This is it."

He gunned the engine and started up the steep drive. "Where's the house?"

"Bryn said it's set a ways back from the road. I know this is the right place." She unbuckled her seatbelt and leaned forward, watching through the windshield as they bumped up the wooded drive.

The property was beautiful—secluded and peaceful. "It *is* kind of out in the boonies, isn't it?" She turned 360 degrees and only saw one farmstead within walking distance. The talk of boogeymen and coyotes made her imagine how it would look out there after dark.

But Lucas looked taken with the place. "It's perfect. Far enough out that you get the quiet, but close enough you could practically walk into town if you needed to."

"I don't know . . ."

"You could get a dog."

She turned to glare at him, then swatted his arm

when she saw the mischievous glint in his eye. "Very funny."

He laughed and patted her knee in a way that made her forgive him.

"Where's the house?" She turned and looked behind them, wondering if they'd somehow missed it.

But as they rounded a curve in the lane, a flash of white and turquoise glinted through the trees.

"There it is." Lucas pointed, wrists lopped over the steering wheel.

She followed his line of vision and her heart sank. "It's . . . a trailer house."

"You didn't know that?"

"No." Hot tears threatened, but she swallowed them back. "I thought it was a house. A real house."

He laughed softly. "A mobile home is a real house, Jenna."

She shook her head. "No. Turn around. Go back."

He looked at her askance. "You're not even going to look? It looks to be in pretty good shape. And it's a double-wide. Those things are a lot bigger inside than they look."

"No. Go back. I'm not interested."

He stopped the truck and turned toward her. "Jenna, are you serious? You don't even want to go check it out? Is it because of what I said about wolves and coyotes? I was kidding. You'll be perfectly safe out here. You're practically *in* town.

I'd live out here in a heartbeat! Besides, you'll never find anything this great for the price."

She folded her arms across her chest and stared at the property.

"At least take a look," he coaxed.

She half expected a rottweiler to come racing around the side of the house. Why hadn't Bryn mentioned that it was a *trailer* house?

She felt a familiar touch on her arm and took a deep breath, preparing to face Luc's scrutiny.

"What's wrong, Jenna? There's something you're not telling me."

How could she make him understand? Maybe she was being ridiculous, but she would live in her car on the streets before she'd move into a trailer house again.

The thought stopped her in her tracks. Hadn't she thought those very words about the homeless shelter that first night she'd fled the Morgans' home? Did she think she was too good to live in either of those places? She hadn't been too good to grow up in a trailer.

She dropped her head, completely blank for words to explain everything she was feeling to Lucas. But he deserved an answer. "Luc, I grew up in a trailer house—a turquoise and white trailer house, if you must know." She gave a humorless laugh that threatened to turn into a sob.

"So?" His tone was far gentler than the word itself.

"So . . . I don't want to go back."

He tapped a staccato rhythm on the steering wheel, and she knew he was praying for the right words, words to reason with her.

When she looked up, he was waiting with a gentle smile. "Listen, sweet woman. I don't know what your life was like growing up, but whatever that turquoise trailer represents, *this*"—he spread his arms to encompass the property—"is not it. Don't get the two mixed up."

"How could I not?"

He shook his head. "For starters you could go look at this place. If it's awful, fine. At least you gave it a chance."

She siphoned a breath, feeling unreasonably panicky. But she nodded. "Come with me."

He gave a little laugh. "Of course. You didn't think I was going to wait out here, did you?"

"Luc . . . Don't tease. This is hard."

Something changed in his eyes—a softening . . . pity? But he drew her into a hug. "I'm sorry, Jen. I know it's not easy for you."

Now she felt bad for making him feel the need to apologize. She pulled away, hugged the door of the truck, steeling herself. "I'm okay." She forced a smile. "All right then . . . let's go take a look."

31

Jenna waited for her eyes to adjust to the dim light, suddenly aware that she was clutching Luc's hand as if she were drowning. Before they'd climbed the rickety steps to the front door, he'd propped his crutches against the side of the trailer.

The trailer smelled stuffy. But in a different way from where she'd grown up. This kitchen carried the smells of old cooking grease, bacon, and garlic—musty smells a good airing would drive away. The room was surprisingly spacious with an eating bar that divided the kitchen and dining room—much like the one in the Vermontez home.

Lucas let her hold his hand—maybe as much to keep his balance as to give her moral support.

"Hey, this is great. Really great, for the price." He looked around the open floor plan, then sought her gaze. "What do you think?

She looked away, not ready to let him see whatever might be written across her features. Slipping her hand out of his, she led the way down the narrow hallway, peering into a tiny bathroom and next to it, a bedroom that looked as if it would barely hold a double bed.

"This is convenient."

She turned to see Lucas bracing himself between the two walls of the hallway.

"Wouldn't even need my crutches here." He grinned, trying, she knew, to elicit a smile from her.

She didn't feel like smiling right now.

At the end of the hall was a bedroom almost as large as the guest room at Bryn's and, beyond that, a full bathroom with a deep whirlpool tub. Okay, so maybe they'd come a long way in designing trailer houses in the last twenty years. Still, the low-hanging ceiling, the feeling that the whole house was rocking and swaying beneath their footsteps . . . It all brought back too many memories.

And where would she go if there was a hailstorm or a tornado? How many times had her mom awakened her and Becky in the middle of the night to drag them halfway across the trailer court to the cramped cellar in the community building to wait out the storm?

She shivered at the images flooding her mind, coming faster than she could deflect them. No. She couldn't stay here. Not even one night. She would not go backward.

She sidestepped Luc and headed back down the hall.

"Hey, did you see this?" he called after her.

"I've seen enough. I'm not interested."

She made a beeline for the front door and went straight to the pickup. She climbed in and wrapped her arms around herself. She was still huddled there, staring at nothing, when Lucas finally emerged from the trailer five minutes later.

Watching him navigate the uneven terrain between the front door and the car, she had a sudden sense of what he'd lost in the fire. It moved her—and scared her a little, too.

He went behind the truck and spoke to Sparky, then came around and slid his crutches under the seat. Lucas would carry his disability long after the cast was removed and the doctor gave permission to abandon the crutches. He would always walk with a limp. If they were . . . together, his disability would be hers in many ways.

"What took you so long?" she asked, not meaning for the words to come out as sharply as they had.

He looked at her as if she'd just slapped him, and his retort was equally sharp. "I was turning out lights and locking up. What's the problem?"

She immediately felt repentant. "I'm sorry. I . . . I didn't mean to snap at you."

Without responding, he turned the key in the ignition and backed the truck until they came to a wide spot in the lane where he could turn around.

But instead, he stopped and reached across the seat to put a hand on her shoulder. "Hey." He put the truck in Park and angled his body toward her. "Jenna . . . It's me, remember? Your friend?" He brushed her bangs out of her eyes in a way that didn't feel like "just friends."

She felt paralyzed.

"Would you please talk to me? Jenna?"

But she couldn't. How could she possibly make him understand everything that was swirling through her head? She couldn't explain what that trailer represented. That it was everything she'd spent the last decade of her life trying to overcome, trying to put behind her.

She may have lost the status and wealth she'd had with Zach—or the appearance of wealth anyway. But she would not go back to ground zero.

*L*ucas sat with his hands at ten and two on the steering wheel, waiting, praying silently for Jenna. He'd never seen her like this. She was actually trembling in the seat beside him. Yet she refused to tell him what was wrong.

He wanted to take her into his arms, to just hold her until she stopped shaking. But he knew from past experience that it wasn't possible for him to "just" hold Jenna Morgan. And he'd promised her they'd just be friends for now. "How can I help if you won't talk to me?" he prodded, risking a hand on her shoulder.

"Maybe I don't want your help." She slid the little goldfish charm back and forth on the chain at her neck.

"Fine."

Silence.

He shook his head in frustration and started the

truck's engine. They drove back to his house in silence. This wasn't going to work. They were too different, wanted different things.

He knew Jenna thought they'd had an open and honest conversation that Christmas afternoon when they'd driven out to the country to talk. But there was too much they *hadn't* talked about. He hadn't revealed the biggest of his concerns: Jenna believed in God, but it was a stretch to say they shared the same faith. He'd always felt free to talk about his faith with her, and sometimes it felt as if she was close to understanding what it meant to him. But if there was any possibility of this friendship turning into something more, he needed to be sure where she stood. Dogs might be negotiable in their future, but faith wasn't.

He couldn't hold back the sigh that escaped him as they pulled into the driveway at his house. He pulled the truck up close to her car.

She turned to him with a sad smile. "Thanks for going with me, Luc. I'm sorry it was a wasted trip."

"I'm sorry, too. I'm sure you'll find . . . a place that's just right for you."

She looked at him as if she was trying to decipher a deeper meaning from his words. He hadn't intended one, but now that he thought about it . . .

She opened her door. "I'd better go. I have to work at four."

"Okay." He was tired of trying to pull

meaningful conversation out of her. Tired of trying to make their friendship work when he wasn't sure it was meant to.

He watched her get into her car and waited until she'd backed out of the driveway before he got out and went into the house.

How could one woman have the power to put him on top of the world one minute and in the depths of depression the next?

32

Ma was in the kitchen fixing a sandwich when Lucas came in. She must have come home for lunch when he was out with Jenna.

She looked up from the counter with a cheery smile. "Hey, you. Where have you been?"

Great. He was in no mood to talk. He just wanted to medicate himself with a strong cup of coffee and be left alone.

"I went to look at a house with Jenna."

"Oh? Did she find something?"

"No." He deposited his crutches in a corner of the kitchen and went to clean out the coffeemaker from breakfast.

"Is she looking to buy?"

"No. It was a rental." He drew fresh water and measured coffee into the filter. "Not what she was looking for, though."

"Oh? What *is* she looking for? I'll keep my ears open."

"I don't know what she's looking for, Ma." He felt bad for being short with her. He just didn't want to talk about Jenna Morgan.

Ma must have gotten the hint because she took her sandwich to the table with a magazine.

He waited for the first cup to brew, then filled a mug and headed down the hall to his room.

"Oh, Luc! I almost forgot." Ma's voice stopped him. "You've got a letter. It's with the other mail by the phone."

He went to flip through the stack of bills and junk mail until he came to a white business envelope addressed to him. The return address was handwritten and contained only a post office box number and zip code, but he recognized the address. It was from the guy at the training center in Tulsa, Wyatt Barnes.

He ripped open the envelope and extracted the single sheet it held.

Dear Mr. Vermontez,
Re: your application for our Accelerant Detection Canine Training Program.

Your résumé has been reviewed by the committee and placed on file with our Tulsa facility. As noted on the application, we typically place our trainees up to one year in advance. However, we have had a cancellation for the upcoming February-March training session in Tulsa, and your application is among those selected to fill the vacancy.

Providing both handler and canine still meet eligibility, can supply all necessary documents, medical/veterinary releases, etc., and handler/canine team can be available to report to the Tulsa facility by 8 a.m., Monday, February 9, for initial evaluation, you will be considered for inclusion in this session.

He felt like he was on a roller coaster.

"Is it good news?" Ma asked.

"Maybe. There's an opening in that training program in Tulsa."

"Tulsa?"

"I told you about it, Ma. The accelerant detection training." Why did she think he'd been spending every spare hour working with Sparky, especially since Gina had gone back to school?

She frowned. "I don't remember anything about it being in Tulsa."

Searching for the phone number on the letterhead, he fished his cell phone out of his pocket. "I need to go call them before they close for the day." Without giving his mother a chance to grill him, he headed down the hall to his room.

The letter said he was *among* those selected. So

it wasn't a done deal. Given his circumstances, he was probably at the bottom of their list. But it was worth a try.

He went back to his room, gently pushed Lucky off his desk, and settled into the chair. Dialing the number on the letterhead, he rehearsed how he'd describe his physical challenges. It struck him that his recent injury might actually be to his advantage since it camouflaged his injuries from the fire and appeared more temporary than his actual disability.

But life had been cruel to him too many times over the past year. He wouldn't let himself get too worked up yet. But even as that thought fired the synapses of his brain, a new flood of hope rushed through his veins.

Jenna adjusted the straps of the smock apron and straightened the Welcome to Hanson's pin on her left breast pocket. She'd been checking for three hours straight and her feet were killing her.

Things usually quieted down after six o'clock on Fridays, but she was the only checker up front tonight. She heard several women chattering and laughing back in the floral department. She hadn't seen them come in, but she was pretty sure they were the only customers in the store.

Maybe once they left she could take her break a little early, at least get off her feet for a minute. An idea had been brewing since she'd driven away from Luc this afternoon, and she was eager to get to a computer.

The feminine voices grew louder, and she turned to see a group of four women headed toward her. They were dressed to the nines and sporting enough bling among them to open a jewelry store.

Her breath caught. It was Vincette Gregory and Mallory Thames—and three other women from Clarissa's book club group. Vincette and Mallory were probably in their mid-thirties—closer to Jenna's age than Clarissa's. She'd never quite felt she fit in with Clarissa's social circle. Still, she'd considered these women friends at one time. Of course, she hadn't heard from any of them, from *any* of the Morgans' friends, since she'd been staying at Bryn's.

She'd always wondered how Clarissa had explained her absence from Hanover Falls' version of high society. Clarissa could be vindictive, but not if it reflected badly on the Morgans. And explaining why her daughter-in-law had been reduced to working as a checker at Hanson's definitely qualified.

Jenna finger-combed her hair and straightened the charm on her necklace, feeling like a seventh-grade nerd facing the cheerleading squad.

"Hi, Vincette. Hey, Mallory. You guys look nice. Out on the town tonight?"

"Oh, my gosh! Jenna, is that you?" Vincette turned to her posse. "Girls, look, it's Jenna!"

They all clustered around, offering friendly greetings, but she got the impression that some of them were feigning surprise at seeing her here.

"I haven't seen you for ages, Jen," Mallory gushed. "We'll have to get together sometime. I heard you sold your house. Are you still in the Falls?"

"I'm . . . staying with a friend—while I look for a place."

"Oh, listen." Mallory's eyes went wide. "The Jimersons *just* listed their house. It would be perfect for you, and you'd love Laurie's colors. You wouldn't have to change a thing."

Jenna had been to a Christmas party at the Jimersons' house two years earlier. It was a beautiful home. And so far out of her price range it boggled the mind. "That's . . . a little more than I'm looking for," she said.

She took a package of burp pads from the cart and scanned them, along with an assortment of baby items and a stork gift bag. "You must be going to a baby shower."

"Cinda Larson's." Mallory's smiled turned sheepish, and Jenna knew it was just dawning on her that Jenna hadn't been invited.

Cinda was another one from the book club group. Clarissa would be at the shower, too, no doubt.

Jenna finished ringing up their gift items and miscellaneous gum and snacks they'd collected at the checkout.

She somehow managed to keep her smile—and her dignity—pasted on until they were gone. But she wanted to curl up in a corner and weep.

Grow up, Morgan. These women had been as friendly as ever to her. It wasn't their fault she'd spent the afternoon looking at a trailer house to rent.

33

*J*enna arrived back at the apartment that night just as Bryn pulled into the parking lot. Jenna jumped out of the car and took an armload of groceries from her friend. "You're off early, aren't you?"

"Myrna let me leave after my break. Things were pretty dead in library land tonight."

"Lucky you." Jenna unloaded groceries onto the counter, and they worked together to put them away.

"Well, unfortunately she's not paying me to take off."

"Oh . . . Ouch. Hey, I got paid today. I really would like to write you a check for the rent." There went her savings. But it was only fair.

But Bryn's face fell and she held up a hand. "Oh, Jen, I wasn't hinting. Honest. I've told you before I don't want you paying. Shoot, I should be paying you for all the cleaning and laundry you do around here." She gave a lopsided grin. "Besides, you need to save your money. D-Day is upon us. I got the lease papers today. We've got exactly two weeks and one day to be out of here."

She blinked. "Wow. Are you ready . . . for the wedding, I mean?"

Bryn's eyes lit. "Honey, I've *been* ready." She giggled, but all at once her eyes brimmed with tears. "Oh, Jen, I can hardly wait."

Jenna reached across a bulky package of paper towels to give her friend a quick hug. "I'm so happy for you. And you know if there's anything I can do to help get ready, you just say the word. My mornings are free almost every day."

"There's really not much left to do. I'm telling you, I can't recommend this small-wedding-no-reception plan highly enough."

"Straight to the honeymoon, huh?" Jenna teased.

"Got that right."

They laughed and finished putting groceries away with Bryn chattering about the plans she and Garrett had made for a delayed honeymoon this summer when he was off from teaching. Listening to her, Jenna wondered if she would ever know this kind of happiness.

She was happy for her friend, but she was relieved when Bryn headed for her room and she could do the same.

She changed into her pajamas and brought her laptop to the bed. Sitting cross-legged on top of the quilt, she opened a browser and started exploring the possibility of selling some of her belongings. Judging by the prices people were getting for furniture and electronics and even clothing on craigslist and eBay, she had a gold mine sitting in the Morgans' garage.

She needed to get her stuff out of storage there. Surprisingly, in the six weeks since she'd left, they hadn't hounded her about retrieving her things. But if she could raise enough money selling some of her belongings, she'd be in good shape for getting an apartment, maybe even paying Bill and Clarissa a little. She'd felt as if she'd taken advantage of them, but under the circumstances she hadn't had much choice. Still, she didn't want to be beholden to them in any way. She would honor Zach's parents and have as much of a relationship with them as they would allow, but she also needed to cut the ties she could.

She would have to get photographs of everything she wanted to sell and then find a place to store it—a place where people could come and inspect things and where they could pick up any items that were too big to ship.

She'd check about renting a storage unit, and maybe Lucas would let her use his pickup to move things. She felt bad about the way they'd left things this afternoon. She knew he wasn't too happy with her about refusing to rent the trailer. Or maybe it was because she wouldn't talk to him about why.

But how could she explain it when it didn't make sense even to her? The trailer really wasn't bad. With decent furniture and her eye for decorating she could make it presentable—inside anyway. Short of camouflage, there wasn't much that could disguise the ugly turquoise and white outside.

She put the idea out of her mind. If she sold all her nice furniture, it was a moot point anyway.

She logged onto her bank's website and checked her balances again. Even if she could find an apartment as cheap as that trailer, it was going to stretch her thin to pay the rent every month, never mind utilities and groceries and gas for her car. How long would she have to live from hand to mouth like this? *Forever.* At the rate she was going, that was the only realistic answer.

She was starting to see how a woman could marry a man for his money.

The thought was like a knife to her heart. How could she have had such a casual thought when marrying a man for his money was exactly what she had done with Zach?

Yes, she'd been young and she'd been pregnant, but she hadn't been ignorant about the family she was marrying into. About the things the Morgan name had to offer. She hadn't figured on Zach dying. Or on his parents disowning her if she didn't conform to their wishes.

She stretched out on her belly on the bed and

started making a list of things she had to sell.

On a whim she grabbed her cell phone off the nightstand and dialed Lucas.

"Hey." His cheery reply made her wonder if she'd misread him this afternoon.

"Hi. You sound like you're in a good mood."

"I am."

"Any special reason why?"

"Maybe. I'm . . . not really ready to say anything about it yet."

"Oh? Well, now you have me curious." Was he just giving her a taste of her own medicine?

But he didn't sound angry at her. "I'll tell you in due time. It's no big secret or anything, but I don't want to say anything till I know for sure."

Now she was really curious. But she didn't dare push him.

"So what's up with you?" he asked.

"I have a big favor to ask."

"Okay . . ."

She told him about her plan to sell her stuff online. "Would you mind loaning me your truck? Maybe this weekend? You could have my car in exchange."

"How about I come and help?"

"You're still on crutches. I wouldn't ask you to do that."

"Well, I won't be much help, but I can carry the lighter stuff. I'll come and keep you company at least."

"I'd like that."

"I can order you around and tell you what you're doing wrong."

"*That* I wouldn't like." But she smiled. The thought of having him there made the whole ordeal seem far more palatable. "I'll let you know after I've talked to Bill and Clarissa and made sure I can get a storage unit. How does Sunday afternoon sound? I'm off work then."

"Sure. Just let me know what time."

"Thanks. And Luc? Thanks for offering to go with me this afternoon. I'm sorry I acted like a brat."

"You *can* be a brat," he said.

She didn't hear the laughter in his voice that she expected with a comment like that. "You almost sound like you meant that."

"Well, I kind of did." He cleared his throat. "I'm sorry. You *can* be a brat, but it wasn't my place to point it out."

"And just whose place do you think it was to point it out?" He still sounded dead serious, and she didn't know whether to be angry or hurt—or if this was just his sorry attempt at humor.

"That's why I said something. Because I don't think anyone else *would* point it out. Except maybe the Morgans—and you probably wouldn't listen to them."

She sat up on the bed and pressed her back against the headboard. "*Where* is this coming from?"

"I'm sorry, Jen, but it really ticks me off when someone is given a gift—a blessing—and they throw it back in God's face."

"*What* are you talking about?"

"I'm talking about the trailer house. The perfect place in a beautiful spot, at a price that's perfect for you. And you can't even give me one good reason why you're turning it down. I'm sorry, but that makes no sense to me."

Now she was angry. Furious. "What do you care where I live? And I sure don't have to explain anything to you, but for your infor—"

"Maybe because you asked me to go with you, I somehow got the impression that you wanted my opinion."

"Well, you got it wrong, buddy. And for your information I grew up in poverty and it stunk—big-time. I'd rather not be reminded of it every single day. In case you haven't noticed, I've had to give up a lot in the last couple of months. Is it too much to ask that I at least have a decent place to live?"

"That *is* a decent place to live. More than decent." His voice softened and she waited for the apology he owed her. "Jenna, I'm sorry you've lost so much. I know life hasn't been easy for you. But even if you were living at the homeless shelter right now, you'd be living in more luxury than half the world. You act like you deserve a house like the one you sold. And you make it like

Clarissa Morgan is such a snoot, but maybe you're more like her than you want to admit."

Okay, now he was hitting below the belt. How had a simple request to borrow his truck turned into an attack on her character? She gulped back a sudden flood of tears. "You know what? Never mind about the truck. I'll work something out. It's obvious you don't—"

"Jenna . . . Wait, Jenna. I'm sorry. I was out of line. Forgive me."

He did sound sincerely contrite now, but why had he spat those cruel things at her?

"Can we talk about it on Sunday?" His voice turned pleading now.

"I guess . . . I'll let you know if it works to go then." She worked to keep her tone cool and said good-bye quickly. She hung up and let the tears come. It was so unlike him to spout insults like that. Undeserved insults!

What was going on with him? She only hoped she could get the arrangements set up for Sunday. She did not want to go through another day with things the way they were between her and Luc.

34

"And for your information, I am not snooty." Jenna heaved one end of a hulky sofa table onto the tailgate of the pickup.

Lucas leaned on a crutch and balanced the other end of the table on one shoulder, looking decidedly unconvinced.

"I'm not! I've worked very hard to *not* be snooty because I've seen what that looks like." She looked pointedly toward the front door of the Morgans' house, feeling certain that Clarissa was watching them from behind one of the curtained windows.

They'd been arguing—albeit half-heartedly—all morning about the way he'd attacked her on the phone the other night.

Luc adjusted a bungee strap across a stack of crates and tugged at the Cardinals ball cap he wore. His dark hair curled out from under the bill in a way that made Jenna think of a little boy. A very cute little boy.

"Sometimes," he said, "being snooty isn't about what you say. It's more of an attitude."

"Oh, like when Clarissa pranced out here and offered to haul some of this stuff off to Goodwill."

"Yes, or like when someone looks down their nose at the idea of living in a certain trailer house."

"You don't have any—"

"Hang on." He held up a hand. "Let me finish. All I'm saying, Jen, is that you insult everyone who's ever lived in a trailer house when you refuse to live in one yourself."

"I don't see you moving to the homeless shelter."

His grin said she'd scored on that one. "Okay, good point. Let me rephrase that. All I'm saying is, just because you used to live in the ritzy part of town doesn't make you any better than the rest of us."

"I never said it did, Lucas." She was incredulous. Where was he getting this stuff?

"You don't always have to *say* something for people to know how you feel about it."

"Well, I didn't intend to come off that way."

"Fine. Where do you want these?" He balanced a stack of shoe boxes in one arm.

She did a quick tabulation. How much of the hundreds of dollars she'd spent on shoes could she recoup on eBay? Probably a fraction. How could she ever have thought it was okay to spend two hundred dollars on a pair of shoes when her credit cards were already maxed out?

Still, almost all of those shoes had been on clearance. And Clarissa had encouraged her, assuring her those were bargain prices for such top brands. It was all about brands for Clarissa. Of course, she'd had an eager student in her daughter-in-law. Jenna closed her eyes and saw only the astronomical credit card bills she was still struggling to pay off.

Clarissa had always joked after their spending sprees that shopping was cheaper than therapy. Now Jenna wasn't so sure. Though she was starting to see that the shopping had indeed been a sort of therapy for her—it filled a void in her life.

She knew what Lucas would say about that: a *God-shaped void.*

She pushed the thought aside and looked over the stacks of boxes and furniture in the back of the truck—not even half of what was still in the Morgans' garage. Maybe by amassing all this "proof" of her financial status, she *was* trying to prove that she was not that little girl who'd grown up in the Shady Groves Trailer Court—a place which, contrary to its name, had no groves and consequently no shade.

She eyed Lucas. "Can we talk about something else?"

"Please."

"So, are you ready to tell me why you were in such a good mood when I called Friday night? Even though"—she cleared her throat and mumbled under her breath—"you're certainly in a cranky mood right now."

"Hey, I heard that." He grinned and poked playfully at her leg with the tip of one crutch.

Jenna gave an inward sigh of relief. The fight was over and they were back to familiar teasing. She liked this much better.

He hefted a box to his shoulder and balanced it with one hand, the other gripping one of his crutches like a walking stick. "So you're going to put all this stuff on eBay?"

"Are you purposely changing the subject?" She had to know what he was obviously trying to avoid telling her. "Maybe I'm being too snoopy, which"—she winked—"in case you weren't aware, is different than snooty."

"Ha ha," he deadpanned. But she detected a glint of playfulness in his eyes.

"Well?"

He dipped his head. "I'm not sure I'm ready to say anything yet."

"Can I at least have a hint? You've got me really curious."

He backed up to the extended tailgate and hoisted himself onto it. He sat there, legs swinging, spinning one of his crutches like a top. "A clue, huh?"

She jumped up beside him, waiting, trying to imagine what kind of news he could be holding out on.

"I'll just say this: if this thing goes through, it will be Sparky's news as much as mine."

"Oh! Are they taking him at the fire station?"

"Nope." He shook his head.

"Does it have something to do with all the training you've been doing with him?"

"Yep."

She giggled. "Am I getting warm?"

"You said a clue."

"Okay, I give up. Just tell me!"

She got the impression he was itching to do just that. But he made her wait. He jabbed at a clump of mud the pickup's tires had deposited on the Morgans' pristine driveway, seeming deep in thought. Finally he turned to meet her eyes. "Okay, it's not for sure, but I got—*Sparky* and I got selected for an accelerant detection training program in Tulsa. Usually it takes a year or more to get into this place, but apparently there was a cancellation, so we got moved up on the list."

"Wow. That's . . . great." She swallowed the lump that lodged in her throat. "Tulsa, huh?" That was hours away. How was he going to manage that? It was too far to commute. . . .

"Yeah, well, I won't know for sure until next week sometime. It depends on how many of the other alternates could go on such short notice."

"Go? How does that work? If it's in Tulsa, I mean?"

"We go to the Tulsa facility for the training. The program is pretty intensive, but when we get out of there, Sparky should be able to alert on over a dozen different accelerants. Then he can work with a handler for a fire station, or with a fire inspector. There are a lot of possibilities once he's been through the six weeks of training."

"Six weeks?" She pressed her lips together. She hadn't meant that to come out quite so desperate. But six *weeks?* "Will you come home on weekends?"

He shook his head. "The training is pretty much twenty-four/seven. I'll make a quick trip to Springfield for Ma and Geoff's wedding on Valentine's Day, and I may be able to come home for a short weekend or two after that, but even if I do, we'll be in training mode. It's a pretty big commitment."

She felt as if he'd just slapped her. "What about your leg? How are you going to manage on crutches?"

"Same as I do now. Actually, the doc cleared me to get rid of these things next week"—he poked his cheek out with his tongue—"but I knew you'd be slave-driving me, so I thought I'd better bring them along today."

She ignored that. "When do you leave?" Her voice came out in a squeak. Six weeks was an eternity. She quickly did the math. It would be the end of March—spring—before he came back. She'd hoped he would go with her to Bryn's wedding. Now he might not even be back in time. What did it say about their friendship that he would choose to go away for that length of time?

She stopped short. Hadn't she been thinking about the possibility of moving to Springfield herself? When people were "just friends," they didn't make life-changing decisions with each other in mind.

"*If* we get accepted, we'd have to report to the facility on the ninth."

"Of?"

"February."

"I don't like this," she admitted. He may as well know how she was feeling because she wasn't doing a very good job of hiding her emotions.

"What do you mean, you don't like it?"

"You running off like this."

"You say it like you mean running *away*."

She could see his defenses prickle. "Well? If the shoe fits."

He narrowed his eyes at her. "And what exactly would I be running away from?"

"Us?" She was so going to regret her transparency later.

In one smooth motion he pushed off the tailgate, slid the crutches under his arms, and pivoted to face her. "There *is* no 'us,' Jen. You've made that perfectly clear."

She couldn't refute that. He was right. She'd held him at arm's length. Why? All she'd wanted since that first kiss was to be with him. Instead she'd pushed him away. Again and again.

He swung back a step and looked at the ground, rocking between the crutches. "I think it might be best this way. Give us some time to figure things out. And solve some other problems in the meantime."

She studied him. "Other problems? Like what?"

"Like the fact that no matter how much I try to tell myself we're just friends, that's not the way I want things." He took off his cap and raked his fingers through matted curls. "I'm not sure how long I could have stuck around and tried to pretend otherwise."

She opened her mouth to argue, but she had nothing.

Movement behind Luc drew her attention. The door off the side courtyard entrance opened, and Clarissa came toward them bearing a tray with pitcher and glasses and a plate of cookies. "Thought you might like a snack. I'm sorry Bill didn't get home in time to help. Maybe next load? It looks like you still have quite a bit to pack up." She nodded back toward the garage.

"We may not get it all today—I hope that's not a problem," Jenna said.

"Just let us know when you think you can get the rest." Clarisssa carried the tray to the pickup and set it on the tailgate, then poured lemonade into tall glasses, chattering about the weather and wondering why Bill wasn't home yet.

Lucas thanked her for the lemonade and helped

himself to a cookie. "I remember these," he said, talking over a mouthful. "Zach used to bring these to the station. You were famous for your oatmeal cookies."

Clarissa beamed. "He always did have a sweet tooth." She smiled up at Luc, her eyes shiny with unshed tears. "Well, you eat these up. Take home what you don't eat. Bill and I are trying to watch our waistlines."

She started back for the house. "Jen, just bring the tray in when you're finished, would you?"

"I will. Thanks, Clarissa." She felt a tug of her heart as she spoke the words. As much as they'd been at odds, she'd missed Clarissa. She wasn't sure if she could trust her warmth. Maybe she was just behaving for Lucas's sake.

She felt an odd prick in her conscience. Her own attitude hadn't always been that great where Clarissa was concerned. And she knew exactly when things had gone sour between them. It was after she'd lost the baby—the second baby. Since she'd never told the Morgans about that pregnancy—never told anyone—she'd withdrawn from them. Secrets had a way of doing that. Guilt nudged at her.

She'd been at home the night she miscarried. Alone. She'd known right away what was happening. Even though she wasn't nearly as far along as she'd been when she lost the first baby, everything else felt the same.

Maybe if she'd gone to the doctor when the cramping and bleeding first started . . . maybe they could have saved the pregnancy. But she hadn't really wanted that. She'd lived every day since Zach's death in terror, thinking about the prospect of raising a baby alone—the way her own mother had. She could not do that to a child. She couldn't.

When the cramps started, she'd felt hope. Relief. What kind of woman felt that way about losing a *baby?*

And when it was all over, she'd been so afraid that everyone—most of all Zachary's parents—would be able to see in her eyes what had happened, and exactly how she'd felt about it.

To this day Jenna wasn't sure why she hadn't told Bill and Clarissa. Maybe she'd grown so weary of grieving, so tired of having everyone look at her with those sympathetic eyes. Tired of crying with Zach's mother, as if by hanging on to Jenna, Clarissa could somehow hang on to her son.

It would have killed Clarissa to know she'd also lost another grandchild—and one final chance for Zach to live on in the life of a son or daughter. And Jenna knew Clarissa would have blamed Jenna somehow for losing the baby.

She hadn't been strong enough to face that.

But Lucas needs to know. She looked around as if she'd heard an audible voice. It was an odd thought. It was only her subconscious. He *didn't* need to know—unless they were to become more than friends.

And with him moving to Tulsa, that possibility had dimmed until she could scarcely imagine it.

35

Sunday, February 8

*L*ucas sucked in a breath and glanced around his room one last time, making sure he had everything he needed. Making sure he really wanted to do this.

Didn't matter. It was too late now. They were expecting him and Sparky at the training center tonight. Classes started first thing in the morning. Sparky would stay with him in a dorm-style room at the facility for the six weeks of the program. Luc had thought seriously about the possibility of looking for permanent housing in Tulsa while he was there.

Of course, that would depend on whether he could find work there. He hadn't told anyone— had barely dared to think about it—but he'd fantasized about their offering him a job with the center. He hoped they'd be impressed with how much he'd already taught his canine companion.

He mentally rolled his eyes. For all he knew, he might get there and discover he'd ruined Sparky for life with his unorthodox training methods. But he didn't think so. He'd done his research, and though there were differing opinions on the best way to train a dog for accelerant detection, there was no denying what the results with Sparky had been. He was a smart dog, and as Pop would have said, he was "coachable."

Lucas flipped off the light in his bedroom, but at the last second he went back to his closet and grabbed the crutches, adding them to the growing pile of luggage in the hallway. He hadn't used them for more than a week, but if he somehow messed up his leg during a training exercise, he didn't want to have to search all over Tulsa for another pair.

Geoff poked his head around the corner. "You need some help loading the truck?"

"Hey, man, that'd be great. Thanks." He showed Geoff which things needed to go in the back, and working together, they had the pickup loaded and a tarp tied down over everything in no time.

He wondered if Jenna remembered that this was the day he was leaving. He'd thought she might come to see him off. She was probably working. She'd been trying to get as many hours as she could. Maybe he should have invited her.

Oh well . . . he'd give her a call once he got on the road.

After helping her move her stuff to the storage unit that day, he'd gone back the next evening to get the last of her furniture from the Morgans' garage. He hadn't seen her since then, but they'd talked on the phone and e-mailed several times.

He knew she was busy trying to sell her stuff. She'd called him all excited a couple of nights ago because she'd gotten seven hundred dollars for a set of chairs.

He was glad she'd found a way to raise some money. Of course, by the time she finally got her own place, she wouldn't have a stick of furniture to put in it. Oh, well . . . let her figure that out.

She'd somehow wrangled another month in Bryn's apartment. He wasn't sure of the details—something about Bryn using the deposit refund for an extra month—but he worried about what Jenna would do when that time was up. He'd tried to stay out of it since the trailer fiasco.

She'd been a little cool toward him ever since he'd told her about his plans for Tulsa. Maybe she was still ticked at him because he'd called her a brat. The thought made him smile. But no, he thought they'd joked their way past that. And he'd had the good sense not to bring it up again since that afternoon at the Morgans'.

He didn't know what would become of their friendship with him going to Tulsa. Maybe it was for the best. He still felt this crazy magnetic pull toward her—probably any guy with half a brain would say the same thing about Jenna Morgan. But there were just too many things going against them—the miles between the Falls and Tulsa being a biggie. But man, he'd missed her in the two and a half weeks since he'd last seen her. He didn't want to think about putting three hundred miles between them.

He pulled the door to his room shut. Ma was waiting downstairs and there were sure to be tears. They were both leaving this house. Pop's house. It was sad to think of the place empty and forlorn. If he did end up coming back from Tulsa, it would be unbearable to live here without his mom. Sure, his sisters might be back for the summer, but that was doubtful, especially if he stayed in Tulsa.

One day at a time, Vermontez.

Ma met him at the garage door with a brown paper sack.

"What's this?" Lucas unfolded the top and inhaled the aroma of warm chocolate chip cookies. He opened the top wider and peered inside. "Holy cow, Ma, there's enough in here to feed the entire city of Tulsa."

Geoff scanned the kitchen counters. "I hope you saved a couple of those for me."

She patted her fiancé's cheek. "Don't you worry. You're taken care of." She turned to Lucas and folded the bag closed again. "Don't you eat all these on the way there either. I made enough to share. I thought it might be a good way to make friends."

He laughed. "Right, and I'll be sure and change my socks and underwear every day, too."

"Yes, and brush your teeth at least once a week," she said. But her laughter caught on a sob.

He pulled her in for a hug. "It's only a couple hours from Springfield, and hey, I'll be there next weekend. You can surely live without me for a week."

She pulled out of his embrace. "Just go. Let me have a good cry and I'll be okay. You call the minute you get there, you hear?"

"I will, Ma. Love you." He gave her another quick hug, then shook Geoff's hand. "I guess you'll be wearing a tux next time I see you."

Geoff stole a glance at Ma and chuckled. "We're still debating that."

Ma gave Geoff the evil eye, then looked back at Lucas. "He *will* be wearing a tux."

"Just so *I* don't have to." He shot Geoff a smug grin.

"Hey, that reminds me," Ma said. "I know you're not coming back to the Falls before the wedding, but I'm sure Jenna told you I invited her. Where is she, by the way? I thought she might come to see you off."

Yeah, me too, Ma. "She usually works weekends."

"Oh." She studied his face. "Well, anyway, she e-mailed a lovely note, but she didn't think she'd be able to come. I wish you'd convince her. The girls enjoyed her so much at Christmas, and I know Abi and Baba would love to see her again."

Jenna hadn't said a word about Ma's invitation. Interesting. He'd have to ask her about that. She surely hadn't planned to surprise him and just show up at the wedding in Springfield next weekend. The possibility cheered him more than it should have.

"I'll talk to her, Ma." He looked pointedly at his watch. "I'd better hit the road."

*W*hen the Hanover Falls water tower disappeared from his rearview mirror, Lucas dug his cell phone out of his front pocket and called Jenna. "Hey. It's me." As if she didn't know from the caller ID.

"Hi."

"I just thought . . . I'd give you a call."

"Oh."

"Are you at work?"

"No, I'm home."

This wasn't going well. "So do you work tonight?"

"Not till tomorrow night. Are you in Tulsa?"

"Just leaving town."

"Oh . . ." Her voice warmed a little.

"There's zero traffic on the Interstate, so I should make good time. I'll probably get to Tulsa by eight or so."

"Oh. So you're already . . . gone?"

It struck him then: when he'd said "just leaving town" she must have thought he was planning to stop by to see her before he left. "Yeah, I'm gone. I thought you might come and see me off."

"I didn't want to come uninvited."

"Jenna, you're always welcome."

"Oh, good. Nice to know that. I'll be right over."

Uh-oh. She was not a happy camper. "I'm sorry. I should have called you—before I left."

"That would have been nice."

"I just didn't want you to feel obligated to come. I figured you'd probably have to work and—" He stopped abruptly, fresh out of excuses. "I'm sorry. I wish I'd called."

"Well . . . you called now. I guess that's something. Unless you called to tell me not to call you ever again."

He was disproportionately grateful for the smile he heard in her voice. "Not a chance. I miss you already."

She blew a sarcastic "ha" into the phone.

"Actually . . . I really do. Miss you, I mean."

Silence on her end.

"You there?"

"I'm here," she said. "I'm just trying to figure you out."

"Good luck with that. *I'm* still trying to figure me out."

"Yeah, tell me about it."

He laughed. And briefly considered turning

around at the next exit and driving back to the Falls to tell her a proper good-bye. But he kept driving.

And they kept talking, finding—finally—the easy, teasing repartee they'd started out with that night in the coffee shop.

Almost three hours later he started seeing billboards for Tulsa businesses. And his cell phone was chirping at him about a low battery. "Hey, Jen . . . I need to let you go." Oh, he did not mean those words. Letting her go was the last thing he wanted to do.

"Thanks for calling. I hope everything goes okay for you there."

"Yeah, well . . . I'm a little nervous. I'd appreciate your prayers."

A brief hesitation. "I'll pray for you, Luc."

Her response made him pull the phone away from his ear, not sure he'd heard right. He'd said the words without really thinking. The kind of generic request for prayer he'd make to Ma or his sisters. "Thanks, Jen. That . . . means a lot."

"Tell your mom I'll be thinking about her next weekend."

"She said she invited you to the wedding. Why don't you come?"

"I don't think so."

"Why not? I know it would mean a lot to Ma. It would mean a lot to me, too." May as well be honest.

"You'll be busy. I'd just be in the way."

"No, you won't. I need somebody to sit with. And Ma and Geoff will run off on their honeymoon right after the wedding and I'll be all alone and lonesome."

"What about your sisters?"

Busted. "They'll be there. But you know how it is . . . three's a crowd."

"Poor baby."

"Besides, they want you to come as much as I do."

"Yeah, right."

"No, I'm serious. Ma said so herself just this morning." He didn't tell her he suspected his mother was doing a little matchmaking.

More silence on Jenna's end.

"I'll take you out to dinner after the wedding."

"Deal," she said quickly.

That made him laugh. "If you're serious, I'll call you later this week and we'll figure out where to meet."

"I'm serious. Now you'd better go before your phone dies." She cleared her throat. "Hey . . ."

"Yeah?"

"You'll do great tomorrow."

"Thanks, Jen."

Great. Just great. The woman waited till he was headed out of state to make up to him?

Still, his heart hadn't felt this light in a very long time. And he would see Jenna next weekend.

36

*T*hanks for shopping Hanson's. Did you find everything you need?"

Jenna looked up from her spiel to see Emily Vermontez smiling at her. "Hi, Jenna. How's it going?"

"Emily! Hi there. Are you ready for the wedding?"

"We're ready." Emily placed a carton of yogurt and some bananas on the conveyor. "Lucas tells me you're coming after all. Geoff and I were so happy to hear that."

"I'm looking forward to it." She didn't mention that it was more Luc than the wedding itself that she was looking forward to. "I'm glad he remembered to tell you. I hope it was okay to send my RSVP through him."

"Absolutely. It's just a small ceremony. Nothing fancy. But we'll love having you there." Emily handed her a five-dollar bill and waited for her change. "Hey, have you found an apartment yet? Luc said you were still looking."

Jenna wondered if Lucas had told his mother about her meltdown at that stupid trailer. She hoped not, but she was discovering that he and his mom were pretty tight. "I'm still looking."

"You're still staying with Bryn—is that right?"

She nodded and put Emily's groceries in a bag. "Yes, but I have to be out by the end of the month." She was starting to feel a little panicky at the thought.

"That's what Luc said. Well, I just want you to know that you'd be more than welcome to stay at our place for a few weeks. Geoff's been helping me move my things to his house this week, and with Luc in Tulsa until spring, the place will just be sitting empty. I can't offer you anything long-term, but I'd be glad to have you stay there while you're looking."

"Thank you." Jenna was stunned at the offer . . . at the timing of it. "I'll definitely keep that in mind. I mean—I'll let you know right away so you can find someone else if I decide—"

"Oh, no." Emily waved her off, then winked. "This is an exclusive offer for you only. I'm sure you'd rather not move twice if you can help it, but it just struck me as an idea if you need a place temporarily."

"How much would the rent be?"

"Oh, goodness, no. I wouldn't dream of charging you. You'd be doing me a favor. I would be relieved to not have the house sitting empty for so long. I guess you could pay the utility bills for the weeks you're there. And I may leave some plants there that I'd want you to water. You just let me know."

"Wow . . . thank you again. I'll let you know as soon as I can."

She watched Emily leave the store, grateful she didn't have another customer in line.

She grabbed a spray bottle and started wiping down her conveyor. It could just be a coincidence. She didn't want to jump to conclusions. But it seemed awfully strange that less than two hours after praying the second genuine prayer of her adult life, she had an answer to that prayer.

Out of the blue.

If this was God—and she had to believe it was—she hoped He'd answered her first prayer, too—that Lucas was getting along well with the training, and that he was happy in Tulsa.

Just not too *happy, God.*

Thursday, February 12

9 think you'll be very comfortable here." Emily switched on the light to reveal a large cozy room with sloped ceilings, white wainscoting on three walls, and cushy carpeting underfoot. "There's a three-quarter bath in here, but you'll have to go down the hall if you want to soak in a tub."

Jenna couldn't curb the smile that came. "It's beautiful. Just perfect."

It really was. A far cry from the master bedroom in the Brookside house with its Jacuzzi tub and twin walk-in closets. And not even on the map

327

compared to Bill and Clarissa's master suite. But it was a lovely room, and it suited her somehow.

"Well," Emily said, "since all my kids still have stuff in their rooms, I thought you may as well use the master bedroom. And I got most of my things moved over to Geoff's earlier this week." She thought a trace of sadness flashed across Emily's countenance.

As happy as she seemed with Geoff, it had to be bittersweet moving from this home where she'd raised her children—and this room she'd shared with Lucas's father.

"I can't thank you enough, Emily. I wasn't sure what I was going to do. Are you sure I can't pay you at least a little something for rent?"

"Honey, if you just pay the utilities for the few weeks you're here, I am money ahead. Believe me, you're helping me as much as I'm helping you."

Jenna doubted that, but she loved Emily for saying so. "Well, thank you again. I'm saving as much as I can toward an apartment, but I have . . . quite a few bills to pay off, too. That's made it tough to put anything aside." Again, she wondered what Lucas had told his mother about her situation. Somehow, though, with Emily it didn't matter. She didn't feel judged by this woman—only embraced and accepted.

"I'm happy it worked out this way." Emily went to smooth the quilt on the queen bed. "You're actually an answer to my prayers."

There it was again. Answered prayers.

"Oh," Emily said, "I forgot to say something when we talked before. I hope this isn't a deal breaker, but Lucas left his cat." She stuck her head out into the hallway. "Lucky? Here, kitty, kitty . . . You're not allergic or anything, are you?"

"I don't think so. I've never had a cat." She'd never had a *pet,* but she didn't tell Emily that.

"Well, Lucky's around here somewhere. He usually hangs out in Lucas's room. He mostly makes himself invisible, but if he bothers you, you can put him out in the garage. He's used to being outside when it's not too cold."

Closing the bedroom door behind them, Emily clucked her tongue. "I don't know what we're going to do with that cat if you find an apartment before Lucas gets back. Geoff's not crazy about the idea of having a cat, and the girls can't have pets in the dorms, of course. I guess we'll cross that bridge when we come to it." She sighed, then brightened. "Well, I guess I'll see you in Springfield in a few days."

Jenna was glad Emily seemed happy about the fact.

"I'd offer you a ride, but I'm heading down there this evening."

"Oh, I don't mind driving. I'm looking forward to it."

"The wedding? Or seeing a certain tall, dark, and handsome fellow who will be in attendance?"

Jenna felt a flush creep up her neck. "Um . . . both."

"Good answer." Emily's wink put her at ease again.

They finished the tour of the house, and Emily showed her where everything was, advising her about trash pickup day and where Lucky's food and litter were stored.

Walking through the tidy house with Luc's mother, Jenna began to see it in a different way from the first time Lucas had brought her there.

Perhaps it was the fact that Emily had moved some of the furniture and decorative items to Springfield and rearranged the rest in a scaled-back style that was more Jenna's taste. But for whatever reason, what had first appeared a mite shabby and out-of-date now seemed only warm and inviting.

It probably also had something to do with her memories of spending Christmas here and of the warmth she'd felt from Luc's family. But it was something more. There was a spirit about this house that was gracious and welcoming and embracing.

Of course that spirit was embodied in the people who lived here, but those qualities lingered in her memories, and even in the fragrance of the house—a heady mixture of cinnamon and coffee and something piney and clean.

She could easily picture herself coming home to this place after a hard day at Hanson's. She could set up her laptop at the dining room table and work her eBay sales. Or do some baking in the large kitchen—a hobby she'd enjoyed at the Brookside house but had scarcely thought about since she'd had to let it go.

She sighed. She hadn't even moved in and she was dreading the day she'd have to move out of the Vermontez home.

Slow down, Morgan. She had to get out of Bryn's apartment first. Her friend had been so gracious to let her stay all these weeks, but she knew Bryn was getting nervous about "kicking her out." Lucas had jokingly called her a "sofa surfer." Ordinarily she liked his teasing—and she knew he hadn't meant anything by it—but it had hit a little too close to home.

On top of that she was starting to feel a little like a fifth wheel now that Garrett was spending more and more time at the apartment while he and Bryn worked to get ready for their wedding and plan their honeymoon.

Weddings. It seemed as if everyone she knew was headed for the altar.

"I'll go ahead and give you the key now," Emily was saying.

Jenna shook herself from her reverie and took the key Emily held out. It was on a little plastic house-shaped keychain, and Jenna read the fancy script beneath the logo: *As for me and my house, we will serve the Lord.*

She shook her head. She was starting to think Someone was trying to tell her something.

37

Friday, February 13

"How's it going, Vermontez?"

Lucas wiped the sweat off his forehead with the sleeve of his T-shirt. His ankle throbbed and his back was in spasms, trying to compensate for the trauma he'd put his leg through, but he and Sparky had performed well and he was feeling elated in spite of his pain. "It's going good, Wyatt."

They were on Day Five of the program and already Sparky was alerting on two new substances. He'd had to unlearn a few bad habits that Lucas had unintentionally reinforced working with Sparky at home. But they'd both adjusted quickly to this facility's training methods.

"You let me know if you need to back off a little," the director said. "No sense in you getting injured again. It's not like this is life and death or anything."

"Not today maybe, but someday it could be." Who knew that better than him?

"Okay. I'll trust you to know your own limits, Vermontez."

He hadn't worked this hard since he and Zach were going through training as rookies with Station 2. It felt good, even if he was discovering muscles he'd forgotten he had.

He liked Wyatt Barnes, the guy who ran the program. Barnes had a good reputation and good connections to place the dogs he trained. Lucas was finding it fulfilling work, and Sparky was doing him proud. The dog was eager to get out to the field every day and was undistracted by the other animals—at least after that first day, when it had been a zoo.

He leaned down and scrubbed his buddy's head. "Good job, Spark. Way to show 'em out there today."

A couple of the other guys in the training program walked by, headed to play their usual round of noon-hour pickup basketball. "You coming, Vermontez? We're going for pizza after." Barnes had given them an extra hour for lunch today.

"No, man . . . thanks anyway. I'm beat. Think I'll just get a sandwich out of the vending machine." Oh, for the day when he could have worked this hard all day and still gone to play some ball.

His ankle was holding up pretty well, but he knew his limitations and he was pretty close to the edge of them right now. About all he was up for was a hot shower, a handful of aspirin, and a nap. Maybe he'd call for a pizza later. If he could stay awake long enough to eat it.

He was grateful for times like these that allowed him to come back to his room and crash. Any day that left him with an ounce of energy he only burned up worrying about the future. About whether he'd be able to find Sparky a working gig when this was through, about whether that would mean giving Sparky up.

The first few days he'd worried about whether he could even finish the course, but he'd managed to keep up with the rest of the handlers pretty well. The instructors had made a few minor concessions for him—he hadn't had to climb any ladders or scale any walls—but that was more a concession to his most recent injury than to his permanent disability. He was encouraged by what he'd accomplished, even if it had cost him some major pain.

He'd had nothing to offer Jenna before. But this training program had the potential to change that. And he was starting to think that once his ankle healed completely, he'd be able to hold his own in any detection exercise, real or staged, or in any fire scene inspection.

Still, a heavy truth weighed him down whenever he stopped long enough to turn it over in his mind: he would never again be in the physical condition required to be a working firefighter. Those days were over, stolen by the Grove Street fire and his own stupidity.

Here in Tulsa, alone in a drab dorm room, Lucas found the dreams of that terrible night returning, the tape rewinding and playing again and again, always with the same outcome: Pop dead. Zach and the others dead. Lucas done with firefighting. For good.

The difference now was that he was able to wake up and shake it off. Then he gave himself a different version of the same lecture he'd given Jenna about being grateful for the blessings, the advantages he'd been given.

He'd thought a lot about his blessings here. He'd had a father who'd loved him and sent him out into the world with all the tools he needed to make something of himself—even now, after tragedy had stolen so much that he valued.

Even though it had been short-lived, he'd been blessed to have the experience of being a firefighter. Even of saving a life or two in his brief career. Not everybody got such a privilege in a mere twenty-seven years of living.

Remembering the day he'd chewed Jenna out, he cringed, even as he chuckled to himself. She'd deserved it. He probably could have been a little more diplomatic in his delivery. Still, he was grateful they'd ended on a rather sweet note.

He needed to remember to e-mail her tonight. She'd asked him to send directions to the chapel in Springfield. He'd see her tomorrow. Now there was a seriously cheerful thought.

She'd asked him for pictures, too. Of the training facility and of him and Sparky. "I want to be able to picture where you are, and to see you and Sparky in action," her e-mail had said yesterday. He hadn't gotten around to taking any photos yet. Maybe he'd have one of the guys take some shots during training drills this afternoon.

His energy returned in a surge and he decided to get out of there. Maybe go for a burger and fries. And he could use a haircut before tomorrow. He grabbed the leash from its hook. "Come on, Sparky."

His loyal sidekick gave him a look that said he was up for anything.

Lucas stowed his gear in a locker, snapped the padlock shut, and headed out to his pickup with Sparky at his heel.

He hadn't left the parking lot yet when his phone buzzed. He looked at the caller ID and smiled. "Hey, Ma." They hadn't talked since he called Sunday night to let her know he'd arrived safely in Tulsa. He knew it had taken everything in her to wait this long before calling him again.

"How's everything going? Are you liking the school?"

"It's going good." He told her a little bit about his days, trying not to let her hear the weariness in his voice.

After making small talk for ten minutes, he made excuses to hang up. "I'm headed downtown for a haircut. I should probably let you go."

Ma hesitated on her end, then blurted, "Have you been hearing our news? About the shelter."

"The homeless shelter?" Something in her tone put him on alert. "No, what's going on?"

"There was another fire."

"You have got to be kidding me! When? Was anybody hurt?"

"Last night. Nobody hurt, but they were saying on the news this morning that they're probably going to shut the shelter down."

"Was it that bad?"

"No, I think once again they caught it before it did any serious damage. But it's obvious somebody is setting these fires, and the Hanover Falls police don't have the manpower to watch the place twenty-four/seven. It's not safe to have people staying there when the place has been a target so many times now. I don't see how they can keep it open."

"Yeah, and that's probably exactly what the sicko doing this is hoping—that they'll shut the place down." He let out a growl of frustration. "Why can't they catch this guy?" He wondered what his buddies at the station had to say about it. The old longing came back with a vengeance. He would have given anything to be back at Station 2 with his crew right now.

337

Ma must have read his thoughts. "You have more important things to worry about, Luc. I hated to even say anything, but I figured you'd hear it anyway. For now, you just concentrate on that training. Except for tomorrow," she added quickly. "Then you just concentrate on getting to the church on time."

"Don't you worry. I'll be there."

38

Saturday, February 14

Jenna put the car in Park, quickly changed into a pair of heels, then climbed out of the car, searching the parking lot for Lucas's truck.

Emily was being married in the chapel on the campus where Geoff taught, and Luc had said he'd meet her here, but she didn't see any sign of him yet.

She locked the car and straightened, smoothing out her suit jacket. She tried unsuccessfully to pinch pleats back into her wool pants, but they'd suffered from too many days in the cramped closet at Bryn's, and she couldn't afford to take them to the cleaners. She caught her reflection in the car window and hoped she was dressed right for a chapel wedding.

She couldn't remember when she'd been so

nervous. It had been years since she'd darkened the door of a church. Early in their marriage she and Zach had let Bill and Clarissa talk them into going to church with them a few times, but once Zach figured out that his father was mostly there to troll for clients, that had been the end of it for them.

Using the car's side mirror, she rearranged the silk scarf around her throat.

"Hey, beautiful."

She jumped and whirled around to see Lucas walking toward her. He looked handsome as all get-out in a dark suit, crisp white shirt, and baby blue tie that complemented his olive complexion. He was off the crutches and back to using his cane. She didn't think she was imagining that his limp had diminished.

"You don't clean up bad yourself," she said, unable to stop smiling.

He held out his arms and she walked into them for a much-too-brief hug. Her heart revved uncomfortably and she took a deep breath, trying to get it under control.

"You didn't bring Sparky?"

"A buddy agreed to watch him for me tonight. Why? Do you miss him?"

She rolled her eyes. "I didn't say that."

Laughing, he glanced around at the complex of buildings. "Have you figured out where the chapel is yet?"

"Didn't you have a rehearsal last night?"

"No. I just drove in from Tulsa. Ma said it's going to be pretty low-key. I guess they decided they didn't need to rehearse."

She pointed to a sign across the parking lot. "That looks like a directory." They walked together over to the map and figured out where the chapel was.

The air was chilly, but she quickly forgot about how cold it was as they caught up on each other's news.

They found the chapel, and Geoff and Emily greeted them just inside the foyer.

"Oh, good . . . you found it," Emily said, giving Luc a hug. "The girls are already here . . . and Abi and Baba." She pointed toward the sanctuary. She reached for Jenna's hand and squeezed it. "I'm so glad you came, Jenna."

"You look beautiful," Jenna said, genuinely admiring her elegant street-length dress of ecru lace.

Lucas shook Geoff's hand and nodded his way with a smirk. "Nice tux."

Geoff rolled his eyes, and he and Emily laughed along with Luc. Jenna looked on with a weak smile, not getting what was so funny.

"You guys go on in," Emily said, herding them toward the sanctuary. "Don't forget, we'll see you afterward for dinner."

"Don't worry, Ma, we're not about to miss dinner."

Jenna counted about twenty people scattered throughout the tiny chapel. As they walked down the aisle, Lucas quietly greeted several people before leading her to the pew where his grandparents and sisters were already seated.

She gave a little wave to Victoria and Gina and slid in beside their grandmother. Luc put a hand lightly on Jenna's back, leaning across to speak to his grandparents. "Abi, Baba, you remember Jenna—from Christmas?"

"Of course." Mrs. Vermontez patted Jenna's knee. "Don't you look pretty today."

Jenna felt herself flush. "Why, thank you." She glanced up at Lucas, grinning. "Your grandson looks pretty spiffy, too, don't you think?"

Luc's grandfather winked at her. "We Vermontez men make a point of always trying to look spiffy."

Jenna laughed, charmed by Luc's Baba, and nursing a pang of envy that she'd never known her grandparents. She hoped Lucas Vermontez realized how very lucky he was.

Music spilled from the speakers at the front of the small chapel, and a hush fell over the group. A young man wearing a clerical collar came through a door at the right side of the low stage, followed by Geoff and Emily. She carried a simple bouquet of lilies, and Geoff had a small leatherbound book in his hand.

Jenna gave a little sigh. There was just

341

something about weddings . . . no matter the age of the bride and groom.

Lucas must have felt the same stirrings because he reached for Jenna's hand. She glanced up at him. He kept his eyes to the front of the chapel, but he laced his fingers with hers and gave her hand a little squeeze as the minister began reading from a Bible on the lectern.

*W*atching his mother standing beside Geoff, smiling up at him that way, Lucas felt a lump in his throat.

I miss you, Pop. Man, I miss you. . . .

Ma's face glowed with joy. How could he not be happy for her? But so many memories flooded his mind. And a haunting sense that things would never again be the same. Ma would make a new life with Geoff, and memories of Pop would fade.

The minister finished his reading from Song of Solomon—a rather racy passage for his mother's wedding, Luc thought. But as he recalled the entire book, he supposed the guy could have chosen worse. Acutely aware of Jen's hand in his, he listened as the minister shared a few words on marriage.

After the couple had made their vows, Lucas was surprised to see his mom and Geoff turn to face their guests.

Geoff picked up a microphone and looked over

the audience with the confidence of a professor. "Emily and I want to thank you for coming to share this day with us. As most of you know, these past couple of years have been very difficult for both of us." He took her hand, smiling down at her. "We have been blessed to enjoy long, happy marriages—and in Emily's case, the gift of children." He nodded at Lucas and his sisters. "We've learned the hard way that the Lord does give, and sometimes take away. But we are grateful that He also restores happiness after sorrow. Emily—" Geoff's voice broke and he lowered the mike, composing himself.

Lucas felt his own throat swell with emotion, and from the corner of his eye, he saw Jenna swipe at her cheeks. He wondered if she was remembering her own wedding day.

Geoff cleared his throat and continued. "Emily is God's gift—a gift beyond belief to me—and I thank each of you for coming today to witness our vows and to share our joy as we commit our lives to each other. On this day—this sacred day—we want to first of all honor the memory of Manny and of Cynthia. Our loved ones are safe in God's care now, and we'd like to think they both approve of the choices we've made."

A low murmur of approval rose from the wedding guests, and Lucas held his breath as Geoff handed the mike to Ma.

But when she spoke, her voice was strong and

clear. "It *has* been a rough year—two years—"
She looked up at Geoff with a sad smile.

It struck Lucas that he didn't know much about
Geoff's first wife. For some reason he'd always
assumed she'd been gone for some years, but
apparently her death had occurred within the past
couple of years. That explained why his mom and
Geoff understood each other so well.

He felt himself warm a little more toward this
man his mother was marrying.

Facing the wedding guests, Ma hesitated,
collecting herself, Lucas knew.

Then she looked up, smiling, eyes shining. The
Ma he remembered from before the fire.

"Geoff and I found each other," she said, "at a
time when our worlds had been shaken, when our
faith had been tested. I will never doubt that God
gave us to each other when He knew we
desperately needed each other. Because that's the
kind of God we know. We wanted this day—this
Valentine's Day—to be a celebration of the hope
God has given us, of the healing we've
experienced at His hands. Painful, sometimes—
like a surgeon's wounds—but ultimately for our
good."

She paused and looked up at Geoff. He gave an
encouraging nod, and she continued. "What God
has done for us, He wants to do for each of you.
Whether your problems are large or small,
whether your pain is deep or . . . fading, God

knows the burden you carry, and He knows your needs better than you do.

"Now, before my kids accuse me of preaching a sermon"—she looked from Lucas to each of his sisters and winked—"I'd better sit down."

"Oh, no you don't!" Geoff laughed and pulled her close. "You can't sit down before we seal the deal."

The minister pronounced them man and wife, and Geoff kissed Ma soundly. The laughter floating through the chapel was musical.

Lucas glanced at Jenna, expecting to share a smile, and was stunned to realize she was weeping.

39

The hotel restaurant was packed, and even though they had a table in the back of the dining room, Lucas had to shout over the hubbub to talk to his sisters.

But it was joyous noise. It seemed everybody in the restaurant was in a celebratory mood, and their party of fourteen—all of his family, Geoff's elderly father and several other relatives, plus the minister and his wife—were no exception.

At the head of the table Geoff beamed and Ma absolutely glowed. It was impossible not to be happy for them.

They lingered over dessert and coffee, laughing while Baba told stories about Victoria, Gina, and Lucas. Luc squeezed Jenna's hand under the table. Though she joined in the conversation and smiled in all the right places, he could tell there was something on her mind. He was eager to talk to her alone. It worried him that she'd been crying during the wedding. It had seemed like far more than the usual weepy female tears he'd seen at weddings before.

When they'd finished dinner, they sent Geoff and Ma on their way—back to Geoff's house, Lucas suspected. *Ma* and Geoff's house, he corrected. That would be hard to get used to.

After Geoff's relatives had said their good-byes, Luc and Jenna stood in the lobby of the hotel with his sisters and Abi and Baba talking. They were all staying the night here in the hotel, but Jenna had to work tomorrow, so she was driving back to the Falls and he'd decided to head back to Tulsa to save a little money.

She touched his arm. "I probably should go," she said, stepping away from the noisy knot of Vermontezes.

He held up a hand. "Hang on . . . Let me say good-bye and I'll walk you to your car."

"It's okay, Luc. You stay and spend time with your family."

"No. I need to get on the road, too."

They said their good-byes and walked into the

brisk night air. A few random snowflakes peppered the sky, and their breaths mingled in puffs of white.

"I'm glad I got to come," Jenna said, wrapping her scarf tighter about her neck.

"Are you cold?" Without waiting for an answer, he opened his suit coat and drew her inside the folds, keeping his arm around her. "I'm glad you got to come, too."

They fell in step beside each other and walked in silence for a few minutes. Her hair smelled like one of the flowers in Pop's garden—the name escaped him just now, but he inhaled her scent, soaking in simply being with her again. It seemed much longer than a week ago that he'd left the Falls.

She fit beneath his arm as if she were made to go there. He even seemed to walk with less of a limp with her beside him.

She must have noticed, too, because she leaned her head back and looked up at him. "I just realized you're not using your cane."

"Who needs a cane when I've got you for a crutch?"

She smiled at that.

"No," he said, "I've been doing pretty well without it during the training. I start to get a little gimpy toward the end of the day, but not too bad."

"That's great, Luc. Really great. So, you like it there?"

"I do. Sparky is already an old pro. He makes the other dogs look like . . . like cats."

That cracked her up. "That's pretty funny coming from a guy who's supposedly more of a cat person." Her smile faded. "Speaking of cats, did your mom mention that I might be getting one?"

"You're getting a cat?" *Why would Ma have known that?*

"I wondered about that." An enigmatic smile played at the corners of her mouth. "So your mom didn't tell you about . . . my new housing situation?"

He shook his head. What was going on? And what did any of this have to do with Jen getting a cat?

"I'm not sure how you'll feel about this," she said, "but your mom offered to let me stay at your house while you're in Tulsa—just while I look for a place."

"She *did?*" He tried too late to conceal his shock.

"Are you upset?"

"I'm just . . . surprised." To put it mildly. Why hadn't Ma said anything? "Have you moved in yet?"

"No. I'll probably start moving out of Bryn's next week—her lease goes till the end of the month. I am taking care of your cat this weekend, though."

"Ah, so that's the cat you're talking about?"

She nodded.

"How is Lucky? Hasn't chased you up on any countertops yet, has he?"

That earned him a slug. But then she bit her lip, her gaze turning serious. "I hope you're not mad. If you ever come home for a weekend, I promise I'll vacate the premises. Just say the word."

He shook his head. "I won't be coming home until the training ends. Ma knew that."

"Yes, that's what she said. But I'm serious. . . . If you want to come home, I can get out of there on a moment's notice. I'm putting most of my stuff in storage. I'm looking at it as if I were staying in a quaint bed and breakfast for a few days." She looked up at him, apprehension on her face. "You're upset."

"No, I'm really not. I'm just . . . a little surprised Ma didn't say anything. And honestly—I don't know why I didn't think of it myself."

She blew out a breath she hadn't realized she was holding. "It might have been a tad awkward for you to ask me to move into your house."

"True." If she only knew how much he was beginning to want to ask her just that.

The parking lot came into view and he missed her already. "Do you have time to go for coffee?"

She looked at her watch and made a face. "It's getting late. . . . You're the one who has a long trip back. How about if we drive through for coffee?"

"Deal. Come on, we'll take my truck. I know

where there's a Starbucks not too far from here."

They climbed in his pickup, and while they waited for the windshield to defog, he called Victoria to tell them not to wait on him. With the heater blasting, it was cozy in the cab of the truck. He was glad she'd had the idea to drive through, and sorry she wouldn't be here to keep him company on the drive back to Tulsa.

When they were settled in the parking lot with warm coffee cups in hand, he dared to ask the question he'd been wondering about since the wedding. "Were those just the usual girlie-girl wedding tears today, or were you crying about something else?"

She stared at the cup nestled between her palms and absently flicked the plastic lid with a pearly thumbnail. "I was just . . . really moved by Emily and Geoff's words. By your whole family. There's something about the way you all . . . see God." She looked up at him from beneath hooded eyes. "It seems so effortless. For all of you. You seem to take it for granted—not just that God exists, but that He cares about you. That He wants the best for you. I could understand if it wasn't for what your family has been through . . . what happened to you"—she nodded toward his legs—"and losing your pop."

The way she said "your pop" touched him deeply. Hope surged within him and he breathed a silent prayer that God would give him adequate words to share that hope. "Jen, don't think that we haven't had moments when we doubted . . . or at least wondered what on earth God was doing. I sure have. And I know Ma struggled for a while. My sisters, too. We *all* asked why. We wouldn't be human if we didn't. And honestly, I haven't gotten the answer to that question yet."

She seemed to grab on to his words, as if something vital hung in the balance.

"I've gotten past the need to know. There's just this . . . feeling inside. Peaceful, I guess is the best way to explain it. I know God has everything under control and whatever happens, as long as I know that, I'm okay."

"I wish I felt that way. I really do. Your mom talked about healing being like—"

"A surgeon's wounds." He nodded. "Man, could I relate to that. Sometimes it hurts to heal." He reached for her hand. "The point is, Jen, healing does happen. I hated every minute of all the surgeries I've had on these legs." The pain in even the memories surprised him. "But if not for them, I probably wouldn't be walking today. My surgeons did what they did to help me get better. God's the same."

"I wish I could believe like you," she said again.

"I want that for you, too, Jen. To believe how much God loves you. To have a faith that understands what true love is. It's all I want for you, because it's all that really matters."

351

She opened her mouth as if to say something, paused like a diver uncertain of the water's depth, then dove in. "Do you believe God answers prayers?"

Wow. Where had that come from? He thought for a moment, forming his thoughts carefully. "I heard a pastor say once that God always answers, but the answer isn't always yes."

"I've been praying—like you asked me to."

"You have?" She'd said it like she was confessing a sin, and he took a quick sip of coffee, hiding a smile behind his cup.

She nodded. "Maybe it's not right, but I've been doing an experiment. You said once that we should always ask God when we need something or when we're trying to make a decision."

He didn't remember the conversation, but apparently he'd given good advice.

"So I told God I needed a place to stay until I can find an apartment. That same day your mom came in to the store and offered to let me stay at your house. I didn't even ask. She just offered."

"That's cool, Jen!"

"And then I prayed that you'd have a really good week in Tulsa, and you did." She looked like a little girl who'd just found a quarter from the tooth fairy under her pillow.

Now he was humbled. God was up to something. *Oh, Father, thank You. Thank You for answering those prayers.*

He decided to tell her something he hadn't intended to, but the time seemed right. So right.

He angled himself in the seat, the better to see her beautiful face. "You know, God's been answering my prayers, too. I wasn't too crazy about the way He was going about it at first."

She tilted her head, waiting, curiosity on her face.

"When I first found out about Tulsa, I thought that was God's way of saying it was over for us."

She frowned. "Us?"

He nodded. "I thought maybe that was God's way of solving my Jenna problem."

"Oh, so now I'm a problem?"

"You know what I mean." He looked down at her with a half smile. "I thought if you were hours away, you'd be easier to forget."

"And how's that working out for you?" She shot him an ornery grin.

"Turns out you're pretty memorable."

"Ah-ha!" she crowed. "I knew it!"

"Don't be so smug." He drained his coffee cup. "But seriously, Jen, I have to wonder if this isn't exactly what's best for us right now."

"Never getting to see each other?" She frowned.

He nodded. "We can e-mail and text and talk on the phone. This way we get to know each other without all that kissing getting in the way."

"Oh, yeah, that icky kissing." Her comical face made him laugh.

He ran a finger down the slope of her nose and proved his own point, overwhelmed by the desire he always fought when he was with her. "And on that note, Ms. Morgan, I'd better take you back to your car. We both have a long road ahead of us."

He drove her back to the campus parking lot, pulling up beside her car. "I'll make sure your car starts. But first, I just have one question for you." He took her hand in his, grinning.

"What's that?"

"Will you be my valentine?"

She laughed. "I'd be honored."

He turned serious and held her gaze, caressing her hand with his thumb. It was a good thing they were headed in opposite directions.

She looked away, then caught his eye again. "What? What is it?"

"I think you know what," he whispered. "I really, really want to kiss you right now."

"Well, now." With a self-satisfied smile, her eyes never leaving his, she pulled her hand from his and opened the passenger door. "*That* would mess up God's reason for sending you away, wouldn't it?"

He chuckled all the way back to Tulsa.

40

*O*h, Jen, I'm going to miss you so much."

"Me, too." Jenna hugged Bryn tight, but she laughed through her tears. "Somehow I think you'd trade me in a heartbeat for the roommate you're getting in exchange." She winked at Garrett, who stood with a moving box on his shoulder awaiting her instructions. "That can go in the trunk."

"Got it." He gave a mock salute, hefted another box under his other arm, and headed out the door.

"Thanks, Garrett," she called after him. "He's a keeper, B."

Bryn beamed. "You don't have to tell me that."

Jenna looked around the apartment that had been her home for almost three months.

"Is that everything?" Bryn followed her gaze around the room. "Man, it's starting to look really empty in here."

"You're probably happy to have the space back."

"Only because it's that much less stuff we have to move out Thursday. Garrett doesn't have much room at his place—I mean *our* place—and Dad will croak when he sees the mountain of boxes I'm taking out there."

355

"How is your dad? I haven't heard for a while."

"Better, I think. He seems a little stronger every day, but this winter's been hard on him. I'll be glad when it warms up and he can get outside some."

Jenna would be glad when it warmed up, too, because that would mean it was almost time for Luc to come home.

"Tell your dad I'm thinking of him, B. And thanks again for everything. I can never thank you enough for taking me in and—"

"Forget it, Jen. You'd do the same for me in a heartbeat."

"Well, I hope you never need the kind of help you gave me, but if you do . . ." She swallowed back tears and reached to hug Bryn again.

Jenna had been in a fog ever since she'd left Springfield Saturday night. Her brain was on overload between the move, the new developments in her relationship with Lucas, and most of all, the new development in her relationship with God.

She still choked up every time she remembered that simple moment in the car on the way home from Springfield. In some mysterious way she didn't quite grasp yet, she had met God face-to-face.

There'd been no drama, nothing outward that anyone could see. But inside she felt pure and clean and *right*. The closest thing she could compare the experience to was the way she'd felt the day she'd chosen to forgive Bryn. Except now she understood the source of her peace. Forever after she would look back on the instant she'd believed and know that in that moment she had been changed—profoundly and forever—and she would never go back.

She'd shared a little with Bryn and been rewarded as if she'd done something Pulitzer-worthy. But she felt the need to hold things close to her heart for a while as she tried to understand and sort out everything that had happened inside her.

There was one other person she knew would understand. And she could hardly wait to tell him.

Thursday, March 12

*C*ut it out, Lucky!" Jenna put down her calculator and pushed the pesky cat off her lap, but not before she gave his head a good scratching. She might have to get herself a cat if she found a place that allowed pets.

The television droned in the background, but she tuned the babbling out, looking over the bank statements spread across the dining room table. She'd spent the last hour trying to get her checkbook to balance. Still, she never thought she'd see the day when she'd find it so utterly rewarding to watch her balance grow, penny by penny.

She'd been at the Vermontez house for over two weeks now, and already it felt like home. But she'd promised herself she wouldn't get too settled there. She felt guilty enough about how long she'd sponged off Bryn.

"Oh, God," she whispered. "I'm not asking to be rich, but please let me be able to pay Bryn back someday." She smiled to herself, thinking how natural these little conversations with God had become over the last month.

She'd been watching the papers and talking to Maggie at the real estate office. There was a two-bedroom apartment—much like Bryn's—available, but even with the two thousand dollars she'd made from selling some furniture, she knew she'd be better off with a smaller place and a lower price tag. She'd even thought about calling Garrett to see if that trailer out in the country was still available. But it hadn't been in the classifieds since last week, and she was content to let it go at that. *Baby steps, Jenna. Baby steps.*

She glanced up at the clock. Emily had said she'd stop by sometime today to pick up a few things she wanted for the house in Springfield. Jenna had cleaned the house from top to bottom yesterday and tidied the kitchen again after breakfast. She'd even spent several evenings raking the flower beds in the beautiful garden in back, wanting to prove to Emily—and to Lucas— that she was taking good care of the place, that she didn't take the gift lightly. She hoped Emily would get there before she had to go to work.

She finished reconciling her checkbook, then pulled up the spreadsheet where she was keeping track of her eBay and craigslist sales. She'd sold several of the larger pieces of furniture and a lot of the fancy decorating pieces. She got a fraction of the price she'd paid, but that wasn't the point. She was just happy to be paying off some bills and socking a little away in savings.

She added up her earnings again, absently sliding her goldfish charm on its chain. She looked down at the necklace. Maybe she should sell her jewelry. She'd gotten some nice pieces as gifts from Zach and his parents. She had no idea what this necklace was worth, but it was real gold. Clarissa had made sure she knew that.

Her wedding set would probably bring several thousand. She didn't wear it anymore. It was just sitting in a dresser drawer in the tiny jeweler's box. Would it be wrong to sell it? Maybe she should offer it to Clarissa first. But what kind of message would that send?

Yes, she was ready to move on. Luc made that an easy decision. But she didn't need to throw it in Clarissa and Bill's faces. The Morgans had seemed to be making an effort to be friendlier, to include her in their lives again ever since that day she and Luc had gone to Clairemont Hills to move her things.

Luc. How she missed him.

She and Luc had spoken—or communicated was more accurate—almost daily. They'd talked on the phone a few times since the wedding, but several times a day they shot text messages back and forth or wrote longer e-mails when texting just didn't cut it.

Jenna was starting to believe Lucas was right when he'd declared that his time away in Tulsa was an answer to prayer. In some ways she felt she'd gotten to know him so much better long distance than she had when they were face-to-face. And while Lucas claimed the distance kept them from temptation, she hadn't admitted to him that she was plenty tempted to dream about those kisses they'd shared and wish that there might be more in the future. He'd been so sweet to her when they were together at Emily's wedding.

She heard the lid on the mailbox slam and went out to collect the mail. She'd had her mail forwarded here, not knowing what else to do after Bryn's lease was up. But most days the mailbox yielded only Vermontez mail—usually junk mail, but she saved everything in a box for Emily.

She flipped through today's offering of catalogs and credit card offers, smiling when she came to an envelope bearing a Tulsa postmark—and addressed to her.

It looked like a greeting card. She slipped her finger under the flap and pulled out a card and a photograph. Lucas and Sparky standing in front of the training center, both looking serious and posed. She laughed out loud, her heart warming.

She turned over the card. It was a formal-looking invitation to graduation ceremonies for Lucas Vermontez and Sparky, on Saturday, March 21, at two o'clock in the afternoon. The first day of spring—a day she'd dreaded and anticipated equally. The former because it meant she'd have to be gone from this house. The latter because it meant Luc would be coming back to the Falls.

An image of Lucas and Sparky in tasseled graduation caps made her giggle. She wouldn't miss that event for the world.

She made a note to check her schedule at Hanson's and ask Mr. Iverson for the day off.

41

Saturday, March 21

£ucas Vermontez . . . and Sparky."

Lucas clicked his tongue at Sparky, took a deep breath, and walked across the stage. He'd expected to feel a little silly walking in front of an audience to receive a diploma for a dog, but the announcer had added a humorous touch to the ceremony, and the crowd was eating it up.

They'd impressed everyone earlier in the day

with an exhibition, showing off the skills the dogs and their handlers had learned during the past six weeks. Sparky had performed flawlessly, and Lucas couldn't imagine feeling much prouder if the dog had been his own son.

He took the certificate Wyatt offered, shook his hand, then turned to pose for the professional photographer as they'd been instructed. Stepping off the stage, he caught Jenna's eye and mirrored her ear-to-ear grin. He hadn't seen the woman for five weeks, and it was all he could do to let a look at her suffice.

Finally the diplomas and awards had all been given out, and the handlers were dismissed to kennel their dogs while the audience was ushered to the back of the room for refreshments. When Lucas got back to the reception, Jenna was laughing and talking with his sisters and Ma. She fit right in.

They had cake and punch and he introduced them to a few of the guys he'd gotten to know so well over the past six weeks.

A few minutes later he realized Geoff was missing.

He turned to Ma. "Where'd Geoff go?"

"He went to bring the car around. I wish we could stay and take you guys out to dinner, but Geoff is speaking at early chapel tomorrow, so we need to get on the road."

He leaned to give her a hug. "I understand. I'm glad you guys could come."

"I wouldn't have missed it." She tightened her arm around his waist. "I wish your dad could have been here today. He would have been so proud of you."

"Thanks, Ma." The only thing that could have made this day better would have been having Pop there. "Tell Abi and Baba I'll come visit them on my way back to the Falls. It'll probably be Wednesday or Thursday before I get everything tied up here."

Victoria and Gina were following Geoff and Ma home and staying in Springfield for the night, so Lucas gave his sisters the obligatory punches before drawing them into genuine hugs. "You guys be careful on the road. They're saying it's supposed to get cold tonight. Maybe below freezing. It could get icy."

Victoria rolled her eyes. "Great. There goes our spring break."

"I told you, you could spend it in Tulsa with me," he teased.

"Thanks anyway, big bro, but I think I'll pass."

"Yeah, me too," Gina said, ducking out of reach before he could ruffle her hair.

Much as he loved his family, and happy as he was that they'd come all this way to see him complete the program, he was eager for them to get on the road so he could have a little time alone with Jenna. She had to go back tonight, too, but he'd talked her into staying long enough to go out to dinner with him.

9 have some news for you." Jenna's eyes sparkled and Lucas was instantly curious.

She wiped her mouth on the cloth napkin and put down her fork. They'd decided on dinner at the Cheesecake Factory and were sharing the famous meatloaf plate, anticipating large slices of cheesecake later.

"I found a place to rent," she said.

"You did! I wondered about that. Ma said you were planning to be out of the house by Monday, but you've been all mysterious about it every time I asked. So have you moved yet? Tell me about it."

He waited. She took a sip of her water and swallowed hard. She seemed to be having trouble forming her words. For one awful moment it struck him that maybe she was moving away from the Falls.

But when she looked up, there was a mischievous glint in her eye. "I rented a place in the country."

"You're kidding." He was a little surprised, thinking about the day he'd gone with her to look at the trailer. "How far out?"

"About a mile and a half."

"So what's it like? *Not* a trailer, I presume." He winked, hoping he wasn't pushing it. "When do you move in?"

"I'm already in."

"No wonder you haven't been answering my messages as quickly lately. So what does it look like?"

She bit the corner of her lip, smiling. "The outside is turquoise and white."

"Ha! That's funny!"

"The inside is . . . wide—double-wide, actually. With narrow hallways . . . Oh, and the whole place kind of rocks you to sleep." Her grin grew to a full-blown smile.

"What?"

"I rented the trailer house, you goober."

"No way!"

"It actually looks surprisingly nice with my furniture and stuff in it. You'll be amazed at the transformation."

He regarded her with a soft smile. "I *am* amazed at the transformation."

Tears sprang to her eyes, but she smiled through them. "I . . . I'm seeing things with such different eyes now, Luc. It's hard to describe."

"Well, I like your new eyes."

She smiled and dipped her head.

"I liked your old eyes, too," he said quickly, afraid she might have taken his comment wrong.

"I know you did. Honestly, that amazes me as much as anything. How on earth did you ever put up with me before?"

He chuckled. "If you'll recall, I didn't always."

She frowned. "That's right! You called me a brat!"

He feigned ducking out of range of her fist, which made her laugh harder. He liked making this woman laugh. "Yep, I called you a brat. The day we went to look at your new home, as I recall."

"That's right!" She rolled her eyes. "Oh, brother, how rich is that?"

"Pretty rich, I'd say." He didn't have to work at looking smug.

They had so much to catch up on, they talked nonstop through the main course. But he started to watch the clock. "I don't want you to go, but I don't want you driving back too late either. It's a good four hours back to the Falls. Not to mention my mother will shoot me if she finds out I put you on the road this late."

She laughed, then turned serious. "Your mom seems really happy. Are you . . . okay with her being remarried?"

He thought for a moment, then nodded. "Like you said, she's happy. That means a lot. And Geoff's been good about . . . acknowledging Pop."

"I noticed that at the wedding."

"Yeah, it made you cry."

She shook her head. "It wasn't just that. God was working on me even then." A faraway look came to her eyes. "I just hope . . . that someday I can have the kind of marriage your mom has . . . and had with your dad."

"Yeah, I want that, too." *With you, Jenna Morgan.*

If God agrees that's what He wants for us.

"You two ready for some cheesecake?" Their perky server bounced at the corner of their table.

Jenna glanced at him with a little grimace. "I'd probably better get on the road."

"Would you mind bringing that cheesecake to go?" Luc asked the server.

Ten minutes later they stood in the parking lot talking over her open car door, each clutching weighty hunks of cheesecake in Styrofoam containers.

He held his up like a weight-lifter. "Breakfast tomorrow."

She mimicked him. "Midnight snack."

He laughed.

"Thanks for inviting me, Luc. It was a fun day. And congratulations. I can't wait to see what's next for you."

She was close enough to kiss. The scent of her perfume was tantalizing. Like the honeysuckle that bloomed in Pop's garden in the spring. Man, he wanted to kiss her. He sort of thought she wanted the same thing, but . . . no. He wasn't going to mess this up. He'd play it safe and take it slow.

He settled for a quick hug instead. They'd have plenty of time to work up to a kiss once he came back to the Falls.

He opened her car door wider and waited for her to climb in.

But she surprised him by standing on tipoe to kiss him on the cheek. "Don't be a stranger," she said. "Bye, Luc."

"Awww, just when it was getting good."

She laughed and reached up to touch the collar of his jacket. "I sure have missed you."

"I've missed you, too. Now get in that car."

She smiled, but she obeyed.

Checking his watch, he knocked on the window and she rolled it down. "It's nine-fifteen. With Interstate all the way, you should be home by one thirty or so. Maybe a little after. Call me when you're home. I don't care how late it is."

"I will. Don't worry about me. I'm wide awake." She demonstrated, batting her eyes at him.

He laughed and waved her off. "Get out of here."

She revved the engine and backed out, waving up at him through the windshield.

He watched her drive away, feeling as if she was taking a piece of him with her.

Looking up into the foggy night sky, he sighed. "Lord, help me . . . I love that woman."

*L*ucas had just fed Sparky and settled into his bunk with the Sunday paper when his cell phone rang.

He picked it up off the nightstand, smiling, expecting it to be Jenna. But when he glanced at the clock and saw that it was almost eleven, he figured it was probably Ma, calling to say they were home safe and sorry she forgot to call earlier.

He slid the phone's cover open. Yep. It was her. "Hey, Ma, you made it, huh?"

"We're not home yet, but we're in town at least." She sounded breathless. "Don't you let Jenna drive in this."

"What's going on? Drive in what?"

"We ran into a snowstorm about twenty miles before we got to Springfield. It was awful. Geoff couldn't see ten feet in front of the car and there were cars in the ditch all along the Interstate. It's terrible!"

"Oh, man! She left over an hour ago."

His mother groaned. "You call her right now and tell her to get off at the next exit. The weather people are saying the storm is headed west. Just have her go to a hotel for the night. I'll pay for it."

His pulse raced. "Okay, Ma . . . Thanks. I need to get off and call her."

"Don't take no for an answer. Tell her she's driving *right* into a blizzard."

42

*J*enna turned the radio down and flipped the wipers on high. The sky had been spitting on her for the past hour, but it was raining in earnest now.

The clock on the dashboard had just turned to midnight. She still had an hour and a half to go before she was home . . . maybe longer if this rain kept up. But she didn't care. She wasn't at all sleepy, and the weather was perfect for day-dreaming.

She'd passed the time reliving every moment she'd spent with Luc today. And praying her heart out that God thought she and Lucas Vermontez should end up together as much as *she* thought they should.

Slowing down to sixty, she switched her lights from bright to dim and back, trying to figure out which made it easier to see. The temperature had dropped to freezing, but the road didn't seem to be slick.

The rain hitting her windshield was starting to look like more than rain. She drove another ten miles, and the sky swirled with white stuff. It was snowing! Beautiful white flakes, except they were hitting the windshield ever faster—and beginning to accumulate on the dry grass in the ditches. She blinked a few times, trying to keep the road and the black night sky from blending into one.

"Just watch the center line," she heard Zachary say. They'd driven to St. Louis in a storm like this early in their marriage. She'd been terrified and angry that he wouldn't pull over and drive. But he'd said it was too dangerous to be on the side of the road, and besides, she needed to learn to drive in all kinds of weather.

She tried to recapture thoughts of Lucas again. Maybe she should call him. At least let him know why she would be later than one thirty getting home.

She searched her purse for her cell phone, trying to keep one eye on the white line. But the snow was coming down so hard now that she could barely make out the front of the car, let alone the road.

She opened her phone and hit Luc's number, but saw that she had no signal. She tossed the phone in the seat beside her. She'd try him again in a few minutes when she got near a cell tower.

She turned the heater on high. She wasn't really cold, but maybe running the heater would help keep the windshield clear. The wipers were working overtime and not doing a very good job of it either. Thank goodness there wasn't much traffic at this time of night. Or morning. It was twelve forty. Sunday morning.

She smiled. That meant only three more days till Luc would be home. Or four, if he didn't get back till Thursday. Surely this snow would be gone by then. But it sure seemed to be piling up fast. And blowing some now, too. A blizzard on the first day of spring? This was crazy.

She passed a road sign that said ten miles to . . . somewhere. The name of the town was veiled in snow. She was starting to feel a little disoriented. She knew she was still on 44, but she didn't remember passing a Leaving Oklahoma sign or a Welcome to Missouri sign. She had to have crossed the state line, though. She should be only an hour or so outside of Springfield.

Nothing looked familiar, but how could it? She couldn't *see* anything. She grabbed her phone from the seat and tried Luc's cell again. *Thank You, God.* It was ringing!

Her spirits sank when his voice mail picked up. She'd leave a message. . . . But what was he supposed to do when he got it? He'd just worry about her. The beep sounded and she hesitated. She started to hang up, then thought he'd worry more if he had a missed call from her and no message. "Hey, Luc. It's me. Just wanted to let you know I . . . hit a snowstorm somewhere around . . . well, I don't know where I am, but anyway . . . it's really pretty, but I'm no fan of driving in this stuff. I'll call you when I get to the Falls, but I'm only going about fifty on the

Interstate, so it's going to be a lot later than—"

In the road ahead of her—*right* in front of her—a dark form loomed. Someone must have had car trouble and gotten out of their vehicle. Idiot! The shadow wasn't moving. What . . . ? It looked bigger than a man. Whatever it was . . . she was going to hit it!

Oh dear God! Help me!

She slammed on the brakes, steered sharply to the right, gripping the wheel like a lifeline. The car fishtailed and snow sprayed all around her.

A huge bump threw her forward against the seatbelt. A loud bang split the air inside the car. A flash of light and Jenna's hands were ripped from the steering wheel. Something slapped her hard across the face. The car kept going . . . spinning. She felt as if she were falling from a high place.

Her face stung and she rubbed at her cheek, confusion clouding her thoughts. Had she hit someone? What was happening?

She choked, breathing in a mist of powder—fine and white, like baby powder. It floated eerily in front of the car's interior lights. She heard a hissing noise and looked down to see a puddle of white nylon pooling on the seat and the floor. Relief swept over her. The airbag. It must have deployed.

But the car was still moving, seeming to take on a life of its own. Branches and tree boughs clawed at her windows, dumping their burden of snow as the car plowed through the woods.

The windshield was completely blocked with snow now. She let go of the wheel and buried her face in her hands.

An odd melody played in her head. Country music. She wanted to laugh. This wasn't what she expected heaven to be like. "Jesus, take the wheel. . . ." It was the song from that *American Idol* girl. *Jesus! Please, God. I need help. . . .*

43

*L*ucas stood in the parking lot looking east. It was cold, but the sky was clear. He pulled his collar up over his ears and checked his phone again. He had plenty of bars. Why couldn't he get through to Jenna? He'd been trying to reach her for over an hour now. Surely her phone hadn't been out of service, in a dead spot, all this time.

Dead spot . . . He shivered. Poor choice of words.

He closed his phone and gave a low whistle. Sparky came running, wound up about this after-midnight excursion. "Come on, boy. Back inside." He headed into the dormitory, at a loss for what to do.

She must have turned off her phone. That was the only logical explanation. But why would she do that? Or maybe she'd forgotten to charge her battery?

He traipsed down the cold hallway to his room, which was only slightly warmer. His legs ached in a way they hadn't for a while.

Sparky settled into his usual spot on the rug beside the bed. Lucas shrugged out of his coat and picked up the remote. He flipped to the Weather Channel, keeping the volume low so he wouldn't wake the guys in the rooms on either side of him.

The TV map still showed a line of snowstorms from the Oklahoma state line to twenty miles past Springfield, with high winds reported in many places.

There was no way she'd made it past Springfield before Ma called at eleven. They'd left almost two hours before Jenna, and Ma said they'd barely made it. If Jenna hadn't had the sense to pull off somewhere before she got caught in the storm, then she was right in the middle of it somewhere.

Why didn't she call? She had to know he was worried about her.

He paced the short distance from the bed to the door and back. Finally he put his coat back on. He couldn't just sit here and do nothing.

Sparky lifted his head and watched him, whimpering a little, as if sensing his distress.

The phone chirped and he slid it open. Jenna. Seeing her number, relief flooded him—until he realized it wasn't a call coming in, but a message.

But it was from her. He checked the time stamp. She'd called almost half an hour ago. Why hadn't he heard his phone ring?

He played the message, reassured to hear her calm voice. *I'll call you when I get to the Falls. . . . only going about fifty . . . it's going to be a lot—*

The message turned into static there, and then nothing.

He didn't like it. Something wasn't right.

He dialed his house in the Falls, on the off chance that Jenna had made it home and gone there for some reason. Silly, when he knew she didn't have a key to the house anymore. He'd seen her give it to Ma. But Jenna didn't have a landline phone at the trailer.

He called Ma's cell phone next. Maybe they'd heard from her. Maybe after she couldn't get hold of him, she'd called Ma and Geoff and arranged to hole up in Springfield until the storm passed. The possibility comforted him. *Please, God, let that be it.*

But Geoff answered Ma's phone. She was glued to the Weather Channel and they hadn't heard anything. Geoff promised to call the Springfield police to find out if there'd been any accidents reported.

Lucas played Jen's message again. If she'd called around twelve forty-five, depending on how long she'd been driving in the snow, and judging by when Ma and Geoff hit the storm,

Jenna should have been at least close to Springfield when she called.

Her message said she wasn't sure where she was, but she had to have gotten at least an hour and a half out of Tulsa.

"Come on, Sparky. We've got to find her."

Sparky got up and trotted over to stand at his right leg, on alert, ready to work.

Lucas grabbed his keys off the dresser, then gathered some blankets and water bottles and a box of granola bars Ma had brought him. He flipped off the lights and headed out the door with Sparky at his heel.

It was *so* cold. So dark she couldn't see her hands in front of her face now that she'd turned off the engine. She'd heard horror stories about carbon monoxide building up when a tailpipe got clogged with snow. But she could run the heater again later . . . just for a little while.

At first she'd thought maybe her car was buried in snow, but occasional gusts of wind rocked it back and forth, so she must not be buried. She switched on the headlamps. Barely a glimmer. The front of the car at least must be submerged in snow. She turned the lights off again. She didn't want to run the battery down. Hard telling how long she'd have to wait before somebody found her.

How far off the road was she? Had she rolled the

car? Or plunged into a ravine? The vehicle was upright now, but it had felt as if the car plowed forever through the trees and woods. Everything had happened so fast, it was a blur. But she had to be quite a distance off the highway.

She heard no noise outside the car except for the wind. She was afraid to roll down a window to listen for traffic on the Interstate—or to call for help. She could barely stay warm as it was, without letting in snow and wind.

She reached down to feel her leg and winced when she pressed on her left knee. The steering column was all messed up and the driver's side door was mangled, but at least cold air wasn't pouring in.

She'd tried to crawl out from under the steering column a few minutes ago, but the pain in her knee nearly caused her to pass out.

Was this what Lucas had felt like when he'd been injured in the fire? She scolded herself immediately. She couldn't say how badly she was hurt, but that she was awake and thinking relatively clearly told her it couldn't be too serious. She didn't seem to be bleeding.

Lucas had nearly died. Though she'd never seen the scars for herself, he'd told her that his legs bore the scars of his injuries and the surgeries he'd endured. How dare she compare this to what he'd gone through?

She groped for the glove compartment, found it,

and stretched to feel inside. Why oh why had she never purchased a flashlight and the other emergency supplies people were supposed to keep in their cars?

She turned on the dome light and searched the car again for her cell phone—as far as she could reach anyway. Nothing. It had to be in here somewhere, but it was nowhere she could see or reach.

A flash of memory hit her. A shadow in the road, her headlights illuminating it. *Oh, dear God . . .* had she hit something? She remembered swerving, and then the dark silhouette of some huge animal—a deer maybe? She thought she'd swerved in time, but what was that horrible bump she'd felt?

And the airbag had gone off. . . . She could feel it resting on her lap, draped on the floor around her.

Her feet were freezing. She pulled her coat tighter around her chest and leaned her head against the headrest. Images flooded her. She remembered the night, not so long ago, that she'd slept in this car after Bill and Clarissa kicked her out. What she wouldn't have given now for all the extra clothes she'd had in the Volvo that night.

If she could have seen a glimpse that night into where she would be today . . . How far she'd come! It had all been worth it. Who would have guessed God would get her attention the way He had?

Her teeth chattered and she played mind games with herself, pretending she was in the Vermontezes' warm, cozy kitchen, imagining that she was fixing herself a cup of hot tea. Funny, it was that modest home she'd imagined, instead of her Brookside house or even the Morgans' mansion.

She'd made a discovery that had changed her thinking . . . not only in the most important thing—what she believed about God—but also in what she believed about herself. She'd learned that it was the spirit inside a home, not the material things it contained, that was the true measure of wealth. And that it was the Spirit inside a person that measured true wealth as well.

She smiled to herself to realize that her mailing address now was a turquoise and white trailer house—and she was rich. Richer than she'd ever been in her life.

Sadness filled her to realize the correlation to her discovery: Bill and Clarissa lived in a mansion—in poverty. But whatever their faults, they'd been more than generous to her over the years, and she hadn't always shown her appreciation. She prayed she'd have a chance to right things with them. *Oh, God . . . help them find the riches I've found in You.*

Trying again to free her legs, she gave up at the first knife of pain. She reached over to the passenger seat until her hand rested on the Styrofoam container that held a slice of banana cream cheesecake. She smiled. She'd told Lucas it would be her midnight snack. She wasn't hungry now, but if she was still trapped here in the morning, she'd have cheesecake for breakfast and think about Luc back in Tulsa eating his own slice of Chocolate Tuxedo. With coffee. Oh, a cup of hot coffee would be heaven right now.

She felt herself drifting. Maybe she would sleep for a little while. That would help her forget how cold she was. Help pass the time. And when she woke up she would run the heater again. For just a little while.

44

Sir, we have dozens of cars in the ditch from here to St. Louis. We're working as fast as we can to get everybody out, but it's not gonna be today."

Lucas checked his rearview mirror. He was two hours east of Tulsa on I-44 and had pulled over on the shoulder to call the highway patrol again, trying to locate Jenna. He'd driven on mostly dry roads and had only run into the storm twenty minutes ago. Now it was slow going, but fortunately, at two o'clock in the morning, there wasn't much traffic on the Interstate.

"St. Louis is saying it's stopped snowing there," the dispatcher said. "And it's a little better here in

Springfield than it was an hour or two ago. So that's good news at least."

Lucas pulled his cell phone away from his ear and checked the time. "Do you have a list of the people you've pulled out so far?" He told the dispatcher about the message he'd received from Jenna . . . how she'd been cut off before she could finish.

"Sir, I'm not aware of any serious injuries at this time. We're advising stranded motorists to contact anyone who might be worried about them. But there *are* some dead zones along that route—especially with certain carriers. That may be why you haven't heard from her."

"Okay . . . thanks." He hung up and put the truck in gear. If the snow had stopped in St. Louis, maybe he could get through. The dispatcher had said that crews of county maintainers were already working to clear roads. His pickup could probably make it. If he'd been thinking, he would have let Jenna take his truck. But they hadn't known about the storm when she left Tulsa. Even the weather guys on TV seemed to have been taken by surprise.

It was almost two a.m. It wouldn't be light for at least four or five hours. "Oh, God. I pray she's okay. Be with her. Keep her safe. I love her, Lord. Don't let me lose her." Immediately the thought came—*she wasn't his to lose.* He would give anything for a chance to change that.

Sparky panted in the cab beside him, eager to go.

"Okay, boy. Let's go find her."

*L*ucas sat at the end of the driveway to Jenna's rental and wracked his brain, trying to think where to look next. He'd driven all the way back to the Falls with no sign of her car, and she still wasn't answering her cell phone. On the way he and Sparky had helped emergency crews pull four stranded motorists out of the ditch, and he could only hope that somewhere along the route another crew had done the same for Jen.

The steep drive was drifted shut. Her Volvo would never have made it through, and the only tracks visible came from his truck. And the mobile home was dark. He'd pounded on the door a few minutes ago, just to make sure, but no one answered. It was clear Jenna hadn't come back here.

Maybe she'd gone to his house. She'd returned the keys to Ma, but maybe Ma had showed her where the spare key was hidden. Maybe once she made it to the Falls, she hadn't wanted to risk driving in the country. But when he got there, it was the same story. No lights on in the house, and no tire tracks or footprints in the snow to indicate she'd ever been there.

Where could she be? He tried calling her again and got the same message. He clicked off and dialed Bryn. Maybe she'd heard from Jenna. A sleepy voice answered.

"Hey, Bryn, sorry to wake you up, but I'm looking for Jenna. You haven't heard from her, have you?"

"No . . . I thought she was in Oklahoma. With you." He heard her stirring, then a little gasp. "Oh! It snowed! What time is it anyway?"

"Almost five thirty. Sorry." He explained about Jenna driving back in the storm and told Bryn when he'd last talked to her. "But she's not answering her phone now, and I can't think of anywhere else she might have gone, can you?"

"No . . . It doesn't make sense." Bryn sounded as confused as he felt. "You don't think she would have gone to the Morgans', do you?"

"I doubt it, but maybe. Do you have their number?"

"I can find it. I'll call them and give you a call either way."

"Okay. If they haven't heard from her, I'm going to head back toward Springfield . . . see if I can find her, or at least get through on the phone."

"I'll call you in a few minutes."

"Thanks, Bryn."

Lucas drove through Java Joint for a cup of black coffee, killing time waiting for Bryn to call back. The coffee shop was empty except for a lone barista serving the drive-through window. While he waited for his order, his gaze was drawn to the corner table where he and Jenna had first reconnected after the fire. It seemed like a lifetime ago.

He drove slowly through town, trying to think the way Jenna would. Bryn called to say she'd spoken to Bill Morgan and they didn't know anything about Jenna. Turning onto Grove Street, Luc headed for Main. The windows of the homeless shelter were dark, but smoke poured from the chimney stack and swirled against the haze of a streetlight. He wondered how many people were sleeping there tonight. What would they all do on another night like this if the shelter shut down?

Intent on getting back on the Interstate as quickly as possible, he pressed the accelerator. But something made him slow down again. Jenna wouldn't have gone there. Would she?

Movement behind the shelter caught his eye. Dogs maybe. No, something bigger. Deer? They sometimes wandered down from the woods in Ferris Park. He slowed the car and leaned across the seat to wipe condensation from the passenger side window.

A man in a long coat stood at the corner of the building. A shelter resident out for an early-morning smoke, probably. He stood with his head down, appearing to be talking to himself.

Lucas shifted into drive and started to pull away, but the figure turned and walked toward him—staggered was more like it. And it was a woman!

A baseball cap obscured her features, but the gait and mannerisms were definitely feminine. Something about her seemed vaguely familiar. She held a bottle in her hand and seemed oblivious to his presence.

In the cab beside him Sparky pressed his nose to the window, watching the woman, his ears pricking. Lucas watched until it became obvious the woman was drunk. He didn't have time to get involved, but he'd call the Hanover Falls police and have them come and pick her up. He slipped his cell phone out and pulled away from the curb. He looked back just in time to see the woman stumble and fall into the snow. She lay there, stone still.

He hit the brakes. He grabbed his cane and jumped from the truck, crossing the uneven lawn as fast as his leg would allow. Sparky beat him to the still form and dropped at her side with his nose on the ground, as if he was working. Odd. He'd been trained to alert on fifteen different substances, but vodka wasn't one of them.

Lucas punched 911 into his phone as he hurried to the woman's side. He was relieved to hear her moaning. At least she wasn't dead. The stench of vomit and liquor hit him before he dropped to one knee beside her. But there was something else. Something even stronger.

Acrid vapors stung his nostrils and he turned away, covering his nose.

Gasoline.

His phone came to life. "911. State your emergency, please."

"Send paramedics to the homeless shelter on Grove Street," he said. "And you'd better send the fire chief, too."

45

*T*he rearview mirror reflected a rim of light on the eastern horizon that illumined a cloud-free, lavender sky. Lucas was still shaken after the odd encounter with the woman at the homeless shelter earlier this morning. He'd left as they were loading her into an ambulance, still barely conscious. Chief Brennan had arrived on the scene and Andrea Morley was on her way when Lucas excused himself, far more concerned about Jenna than the fact that they'd likely caught their arsonist.

Lucas felt his hopes rise with the sun as he headed west on I-44 past Springfield. At least he could see more than three feet around him now. He drove slowly, keeping his eyes peeled.

His only hope was that as the sun came up they'd be able to spot Jenna's car. Two of the vehicles they'd towed last night had slid thirty and forty feet beyond the shoulder into dense woods. If the drivers hadn't called for help, they'd never have seen them in the dark—certainly not while it was still snowing. But even in broad daylight, a gray Volvo wasn't going to be easy to spot in this monochromatic landscape.

His cell phone rang and he jumped. He slid it open. His mom.

"Any word yet?"

"Not yet, Ma. I'll let you know."

"Where are you now?"

"Probably half an hour west of you. But I'm about ready to turn around and head back to the Falls again. She's got to be somewhere between here and there."

"This is making me crazy," she said.

"Yeah . . . me too. So help me if she just forgot to charge her phone—and if they find her alive—I'm going to kill her." He chuckled, imagining the relief of being able to spring that line on Jenna.

It would make her laugh.

His mother, on the other hand, did not think it was even a little bit funny. "Lucas! What is wrong with you?"

"Don't worry, Ma. We'll find her." His words rang false in his own ears. He was past worried. . . .

He hung up and swung around in the median and headed back east toward Springfield and the Falls. Judging by the time he'd last talked to Jenna, along with the weather reports, she had to have made it at least this far east. He would concentrate his search between this exit and the Hanover Falls interchange.

The sun was climbing quickly and he slipped his sunglasses on, training his eyes on the right side of the roadway, where her car should be if she'd slid off the road. The radio said the temperature was headed for the upper forties today, and thankfully, the snow was already beginning to melt wherever patches of sunlight landed.

His gaze darted from the shoulder of the road—keeping a lookout for errant tracks in the remaining snow—then back to the woods in the distance where the snow was still deeply drifted.

He drove east for three or four miles before he noticed tracks in the median that looked like something more than the usual pattern he'd seen from emergency vehicles and cars that'd decided to turn around and drive out of the storm last night.

Something made him pull off onto the median, and that's when he saw it—the gray top of a car blanketed in snow one hundred feet off the opposite side of the Interstate. How in the world had she gotten clear over there?

He drove his truck as far into the ditch as he could without getting stuck, then flung open his door. "Come on, Sparky. Let's go, boy."

They slogged through snow that had drifted to ten or twelve inches in last night's winds. A trickle of water ran through a ravine at the bottom of the ditch. Sparky leapt over it gracefully, but Lucas picked his way over a natural bridge of stepping stones, praying he didn't slip and fall into the icy water.

His left leg ached like an abscessed tooth and his right one wasn't much better. But he kept going, pushing his way through the woods to where the car rested.

It seemed as if they'd been trudging for hours without getting any closer to the car, but finally they got near enough that Lucas could have seen through the windshield if it hadn't been covered with snow.

Sparky must have recognized Jenna's car because he started barking and raced ahead.

Lucas finally caught up to him and moved through snow that felt like concrete. He shuddered when he pushed away enough snow to see that the front of the car had been crushed like a soda can.

He fell against the driver's side fender, knocking on the door even as he brushed more snow away with the broad sleeve of his jacket.

"Jenna? Open up! It's me!" He tried the car door. Locked.

"Jenna!"

Nothing. He held his breath. "Jenna?" He banged on the windows now, not caring if he broke the glass.

The windows were frosted over and he scraped beneath the remaining snow, clearing a patch big enough to look in and see if she was okay, terrified of what that porthole in the snow might reveal.

He bent and peered inside. She wasn't in the driver's seat, but it was so dark inside the car—the other windows and windshields obscured by snow—that he couldn't tell where she was. She must have climbed into the back, trying to keep warm. He shouted her name again, pounding on the car as he made his way through the snow around to the other side of the car.

He cleared the snow off of there, too and peered into the windows. The interior was well lit now, with light coming through the other side. The airbag had deployed and lay in a heap across the front seat.

But the car was empty.

46

Sparky barked at the trees limbs swaying overhead, and Lucas turned 360 degrees, scouring the woods, trying to figure out where Jenna could have gone. There didn't seem to be a trail leading from her car, but then, the snow had probably obscured it.

She couldn't have been thrown from the car. The windows and windshields were intact. Had she somehow walked out of there?

Or had someone seen her go off the road last

night? Had she been rescued hours ago? He pictured her warming her hands by a fire in some hotel along the road to Tulsa and prayed it was prophetic.

He imagined himself giving the missing person's report and wracked his brain to remember what Jenna had been wearing when she'd left the Cheesecake Factory.

Something purple, he thought. She would have called it plum or magenta or some fancy-sounding name. Her coat was black leather, he remembered that. He couldn't have named one other item she was wearing—except for her goldfish necklace, which she was never without.

A woodpecker drilled in a tree high overhead, and a mockingbird gave his lonesome call from somewhere across the wood. Sparky was having a heyday, barking at the birds and chasing imaginary squirrels. He took off up the other side of the ravine. Lucas called him back, using his sharp I-mean-business voice.

Sparky stopped and turned at the sound of his voice but turned again and kept running until he'd disappeared over the ledge behind a copse of trees.

"Sparky! Get back here!"

In reply a sharp bark echoed back at him.

"Sparky! Come!" Fine time for the dog to abandon all his training.

He waited a moment, thinking surely Sparky

would get tired of chasing whatever he was barking at and obey his command.

Instead he barked again. His dark head appeared at the top of the rise, and he looked down and gave Luc a good chewing out, then disappeared again.

Grumbling, Lucas started the steep climb up the side of the ravine. Using trees for leverage, he prayed he didn't twist an ankle. As the sun rose higher in a blue morning sky, the thaw turned the leaves into slippery mush underfoot.

Sparky must have heard him coming because he chose that moment to charge down the slope. But when Lucas reached for his collar, the dog pranced out of reach and headed back up the ravine.

No amount of yelling could get him to obey a simple command.

When Lucas finally pulled himself over the ledge to the top, he understood why.

Jenna lay on her back, her coat unbuttoned and spread beneath her. Her face was ghostly pale. He couldn't see any blood, but her left leg was bent at an odd angle. Sparky stood over her, alternately nudging her and barking his heart out.

Lucas caught his breath and took off running— as fast as his legs would let him. His mind seemed to work at high speed and in slow motion all at the same time.

He stumbled and went to his knees beside her, telling himself no one could possibly look that beautiful in death. But it was so cold. And how long had she been out here exposed to the elements. How on earth had she gotten up here?

He reached a hand to touch her cheek. She had to be alive. She *had* to.

Please, God.

Sparky nosed her shoulder with a whimper that gave him chills.

"Sparky—?" Her voice was barely a whisper, but Lucas had never heard a more beautiful sound.

"Jenna? Wake up!" He patted her face gently, and when he got no response, he slapped her cheek.

"Ow!" She came up fighting, groping at thin air. Her eyelids fluttered open and she sank back to the ground. Her gaze flitted, then seemed to focus on his face. She put a hand up, as if it were an ordinary day and she was giving a friendly wave.

"Are you okay? Jenna? Talk to me?" He shrugged out of his coat and draped it over her, tucking it around her shoulders.

She gave him the slightest of smiles, then wriggled a hand out of the shroud of his coat and reached out, grasping for him. She caught hold of his sleeve.

"Where does it hurt, Jenna?"

She looked up at him, rubbing her eyes with her freed hand, as if she might be seeing things. "Lucas? Is that you?"

Her tongue seemed thick and he could barely make out her words.

"I'm here," he assured her. "Everything's okay. You're going to be fine."

She grabbed onto his arm and tried to sit up, wincing. "My leg. But . . . it's okay. I can walk. I'm okay. It . . . it just hurts."

"No. You stay where you are. We need to check you out before we move you." He looked back down the ravine to where he could just see the trunk of her car breaching the snow. "How did you get up here?"

He dialed 911 on his cell phone and told the dispatcher how to find them.

Before he could stop her, Jenna struggled to a sitting position. "I thought . . . I don't know what I thought. Oh, Luc . . ." She began to weep. "I don't know if I can ever give you babies. What if I can't? You should have babies—you should be a father."

Was she delirious? He didn't know what to make of her rambling. "Shhh . . . It's okay, Jen. Don't cry. We . . . we'll worry about babies later. For now everything's okay. You're safe. I'm right here." He reached for her hands and examined her fingers, checked the tip of her nose. Amazingly, she didn't seem to be suffering from frostbite. Maybe she hadn't been out in the elements as long as he feared.

He went around behind her and wrapped his arms around her, trying to warm her, encouraged by the fact that she was at least conscious—even if she was delirious.

"I couldn't get out. Of the car." She began to shiver, her teeth chattering. "My legs were stuck."

"Then . . . how did you get up here? And *why* did you get out of the car? Why didn't you stay where it was warm?"

She ducked her head and gave an awkward laugh. "I . . . had to pee."

"But why did you come all the way up here?"

"I thought . . . if I got closer to the road somebody would see me."

"The road's the other way."

"I just . . . followed the lights." She pointed to the north.

He followed her gaze. A cell tower blinked on the horizon.

"Why didn't you call for help?"

"I don't know where my phone is. I . . . I was talking to you when—" She gave a little gasp and a look of horror drained her face of color. "I think I might have hit something. *Someone?*"

She told him about seeing the shadow in the road, swerving to miss it.

"The highway patrol said they haven't had any fatalities." He breathed a prayer of thanks that this woman hadn't changed that statistic.

"Oh . . ." Jenna rubbed her forehead. "I remember—I think it was . . . a moose."

"A moose? In Missouri?" She was definitely delirious.

"No. Not a moose." Her words slurred slightly

and she gave a lazy smile. "I meant a deer. A big one. With antlers."

"Shhh. You just rest." He tucked his coat tighter around her, worried that she seemed a little out of it. Except for her knee, there were no signs of trauma, but maybe she'd hit her head when the car crashed.

Sparky barked and raced to the ledge overlooking the Interstate.

Lucas heard voices near the highway and relief turned his bones to jelly. "Somebody's here to help you now."

"Sparky?" She leaned forward, looking to where the dog was standing at attention.

"He's right here. What's wrong?"

She looked up at him, and a slow smile started at one corner of her mouth and turned into a full-fledged grin. "I never . . . I never in my life thought I'd be so glad to see a big dog."

Laughing, Luc gathered her into his arms and covered her face with kisses.

47

Thursday, May 7

Jenna filled the teakettle with fresh water and put it on the burner. She looked across the counter at the cozy living room in the trailer house, *her* house. It amazed her all over again how different this place appeared to her eyes now from the way it had that first day Luc had brought her out here.

With fresh paint on the walls and some of the curtains and furniture from the Brookside house, the place actually looked quite charming. Outside the wide living room windows, the forest wore a hundred shades of green, and pink and white dogwood petals fluttered in the breeze like tiny garments on a twig clothesline. She couldn't deny that she was very happy here.

Of course Lucas Vermontez had far more to do with that than any house. She smiled at the thought of him and knew he would give her fits if he thought she'd given him credit for the new joy that welled up in her when she least expected it.

"I'm a great guy and all that," he'd say with that crooked smile she loved so much. "But you give credit where credit's due."

He was right, of course. Her newfound faith never ceased to delight her. She touched the necklace at her throat. She'd always liked that the goldfish represented prosperity and wealth. But now she decided it meant something far more precious to her. The symbol of her new life. An *ichthys*, Lucas had called it. He'd redeemed the jewelry's meaning for her.

Redeemed. When she thought about all the years she'd ignored God—and all she'd missed out on because of it—she wanted to cry. But she'd been going to church with Luc the past few weeks, and only last Sunday the pastor had talked about regrets, and how they served no purpose unless they helped you move ahead to do the thing God had created you to do.

She wasn't exactly sure yet what that thing was for Jenna Morgan, but Lucas reminded her that figuring out God's plan wouldn't be an overnight discovery.

One thing she was sure of: she hoped Lucas Vermontez was part of that plan.

They'd grown closer than ever over the last few months. And as they shared their stories with each other, she had finally gotten up the nerve one night to confess her deepest secrets to him—about the babies she'd lost, about not loving Zachary the way she should have.

It was one of the first warm days of spring, and they'd sat out on her front stoop late into the evening, listening to the crickets chirp and the birds sing in the green canopy over their heads. She sat on the step below Luc, and he put his arms around her, resting his chin on the top of her head. She told him how she'd learned to love her little place in the country. And then something clicked and she knew the time was right to tell him.

He'd listened in silence, his expression revealing his shock. When she finished, he pulled away from her and struggled to his feet. He went to sit on the opposite edge of the porch and stayed there, with his head down, for a long time.

She wanted desperately to reach out for him, to take his hand and feel his pulse against her fingers. But she let him be.

"Why didn't you tell me before?" he said finally, not looking up.

"I'm sorry, Luc." Trembling, she whispered, "I should have."

"I wish you would've. I don't like secrets."

"I know. I'm so sorry."

He stared off to the west, where the sun was dropping off the edge of the horizon.

She swallowed hard and tried to imagine what her life would be like if she lost him. A sick feeling overwhelmed her. "I know you've always wanted a house full of kids."

"I've always wanted a wife who truly loved me, too."

"Oh, Luc . . . I would. I *do*. I love you." It wasn't how she'd wanted to tell him for the first time. But there it was. Another secret revealed.

He studied her as if trying to decide if he could believe anything she said.

"With Zach—oh, Luc, I didn't know *how* to love anybody then. Not even myself. I'm different now."

"I know you are," he finally said. "I know." But she didn't hear the conviction she longed to hear in his voice.

He'd gone home not long after, and she spent an agonizing night begging God not to take him away from her.

But when she got off work the next evening, he was sitting on her stoop again, waiting for her. He held out his arms and she fell into them.

"Thank you for trusting me with your secrets, Jen. I know that wasn't easy."

Again, they'd talked late into the night. He'd struggled with the things she'd confessed. He wanted to know she would never keep secrets from him again. "And I won't lie to you, Jenna. I want babies. And lots of them. But there are other ways to get babies. And I'm willing to trust God on that one."

Her heart had soared. He was talking about a future with her. And he'd forgiven her. She never should have doubted.

The doorbell pulled her from her reverie. Luke was here. She ran to let him in, her heart hitching the way it always did at the sight of him.

He stood on the rickety porch wearing a grin as wide as the Missouri sky. It took her a minute to register that something was squirming beneath the Daylight Donuts bag in his hand.

She took the bag from him, and a brown puppy with floppy ears wriggled to get free.

"What in the world . . . ?"

Still grinning, Lucas slipped inside and set the pup on the tiled entryway, closing the door behind him. He pushed the dog's hindquarters to the floor. "Sit, boy. Be nice now. Jen's not a fan of your kind."

She tried to look stern but couldn't pull it off. "What is he?"

"He's yours," Luc said, mischief in his eyes.

"Very funny."

He turned serious. "He's a chocolate Lab. I bought him from a guy up in Fenton. Just picked him up this morning. He's my next training project."

"What's his name?"

"Smoke." Lucas looked like a proud papa.

The puppy looked up at her with droopy eyes. "He looks more like a Mud."

"Hey! Be nice."

She knelt and gingerly touched the pup's head.

"He won't bite," Lucas said.

For Luc's sake—and only for his sake—she made a show of stroking the soft mink-colored fur. The little guy *was* pretty cute—for a dog.

Since his graduation from the program in Tulsa, Luc had been talking with Andrea Morley about putting Sparky to work with her fire investigation agency. He'd also gotten Sparky a gig next week at the school where Garrett Edmonds taught. Luc would be demonstrating Sparky's accelerant detection skills for the fifth grade class.

The kettle whistled and she jumped up to get it. "You want tea?"

"Sure." He picked up the pup. "Let me go get his carrier."

He came back a minute later with the pup in the crate and a rolled up newspaper in hand.

"What's that? Puppy toilet paper?"

Luc shook his head, but she didn't get the smile she expected. Instead, he shook out the paper and spread the front page open on the kitchen table.

Jenna brought steaming mugs and set them on the table, curious about the news.

Woman Confesses to Setting Arson Fires, the headline in the *Courier* read.

"She gave a full confession."

Her eyes widened. "The woman you found outside the shelter?" That morning seemed like a lifetime ago now.

"I stopped by the station and they said it was in the Springfield papers this morning, too."

"Did she say why? Was it just to protest the shelter?"

"I suppose you could say that."

"What do you mean?"

"Remember the guy who assaulted that sixteen-year-old girl—back at the old shelter?"

"James Friar, right? He was still in jail for that, last I heard."

He nodded. "This woman is Friar's mother."

"You're kidding."

"I can't be sure, but I think I saw her hanging around outside the shelter that night they had to evacuate. They say arsonists like to stick around the scene of the fire to see the chaos they've created."

She shook her head. "But why the fires? What did she hope to accomplish by that?"

"According to the news stories, she has a history of mental illness, so who knows? But apparently she blamed the shelter for her son being arrested. Maybe this was her way of getting revenge."

Jenna read the story, and her heart went out to the woman. And strangely, to the son, too. A tiny shiver went up her back. *There, but for the grace of God . . .*

They shared the newspaper over tea and donuts, listening to the birds chatter in the trees outside the kitchen window. The pup barked sharply from his carrier by the door, and Luc hushed him.

A depressing thought struck her. "Does this dog—does Smoke mean another six weeks away in Oklahoma for you?"

"If he's worth his salt, it does." He reached across the table and ruffled her hair as if she were a puppy. "That won't be for a while. You don't need to start worrying for a few months yet."

She rolled her eyes and heaved a sigh. It appeared that, if Lucas was going to be a part of her life, so were dogs. May as well get used to it.

"Besides," he said. "I have a proposition to make about that. . . ."

She shot him a wary glance. "What's that?"

"I was thinking maybe you could go with me this time." His dark eyes danced. "As my wife."

She'd thought this might be coming. Lucas had been dropping hints for weeks. But she hadn't expected the rush of emotions that paralyzed her now. She tried to speak over the fullness in her throat, but nothing came out.

Lucas laughed and struggled to his feet. He came around the table and pulled her up into his arms. "Is that a yes?"

She buried her face in the crispness of his shirt, holding him close. *Oh, God. I don't deserve to be this happy.*

After a minute he spoke. "I was thinking we could get you a puppy, too. We could train them together—"

She shook her head against his chest. "Not even funny, Vermontez."

"Aw, come on . . . Why not? We could name yours Fire."

She looked up at him, laughing, hoping to goodness he was only teasing. "Fire? A dog named Fire?"

"Yeah. They'd be best friends. You know . . . where there's Smoke, there's Fire."

She groaned. "Listen, mister, you may not realize it, but this is the engagement story we'll be telling our kids for the rest of our lives. You'd better come up with something better than that."

The twinkle in his eye turned into a look that was pure love. "Just tell 'em about this." He cradled her head in his hand and kissed her long and sweet.

When they came up for air, she giggled.

He pulled away and looked at her. "What?"

"I might have to stick with the Smoke and Fire story. That was *not* rated G."

He grinned. "You tell it however you want, babe. Just be sure the story ends with you saying yes, will you?"

"Oh! Yes, Luc! Definitely, *yes.*"

Though you have not seen him, you love him;
and even though you do not see him now,
you believe in him and are filled with
an inexpressible and glorious joy . . .

1 PETER 1:8

$\mathcal{D}$ear Reader,

Note to self: be careful what subjects you choose to write about.

As I begin work on my twentieth novel, it shouldn't surprise me when my life starts looking an awful lot like the lives of my characters. And yet it seems to catch me by surprise every time.

Although we haven't had to give up our home (yet), between having a daughter in college and a husband laid off from his job, ours has been a year somewhat like Jenna Morgan's. As we have struggled through the months, wondering what God has in mind for the next chapter of our lives, we've learned a lot about what really matters, about the difference between having material wealth and being rich in friends and family, love, and joy. We've decided we'd choose the latter any day. (But I won't kid you, it's not been easy letting go of the former!)

The day he got the news of his layoff, my husband took me in his arms and said, "God has taken care of us for thirty-five years. There's no reason to think He's going to stop now." A year-and-a-half later, we can testify to the truth of that statement. God has taught us so much through the pain and fear (okay, *terror*) and uncertainty of these days. I'm a different—I hope, better—person for the trials He's put in our lives, and as difficult as it's been, I wouldn't go back for all the wealth in the world.

May God bless each of my readers with just enough joy to keep you from discouragement and just enough difficulty to keep you close to Him.

Deborah Raney
July 8, 2010

Reading Group Questions

1. In *Forever After*, Jenna Morgan had the difficult task of grieving a husband she never really loved. Have you ever faced a similar situation, feeling the need to pretend grief for someone you're actually relieved is gone? How did you handle the situation? Did you share this truth with anyone? What was their reaction?

2. Lucas Vermontez felt his life was not worth living if he couldn't get back on the firefighting crew. Have you ever been prevented from holding a job or answering a calling you feel you were created for, but for some reason didn't qualify for? How did you handle it? Were you ultimately able to do that task, or is it something you continue to be denied? In either circumstance, how did that make you feel?

3. Jenna was essentially kicked out onto the street after an argument with her in-laws. Her pride dictated that she spend the night in her car on a freezing night rather than go to the homeless shelter. Would you make the same decision if you had no place to go? What other options might Jenna have explored? Do you think sleeping in her

car was a less humiliating choice than going to the homeless shelter? Why or why not?

4. Clarissa Morgan asked Jenna to leave their home because Jenna had chosen to forgive Bryn for her fault in the fire that killed the Morgan's son. Do you believe Jenna should have honored their request that she avoid Bryn? Or did Jenna owe her friend loyalty and forgiveness even though it went against the wishes of her in-laws? Is blood thicker than water? Is family more important than friends? How do you decide?

5. Jenna grew up poor, and the things she experienced living in relative poverty colored the way she looked at life. But marrying into wealth also changed her view of the world. What traits do these two extremes produce in Jenna, and how do you think she could find balance between the two? How have your financial circumstances—past and present, poverty or wealth—changed the way you view the world? Have you ever gone from one financial extreme to another in a short period of time? How did that experience change you?

6. Lucas had a strong physical attraction to Jenna—one that existed while Jenna was still married to Luc's best friend (even though Lucas never acted on that attraction while Zach was still alive). Do you think Lucas should have felt guilty

about his growing love for Jenna? Why or why not? Are physical attraction and affection good things on which to base a relationship? Explain your answer.

7. Conflict arose between Lucas and Jenna because he didn't like her being estranged from her in-laws (his late friend's parents). Do you believe he was right to be upset with her to the point of pushing her toward reconciliation? Do any of us have a right or responsibility to request that a close family member or friend reconcile with an enemy?

8. Jenna kept secret the fact that she had two miscarriages. When she revealed her secret to Lucas, he was upset not only because she kept this fact from him, but also because he'd always wanted a large family. If you knew someone you were dating could not give you children, would that change your decision to marry him or her? How did you feel about the way Lucas handled it? When you are in a relationship, how do you decide the right time to reveal similar "secrets" to each other?

9. *Forever After* deals with the two extremes of wealth and poverty. Discuss the pros and cons of each from a spiritual viewpoint. In your own experience, how does wealth keep you from

serving God or allow you to serve Him better? How might poverty keep you from serving God or allow you to serve Him better? How does one's financial status affect his place in society? How is it different in the United States than in countries where a class or caste system is in place?

10. At the end of the book, Lucas and Jenna had seemingly overcome their conflict and were looking forward to a life together. Given the struggles they'd been through individually and together, what do you see as potential problem areas in their eventual marriage? If you are married or seriously dating someone, did/do you recognize possible areas of future conflict in your relationship? How can identifying such issues help you deal with them in the future?

About the Author

*D*EBORAH RANEY dreamed of writing a book since the summer she read all of Laura Ingalls Wilder's *Little House* books and discovered that a little Kansas farm girl could, indeed, grow up to be a writer. After a happy twenty-year detour as a stay-at-home wife and mom, Deb began her writing career. Her first novel, *A Vow to Cherish*, was awarded a Silver Angel from Excellence in Media and inspired the acclaimed World Wide Pictures film of the same title. Since then, her books have won the RITA Award, the HOLT Medallion, and the National Readers' Choice Award; she is also a two-time Christy Award finalist. Deb enjoys speaking and teaching at writers' conferences across the country. She and her husband, Ken Raney, make their home in their native Kansas and love the small-town life that is the setting for many of Deb's novels. The Raneys enjoy gardening, antiquing, art museums, movies, and traveling to visit four grown children and small grandchildren who live much too far away.

Deborah loves hearing from her readers. To e-mail her or to learn more about her books, please visit www.deborahraney.com or write to Deborah in care of Howard Books, 216 Centerview Dr., Suite 303, Brentwood, TN 37027.

Center Point Publishing
600 Brooks Road ● PO Box 1
Thorndike ME 04986-0001 USA

(207) 568-3717

US & Canada:
1 800 929-9108
www.centerpointlargeprint.com